MY DARK HORSE PRINCE

BRIDGET E. BAKER

Purple Puppy Publishing

To Tessa
The scrappiest fighter. The tiniest girl. The biggest heart. Even when things look dark, keep on riding.

I've been obsessed with horses my entire life.

It makes sense, really. Warmbloods—the type of horse I've spent the most time with—weigh between twelve hundred and fifteen hundred pounds, and yet their go-to move when they encounter danger is to run away.

A barking dog? They're off.

Gunshot? They bolt.

A car backfires? Sayonara.

Windblown plastic bag? They'll dead sprint the opposite direction.

In that regard, they're just like me. Mom has always joked that when God made my twin sister Adriana and me, he gave her all the fight and I got all the flight.

She's not really wrong.

Horses and I share the exact same reaction to danger.

My mom has always pulled an ostrich. She'd hide. . .kind of. Mostly she'd just try not to see whatever bad thing was happening. But me? I learned at an early age that if something terrible was going down, I didn't want to be anywhere near it.

It's good that I'm not actually more like a horse, because

if a horse's leg stops working, you have to put it down. Horses can't live with a leg they can't stand on. They'll develop laminitis in the other hooves and die miserably.

Meanwhile, I've been hobbling around for almost ten years on my train wreck of a limb. Unfortunately, it's finally gotten bad enough that I can't run. I can barely walk.

"You needed to talk to me?" Brigita already looks exceptionally annoyed. Then again, she always does.

I swallow. *You can do this, Mirdza.* I give myself pep talks sometimes. They don't help, but they play in my bizarre brain anyway. "Yeah. So, you know I had to cancel a few lessons."

She arches one eyebrow. That's how I know she really *is* annoyed.

"Okay. You do know. The thing is, I finally got in to see a surgeon. It looks like that time Emilia and Vilks crashed into me, it dislodged some of the plates and screws that were holding my leg together."

"And?" I didn't think it was possible, but her eyebrow hikes up another centimeter.

"I'll need a surgery to fix it." I cough. "Maybe a series of surgeries, actually," I say. "The reason I've been in such terrible pain is that—"

"Get to the point," Brigita says.

I blink repeatedly. The point. Oh, no. This is where I have to ask her. "I'm going to need some time off, and I was hoping you might give me a loan to pay for the surgeries." I cringe as I ask, which can't possibly increase my chances of convincing her.

"You need time off?" She sighs. "How much do you need, exactly?"

"I'm not supposed to be on my feet at all afterward," I say. "And if you can loan me the money, I'll get the surgery set up right away. Then, if I need a second, which they think I could, that would be as soon as thirty days after. Really, it would be just about two months before I could be up and teaching again with a brace."

I don't mention that the surgeon said a minimum of three months. I'm sure I'll be fine in two. Maybe less.

"How much money would you need to borrow?" Her lips are pressed into a tight line, and she's picking dirt out from under her fingernails.

"Fifty thousand euros." I close my eyes at the end, because I can't stand to see her scowl at me.

But the sound she's making almost sounds like. . .laughter.

I open my eyes, and I was right. She's laughing.

"You're not upset?" Have I been misreading her this entire time? Is she more understanding than I realized? Maybe Danils has told her good things. Maybe—

Her laughter abruptly stops. "You're fired, of course."

My heart stops. "I'm. . .I'm what?"

"You're *fired*. Clean out your locker, if you can manage it with your bum leg."

"But I brought so many new clients with me," I say. "More than half the riders at this barn followed me here."

She clucks. "Oh, Mirdza. You're such a naive little thing. Did you really think I meant to keep you around? Even if you hadn't given me such a beautiful excuse to fire you, this was always the plan."

I swallow. "The plan?"

"I only hired a broke-down nag like you to teach here because—"

"You said Danils convinced you."

She's laughing again. "You believed that? That my boyfriend recommending his *ex* to me would be beneficial to you?"

"But you also said that even though we don't show

together any more, you had a fondness for me from when we were in the ring."

"A *fondness*? You should never have beat me—not when all you ever had were hand-me-down horses your loser friend gave you out of pity. I hated you when we were in the ring together." This time, her laughter's high and light. Airy. Like the tinkling of demonic bells. "You do know that naive is just another word for stupid, don't you?"

My leg's throbbing like someone hit it with a poker from the fire. My head's pounding now too. "You always meant to fire me?"

"It was actually Danils' idea all along. Did you really think he'd encourage me to hire his *ex-girlfriend*?" She rolls her eyes. "But now you can't teach your students, so they won't even have to feel bad for staying here with me."

"What about my horses?" I ask. "You don't have enough lesson horses without mine."

"As if I can't find some old, janky horses to replace them." She sighs. "I'll give you a month to find them a new barn," she says. "And if you can't find one, then they'll become *my* horses and I won't even need to find new ones, per the terms of our contract." Her smile this time is wicked. Malicious. Pure evil.

"Oh, I'll find them a new place." And I don't plan to roll over and let her steal my clients, either. After enduring a few weeks of her teaching, they'll realize what a mistake it would be to stay, I'm sure of it. I hate how heavily I have to lean on my crutches as I limp toward the tack room to clear out my locker.

She starts to yell when I just walk away, but she shouldn't be too surprised. Even dogs dodge when someone's kicking at them.

It's hard to manage all of my gear on the bus with my crutches, even though I left all my tack behind with my animals. Horses come with a lot of stuff.

When my phone bings, I almost ignore it. But on the off chance it's Kristiana, finally returning one of my messages, I dig it out. If she has room for me back at her barn, that would solve a lot of my problems at the same time. While digging in my bag for my phone, I inadvertently drop my bag of grooming brushes, and the lady next to me kicks them away from her.

Sometimes it feels like there are no decent people left in this world.

By the time I finally recover all my belongings, my leg vehemently protesting the movements, my hand is shaking. It makes it hard to read my text. Once I do, my spirits sink even further. It's from Danils. I should have expected that.

HEAR YOU'RE IN TROUBLE. CALL ME.

I may be in terrible pain without a solution in sight, and his girlfriend may think I'm an idiot, but I'm not even close to stupid enough to ask Danils for aid. I wouldn't touch his help with a three-meter lunging crop.

I delete the text with a shudder.

By the time I get home, I still haven't come up with a better solution. Adriana's face in the front window is pressed against the glass. Her long blond hair and bright blue eyes look so similar to Kristiana's that it's almost startling. Adriana looks just like my mother, but high cheekbones and slender frames are the only things we share, in spite of being actual twins. My hair's so dark it's nearly black, and my eyes are a dark chocolate brown. Apparently I look just like my father, but I don't even have a decent photo of him, so I have to take my mother's word for it.

As if our looks reflect our insides, our personalities are entirely different as well. Adriana's forever making sure I know how lacking I am, and how much better it would be if I were like her—brave, outspoken, and bitter. She's standing by the time I finally hobble through the door. "She laughed, didn't she?"

My jaw drops. "How could you know that?"

"She's a vindictive, nasty piece of trash," Adriana says. "That's how." Her hair's pulled back like it always is, and her muscular arms flex when she slaps a bug on the wall. "You never should have gone to work there." There's another one crawling up the wall behind her, but I don't bother pointing it out. It'll only make her more irritated than she already is.

"Not like I had much of a choice," I say. "Kris had to sell up."

"So that witch laughed at you and now you have to walk back in there and try and act professional."

"Not exactly." I wince. "She fired me for not being able to work, and she's planning on keeping all my clients."

Adriana's string of expletives is actually impressive. When she finally calms down a little, she says, "I've had a bit of luck, so I can cover our rent this month, and you can borrow the money for the surgery from Danils. Do you know how pissed she'd be about that?"

I grit my teeth. "He told me to call him."

"Great," she says. "Do it."

"Not if flesh-eating beetles were stripping the skin and muscle from my body," I say.

Adriana rolls her eyes. "Always so melodramatic. Look, you said Kris still hasn't called you back."

"Her dad says she's in Russia, and she just won the Grand National a few days ago. I'm sure the press is hounding her, so she's turned off her phone. I should just wait for her to get back. Asking someone for money isn't something you should do over the phone, anyway."

"Well, maybe a few hundred," Adriana says. "But not fifty thousand euros." She flops onto the very worn, very dirty couch. "Do you think she even has it? Or will she have to call her rich little banker ex?"

"I wouldn't even ask her to do that. I'm hoping that she

can pay me out of the winnings from her race, but with her dad's gambling, you never know."

"You're unemployed now, thanks to her selling her land. She owes you."

"I only know how to ride thanks to her, and you're the same. She's given me countless horses over the years, and she brought me in as an instructor when no one else would have. I won't have you saying anything nasty about her."

"Fine." Adriana rolls her eyes. "But don't tell me it never bothers you when she complains. She was born with a silver spoon, and we got nothing, but we have to listen to how *hard* her life is."

"I lost my job because of my leg, and that had nothing to do with her. She's only ever helped us both."

Adriana scowls. "But she knew you were stuck working for the devil herself, and meanwhile she's doing what in Russia? Sightseeing?"

"Her dad says she's there with her boyfriend." I shrug.

"Hiding from the press with some hot, penniless Russian horse trainer?" Adriana rolls her eyes. "I swear that girl's a pampered princess if I ever saw one. It's not your fault you can't ask her for the loan in person. She's the one hiding out in another country. If you won't call and ask her for the money, I'll call Danils for you."

"You wouldn't dare."

She picks up her phone.

The idea strikes like lightning, fast and quick. "I'll go visit her," I say. "Her dad gave me the address that she sent him in an email."

"With your bad leg and no car, how do you plan to get there?"

"The train, of course," I say. "Since I can't work, I have nothing better to do. And once I'm there, I can ask for the money."

"You can't even afford to get there," Adriana says.

"You just said—"

She stands up and presses a wad of bills into my hand. "This should cover your train ticket." She smiles. "Iron Cross won today." She shrugs. "You know if I don't hide it, Mom'll just give it to Mārtiņš."

We may not like Danils, and after today, I loathe Brigita, but neither of them hold the title of the World's Worst Human. The long-time winner of that is our step-dad, who also happens to be our uncle. The whole thing is disgusting.

I don't really want to borrow money from Adriana either, but she's right. I need the surgery, and I need it soon. The surgeon said the longer I wait, the worse things will get, and the higher my risk of infection will rise.

"Fine."

"Ask her for fifty-*one* thousand so you can pay me back."

I open my hand and examine the wad of bills. "This is barely more than five hundred."

She shrugs. "Compound interest is the worst, isn't it?"

之 2 豰

I used to dream that the hottest, richest, smartest guy in school fell for me. Sometimes, I'd slip and he'd catch me. Other times, it would be raining and he'd offer to share his umbrella with me. Still another time, I was walking home—which happened often—and he'd stop to give me a ride, shocking everyone else around.

When it happened, it was just like a fairy tale. The day started out warm, but somehow, during class, the temperature dropped. When school let out, I walked outside into an almost arctic wind. I stopped, shivering, and wrapped my arms around myself, preparing for the long walk to the bus stop.

I barely went two steps before a nice, warm leather jacket dropped around my shoulders. Nearly every eye was on me, all the girls jealous, all the guys curious, as Danils Ozols steered me away from the crowds and toward his beautiful imported Mustang. "I hear you like horses," he said. "This is my favorite kind."

It was a pretty cheesy line, but it made my heart race. For weeks, I was perpetually on cloud nine, as all my classmates watched in envy. The only person who was truly happy for me was my best friend Kristiana. Even my sister Adriana seemed to be some strange mix of jealous and leery of Danils.

Every girl may dream of Prince Charming, and in Daugavpils, Danils was about as close as it got. His dad owned half the town and his uncle owned the other half. He was good looking, confident, connected, and fairly smart. And he knew it. Over time, I discovered that while he might have loved me forever, it wasn't the kind of love I wanted. His love wasn't unconditional. It was fraught with conditions—I had to do what he wanted, when he wanted to do it, and if I ever said no, I was disciplined.

It was after I refused to sleep with him that he decided to find another girlfriend. After all, we had been together for a 'long time.' He had been *patient*.

That was around the same time that my mother decided to remarry. . . my uncle. That's right. My dad's older brother, whom we had never heard from a single time after my dad died and left us penniless, came through town and needed a place to stay. He flirted with my mother shamelessly.

Then he found a job in town and *moved here*.

On top of it being super gross that he married his little brother's widow, he's also a supersize bag of garbage. He forced my mom to leave the barn apartment at Kristiana's family estate, where she'd been the cleaning lady for our entire life almost, and move into an apartment he found. He spent all his time telling us how lucky we were that he would provide for us.

Mārtiņš was the reason I quit living with my mom before I was even done with school. If Kris hadn't offered to let me use the barn apartment again—her stable has several different groom's quarters, but she saved the best one for me, always—I'd have really been in trouble.

But no matter what my lousy uncle says or does, Mom

won't leave him. Now that I know what I'm looking for, I see guys like him everywhere. Most of them are alcoholics like Mārtiņš, but that's just an excuse. The drinking didn't make them horrible people. They chose their lives, every step of the way.

I used to think I could do something about the evils of the world. We're taught when we're kids that if we're brave, strong, and loud enough, we can make a difference. In some things, sure, but when we're going up against men who are holding all the cards? No way.

My sister Adriana still tries, the idiot.

But I've learned that the only way to deal with men like him is to avoid, to hide, or my personal favorite, to run.

The biggest problem in my life is that I can no longer run. At all.

After boarding the train in Riga, bound first for Tallinn, and then on to St. Petersburg, I can't help feeling a little like a sitting duck. At least they're still speaking my native tongue, but I'm in a strange place, surrounded by strange people, and I have limited mobility. I spent over a hundred euro on a dumb multi-leg train ticket, even taking the cheapest, slowest route, which means I have just under four hundred euro left to pay for food and a hotel if I need it. I know nothing about the kind of place where Kris is staying. I can't think that a Russian horse trainer has much money, so they may not even have a couch to offer me.

After the first few stops, I settle in more comfortably. The train rocks and rattles as we move, rocketing along. My bag's right above me, safely tucked into the overhead storage. My purse sways ahead of me along with the train, stuffed into the mesh compartment on the half wall. I'm sitting in the first seat behind the door—something about being close to an exit makes me feel safer, even if I don't plan to use it.

The downside is that people are almost constantly

moving past me, and each one makes me jump. For a twenty-hour trip, it's not ideal. I steal snatches of sleep in fits and starts, opening my purse to stuff my face with dried, smoked pike and chunks of rye bread when my stomach complains the loudest.

We're sitting in the Moskovskiy Railway Station in Saint Petersburg when a smallish woman dressed in drab grey pants and wrapped in an old grey jacket boards, dragging a tiny little girl behind her. She's also wearing all grey, as if they want to disappear into the background. The sun's just setting, and they keep their faces down.

I recognize them immediately.

They're frightened, and they're on the run.

I recognize them, because I have *been* them. My attempt to leave didn't end well. I wish them better luck in their endeavors. They take the seats just behind me, clearly also wanting to be close to an exit. The little girl whispers, "Will he find—"

Her mother shushes her.

Just like the mother, I hope he won't find them. Oh, please, please, *please* God, let him not find them.

The loudspeaker has switched to Russian, so it's lucky that I speak it mostly fluently as well. Thanks to my mother's family, I've been to Russia many times. I'm not quite as proficient as I am in Latvian, but I don't struggle either.

"Four minutes to departure. Find your seats quickly. The conductor will check for tickets soon."

No one has checked for tickets in at least three stops, so I'm not at all convinced that's true. I suppose it's to make stowaways think twice. A flurry of people board, all of them scanning the rows for empty seats before ducking into one or another, here or there. A hunched-over woman with a head shawl takes the seat next to me, and we share a nod. She looks to be in her sixties, and she smells like pumpkin for some reason. She offers me a piece of gum and

I decline, but I smile to let her know I appreciate the offer. I'm so distracted that I almost don't notice when a large man in a dark coat hops on the train briskly, his heavy footfalls thunking loudly, even against the dense carpet of the train floor.

But when I glance his direction, I immediately forget anything else.

All the alarms in my body go off. He's exactly the kind of man I avoid, always. It's not that he's wearing all black. It's not his closely trimmed beard, scattered with a bit of grey. It's not even his heavy footfalls, his serious visage, or his flinty eyes.

No, it's something else entirely.

Violent men have a kind of aura about them. Something about them sucks in the light and casts a pool of darkness around them. I curl inward reflexively, but my heart freezes dead in my chest when he stops in the aisle behind me.

I knew.

Before he stopped there, I knew.

He's found them.

The light-stealing villain found them.

"Otpravit'sya." His voice is low and menacing. A chill runs down my spine, freezing me in place. The word in Russian just means 'Get off,' but somehow, when he says it, it's like an expletive-laden command. His voice may be quiet, but it's full of promise. He's livid that they had the audacity to leave without his permission.

They will pay for that decision. That much is very clear.

Most people on this train have no idea what's going on. The woman next to me is prattling on about her cat. She says it only eats its dinner when mushed pumpkin is added to the dish—which explains the smell—and she hopes that Vlad can remember to do it.

Who cares about Vlad? Does she really have no idea what's happening behind us? Two lives that were so close to freedom are now ruined. And the penalty for their attempt will be heavy.

"Do you have pets, dear? Anything you love with all your heart?"

As if it's just come back online, I can feel my heart hammering in my chest. This is one of those moments—the moments in life that you never forget. Paths roll out all around you, yawning lazily, beckoning, and only one path really matters.

The one you choose.

I should tell the woman about my horses. They're the reason I'm here. One of them is blind in his right eye. He's a great jumper, but you must always be cautious that no one spooks him on that side. Another is allergic to alfalfa. One bite and he'll break out in painful hives all over his body. Another of my horses is my heart horse—she and I were Olympic-bound when my uncle, a man like the one behind me, decided I needed to learn a lesson.

I wasn't on a train, but I couldn't escape.

He shattered my leg.

A decade later, I'm still suffering from his rage. For the sake of all those animals and more, I should keep my mouth shut. I should chat with the old woman about her tabby cat and forget about the man behind us. I should pretend nothing is happening so I can make it to Russia and keep my animals safe.

But the face of the little girl in grey floats in front of me. Her eyes are wide. Her mouth parts in surprise, and the blood drains out of her already pale skin. Her dark hair's pulled back and plaited, making her baby-round cheeks easy to see.

She could be me.

I was her.

And no one on the train or in my life cared enough to spare me.

Is her life about to be shattered?

What will he do to her mother?

Mine never even tried to escape. She only shook and cried and hid, and eventually, defended him instead of protecting me. What did it take for this mother to grab her daughter's hand and make it to this train? If Adriana were here, she'd already be standing, shouting at the man, her small hands balled into fists of rage. She'd be alerting every single passenger to the threat.

She'd be doing something.

But I've learned.

I know what happens when people like me try to intervene. When we try to fight the Mārtinš of the world, *we shatter*.

"Come," the man says, his voice louder this time. "Now."

"The train will be departing in one minute," the loud speaker bleats.

"Let go," the little girl says, her voice unsteady. "Let my mom go. You make her cry."

The little girl might look like me, but she talks like Adriana. And in that moment, something snaps inside of me. The bands of fear that encircle my heart at all times fray and my heart beats loudly in my ears. I stand up and turn around to face the villain.

"Get off," I say. "Get off the train before the ticket-taker comes and throws you in jail."

The man's head whips toward mine.

I want to cringe and cower and whimper. But instead, I channel every speck of Adriana in my body, and I grit my teeth, and I glare. "You don't have a ticket, and you're threatening a passenger. You need to go."

A man two rows behind the mother and daughter stands up. "Leave."

"Let her go." Another man on the other side of the train car stands. He's scowling.

"Sir?" An actual, honest-to-goodness ticket taker in a uniform steps through the connection and glances our way. "Is there a problem?"

The doors close, and I panic that we'll be trapped in here with this man all the way to the next station. But the villain shakes his head, steps toward the exit, and presses the button. The door opens, and the bad man in black steps off.

Before the doors close, he turns to stare right at me.

He's smiling, and that's not a natural state for a villain like him. His smile isn't full of warmth, or happiness, or generosity.

It's a promise.

A promise I hope he'll never have the chance to fulfill.

My blood runs cold in my veins, but when I sit down, the train starts to move, and we're all on it.

He's not.

I'm shaking. The clueless woman next to me drops a wrinkled hand over mine. "My dear, are you cold?" She unwraps her head scarf and offers it to me. I can't very well explain that I'm trembling from fear to someone this oblivious, so I thank her.

And I take it.

It's not much, but perhaps if the man shows up in my life again, the head scarf will confuse him. It's not like I look very different than the other people around me.

"Where are you headed, dear?" the woman asks.

I don't really want to tell her, of course. I never share anything I don't specifically have to, not with anyone other than Adriana, Kristiana, or a few other trusted friends. "I'm visiting my best friend. She's staying near Novgorod."

"How lovely," the woman says. "We're lucky to be having such nice weather."

I glance outside, becoming more and more positive that this woman is insane. It's terribly cold and it's been raining steadily for at least twenty-five miles. "I guess."

The old woman cackles. "You think I'm nuts, probably."

I shrug, but I can't help my small smile. "This isn't what I would call nice, but the early spring rain does help things start to grow."

"You're in Russia, girl. It's not snowing, so it's nice weather."

About five minutes later, she falls asleep, snoring softly. I can finally shift in my seat to look behind me. The woman's whisper-singing to her daughter, who's nearly asleep. Now that I've noticed what she's doing, I can make out the words to the song.

It's gentle.

It's kind.

It's reassuring.

All the things that man was not.

This mother is caring for her daughter in a way mine never did. What I said—standing up for someone I don't even know—was monumentally stupid, but I'm proud of it anyway. It worked, and other people on the train backed me up. The little girl escaped. That's what really matters.

Once the daughter's asleep, I hear a soft hiss and turn around.

"Thank you," the mother says, her eyes intent.

"You're welcome," I say.

"I mean it," the mother says. "We might be dead if not for you."

The words rock me. I knew it already, but hearing them aloud causes me to tremble again. I should have run. I should have hidden. I should have done anything but inject myself into the middle of that fight. Luckily, post-aid cowardice isn't immediately obvious.

Of course, when the train stops next, the conductor

announcing loudly, "We'll be stopped for five minutes here at Tosno, and then we'll depart for Lyuban. Gather your belongings and depart if this is your stop."

The old woman jerks awake and looks around in a daze. "Is this Tosno?"

I nod.

She scrambles to her feet. "Better get going. Nice chatting." She leans close and whispers, "You're ready to bond, young woman. When the chance comes, take it."

"Huh?"

Her laugh is short and sharp, just like the last time. "You know what bonds are?"

"Like, tying someone's hands, you mean?" I wish she'd just leave already.

Again, with the cackle. "Chemical bonds are when atoms are drawn together and form new molecules. A government bond is when you're stuck in a promise to pay, bound to someone over time. You can bond things with glue. Or people with feelings." She smiles, her teeth as ragged and unkempt as her hair. "But you're ready for a soul bond—a connection that will change you, and him, *forever*. You won't want to do it. It may make you tremble like you did back there with that horrible man. But you need it. It's time."

Then without explaining anything else, she just ducks off.

It was nice, in a way, her ranting. It distracted me from my fear of the *horrible* man, as she called him. He could easily have looked up where our train's headed, and it would have been a snap for him to drive here faster, if he had a car.

The minutes tick down slowly, but finally, the doors close.

And he doesn't show.

I breathe a sigh of relief as the train once again sways and rocks and rattles along its path.

A moment later, someone drops into my seat.

I look up, surprised, but it's the mother in grey. Her eyes are weary, and I'm sure that she's even more relieved than I am that the man didn't show up at the stop. Escaping once was a near miss—but he wouldn't come alone if he returned.

"I put sand in his gas tank," she says. "I saw it on a movie. I hope it works."

My heart swells. Not only did she leave, but she took steps to stymie his attempt to follow.

"My daughter's exhausted, and she wanted to stretch out. I hope this is alright." She tosses her head behind her.

I turn around and look at her little girl, sprawled at an angle across two seats, her hands wrapped around their small bag as if it's a pillow.

"Of course," I say.

"May God bless you for your bravery."

"I'm impressed with you," I say truthfully. "My mother never left."

A shudder runs through the woman. "This is my fifth attempt."

Fifth attempt.

The words practically hang in the air between us. She's failed four times. I wonder about the cost of all those efforts.

"A nice, quiet man," I say finally.

"Excuse me?" She turns toward me, her lips slightly parted.

"The old lady, as she left, told me I'm ready for a soul bond with someone." I laugh. "A soul bond. Can you even imagine that?"

The grey mother shakes her head. "Not in the slightest.

I'm pretty sure my soul is a crumpled, worn-out thing, if it even exists."

"My sister has never dated," I say. "She fights with men. Spits on them. Attacks them sometimes. But she's never dated a single man."

"But you have," the woman says.

I nod.

"He was terrible, too."

I can't help nodding. "It was a big mistake. I thought he was different, but he dictated what I had to do, and he grew impatient if I didn't follow his directions."

"They're all the same," she says. "And the only hope you have is to find the biggest, baddest, and scariest one."

"What?" I'm shocked to hear her say that.

"In school, I met a guy who everyone else was scared of. He liked *me*."

I know this story. I could tell this story.

"I was delighted."

So was I.

"And then to get away from him, I found someone even scarier."

Oh. I disappointed him in small ways until he was utterly disgusted, and then I let him discard me, like it was his decision. "And to get away from him?"

She looks at her hands.

"That's how you met. . ." I toss my head at the door.

"Exactly."

"I don't want someone who's powerful enough to protect me," I say. "I'm fine hiding in the shadows. If I'm going to find a soul-bond, it's going to be with someone who will hide right alongside me."

The woman smiles. "Good luck. It's too late for me. I'd have to entice the devil himself to keep me safe from Yevginiy. He's pretty much the worst man in Saint Petersburg."

A shiver runs through me. "But you're free, now."

"He doesn't know about my cousin in Novgorod," she whispers. "It's my last hope."

The woman and I tremble through the stops at Chudovo and Myasnoi Bor, but the man never shows. We're nearly to Chechulino, the train rocking, her daughter sleeping, when the sliding door separating train cars opens.

I barely notice it.

After all, only existing passengers can even move from one train car to the next. Usually it's only the ticket takers, and they appear less and less often as we travel deeper into Russia.

But then the bootsteps register at almost the same time as the woman stiffens next to me. It's not one set of footsteps, either. There are dozens, like a regiment marching in step, but less organized. Heavy, ponderous steps, the sound made by heavy boots worn by large men.

I bite my lip and my fingers grip the arm rests, and then I turn.

At the front of a large group of men—at least ten—is the man in black. Yevginiy. He looks exactly the same as before, just as angry, just as eager, and just as resolved. Only now, he's not alone. The man next to him is broader and, somehow, even darker. The man behind him is so tall that his head nearly brushes the top of the train ceiling.

And they're armed.

One of them's holding a knife that gleams softly in the incandescent light of the train. Another taps the end of a dark grey gun against his thigh.

"Put that away," the man I assume is Yevginiy says. "Gunfire would attract too much attention."

"No." The little girl behind us has woken up, and she stands. "You need to leave us alone. We don't want you anymore."

"I thought you were cute for a while, but you aren't

even my daughter," Yevginiy says. "You need to learn to keep your stupid mouth shut before I get truly sick of you." His closed fist flies backward, slamming into her small face almost absentmindedly.

Her small frame collapses, like a fork sliding through cake.

The woman at my side cries out and tries to push past Yevginiy, her arms thrown out in front of her, yearning to hold her daughter.

But her big, bad lover isn't done yet. Just as casually as before, his hand reaches for her, his large, strong fingers wrapping slowly around her upper arm, yanking her back against his side. "I didn't tell you that you could leave. In fact, I told you *not* to go."

She turns her head upward. "You promised me when we met that you never hit women. You said your mother made you swear."

His laugh is dark and terrifying. "She's a little girl. I've kept that promise. I would never hurt you." And then he turns, and commands his men. "That girl there, the cripple." My crutches are leaning against the corner of the train, wedged into the short space against the doorframe, but my leg brace is hard to hide.

I can't put any weight on my leg right now without it.

Every single person I meet can immediately tell that I'm broken.

"Kill her and toss her out the window."

"No," the woman shouts. "No, Yevginiy, don't. I'll go back with you. I won't run away again."

"Do it," he says, ignoring her pleas. "If I don't follow through on her punishments, how will she ever believe me in the future?"

"No, please don't." The woman drops to her knees in front of him, her hands grasping at his. "Please, I beg you for mercy. She was only trying to help." Tears run down her face, and she's shaking so much that her words are distorted. "Please, please, leave her be."

"At first it amused me, you know." He tilts his head. "You leaving. It felt like a game, like you were flirting, almost, like you wanted more of my attention." He crouches down closer to her. "But this is pissing me off. You're doing it too often now, and I've told you before that I'm the only one who can give you toys. When you find your own, you force me to take them from you." He scowls at me. "*She* can't keep you safe. No one can keep you safe, except for me."

"Yevginiy," she pleads, "don't hurt her. Please, don't. I don't want to keep her. Just let her go." She sinks to the ground, her hands covering her face. "Please. Please." She repeats the word over and over like a rosary, like a chant.

That's when I realize that she already knows he won't change his mind. Without even thinking, I reach back and grab one of my crutches. The wide man he ordered to kill me is close now, his knife raised, his mouth half-smiling. He has a small scar on his jaw, just under his left ear.

He likes hurting people, that much is quite clear. There's a reason Yevginiy told him to do it. So when I bring my crutch around, pretending to use it to try and run away, his smile broadens.

"I'll make it quick," he lies.

As if someone like him would miss out on enjoying any part of this.

I don't even feel bad when I bring my crutch around the door frame and slam it downward into the space between his head and his shoulder. A broken clavicle is painful—I know from personal experience—and it's an easy bone to snap.

When I hear the crack, I smile. He drops the knife. My leg screams at me as I crouch to snatch the knife from the ground. I stumble forward, bracing myself with my other hand.

"Durak, you idiot!" Yevginiy shouts. He sighs with disgust and waves his hand. "Someone else get her. Now."

I force myself back to my feet and turn for the door. No passengers in this car have done a thing to help, but maybe in the next—

The knife hits my right shoulder, sinking in deeply enough that it protrudes through the front. Blood sprays all over the wall. I expect the pain to be worse than anything I've ever felt—Mārtinš never used blades—but it's not so bad. It feels like a sunburn that's been scratched, maybe, burning and tingling, and it's a sharp pain, sure, but it's not nearly as bad as the radiating pain I feel from my leg every single day. I don't even drop the knife I'm holding in my right hand.

I keep walking, using the one crutch I've got, and I make it as far as the door, my left hand releasing the handle of my crutch to reach for the button that makes the door open.

But another set of hands yanks me back, and a much longer knife stabs me in the lower back. This one hurts far, far worse. I can feel the warmth of my own blood flowing down and out, stealing over my back as I sink toward the floor.

Someone picks me up, and then I'm jostled pretty badly, and then they make good on their threat to shove me out the window of a moving train, my injured shoulder slamming into the side of the window at first, twisting my entire body sideways, before they finally succeed in shoving me out.

I duck and roll, so that when I hit the undergrowth below, on the same side as my shoulder stab wound, at least it only snaps my clavicle and not my neck.

The train rockets past, drowning the sounds of my sobs,

and I realize that maybe I wasn't so smart to duck and roll. Snapping my neck might have killed me quickly. The throbbing of my leg, the sharp pains from my shoulder, my clavicle, and my back would all end instead of dragging on and on. Because there's no way I survive this, badly injured, in the middle of the night, in the middle of nowhere.

Without a coat.

In the rain.

Bleeding to death as nature covers up the gory details.

It's really just a question of how long I suffer.

We have discussions about this with the vet, when a horse is injured. How long should we make him or her suffer before we throw in the towel? And when that time has come, what's the most effective way to kill the poor creature?

Now it's my reality.

I can't help thinking how sad it is that my mom, my sister, and my dear friend Kris will have no idea what happened to me. My belongings are still on the train, including my phone, my identification, and all my money, but I imagine Yevginiy's men will dispose of those. So the Russian authorities, if they even find me, will just find an unidentified Jane Doe.

I must be bleeding quite a lot, because it's not long before my world begins to become hazy. My thoughts are disconnected. My body, blessedly, stops hurting and is no longer cold.

My last thought is that I wish I could have ridden a horse one last time. I've avoided it for a decade because it was too risky. One fall and my leg could have been unable to bear weight. One misstep and I would have been confined to a wheelchair for life.

But now I'm dying anyway. . .

In my final moment, as darkness closes in around me, the strangest thing happens.

A vision of a huge, dark horse appears on the horizon, running toward me. He's got the most beautiful white blaze down his face, and he's looking right at me, neighing loudly as my world drifts into nothingness. Maybe he's come to give me a ride to heaven. It's not a bad way to go.

❧ 3 ❧

I'm warm.

The air blowing past my face is cold—frigid, even—but my body is somehow warm.

How can that be?

The sun's rays are just peeking over the horizon as I open my eyes, and I blink repeatedly to clear them until I can look around. I'm in the middle of nowhere, lying on the cold, hard ground, and it's still lightly raining, but my back is warm.

Suddenly, I remember it all in a rush.

The train.

The woman.

The villain.

The knives.

The window.

My body, broken.

The dark horse, pounding toward me.

Something nudges my hand, and it's soft and fuzzy. I turn my head slowly, and my eyes meet one big, dark blue one. The dark horse from last night is lying at my back, nuzzling my hand.

I shout and lunge forward, wondering how those stab wounds didn't kill me.

And more bizarrely, why don't they even hurt?

Am I in heaven? Is that what happens? You just *blink* and you're in the same world, but now you're not part of it? Is that why I'm warm?

Goosebumps explode all over my arm now that I'm not lying next to the long, warm body of the horse behind me. Apparently heaven can still be cold.

He whuffles then, the horse at my back, and scrambles to his feet. He has three gorgeous white socks, and one entirely black leg on his front. He's beautifully proportioned—absolutely enormous, probably at least seventeen hands, and thick, like a Belgian Warmblood.

It should be terrifying, waking up next to a horse I don't know, in a place that's unfamiliar. The horse could be a wild maniac, and I have no idea how it will behave or why it's here.

But somehow, I'm not scared at all.

Horses are huge, and they're powerful, and they're unpredictable.

Even so, they're still one hundred and ten percent better than humans on almost all counts. Now, if I could only figure out how or why my knife wounds that should have killed me. . .disappeared, and how my broken clavicle healed, then I might know where I am and what I'm doing here.

Could I have dreamed all of it?

But I'm next to a train track—and if I did imagine it, where are all my things? Where are my crutches, my warm coat, my phone, my purse, and my bag?

How did I wind up here?

I look around slowly, taking in my surroundings. We were nearly to Novgorod when the men showed up in the train car last night. I shudder just thinking about it. I wrap my arms around myself and rub my hands up and down, trying to warm up a bit in the brisk, early morning air. The sun is low in the vast, wide blue sky, the clouds moving past above us quickly, forming a tapestry of motion that in other circumstances I would have enjoyed watching. There are no buildings anywhere that I can make out—not even dilapidated ones. The grass is mostly dead, but here and there, bushy patches of it are starting to grow in clumps, like the sprigs of bull grass that always sprout near Daugavpils in the spring rains.

The dark horse has inched closer, one slow step at a time, until his face nudges my arm. Sleeping next to me was already odd. Sure, it's cold, but horses don't huddle for warmth. They do lie down, but not next to people. They're prey animals and would typically be in a herd. They don't like to be prone around strangers. And sticking close, nuzzling my arm? It's all very strange behavior for a horse. Where did he come from? Why's he here?

And what drew him to me?

He might be wild, but those horses are typically afraid of people. There may not be a lot of them around, but they'd usually be in a herd. They'd also typically have had enough interactions in a populated place like this to be wary.

That makes me think he must have been broke, but if he's trained, how did such a beautifully fed, clearly healthy horse escape and come to find me? Alone? In the middle of essentially nowhere? I scan him for signs of ownership.

His hooves look well-trimmed, but he's barefoot—no shoes. That's no help. He has no halter or bridle, obviously, and no signs of having worn a saddle, either. No tell-tale white fur spots where someone regularly cinched him too tightly, but then again, proper riding wouldn't have resulted in those without advanced age, anyway.

I could try checking to see whether his teeth have been

recently floated, but to do that, I'd have to stick my hand in his mouth. Probably a bad plan. All in all, I have no idea why he's here.

Except for the heaven thing.

My last wish was to ride one last time. Could I be dead? Is this what happens when we die? Our last wishes are granted? I struggle to stand, and my leg screams in pain. I grunt and sink back to the ground. If it's heaven, then this sucks. I was counting on my leg being healed at the very least, and it feels exactly the same as before.

Destroyed.

Surely if I've died and moved on to some kind of after-life, I wouldn't take my mortal aches and pains with me. Right? Part of me wants to look upward and shout and rail and scream. Maybe God will strike me, but at least I'll get some answers.

"Who are you?" I ask.

The dark horse doesn't spook or shy away at the grating sound of my demand, like I expect him to. Instead, he tilts his head slightly, and then he tosses his head in a small, controlled way.

It almost seems like he's saying, "I hear what you're asking, but I'm a horse so I can't talk. Duh."

"Right, so I know you can't answer me," I say. "But I can't figure out how you found me or why you kept me warm. If you belong to someone, maybe they can help me."

That makes me think. No matter where I go, people are going to have a lot of questions. How did I get here? Why don't I have a coat?

I'm shivering now, and wishing I'd had it with me when I was, well, almost murdered. What was I thinking? I should never have let myself be thrown off a train to die without at least having a coat clutched in one hand.

The more I go over my story, the crazier it sounds, even to me. I clearly wasn't stabbed in my shoulder or back—I'd be dead. But I recall it happening *vividly*. I can still hear the crack of my clavicle as it struck the hard ground. Still feel the raindrops as they slap against my crumpled body. The smell of the mud and the spring rain. The sharp, searing pulsing from both knife wounds.

I glance down then, finally thinking of examining the injury sites. My dark jacket—far too thin for this weather—is battered and filthy. Landing in the mud did it no favors. My khaki riding pants are torn above the knee and just as dirty as my jacket. My boots appear scuffed, but otherwise are fine.

Perhaps because of the rain, nothing seems to be too bloody—but there's a small, flat slit in the right shoulder of my jacket where the knife tip protruded from the front of my body last night.

But if I *was* stabbed, I went out the window with a dagger still lodged in my shoulder. Where could it be? My head spins around too fast, dragging my body with it. A flash of silver a half dozen feet closer to the train track has me crawling around the inquisitive horse and toward the edge of the tracks.

I stop cold, a few feet away from a dark, gunmetal grey dagger, the shiny silver hilt gleaming at me, even through a layer of grime. There's a symbol on the handle—it looks like a double headed hatchet—not that it means a thing to me.

"I don't understand," I say aloud, as if giving voice to my confusion will somehow help me make sense of things. "I was stabbed with this knife last night, but now it's here, lying on the ground, and my shoulder is fine." I bounce it up and down without pain or even stiffness.

The dark horse bumps my side gently, his nose staying put this time. I reach for him slowly, my fingers curving around his solid face. He doesn't nip or even lip at me. He holds utterly still, his dark blue eye studying mine.

"You're a strange fellow," I say. "Most horses would run. I can't think of any that would lie down next to me. Did you see me get tossed out of that train window last night?"

He whinnies at that, and I wonder whether he has any idea what I'm saying. Surely not, but perhaps he understands the tone I'm using.

"I thought I was dead for sure." I sigh. "That's what I get for trying to help someone. Every time I've ever done that, it's gone badly for me. I knew better, but that little girl. If you'd seen her, you'd understand. She was so helpless and so cute, and she reminded me of. . .well. Of me."

He bumps my hand again.

"Are you even a boy?" I ask aloud. "I guess I should check, right?" I struggle to my feet, whimpering a little as my leg tries to buckle under me a second time. I stumble a few steps forward and take a closer look at him. "You are a boy, and if I'm not mistaken, you're a stallion, not a gelding. I can't decide whether that makes it more or less likely that you're a wild horse."

I reach one hand out, and he leans his face into my palm.

"A horse this nice needs a name. I can't just call you, 'hey you.'" I think for a moment. We're in Russia. He's big and bold and beautiful. "How about Khan? For Ghengis—"

He snorts loudly, flinging snot on me.

"Okay. Not that," I say. "I get it." I think for a moment before I have another idea. "What about Napoleon?"

He tosses his head and then coughs.

"Yeah, he's always drawn with a white horse. Plus, it's probably overused." I scratch under his massive head absently. "Alright, how about Charlemagne?"

The big stallion paws at the ground.

"He was a warrior-king who wasn't super well educated, but he was bright and learned from things around him. He defeated all his foes, and expanded his kingdom a lot."

He snorts.

"It sounds regal—just like you look. Some people around here might have trouble saying it, but it's not like it's really your name. I'm the only one who has to use it, and it sounds posh. You seem posh."

He bumps my hand gently, so I take it that he's alright with the new name.

"I'm guessing that there's someone, somewhere, who's frantic that you're missing. I wonder if they'll come looking for you. Maybe they can help me get back to the civilized world. Maybe I could even bum a phone call off them."

The horse nods again, as if he's agreeing with my logic.

"But what direction to go." I look around. "The sun rises in the east, and sets in the west. Since it's rising now, that must be east." I point. "And we were headed mostly south to get to Novgorod. I'm hoping someone there will take pity on me. One of the few numbers I have memorized is my friend Kris's." I can't help muttering. "If she'd just turn her phone on."

I take a slow, ponderous step in the direction I think the city must lie—which is also in line with the direction of the train track, so that's promising—and the dark horse takes off at a trot, breezing past me in the same direction I was headed.

It's illogical and ridiculous, but for a split second, I feel abandoned.

He doesn't know me. I don't own him or have any idea what he will do one moment to the next, and I should just be grateful he kept me warm enough last night that I didn't die. Even so, for some reason, I thought he'd stay with me.

I named him, for heaven's sake, and he gave me feedback.

When he stops, turns, and paws at the ground, I marvel again. What's he doing? He's going the same way I am and turning back to watch my very slow, very painful progress?

He calls out then, neighing loud and long, and tosses his head.

"I know I'm slow," I say, "but this is my maximum speed." I look down and point. "My leg. See? It's no good. You're lucky I'm moving at all without my crutches."

The enormous horse trots back toward me, quickly, almost aggressively, and he bows his head lower, his nose inhaling and exhaling robustly. He blows an entire mouthful of air out across my leg, as if expressing his dissatisfaction with my disability.

"Believe me, I agree with you. I hate it, too."

He tosses his head, then. And then he turns his long, graceful neck and tosses his head again. Then he straightens and looks at me almost expectantly.

I have no idea what's going through his bizarre equine brain, so I ignore him and keep shuffling on, one tortuously painful step at a time. At this rate, I should reach civilization in approximately twelve years, three months, and seven days. If I'm lucky, and if my leg doesn't just give out first.

Charlemagne shrieks his disapproval, and then he circles me at a big, showy trot, his dark tail streaming behind him. He tosses his head, his shining mane fluttering in the wind.

"What do you want?" I ask, annoyed now. "I can't go faster. If you have any idea what I'm saying you must understand that. This is my top speed, you big show-off."

But that only makes him angrier. He prances faster and faster, circling me alarmingly close. Finally, I reach out and slap his perfectly shaped rear haunch, praying that he won't kick out at me.

"Knock it off, you big bully. Nothing you do will make me go faster. You can't herd an injured animal."

He blows out air loudly and paws at the ground, and then he drops to a knee in the front, one leg bent, the other stretched out. Charlemagne's head is bowed, and he tilts his nose toward me and tosses it.

Almost like he's telling me to climb on his back.

Which would be entirely insane.

No wild horse would sleep by me, wake up and follow me, and then demand that I get on his back. No broke horse would do that, either.

None of it makes sense.

But then again, neither do stab wounds healing, or people surviving being tossed off moving trains.

"Let's say that you really are telling me to get on your back right now," I say.

His head pops up, his eye wide. He tosses it up and down.

"You are."

He tosses it again and whinnies.

"You want me to climb up onto your back?" I point.

He neighs again and tosses his head.

"Do I really think I'm talking to a horse, and he's responding to me?" I sigh. "Is this really the most insane thing that's happened to me since waking up?" Sadly, it's not. "But here's the thing. Even if you're telling me to do that, I can't listen. I haven't been on a horse in a decade. It's not safe for me. If I fall, my leg will just. . .well, it's like the insides will explode."

He tosses his head again, and then he curls his lips back. Horse people often call it a smile, but it's more like a dramatic lip curl.

"I can't get on you," I say, shouting now. "If you can understand me, which is totally nuts, then you should get this part too. I cannot ride a horse."

Unless it was an inexplicably magical horse, one that didn't spook, or buck, or bolt. A horse that didn't behave like a horse at all. . .

"You're not magical," I say. "And I don't have a saddle or

a bridle, which would make me getting on your back even more insane."

Charlemagne finally stands up, but only to take a few steps closer and bow down again. When his head whips toward me, the only reason I don't move away is that I don't have time. His mouth closes over my sleeve and he chomps down, luckily just on fabric, and then he tugs.

A horse is literally *pulling* me toward his back.

"If I reach up here and climb on you, you won't shy away or freak out and run?"

I've lost my mind to even be considering this.

"I haven't been on a horse in ten years," I say. "I'm not sure I even remember how to ride."

He whuffles this time, and lips the sleeve of my jacket. Then he rubs his head against my arm. For all the world, it seems like he's trying to reassure me.

"If I climb on, will you listen to me? Will you go where I want you to go?"

When he nods his head, it doesn't even surprise me, which shows just how crazy I've become. I *expect* him to understand me and respond in a way that makes sense.

"You're my knight in the form of a dark bay stallion?" I arch one eyebrow. "I should climb on your back and trust that you'll give me a ride somewhere safe? Is that really what you're saying?"

This is absolutely bonkers, but he neighs and tosses his head again. . .and I climb on. When I put all my weight on my bad leg to swing my good leg up and over, I nearly collapse into a heap, but after a few solid seconds of blinding pain, I finally manage to clamber onto his back.

He's utterly still and calm for the entire ordeal.

"I think we should head that way." I point down the tracks, in the direction I was shambling before.

And he starts to walk that direction, slowly, his head turning back to look at me several times.

"I'm fine," I say.

And then he starts to trot.

My legs squeeze to grip, and pain shoots upward from my injured one. "Ow," I grunt.

And he drops to a walk again and sighs loudly.

"I'm sorry," I say. "I hate slowing you down."

He shakes his head then, back and forth, as if to tell me he's not upset. Then he neighs. His walk speeds up a bit, and I don't complain, so he holds that speed.

It's at least three miles before we encounter an outbuilding. I'm excited at first, but as we approach, it's clearly abandoned. Within another half mile, we start to see more and more. I try to angle him toward a small hut with smoke curling out of the chimney, but he won't deviate from his path.

"I think people are there." I tug on his mane. "See, there?"

He tosses his head and neighs.

"You think that's a bad place?" I squint. There's a clothesline and a very old, very ramshackle old truck parked out front. "They might have a phone."

He tosses his head again, and speeds up until it's almost uncomfortable for me.

"Seems like you have a plan."

He snorts.

"If you're sure." He whinnies softly, so I let him be.

Not half a mile farther down the road, an enormous mansion with several outbuildings comes into view. It's made of a bright, grey stone, and there are two large onion domes on the front towers, with a huge one in the center of the building, reminding me of the architecture I've seen in Moscow and Saint Petersburg on churches, mostly, but also on lavish buildings and homes.

Charlemagne angles right toward it.

"Whoa." I tug on the dark horse's mane until he stops.

"A shack may have been a bad idea, but this is for *sure* a bad plan. There's no way that whoever owns that will want me knocking on their door."

But after listening to me, he snorts and starts forward again.

"Hey." I yank harder. "Listen here. I didn't insist that we approach that tiny house before, so you need to listen to me here. This is a bad plan. We can't go there." I point at the imposing iron gate we've nearly reached. "Those people do not want vagrants coming and asking for help."

But he ignores me yet again, and picks up speed until he's trotting for the gate.

"Hey." I'm shouting now, and pulling on his mane. Fear spikes inside of me. What's Charlemagne's deal? Did his owner train him to bring people to him? Is he some kind of honeytrap? "I can't go there."

The kind of people who own massive estates like that are people like the man on the train. My ex, Danils. Others like him.

But it's too late. By the time the stupid stallion finally stops, we're standing mere feet from the wrought iron gate in front of the estate, and someone has seen us.

"Hello?" A short, stocky man wearing a dark uniform and an ushanka, with the ear flaps dropped down and tied under his chin, salutes. "Who are you, and what business do you have here?"

I yank again on the stupid horse's mane, but he still doesn't budge. Instead, he whinnies. Loudly.

"Um." I clear my throat, trying my hardest to sound legitimately Russian. "I'm hoping to use your phone." I sound like an idiot. "I was recently, er, I'm lost. And I'm cold."

"You're in Russia in April." The man scowls. "Where's your coat?"

I pull my jacket tighter. "If I could just use a phone."

"This is not a halfway house," the man says. "Nor is it a government owned property any longer. It's a privately owned estate, and you need to keep on going into town. Maybe someone there can help you." The man sniffs.

Charlemagne is, inexplicably, furious. He paws at the ground and neighs. He snorts and prances. And then he takes off, trotting quickly enough that my leg protests.

No, it screams.

"Ow," I say. "That hurts. Can you slow down, at least?"

But apparently, he cannot slow down. Moments later, we're circling the edge of the fence, and I realize where he's headed. There's a low spot—where the gate has broken down and sags sideways. Charlemagne circles around and heads straight for it.

With me on his back.

"No," I shout. "You have to stop and let me off."

But he doesn't stop. He glances back at me over his shoulder, and he bobs his head and whinnies, and then he picks up more speed, and before I can even object, we're sailing over the low spot.

Without even thinking, I drop into jump position, my hands gripping his mane tightly, my thighs gripping his body, and then we land. The staccato force of the landing, front and then back, slams into my leg like a freight train.

I choke on my shout, because the man must have known where we were going. He's standing in front of us now, glowering, and a half dozen others are filtering toward us from the big house, clearly responding to his agitated shouting.

"I've called his lordship," the man says, "and he was already on his way to check on the progress with the bathrooms. You'd better stay right there, because when he arrives, he's going to be livid."

"I told him to repair that fence." A matronly woman near the top of the rise is shaking her head. "I told him, and he said we could do that after we finished cleaning up the house."

My horse takes it into his head to circumvent all of that, and starts moving again, heading up the hill. I yank and pull, and I even sit back, remaining as stiff as possible, in spite of the pain it causes my leg, hoping the discomfort will make my idiotic horse stop.

None of it works. We're nearly to the front of the house, with servants and grounds staff jogging after us and shouting, when a black sports car roars around the corner and stops at the front gate.

"He's here." The sour-faced ushanka man from the front gate shouts and points. "His lordship's here." The smug smile on his face makes me all kinds of nervous.

But my horse seems utterly unconcerned. He neighs loudly and dives forward again, heading for the front of the home.

Clearly possessing some kind of entry button, the gate swings open for the black car, and it revs loudly and flies up the drive until it reaches the circular driveway in front of the home. It screeches to a halt, and the driver's side door's thrown open.

"Grigoriy?" A tall man with dark hair who looks familiar leaps from the car. His eyes are wild, and his hands are gesturing broadly. "Grigoriy!?"

"Aleks?" My best friend in the world, Kristiana Liepa, opens the passenger side door and hops out. When she turns around, her eyes meet mine and widen. "Mirdza?"

4

My mom's always been a pretty decent mother. She loved us. She fed us and cared for us, and unlike a lot of other moms, when things got hard, she didn't drown herself in a bottle. If it hadn't been for meeting and marrying Mārtinš, which she thought was prudent at the time, she'd have been practically perfect.

She worked hard to support us after Dad died, and that's how I met Kris, actually. My mom got hired to be their housekeeper, and it came with a little apartment in the corner of their barn. We moved in there, and a window to a whole different world with a very kind and welcoming window-keeper opened up.

My mom's general goodness is why I felt so guilty for pretending, after we moved, that Amelia Liepa was my mother.

She was just so beautiful, and so graceful, and so talented, and while my mother worked hard to clean and cook inside her home, Amelia spent all her time outside, working with the most majestic creatures I'd ever seen. Horses were animals I'd never have the funds to own or the knowledge to work with at all.

Except, that angel of a woman taught me.

Right alongside Kris, she taught me and my sister Adriana everything she knew about horses. Amelia Liepa, with her softly accented Latvian, would teach the three of us a lesson every single day. Once we progressed enough that we could ride competently, she'd use us to work her horses. And eventually, she had us help her train the new ones.

Shortly after I transitioned into a somewhat helpful role. . .she died.

That's when my lessons stopped, too.

For a while.

But her daughter was just as kind, and Kristiana welcomed me and Adriana to join her in training with John, their long-time horse trainer. I was able to gain a life skill and pursue my passion, thanks to the largesse and generosity of some very wealthy, very gifted friends. Most people of the same social strata as Kristiana would've refused to rub shoulders with the children of the house-keeper, but her American mother had different notions. She felt that we were all the same—our jobs differed, but our value didn't.

They were radical ideas, but they stuck with me as much as the equine knowledge I gained. All of it shaped me into the person I am today.

Sometimes I wonder whether I'd have been happier if I had grown up on the same steady diet of misogyny and elitism that the rest of my friends and colleagues were fed. But for better or worse, Kris and her mother made Adriana and me into feminist egalitarians.

My poor sister Adriana, ninety-nine percent spitfire, always resented both of them, probably because of their teachings. She was born with nothing in a world that always seems to take. It filled her with an almost bottom-less rage and desire for more. She has the energy and resolve to change her fate, and has done everything she can to do it.

Not me.

I've never had anything but gratitude and love in my heart for my best friend. That's why, when I find myself broken and alone, riding a dangerous and unknown horse in the middle of an unfriendly and freezing environment, my only hope was to find someone who would let me borrow their phone so I could reach out to dear Kristiana Liepa and beg for her help just one more time.

My shock when she drives up in a sportscar driven by 'his lordship' and climbs out after the very same—penniless—horse trainer I met in Dauvavpils at Liepašeta is utterly and completely unfeigned. I have absolutely no idea what to say or how to react.

"What are you doing here?" I almost forget I'm on horseback for a moment, until the stupid stallion beneath me stamps and paws the ground.

"I should be asking *you* that," Kris says.

"Wait." Aleksandr turns. "*Mirdza?*"

"Who's Grigoriy?" I ask. "Is he that rude butler guy? He's really angry that I came in here, and he said you'd kick me out."

"Why did you come?" Kris asks. "I mean, to Russia, but also, why are you *here?*"

My stallion's clearly not liking being ignored. He screams in frustration, and my anxiety at being mounted—especially without a bridle, saddle, or anything approaching a medical clearance—escalates.

"Can you help me off?" I'm shaking, I realize. "This horse—I kind of just *found* him. Or, maybe he found me. I'm not really sure. He's the one who insisted we come here, and even when I kept saying no and tugging on his mane, he vaulted over a low spot in the fence. It's a miracle I haven't fallen to my death."

"Wait, here, as in, the horse insisted you come to this house?" Aleks has walked closer, and he's studying my horse.

I forgot, for a brief moment, that he's an actual horse trainer. People all say he's crazy, but he did tame the big black stallion Kris bought last year. Maybe he knows this horse? Could *Charlemagne* be Grigoriy?

"Yes. He wouldn't stop elsewhere, no matter what I did. He came straight here." I shudder.

"Hey there." Kris steps closer, her hands upraised. "I can help you down."

Of course, she's about five foot one, a hundred pounds. Since this stallion's at least seventeen hands, dismounting toward her would be a bit like leaping to my death.

"Don't be ridiculous." Aleksandr towers over Kris. He rolls his eyes and smiles at her fondly as he steps past her and offers me his hands.

Unfortunately, my idiot horse freaks out, shying sideways, nostrils flaring, and snaps at Aleks.

"Stop that." I pat his side with one hand and grip his thick mane as tightly as I can with the other. "I need help getting down, you idiot. I have a bad leg, remember?"

Aleks glares at the horse as if that will have any impact. Then he mutters, "Knock it off, moron," in Russian. "I'm helping." But when he approaches again, the stallion shies away just the same.

This time, his ears are pinned as he screams.

"Look." I point at Kris. "This is my best friend. She's the person I was trying to call. She's the whole reason I came here to Russia to begin with. I'll be fine, now. You got me to safety."

The dark bay paws at the ground again, this time with his one dark front leg.

"Listen, you stupid, bloody idiot," Aleksandr practically growls. "If you don't let me get her off your back this very moment, I'm going to *bury* you, and you know I can put you underground." He doesn't approach again—he just glares.

Charlemagne's nostrils flare. He huffs. He paws. He snorts. But finally, he drops down and bows.

I slide off his back to the ground.

"Finally." Aleks shakes his head. "Was I this moronic?" He quirks an eyebrow and stares at Kris, as if his question makes any sense at all.

"You were way worse," she says.

"What's going on?" I'm so confused.

Aleks sighs. "The thing is, I know this gu—"

"Horse. He knows this horse." Kris takes his arm and leans against him. "Aleksandr trained Grigoriy." She beams, but something's off. She's forcing her cheer, and I definitely need to know why.

Oh, no. Is the horse nuts? Did it break free, and now it's running wild, kidnapping women?

That makes no sense. Horses don't kidnap people.

But their bizarre shared glances, which are now getting more intense, make even less sense. Kris is shaking her head, and cutting her eyes toward me. Aleksandr's gesturing and throwing his hands up in the air.

"No, she speaks English and Russian, too," Kristiana says. "I told you that my mom taught us at the same time."

"Hello?" I say. "Are you guys practicing some kind of pantomime?"

Kris spins around and smiles at me again.

"That smile's freaking me right out," I say. "And that's shocking, really, after the night I've had."

"Let's start there," Kris says. "How did you get here?"

"By train, mostly," I say, taking a step toward her. "This is *so* not how I planned to tell you this." I wince. Even one single step hurts. "But the thing is, while I was at Brigita's, I had an accident. That one horse I told you about, the crazy one that little girl bought, freaked out, and I got her off, but it slammed me against a wall in the process."

Kris closes her eyes.

"The government docs told me it was not fixable and offered me a wheelchair. They said if it gets infected, they'd amputate at this point, and I'd get a new, top-of-the-line prosthetic." I can barely say the words. "I decided to look into private options."

"Obviously." Kris looks ill. "And?"

"They would need to do another round of surgeries, hopefully just two, to try and reconstruct the bone into something that will hold my weight. They think there's about a fifty-fifty shot that it will work and I'll be able to keep walking."

I haven't said that out loud to anyone else.

It means that loaning me the money is a tremendous gamble. I didn't even tell Adriana. It's too depressing. I could borrow fifty grand and never be fit enough to earn the money to ever repay it. The surgeries—costly, arduous, and painful—have as much chance of failure as they do of success.

I can't even blame Brigita for firing me. It's what she should have done. It's what anyone would have done if I was honest with them. But I can't lie to Kris, especially not when I'm asking her to give me money for it.

"But how did you meet this horse?" Aleks asks.

"Charlemagne?"

"Wait, you're calling him. . .what?" Kris glances back at Aleksandr with a twitching lip.

"I went through a few, and he seemed to like that one best," I say. "I'm sorry. I forgot you said he has a name. Grigoriy." I can't help thinking that's a terrible name for a horse. It sounds like a Russian business mogul or something, not a horse. "Well." Now that I have to explain it,

I'm not sure quite what to say. "I was on the train for a long time. We'd almost reached Novgorod."

"Okay." Kris's brow furrows.

I notice that the people who were at the gate of this estate, barring my entry initially, are all lined up now, standing in a semi-circle behind Kris and Aleks. "Maybe we should talk about this somewhere else." My leg's aching and sending periodic shooting pains through me all at the same time. "Is there somewhere I can sit? Maybe where there aren't as many people?"

"Right." Aleks shakes his head. "Let's go inside."

"Wait, is this your house?" I glance behind me again, somewhat in awe. Kris's penniless trainer owns a *mansion*?

"Not exactly." Kris smiles. "This one belongs to someone who's been away for a long time. Our house is—"

"Wait, did you just say *our*?" My brain feels fuzzy. I clearly didn't get much sleep the past two days.

Kris beams, and this time, her wide, open grin isn't forced. "We have a lot to catch up on."

"Clearly," I say.

"Let's head back, feed her, and then maybe call some doctors." Kris doesn't look like she's asking, the way she's staring at Aleks expectantly.

"Wait," I say. "Did you switch to Latvian? When did Aleks learn Latvian?"

"He's known it for a long time," Kris says, at the same time Aleks says, "I just learned it."

They laugh.

Like something really funny is happening.

"So you want to tell her?" Aleks's eyes light up. "Are you sure?"

Kris's smile is forced again. "About how we fell in love and kept things private so people wouldn't pry?" She nods. "And about how you lost this horse, and we've been looking for him for a while?" She bobs her head again. "Of course."

Aleks frowns. "How about you drive back to my place, and I'll bring the lost horse back in a. . .trailer?"

"Right." Kris bites her lip. "Well." She glances at me. "I mean, he found her or something. May as well try this real quick." She marches toward me, shifting at the last second and practically running into the stallion. Her hand presses firmly against his shoulder, and she says, "I wish you were a man."

She wishes. . .*what?* Clearly she and Aleks have some bizarre inside jokes or something.

The stallion's head whipped around when she walked toward him, and his ears went back. But now that she's still just standing there, her hand on his shoulder, he bares his teeth, almost like a dog.

"Okay." Kris snatches her hand back and trots back toward Aleks. "So, that didn't work."

"Did you *actually* think he'd turn into a human?" I can't help laughing. "You've been reading too many books. I saw that *Night of the Wolf* on your bedside table," I say.

Okay, that's a lie. I didn't just see it. I swiped it and read it. Along with *Wolf's Mate, Wolf Girl, Wolf Born,* and *Wolf's Destiny.* They were all pretty good. I mean, they weren't my usual read, but I could see why Kris had gotten into them.

"You know that werewolves—and also horse shifters, by extension—don't exist, right?"

Kris's lips twitch.

Clearly she *does* know, and now she's mocking me. Awesome. "If Aleks grabs me a halter, I think I can put it on him."

The look on Aleks's face is hard to interpret. He looks either amused or horrified, and I don't know him well enough to be sure which it is. "I think I can handle it."

Fine. He's a trainer. He's healthy and strong. Good luck to him. I start to limp toward the sports car. "I'll see you back at your apartment or whatever, then."

I may not have stab wounds, somehow, and I must not have broken my collarbone when I hit that window like I thought, but it didn't help my leg at all. If anything, it's gotten worse.

A spear of pain shoots up my leg and into my butt and I nearly fall. *Much* worse, apparently.

I miss my crutches, and I start looking around for a stick that might work, like an alcoholic in desperate straits might start looking for hairspray, or mouthwash. No luck. This estate is too well kept, other than that sagging fence, apparently.

"Uh," I stifle a groan as I make my way toward the car.

Before I can take another step, the stallion's rushed over next to me, bumping my shoulder with his head.

"What?" I whisper. "I found my friend, thanks to your help. I'm pretty sure you kept me warm overnight, and then you got me here. You have no idea how grateful I am. But someone owns you, and you need to be a good boy and let Aleks take you to them." I rub his nose. "Alright?"

He snorts. Loudly.

"I mean it."

He slides his head up under my shoulder, and I realize that he's bracing me to help me walk.

Tears well up in my eyes.

No one, other than Kris, has ever helped me. Even my heart horse, who's amazing, has never really paid enough attention to when I was hurting and tried to lend a hand— er, or a head, as the case may be.

"I'll be fine," I whisper. "I swear I will. Kris will help me find a doctor."

I realized it the moment I said the words aloud—she will do whatever it takes to help me. In fact, my best friend has already opened the passenger side door for me. Her face is earnest, concerned, and attentive.

"I'm sure you called," she says. "I'm so sorry. My phone

broke.”

“She dropped it in the toilet.” Aleks’s lips are twitching again. “She was too preoccupied playing that stupid game.”

“Not Clash of Clans again?” I’m laughing too. “I told you to quit wasting time on that.”

“There was a war attack I had to do, alright? I can’t let my team down.”

“I did try to call,” I say, “but I didn’t want to ask for this kind of help on the phone anyway.” Plus, now I get to see what she’s doing out here. Even though I’m the one begging for help, I can’t stop feeling like she might need me almost as much as I need her. Something about her and Aleks feels. . .strange.

“I’m so sorry. We’ve been so busy I just haven’t had time to go get a new phone yet.”

“I’m unbelievably lucky that you happened to be coming here,” I say. “What are the odds?”

“Actually, the crazed butler from earlier called Aleks,” Kris says.

I’m releasing Grigoriy the stallion to slide into the car, but I freeze. “What?”

“Aleks is the caretaker for this place right now, while its owner is lost.”

“He called Aleks ‘his lordship.’” Maybe that was a stretch, but being a caretaker is still a much better job than a traveling horse trainer. But does it mean that Kris will be stuck here? I selfishly hope not.

“We can talk more later. We’ll see Aleks soon, I’m sure?” She glances his way.

He nods, but he’s too busy staring intently as he approaches the stallion to pay much attention to us.

I slide into the seat and close the door. Kris presses a button to turn over the engine, and the car roars to life. But the second she puts it into gear and starts to drive, my beautiful bay begins to freak out, bucking and rearing and tossing his head like a lunatic. Kris slams on the brakes to avoid hitting him.

Grigoriy's rearing back and screaming so loudly I can actually hear him over the growling of the engine.

"What's going on with him?" I ask.

Kris blinks, and then she turns slowly toward me. "I think we'd better not try to leave." She kills the engine and climbs out. "Aleks, why were you freaking out after the Grade One? When they kept sedating you?"

He freezes, her enormous, beautiful boyfriend. His head turns slowly. "I was panicked."

I can barely hear him, so I open my door and use the frame to stand up next to the car. "Panicked? Wait. They sedated *a person* back in Ireland?" What are they saying?

"After the race ended, they dragged me away from you," he says.

"That's what I thought." She claps her hands and raises her voice. "I need all of you to turn and go inside the house, right now. No questions. No peeping out windows. Just go."

"There aren't any windows facing us from the house," Aleks says.

"I know," Kris says. "And that's a good thing." She and Aleks exchange yet *another* glance that I do *not* understand.

But finally, after the people have left, Kris turns toward me slowly, as if I'm a horse she doesn't want to spook. She *should* be afraid of the total lunatic animal that practically ran over our car, but it appears she's afraid of *me* for some reason. "I've known you for a long time."

I nod.

"You trust me, right?" Her gaze is intent.

"Of course." Why else would I be here? "I got stabbed on a train last night, chucked out the window, and somehow made it back to you." How's that for sounding crazy?

Her mouth drops open.

"By whom?" Aleks is now standing like a soldier, and he looks ready to attack something, his shoulders square, his eyes sparking, and his hands fisted at his sides.

Grigoriy's nostrils are flaring, and he's looking around as if he might find an enemy behind a bush as well.

"It was some mob boss whose girlfriend I tried to protect." I shake my head. "Did I mention I had a fit of stupidity on the train?"

"Wait, are you serious?" Kris's whole face looks terrified. "Do you think it really was someone with the mafia?" She's looking at Aleks now.

He shrugs. "We have a lot of things to ask her, but it's fine. Whatever the answers are, it's fine." He beams. "Because we found him, and we finally have people who might answer them."

Kris is smiling, too. "If I ask you to do something, will you just do it, no questions?"

The last thirty-six hours have been some of the most painful, and definitely the most bizarre, of my entire life. First I was fired and betrayed. Then my sister actually had enough money to send me here. I stood up for someone, was nearly killed, somehow miraculously healed, and then found by a horse—which I rode for the first time in a decade—and now I've found my friend and she's acting like we're in some play, but I lost the script and don't know my lines.

"Sure," I finally say. How much stranger could today really get?

"I want you to walk up to Grigoriy," she says softly. "Place your hand on him." She pauses.

"Okay."

"And then say, 'I wish you were a human man.'"

I laugh.

"I'm serious."

The same thing she said earlier? "What's going on?"

"Just humor me," she says. "And prepare yourself for something very, very strange to happen."

Aleks strides toward her. "Are you sure—"

Kris holds up her hand. "I'm almost positive she's involved somehow. She said *he found her*."

Aleks frowns.

I don't have to move to touch the stallion. He's circled the car to stand right beside me. His head slowly lowers toward mine, and I hold out my hand. My fingers part slightly, and I place my hand right in between his eyes. "I wish you were a human man," I lie. Because who would *ever* prefer a human man to a horse?

An electric pulse shoots through me then, as if I've brushed against a very high voltage electric fence. A stallion fence, maybe. And then I'm flung backward, my head slamming against the frame of the car's door.

"Ow." I straighten slowly, rubbing one hand over my eyes and face. "What the hedge was that?"

Kris isn't even listening to me.

Neither is Aleks.

They're both staring, their mouths gaping open.

I turn to follow their gaze, and my mouth drops as well. Right in front of me is a very large, very muscular, very naked man.

His longish, dark brown hair is shaggy, and he looks like a copycat carving of the ancient Greek gods, with perfectly sculpted muscle covering his upper and lower body.

With one notable exception.

He would need an *extra* large loincloth. No simple Speedo would work to keep him modest.

I can't help swallowing, in spite of the dryness of my mouth. "What—who—Where's Grigoriy?"

The very hot, very large, very *hung*, naked man arches one dark eyebrow over a startlingly cerulean eye. "I'm Grigoriy, and I'm very pleased to finally meet you, Mirdza."

5

Once, when I was seven years old, I went to a birthday party for one of the rich kids in my school class. They had a lot of things at that celebration that shocked and amazed me, from a cake almost as tall as I was to people walking around the room with trays of food. They were carrying them so that the guests could pluck things off to eat. Why they didn't just put them on the table and let us walk over to the table? It's still a mystery.

But the strangest thing of all was something we did as an activity at the party. A man showed up and helped us—in our party dresses and Sunday-best shoes—to pour white glue into a bucket... and then to add shaving cream to it. He asked Elmira what her favorite color was—she said blue —and he dumped blue food coloring into it.

It turned into *slime*.

The feel was odd. The look was bizarre. None of us had ever felt anything quite like it. We all shrieked at the feel of it against our skin. The party girl decided she wanted someone to take off their shoes and stand in the bucket. It was a weird request, but seven-year-olds are odd.

For some reason, she chose me to do it.

Pretty soon everyone in the room was chanting my name. It was exhilarating, and terrifying, and exciting. I unbuckled my shoes, and then I stepped in the bucket. The slime squished between my toes and I sank and sank and sank. . .and then another hand slid into mine, our fingers interlocking.

The whole thing—all the eyes on me, the slime in my toes, and my bare feet in a bucket—was terrifying. But it was far less scary than it would have been without Kristiana's hand in mine, her calm demeanor, and her reassuring words in my ear.

That day, I learned that scary things aren't nearly as frightening when you're doing them with a friend at your side. So today, after watching a horse transform magically into a human man, who then turned and addressed me by name, I turn to face my friend.

She smiles at me reassuringly.

Kristiana doesn't look alarmed, shocked, *or even surprised.*

"What's going on?" I angle away from the naked man, and if I do it partly because a small part of me wants to keep looking and looking and looking, well. I'm proud of myself for doing the polite thing.

"Okay." Kris smiles and bobs her head like a cheerleader at a pep rally. "Wow, you're taking this really well."

"Taking this?" I blink.

"The first time Aleks shifted in front of me—"

Aleksandr hisses.

"I'm pretty sure the halter's off this wild horse, hun," she says. "She just watched Grigoriy shift, and also, 'Yay! He shifted.'" She smiles at him. "That means I was right, and she's involved. Now it's time to make sure my dearest friend of all time is also on board with keeping this secret?"

She turns back toward me slowly, biting her bottom lip and half-smiling.

"On board with *what,* exactly?"

"So, I never really told anyone, including you, but it's not personal," Kris says. "I wanted to tell you."

"You wanted to tell me. . .that your boyfriend is a horse?" I can feel my brows pulling together.

"Yes." Kris smiles again. "Look how fast she's accepting it!"

"Accepting *what?*" I ask. "None of this makes sense." But the fact that the horse in front of me who was so helpful, and so insistent, and so, well, so human, *is a human,* well, it makes sense. I mean, it doesn't. But also, it does.

"Aleksandr Volkonsky is a Russian prince who comes from a long line of princes who have magical powers and can shift into horse forms." Kristiana looks totally serious.

So does her boyfriend.

I can't bring myself to look at the naked man, who must be part icicle by now. At least it stopped raining. "And?"

"He and his two best friends fell victim to some part of the magic that made them the way they were by refusing to help some other friends of theirs."

Aleksandr coughs.

"Okay, more like, acquaintances of theirs. It triggered some kind of curse."

"A curse?"

"We're looking into it," she says. "But until today, we haven't had any luck at locating his friends or figuring out the details of the curse."

"Grigoriy?" I ask. "That's one of his friends?"

She nods. "The good news is, this is Grigoriy's house." Kris points. "So the fact that he popped up here, close by, is really good."

His house. The enormous mansion is. . .the naked man's house? "Wait. He owns that?" I can't help turning around to look—and seeing a very naked, still quite hot, and also covered-in-goosebumps man behind me. "Someone get that guy a shirt and some pants." I shake my head.

Aleksandr springs into action, shedding his coat. "You're never cold, so I didn't think about it as an urgency."

"My powers aren't working for some reason," Grigoriy says softly, clearly shivering. "Wha-wha-what's going on?"

"You're lucky I was here," Aleks says. "No one else was awake when I woke up, stuck in my equine form. I was taken by some horrible men, sedated heavily over and over, broken to be ridden, and made to race with men on my back."

Like a ton of bricks being dropped on my head, it all starts to make sense. "Wait." I turn back to face Kristiana. "*Obsidian Devil?*"

She nods.

"*He's—Aleksandr* is Obsidian Devil? They're the same— er—not person, but they're the same. . .entity?"

"The very same," Kris says.

Of course. "That's why I never saw him with the horse he was supposed to be training."

Kris shrugs.

"You have no idea how many jokes the grooms made about him. They all thought you were sleeping together, but no one could figure out why you kept him around just for that." I should not have said that, judging by the look on her face. I throw my hands up. "I defended you."

"How classy of them." Kris looks irritated as she turns to face Aleks. "Now that she knows, maybe we. . ." She tosses her head up the hill, toward the mansion this man apparently owns.

"Yes, that's a good plan. I could use a very stiff drink." Grigoriy sounds far too calm for someone who was recently bucking and rearing back *as a horse* and who was apparently stuck sleeping for a long time under some curse. "I assume

Heinrich stuck around, even if many of the staff left. He'll have kept the best vodka safe."

"Is there any good vodka?" My joke falls a little flat with this crowd.

Even Kris, who should have laughed, looks preoccupied. "About the staff."

"Clearly, given the state of my home, not many of my people stuck around once I disappeared."

Aleks cringes. "Yeah, so."

"So, what?" Grigoriy glances from Aleks to me and back again, as if I might know what's making his friend nervous.

"Don't look at me. I haven't met anyone. I have no idea who Heinrich is."

"It's been a hundred years and change since we were cursed," Aleks says. "All your staff, whether they stuck around or not, are now dead."

This time, Grigoriy's the one sputtering. "What?"

"It took me the better part of a month to get this pile of rubble looking as good as it looks right now. It's a work in progress, but it's much better than it was."

"Wait, how old are you?" I ask. "Are you, like, a vampire?"

Kris laughs, then claps a hand over her mouth. "Sorry. I wondered that, too."

"Am I a what?" Grigoriy frowns.

"It's a dead person who walks around drinking blood," Aleks says. "Apparently some horror novel published just before the famine has everyone believing there may be corpses walking around among humans."

"I don't actually believe it," I mutter. "But is that really any crazier than a horse-shifter magician?"

"We prefer the word mage," Grigoriy says.

"And for the record, vampires are hot," Kris says. "Don't knock them."

That makes Aleksandr scowl for some reason.

"Inside," Kris says. "Go. Before your powerless friend who just came back freezes to death." She starts walking up the hill, and Aleks follows, so I start walking, too. Or at least, I try. I close the door of the car and attempt to put my weight on my bad leg, but not with any success. I make it about half a step and nearly topple over.

Before I can say a word, Grigoriy takes my arm in his, and then he wraps his other arm around my shoulders, bracing me against his enormous, very solid body.

And I realize that Aleks's jacket does not cover nearly enough.

"Kris!" My voice is ragged—almost panicked.

"What?" She turns around, and swears under her breath. "I'm so sorry. I forgot about your leg again." She glances at Grigoriy. "In my defense, until a few moments ago, I thought Mirdza could walk. Her leg wasn't solid enough to risk a fall from riding, but she walked around just fine."

I shake Grigoriy's arm off.

"I'll just carry her." Aleks is following Kris back down the hill. "That'll be the fastest way—"

Grigoriy's head snaps toward his friend. "You will not."

"Excuse me?" I ask.

"I'm fully clothed and won't show any parts of anything to anyone," Aleks says. "They care a great deal about that these days."

"People didn't care about nudity a hundred years ago?" Kris asks. "I find that hard to believe."

"Our people were accustomed to our occasional shifts," Aleksandr says. "They didn't react as irrationally as you do." But the set of his lips tells me that he just likes messing with her.

"I'll help her." Grigoriy tightens his grip on my arms. "She can avert her eyes, if the sight of my body bothers her that much."

"I'll be fine," I say. "I may move slowly, but—"

Suddenly, strong arms are shifting, pulling, and with a whoosh, I'm being carried. "Enough."

Just as he forced me to ride him before, now Grigoriy's striding quickly up the hill, gaining on Aleks and Kris, and then passing them. "Who's running this place now?"

"A man named Sergey," Kris says.

"Servant?" Grigoriy laughs. "Really?"

"It's a common name now," Aleks says. "No joke. I've met dozens of people with that name."

Grigoriy's shaking his head, his long hair shifting across his shoulders to brush against my face.

My hand itches to reach out and touch it, and I'm horrified. What's wrong with me? I should be reeling still, struggling to process that the horse who saved me, the horse who gave me a ride *here*, is actually a *man*.

Then something he said registers. My brain is like that when I'm tired. It works in fits and starts. I look over Grigoriy's shoulder and direct a question at Aleks. "What powers would usually keep him warm?" I ask. "You said that, usually, he wouldn't be cold."

"You can ask me," Grigoriy says softly, his voice gruff, his breath warming my face. "I'm right here."

How do I explain that it's strange to talk to someone who was a stallion four minutes ago? I can't really tell him that I'm trying to pretend the man who's carrying me doesn't exist. "Right."

"Normally, I can harness the wind," he says. "Using its currents, I'm always precisely the temperature I wish to be."

That must be nice.

"I don't understand how they could not be working. I used my powers last night," Grigoriy says.

"You did?" Aleks jogs up next to us. "When?"

"Twice," Grigoriy says. "First, to heal her, and then to keep us warm."

"So I really did get stabbed," I say. "That's not all in my head."

"You were nearly gone when I found you." Grigoriy's arms tighten around me, and his voice drops, its timbre deepening. "I'm going to find that man who—"

Aleks clears his throat. "I could use my powers as well, but only when Kris was touching me."

Grigoriy slows down, mere steps from what looks like a massive side door to the palace. A half smile turns the corner of his mouth up. And then the wind whistles all around us, tossing my hair up and flying past.

"Yes," Grigoriy says, his voice rumbling against me. "Yeees."

Suddenly we're lifting up off the ground, and I can't help it. I panic. "No!" I shriek. "Put me down."

As quickly as we lifted into the air, we drop back down, lightly, and I can breathe again.

But Grigoriy doesn't release me. If anything, he tightens his grip yet again. "Let's get inside first."

Without even touching the massive wooden double doors, they fly open. A maid in a black and white maid costume, that would totally be sold in stores as a Halloween joke, squeaks and runs down the hall as if we're marauding invaders.

As if he wants to reinforce the impression that we don't belong, or that we're delusional, Grigoriy announces himself, like they do for lords entering balls in movies about Victorian times. "Grigoriy Khilkov, Prince of Dolgovo, has returned."

"Cool it, Storm," Kristiana says. "If you're not careful, your new servants will call the po-po."

"The who?" Aleks asks.

"What's storm?" Grigoriy asks.

Deciding to respond to the more easy-to-explain question, I say, "She means the politsiya," I say in Russian. "And

I'm more worried they'll call a doctor and have you admitted."

"Our resident wind superhero is currently naked and ranting," Kris says. "Aleks, you should probably stop your friend before they come take him away."

"What am I supposed to do while he's holding her?" Aleks asks. "You should have let me take her earlier."

"No one's *taking her* anywhere." Grigoriy sounds a bit like a toddler. If toddlers had rock hard pecs, abs that could double as a washboard, and voices that sent little thrills up my spine.

The problem is that I've had plenty of boyfriends who wound up being far, far too toddler-esque, so now I hate any man who acts this way. "You can put me down," I say. "I think now that we're inside, I'll be able to hop anywhere I want to go."

He turns to look at me, and a strong, deep shiver runs down my entire body when our eyes meet at such close range. Clearly my errant body did not get the memo that I'm unimpressed by domineering men. His voice is low and rough when he says, "I don't want to put you down."

"Too bad," I say. "In the twenty-first century, women have rights."

He frowns. "You had rights a hundred years ago, too."

"We have more now. Take my word for it."

"You can't walk," he says. "Once we find a place for you to sit, I'll put you down."

"You're naked," I hiss. "Put me down now."

"She has a point," Kris says.

"I'm not naked." Grigoriy grits his teeth. "But I see your meaning. We'll go to my room, we can both get cleaned up, and then we'll meet you back here in an hour." He cuts his eyes toward Kris, and I realize that when he said 'we,' he meant himself and *me*.

"Oh, no," I say. "There will be no 'cleaning up' together.

No going back to your room, either." I struggle in his arms. "Put me down. I'll go find a place to clean up myself."

"You're not safe—"

Irritation pulses through me, and I pick up my hand and flick as hard as I can on the end of his nose. It works.

He drops me.

Although, it could have worked better. Landing hard on my butt isn't exactly comfortable, and shooting pains claw their way through my leg. At least I'm not being held by Conan the Barbarian anymore.

"You're hurt?" Kris drops down at my side. "How bad is it?"

"She's hurt?" Grigoriy bends toward me.

Kris throws an arm up. "Not so fast, Mike Tyson."

"Who?" Aleks asks. "Why do people keep calling him storm and Mike? His name is Grigor—"

"We know," I say. "And I think Kris and I just need some space."

Grigoriy's frown deepens. "But—"

"Listen to them," Aleks says. "You and I need to talk."

Grigoriy still looks just as upset, but he stops arguing as Kris helps me stand and leads me down the hallway. "We can use the room Aleks and I stay in when we have contractors to meet."

"Whoa, you stay in the same room?"

Kris smirks. "Did I mention. . .we're engaged?"

I can't help squealing. "You are?"

"Don't be too hard on Grigoriy," Kris says. "He may not be nearly as bad as he seems. He's been unconscious for a hundred years, and—"

"How is his house still *his*?" I ask.

"It wasn't," Kris says. "But Aleks bought it for him."

"Your pauper of a horse-trainer bought this?" I can't keep the incredulity out of my voice.

Kris laughs. "He's not really a pauper, as it turns out. In fact, we're quite wealthy."

I pause for a moment to process that. "Wait. . .wealthy?"

"He's buy-a-small-island-and-stock-it-with-whatever-we-want-and-travel-with-a-private-jet wealthy," she says.

The hope that rises in my chest is terrifying. "Does that mean. . ." I swallow. "Does that mean you can loan me the money for my surgery?"

Kris spins me toward her and wraps her arms around me, squeezing as tightly as she can. "Oh, Mirdza. I'm so sorry I lost my phone and you had so many bad things happen on your way here. Of course I'll loan you whatever you need." She snorts. "Actually, forget loaning it. I'm going to have to insist that you let me just pay for it. Alright?"

In the past two days, I've been deprived of sleep, terrorized, thanked, criticized, attacked, left for dead, healed, toted around horseback and by a huge naked man, and I've seen a horse turn into a man.

But it was all worth it.

Other people may have wind powers and magical horses and piles of gold. But for me, the biggest magic in my life is this—a chance to fix my leg. It means that, very soon, if I'm lucky, my life might be worth living again.

🦋   6   🦋

Nothing in my life ever goes this well.

Being fired? Being stabbed on a train and chucked out the window? Those are the types of things I expect to have happen to me.

Even having a horse turn into a man right in front of me feels more likely than having someone offer to pay for an expensive surgery. Magic wands saving the day? It's just not how my life works. Not ever.

Bad gets worse. Terrible days fall apart. Everything goes into the crapper.

That's my life.

"Mirdza?" Kris's brow is furrowed.

"Yeah." I meet her eyes.

"Are you alright?"

We're standing in the room she says they just finished remodeling. It's absolutely beautiful, and it's peaceful too. I can tell that Kristiana chose all the furnishings and tile and wall colors. Everything is white and blue and bright, just like her. I'm sure she's wondering whether I'm okay with watching a horse turn into a human.

"I can't figure something out. Grigoriy says he healed

65

me?" I blink. When I open my mouth, the words barely come out. "How? Because I think I should have died."

She bites her lip.

"Just tell me. I've accepted the rest of this just fine, haven't I?" I have to. After all, I lived it.

"Aleks can heal people too," she says. "But it's strange. It's linked to their elemental power, and each of their abilities differ a bit."

"Wait, who's they?"

She winces. "I mean, if you know about the others, it can't hurt to tell you there are two more men whom we don't talk to—they cursed Aleksandr and Grigoriy and Alexei somehow."

"Where's Alexei? Relaxing in a nearby mansion?"

Kris smiles. "That would be nice, but no. We aren't sure where he is. If I'm being honest, before today, I think Aleksandr was starting to give up hope of finding them. It's been a horrific day and a half for you, but this is the happiest I've seen him in a long time."

"Glad my nightmare has been good for someone."

Kris pivots on her heel and pulls me against her chest, tightly. "I'm so glad you're alright. I can't even imagine how terrifying that must have been."

"It's fine." But tears roll down my cheeks now that I finally feel safe. "To be honest." I hiccup. "I remember thinking that it would be better to just die than to never get my leg fixed. Even if I had to choose again, I'd still get on that train to come ask you for money."

"I'm so sorry my phone broke, and I'm sorry such horrible people are out there, controlling the world." She finally releases me. "I promise, we'll take care of you from here on out."

"Violent men are more common than the alternative," I say. "Sadly."

"Aleks is a little violent," Kris says. "Or maybe a *lot* violent, but not with me."

I don't argue with her. I hope it stays that way, but in my experience, violent men are just violent, period. The interchange between Yevginiy and that mother is evidence of that. One of the things she said was that he promised he never hit women. His ridiculous exceptions show how stupid it is to trust that one violent man may be different than the others, at least with regards to you.

"Let's get you cleaned up." She points at a bathroom, and I don't even wait for her help to hobble inside. I nearly cry when I see there's a tub. Sitting in a shower to clean myself off feels. . .more pathetic somehow, and there's no way I can balance on one foot and do it all standing. I'd risk slipping in the tub, and with the way my leg is right now, I can't even contemplate how that would go.

I close the door and start the arduous process of removing my clothes. Every single article of clothing somehow jostles my leg, and each movement causes shooting pains. I sit on the top of the toilet seat and nearly pass out while peeling my filthy pants off.

Yet, my shoulder's perfect. There's not even a scab or a mark where I was stabbed. It's baffling.

"If he could heal me, why didn't he fix my leg?" I shout.

"Aleks can only accelerate the healing process. So if something won't heal on its own, he's useless. I'm not sure about Grigoriy. We'll have to ask."

"Can I pass these clothes out to you? Or would you rather I wash them myself and maybe use a blow dryer on them?" The thought of putting my dirty, shredded clothing back on makes me cringe, but it's still going to be so much better than wearing them while filthy.

"Yes, pass them out. If you really want to keep them, I can have them washed, or I can just toss them."

"It's not like I can borrow your clothes," I say. "You're

like a size double zero." I'm not large by any means, but I'm much taller than she is. We haven't been able to share clothes since elementary school.

"Please," she says. "I sent Aleks for clothes the second we got in here. I told him his friend can surely wash up alone. His driving terrifies me, so he should be back from town any time. Even so, no rush washing your hair or blowdrying it."

"You're saying that giant of a man is going to pick out clothing for me?" I hate how skeptical I sound.

"He's surprisingly fashionable," Kris says. "He picks out my clothes sometimes. Don't worry so much."

A wave of relief rolls over me. To be clean was one thing. To be clean and wearing new clothes is another. After losing everything—my phone, my clothes, my wallet—I feel a little safer knowing I'll at least be presentable.

An hour later, I feel like a human again. My hair's dried and my body's clean and smooth, even if I am wrapped in a towel. When Kris passes a bag through, I expect things to be *way* off. I'm prepared for it.

"He bought me a bra?" My face heats, and I'm glad no one else can see me.

"Calm down," Kris says. "He does whatever I say." She laughs. "Hope it's the right size still."

"Haven't changed there since high school."

And everything fits, more or less. Dark pants, a cute, chunky sweater, and even a stunning, supple, black leather jacket. It all cost more than my rent, I'm sure, which causes me a little anxiety. I open the door, and Kris hands me some crutches.

Which promptly makes me break down in tears.

They've done way too much. "I'll pay you back," I say lamely. "It may take me a bit, though."

"Stop." Kris slides the crutches under my arms and takes the coat I don't need to wear right now. She tosses it on the bed and tilts her head until we're finally making eye contact. "I wish I'd been a better friend. I got so caught up in Aleksandr and my own drama that I didn't even think about you. You always seem so tough, so capable, and so self-sufficient that I didn't even think about it. I should've been paying better attention."

That just makes it worse. Kristiana, no matter what my sister Adriana says, has always been the best friend anyone has ever had. Things have always gone one direction with us. She gave me horses that had an aptitude for jumping, but no particular speed. She found me work, and then later, let me run a lesson program at her barn. She gave me a place to stay, no questions asked, whenever I needed one.

The one time I've had to handle things on my own, when she was in the middle of her own personal misery and losing her family farm, I completely botched things, got injured, and fell apart. That's not her fault. It's mine. "You're the best friend."

"No, you are." She hugs me then, ignoring the crutches, and whispers. "Please, just let us buy you some stuff to replace what you've lost, and let us pay for your surgery? Okay? No arguing and no more awkward promises that you'll repay me."

"But—"

She releases me and pushes her hand against my mouth. "No. That's what I'm talking about. Just, stop. Aleks has a *lot* of money, and that means I do too. Let us pay for the *medical care* you need. Alright? It won't cause me any problems, I swear." She snorts. "If you insist, we can call it an early birthday present."

My lip and my voice both wobble, but I manage an "Okay."

She points at the table. "Pain killers. A phone Aleks grabbed—we can try and get you a new one tied to your number and account soon, but at least you'll have one for now. I'm sure your mom and sister are worried. You can call them. Aleks lined up an appointment with a surgeon for tomorrow afternoon."

It's too much, too fast. I sit on the edge of the bed and drop my face in my hands.

"Do you want to take a nap?"

My head feels like it's spinning, but I manage to shake it. "No. I'm not tired. I feel. . .hopeful." I force myself to take the pain meds, down them with some water, and then I square my shoulders. "I think I need to talk to Grigoriy. If he's a horse shifter mage or whatever, why didn't he fix my bum leg?"

"Let's go ask him." For some reason, there's a sparkle in Kristiana's eyes.

I arch one eyebrow. "None of that."

"What?" She feigns innocence.

I give her my best solid glare. "Do *not* try to push me and Grigoriy together just because you and Aleksandr are so happy."

"I wouldn't dream of it." But her lips are compressed a little too hard, and they're twitching. "I mean, why *would* I try to set my best friend up with the ripped—"

"You should not have been looking at him," I say.

"Methinks the lady doth protest too much," Kris says. "For someone she doesn't care about."

I roll my eyes. "I meant, because your *fiancé* was right there."

"I may not be shopping for a pie, but I can ogle the bakery window as much as I'd like."

Even when my day has sucked royally, Kris always makes me laugh. "Well, ogle elsewhere. That pie is—" I snap my mouth shut. I almost said *mine*. What's wrong with me? It must be that I was tossed out a window. Or that I literally rode him this morning. I've always been a little possessive with my horses. Maybe that's it. It's confusing me that he's a horse and a man. I shake my head.

"Yes?" Kris is smirking. "That pie is. . .what exactly?" She arches one eyebrow in an infuriating way.

I clear my throat. "You can't eat it. That's what I was going to say. It's inedible."

She laughs again, this time high and long. "Sure." She walks toward the door, grabbing my beautiful leather jacket and hanging it over her arm on the way. "I think we should all go shopping. We can get you more than the one outfit, and you can get a watch and new shoes—whatever you need."

Again, I'm overwhelmed by her generosity and thoughtfulness.

"And Grigoriy will need all those things as well. After all, he's been cursed for a hundred years and stuck in some kind of hibernation or something."

"That's so long. Since, what? The Russian Revolution?"

Kris nods slowly. "Yeah, I had to teach Aleks most everything. He's wicked smart, so he picked it up fast. Let's hope his hot friend's not a dope." She yanks the door open. "He looked delicious, but he sounded a little caveman to me."

"Who looked delicious?" Aleksandr's just down the hall, his face marvelously scowly.

"You deserve that." I can't help giggling.

"My fiancé, of course," she says.

"I'm not a caveman," he says. "I bought you tampons."

"What are tampons?" Grigoriy asks, almost stumbling over the word.

Aleksandr laughs.

"Nope," I say. "Not a good discussion to have right now." I can feel my cheeks heating up. Aleksandr may have been stuck in some kind of cursed sleep for a hundred years, but he's pretty modernized if he's using tampon purchasing as an example of how he's not a caveman.

Getting cultural references and defending himself with proper behavior gets high marks from me. I'd never have thought he was a horse shifter. . . Even that simple thought makes me laugh out loud. *Who would have thought anyone was an ancient, cursed mage who was actually a horse shifter?*

I may be going crazy.

Kris pats my arm. "I know. I struggled with it, too."

"So are we going shopping? I've been trying to catch Grigoriy up on world changes, but there are too many. I think seeing some things will help."

The idea of shopping with the two men makes me acutely uncomfortable. And it's not only because of the way Grigoriy's looking at me, all intense and smoldery. "Hey, what are we going to do about the car?" I ask. "There's no way we can all fit in yours. Maybe it's a better idea if Kris and I go first."

Aleks's brow furrows. "I think—"

"Or you can go first," I say. "I don't mind waiting. Actually, this outfit is totally fine. We can wash the one I had and mend the shoulders and—"

"Your friend never stops talking," Aleks says.

"Only when she's nervous." Kris lifts her eyebrows at me.

I splutter. "I'm—I'm not nervous."

"Luckily, sports cars aren't Grigoriy's style." He looks, almost apologetically, at his friend. "When I first got back to Russia, I thought I'd find you and Alexei right away." Aleks's smile is rueful. "I ordered you a Range Rover. It finally arrived last week."

"I'm a little bummed," Kris says. "He told me I could have it, since you never showed up. It'll take forever for another one to get here. Imports aren't fast."

"Imports?" Grigoriy looks majorly lost.

That's when it occurs to me that we're all speaking Latvian. "How can you speak Latvian so well?"

"It has to be something to do with the curse," Aleks says. "I speak all three languages that Kris does." He shrugs. "I tested Grigoriy, and he speaks them all, too."

"Does that mean Kris is somehow tied to the curse?" That would be bizarre.

"She must be," Aleks says. "And Grigoriy speaking all three just confirms it. Before we were cursed, we both only spoke Russian. Now we speak English and Latvian as well."

"But Mirdza speaks them, too," Kris says.

"I learned English from her mother, same as Kris," I say. "I kind of grew up with her."

"But her English isn't quite as good, and her Russian is better," Kris says.

She's probably right, but neither's really noticeably different.

"So maybe he could speak them all because of Mirdza." She frowns. "We've been searching for a while with no luck. But Mirdza gets here and bam. He wakes up and finds her immediately."

"Can we head for the car while we analyze?" Aleks asks. "I'm starving."

Kris rolls her eyes. "Lamb *chebureki* again?" She laughs. In all the years I've known her, I've never seen her laugh as much as she has today. It's really nice to see her so happy. "You're obsessed."

"Obsession has such a negative implication," Aleks says. He's moving down the hallway, so I follow him. The crutches are so much better than walking on my own, but I'm still slow. I don't want to fall behind.

"You eat three or four from that same street vendor every day."

"For a few days I did," he says. "But I don't always. It's not a big deal."

"What is it exactly?" Grigoriy asks.

"They're meat pies," Aleks says. "They became popular after the revolution." Aleks looks down, and I get the sense that something that happened long, long ago for us is still very real to him. How strange. "It's the only good thing that came out of the Soviet occupation." The set of his mouth is pretty grim.

I wonder what it would be like to go to sleep—or whatever happened to them—and wake up a hundred years later. Everything you knew, everything you cared about, would just be *gone*.

It hits me then that Grigoriy is going through that right now.

He falls into step next to me, modifying his giant stride to match my hobbling one. "Are you alright?" he asks, his voice low.

"Are you?" I ask. "Today must have been a really rough day."

He shrugs. "Aleks had it way worse than I do. His mother and sister were still alive. My parents had both passed—no siblings. He was stuck as a horse for months—I managed to shift back to human within a day." His smile is half playboy, half adorable teenager. "Thanks for that, by the way."

He's thanking me. . .because I shifted him. "I mean, I guess you're welcome?"

"Oh, it was you. Only Kris could change Aleks, and then she tried, and nothing. Only you could change me. I hope you'll keep doing it, at least until we can figure out how to break whatever's keeping me from my magic."

"Sure," I say. "But it's not like I got nothing from it. You healed me, right?" For some reason, all my brash desire to grill him about it is just. . .gone. Why am I shy about him healing me? For some reason, it feels sort of scary, almost, to ask him about making my stab wounds disappear.

He slows, making me half-halt to look him in the face. "It was my pleasure to do that." His hand balls into a fist at his side. "I vow that I'll find the men who—"

I shake my head vehemently. "No, please vow the opposite. Never try to locate those men. Not ever."

He frowns. "But—"

My voice is raw when I beg. "Please. Promise me."

"Mirdza?" Kris and Aleks have reached the doorway into a large garage. "Is everything okay?" Kris asks. "Because you've had a bad enough day. No one better make it worse." She glares spectacularly at Grigoriy, not that he even notices.

"Let's go," I say. I can always push the promise out of him later.

I'm utterly unprepared when I walk through the wide doorway. "What. . .how many cars did you think he'd need?" The garage has at least ten spaces. There's a sports car—Aleks's car. Someone must have pulled it around. And a shiny, black Range Rover. I've never even seen one up close. They aren't common in Latvia.

"Aleks has developed quite the taste for nice cars," Kris says. "When they asked us how large we should make the renovated garage, he didn't want to have limited space." She laughs. "He's adjusted to modern times fairly well, don't you think?"

"One car?" Grigoriy asks. "You only thought I'd want one car?"

I cannot believe he's hassling his friend who restored his home and bought him a ridiculously expensive import. What kind of friends were they?

Aleks smiles. "I didn't want to deprive you of the opportunity of buying them yourself."

"But you said I'm broke." Instead of looking worried, Grigoriy looks irritated. "You said I won't even be able to pay the taxes on this estate you bought back from the stupid government for me."

Kris slugs Aleks on the shoulder. "You're mean."

"It's always better to know the truth than to be unprepared," I say. I should know. As the poor friend, I've learned this the hard way.

Aleks rolls his eyes. "Not for long, though. I already told you I bought all those wind turbines when the government offered those subsidies."

"*You* bought them." Grigoriy sounds downright grumpy.

"I had them installed on your land, you idiot. You should just be thanking me."

"I actually got mad at him," Kris says. "It seemed like a huge waste of money. They're generating nothing at all right now."

"Not nothing." Aleks laughs. "But not what they'll produce once we make a little trip out there."

Grigoriy jogs down the steps toward the Range Rover effortlessly, not even thinking about it. Then he turns back to see me, awkwardly navigating them as best I can.

Stairs suck.

"Here." He jogs back up before I can stop him. He slides his arms behind my back and my knees and picks me up like he thinks I'm Kris's size, my crutches dangling at strange angles.

"I'm so sorry. I didn't think."

We're past the stairs before I can even protest, but instead of putting me down, he keeps right on walking toward the car.

I must have been a real nuisance, slowing everyone down as I did, or he'd have put me down again. My cheeks heat. I hate being a burden or a nuisance, but it's even worse that he's carrying me like I'm a child.

"Put me down," I hiss.

He grins at me wickedly. "Make me."

My right hand slips, and one of my crutches clatters to the ground. Kris had her hand on the passenger door, but she spins around, her mouth gaping, her eyes widening. "Grigoriy. Put her down this instant."

His head whips toward her. "Why?"

"She's not a child or a dog or a toy. You don't carry people unless they ask."

His brow furrows, and then slowly, he lowers me to the ground. "I'm sorry." His words are gruff, but they seem sincere.

"It's fine." Embarrassing, but fine. At least I'm used to being humiliated.

This time, his words are soft. I doubt Kris or Aleks can even hear him. "I liked holding you, and I just didn't want to let go. I didn't think about that being rude."

Something shifts inside me, at his explanation. Is he for real? "It's fine," I say again, but this time. . .I mean it.

"I'll need your help," he says. "To get the wind turbines working."

He knows what they are? "Okay."

"Apparently my powers only work when I'm touching you."

Something about the word *touching* makes a tiny zing fly up my body. "Okay."

"You don't mind?" Is he really serious? The man who grabbed me and carried me like a sack of flour down the stairs cares whether I mind?

I shrug.

He drops to one knee and grabs my crutch and offers it to me carefully. "I'll be more polite, I swear." He looks so earnest, his dark hair falling forward in front of his eyes. Now that he's wearing Aleks's clothes—presumably, because they're a little too tight—he looks modern, too.

If I weren't all broken, and if I met him at a club or at the barn, I'd probably leap on him and attack. He's got a killer physique, an absolutely dreamy grin, and beautiful hair.

Which is why I should keep things really, really professional. There's no way the crippled horse girl friend of Kristiana is anything more than a passing fancy to him. He hasn't seen any other women in a hundred years, after all. He's probably just impressed that my teeth are all relatively straight—thanks to Kristiana's mother getting me braces when she got them for Kris—and that I'm clean. I hear they didn't get the chance to bathe often before running water was common. Maybe I looked like most women of his era when he saved me.

Who knows?

"Let's just get the shopping trip over with," I say.

"Over with? Aleks said girls still love to shop." He frowns. "Is that not true?"

Kris and Aleks are sitting in the car, waiting, so I gesture. "We better go. They're waiting on us."

"They can wait." Grigoriy crosses his arms and looks at me. "Is this not fun? If you don't want to go, we can just tell them to get clothing for us. After the day we've both had— me back from who knows where, and you being thrown off a train—they'll do it for us."

I sigh. "I would like shopping if I wasn't so poor." Did I really just say that? "I feel terrible, letting them pay for everything for me."

He narrows his eyes. "I know what you're saying, but Aleks says that soon, I'll have money again. Once that happens—which I can only do thanks to your help—I'll give you money of your own. Then you can repay them."

I shake my head. "That's very generous, but it's just *you* giving me money, instead of *them* doing it. It's still uncomfortable."

"But Kris has no money of her own, right? She uses Aleks's money."

"She does have money." Much more than I do, anyway, thanks to her family and her veterinary practice, and her race winnings. I roll my eyes. "Plus, they're getting married."

"Then marry me," he says. "If that means you don't have to feel bad about using mine."

My heart practically beats its way out of my chest. "Stop."

His eyes are wide and terribly sincere looking. That just makes the joke even meaner. "Stop what?"

"Don't make jokes like that."

"It's not a joke." He steps closer. I can feel the heat radiating off of his large body. "If you married me, would you not feel better about using my money?"

"You don't even know me," I say. "And I don't know you. But you should know this. I'm not planning to ever get married."

"Because you've met all the wrong men." His smile is smug, even though I just rejected what really must have been a joke. "I'll change your mind."

This entire day is surreal. "I'm a cripple," I say. "And I have no money. I came here to beg Kristiana for a loan, and I couldn't even get that right."

"We're all broken in our own ways," Grigoriy says. "Yours is just more obvious."

For someone who makes absurd jokes, he's got a remarkable amount of insight. "How did you heal me?" I ask. "And why didn't you fix my leg when you did it?" I hate that tears spring to my eyes, but if we only get one miracle in life, why couldn't mine have fixed my leg, too?

He looks at me for a moment.

Aleks honks the horn and we both startle. I nearly drop my crutches. Grigoriy looks back at the car and shouts something strange in Russian that I don't quite understand. It makes Aleks laugh, though.

When he turns back toward me, he's not smiling. "If I could have fixed your leg, I would have." His voice is low and deep. "My healing comes from my wind power. The wind is fast, temperamental, and powerful. But it's also short-lived. I can heal most anything. . .if it just happened. That's why I could repair your fatal knife wounds. I could repair your snapped collarbone." His voice drops to a whisper. "But that leg wound is old. It's not something I can repair." His shoulders drop just a hair. "I'm so sorry."

He doesn't sound sorry. He sounds broken, too.

"It's fine." I swipe at my eyes before the useless tears can fall. "I'm used to it." I inhale. "Besides. I'm more than grateful for what you did for me. I was just curious, that's all. I'm sorry for making you feel bad."

"Aleksandr says the top surgeon in the area is meeting with us tomorrow, and he'll fix it."

"I hope he makes it so that I can walk again." I don't tell him what the Latvian surgeon said about my success rate. "I'm really, really grateful to Kris and your friend Aleksandr for what they're doing for me."

"I'll pay them back." The playboy smile is back. "Then you can be grateful to *me* for it."

"Are you two going to keep flirting all day?" Aleks asks. "Or are we going shopping?"

My face must be bright red while Grigoriy loads my crutches into the back and helps me into the car. But I feel a little better after he punches the back of Aleks's seat. "Shut your stupid mouth and drive, idiot."

$\approx$ 7 $\approx$

When I was growing up, a trip into town was a big deal. There were so many people, so many shops, and so much happening all at once. It cost a lot to go into town, to buy clothes or house-wares, so we rarely did it. But when we did?

It was so exciting.

The Russian shopping area Aleks drives us to in Novgorod is surprisingly robust. I suppose I shouldn't be surprised. I'm accustomed to Daugavpils, which is the second largest city in Latvia, but still not very massive comparatively. We still don't quite have a hundred thousand people. Novgorod looks much larger.

"How many people live here?" I ask.

"A million and a quarter," Kris says. "I wondered the same. It's way bigger than back home, right?" She smiles warmly.

"It's no Saint Petersburg," Aleksandr says, "but it's not bad."

After he pulls into a space, I realize there's an H&M, a Massimo Dutti, and a Mango store all right in a row. My three favorite places to window-shop, all sandwiched together. Only today, I'm going inside to buy new things for once.

"You look happy," Grigoriy says.

"Oh," I say. "I guess I am." Even if I can't pay for my own stuff, and even if I feel a little (or a lot) guilty about letting Kris pay, it's still fun to have new clothes. It's not something I've experienced often.

"Here." Kris tosses my jacket over the seat. I slip into it quickly, not wanting to make anyone wait for me any longer than they already have to. In my haste, my hand catches on the liner and gets stuck.

"Here." Grigoriy carefully and gently straightens out the sleeve, and I push my arm through.

"Thanks."

Kris is smiling at me from the front seat, turned all the way around like a little kid watching something exciting. Her expression's practically shouting, *You two are so adorable.*

I glare at her.

"Ready?" Grigoriy waits for me to nod, then reaches into the back and snags my crutches. He hops out and jogs around the car to open my door. "Here."

All the attention makes me feel way worse. "Sorry." I snatch the crutches from his hand. "I'm fine, though. I swear." As if to make up for all the unwanted attention, I zoom ahead, making a beeline for the Mango store. I'm nearly there when I realize—I don't even have a purse.

That takes some of the wind out of my figurative sails, and that phrase makes me think about Grigoriy, who has caught up.

His brow furrows. "What did I do?"

I sigh. "Nothing."

"Something," he says. "You were practically running, and it looked painful."

I wince. There he goes again, making it all about my

shortcomings. "I just don't like people to draw attention to my leg."

He frowns, but says nothing else.

"Let's go." Kris breezes past me, her arm hooked through Aleksandr's, and pushes through the doors. "I think you need a purse first."

"I did put in some requests for new identification for you," Aleks says. "We'll need to have it expedited over from Latvia, because they'll want it for your surgery."

Duh. Why haven't I even been panicking about my passport or EU paperwork? "You can do that?"

"Aleks has some contacts within the Russian government now." Kris looks proud. I suppose she should be. Her future husband's connected, rich, and powerful.

"I bought them," Aleks says. "It's not really very impressive."

"Money is its own security." That's something rich people don't often realize.

"That's true," Grigoriy says. "Which reminds me. How soon can we get out to those wind turbines?"

I start to laugh—it felt like a joke—but Aleksandr nods. "I knew you'd want to do that right away. They aren't all wired in yet. I hadn't been rushing it, since we had no leads on you. I called the electrician today and he's rushing the job—should be up and running in a few days."

"You'll have to explain the design to me in more detail anyway," Grigoriy says, "so I can be sure I create the wind funnels correctly."

"Wind what?"

He's smiling a cocky smile when he turns to answer. "I control the wind. It's a snap to make air current patterns and fix them in place. Once I do, those wind turbines will put out consistent energy—and apparently that's something the local grid will pay dearly for."

"I actually ordered more for my rocky fields," Aleks

says. "The areas that are useless for farming, and now that you're here. . ."

"Happy to help," Grigoriy says.

"Oh, I think we should split the profits," Aleks says. "It's only fair."

"Always a pleasure doing business with you," Grigoriy says.

"I think we should split the profits on our horse farm back home." I wink at Kris.

"Yes," Kris says. "I know what you mean. You can jet on by, magically enhance the horse skills, and then I'll use my magical training powers, and voila. We'll be rich." She laughs.

"That's just what I was thinking."

"Yeah, yeah, we get it," Aleks says.

"At least talk about that stuff in Latvian," Kris says. "The people passing by us think you're nuts."

"Or I could shift into a horse right here," Aleks says. "That would show them we're not the crazy ones."

She rolls her eyes, grabs his elbow, and hauls him inside. "Just get your credit card ready, Mr. Hilarious."

"It's always ready when you're around."

They're laughing as they walk past racks of clothing, stopping now and again to take a closer look at a few things. Of course, in the past ten or so years that I've been dealing with my leg injury, I haven't done a lot of shopping. Mostly, money has been tight, and I've been lucky to buy one or two things here or there. Internet shopping when there are steep sales has been my best bet. If I wanted something to purchase in person, I'd usually go to a thrift store. In all that time, I've had plenty of instances when I couldn't walk very easily, usually before or after some surgery or another. But I never went out shopping, then. Today, I'm learning lots of new things, but one of them is not very exciting.

It's very hard to shop with crutches.

I can't exactly reach out and pull clothes off the rack. Nor can I set my crutches down easily anywhere—everywhere I look is full of stands with small things on them or round racks of clothing. None of that even addresses how long it takes me to try new things on. I thought shopping when money was no object might be fun, but this is arduous and depressing.

I sigh heavily, wondering whether I can get by with just an extra pair of pants and a shirt or two.

"How about this?"

I jump at the sound of Grigoriy's voice. He's standing right behind me, holding a reasonably large stack of men's clothes. He must have noticed that I'm struggling—Kris and Aleks each have a similar, albeit smaller, pile, but I'm holding nothing.

"What?" I wave him off with my fingers, releasing my hold on the handle of one crutch. "I'm fine."

"You were probably distracted by how fabulously beautiful I was as a horse, but I actually make an excellent pack mule." He winks.

"Having seen your horse form," I whisper, "I don't think pack mule is a good fit." Frankly, seeing his human form, no part of him fits with me—the broken, damaged girl.

He preens a bit. "I may not be the showy black stallion that Aleks is, but I'm not so bad-looking either."

"I've always preferred chrome on my horses." What am I doing? Kris was right. I am flirting. I clamp my lips together.

"You don't say." He grins so broadly this time that I can see all his shiny, white teeth. I can't imagine they had bleach a hundred years ago, but I swear it looks like they did. He must not drink much coffee, and there's no way he smokes.

"Don't worry about me," I say. "Just go find things for

yourself over there." I toss my head at the men's section. "I'm always the same size. I'll grab a few things and be just fine."

"Aleks says they have rooms where you can put the clothes on to make sure you like them." He scrunches his face a bit. "I can't say that I love the idea of wearing things that have been on some other man's body." He exhales. "But apparently you need to make sure these ready-made clothes fit properly."

"Ready-made?"

"In my day, clothing was made to order, always." He shrugs. "Not as efficient, but much more practical. Things you bought always fit."

I hadn't even thought about that. "Today is your day now though, right? It's not like you can go back in time."

He blinks. "I suppose not." He smiles. "So I may as well get used to it." He plucks a purple blouse off a rack. "This one is nice. It should look pretty with your eyes."

Maybe with Kris's blue ones. "Mine are brown."

He steps closer. "They aren't. They're the exact color of a dark, rich sherry." His voice is so low, so intimate, that it makes me shiver. "This purple will accent them perfectly."

I can't scrounge up the will to argue with *that*, so I just balance on one crutch and snatch the blouse. That's when I realize it's big. Like, really big. "What size do you think I am?" I arch one eyebrow and tilt my head.

"Excuse me?"

"This is a triple extra large."

His brows draw together.

"I'm not tiny like Kris, but I'm not a triple extra large, either." I shove it back toward the rack.

He practically spins around, peering at the clothing. "How do you know the size?"

"It's on the tag." I'm so annoyed that I start to move away.

"Wait." He shoves another blouse at me—same cut and color, but a new size. "Here."

I accept it, far less annoyed than I'm acting for some reason, and glance at the tag. "An extra small?" I heave another sigh. "Really?"

"I'm an extra small." A very cute, very small blond with a huge rack slides up next to us, her lips curved into a coquettish smile. "And I love that color." She's practically purring.

Kris might claw her eyes out.

She licks her lips and gazes up at Grigoriy, batting her eyes.

Maybe Kris would just straight up punch her.

But she's exactly the kind of girl Grigoriy should be with. She looks more than ready to get married, and they're almost a match, in terms of attractiveness.

I clear my throat. "I'll be over here," I say. "Looking for mediums."

"Medium," Grigoriy practically shouts. He bends over the rack again, rifling through them. "Yes, they have one with an m on it." He triumphantly holds another purple shirt aloft. He snatches the other blouse out of my hands and shoves it at the blond. "Here you go." He pushes past her and walks alongside me, pointing. "What about those?"

He's pointing at a black knit dress with adorable cutouts on either side of the waist. It has a beautiful black accent line across the waistline, and a high slit, and white trim along the slit. It's dramatic, classy, and striking. That probably means it's quite expensive.

What he's not doing is paying any attention at all to the woman who's now left holding a blouse she didn't want and staring.

I don't approve of him pursuing me, but I can't help enjoying how uniformly he rejected—that's not the right word—dismissed her. That's better. It was like he didn't even notice she was *there*.

"This would look really great on you." He pokes through the rack until he finds one that says medium. Then he slings it over his arm.

"I hate to rain on your parade," I say.

"My parade?" He frowns.

"Never mind." I sigh. Him not knowing any of these expressions is a bummer. "It's hard for me." I drop my voice. "To try things on. My leg makes it hard."

His eyes widen. "I'm sorry. Again." He sighs. "I'm really bad at this, but I swear it's because I'm not used to this two-thousand era world."

"It's not your fault."

"Let's buy it all." He shrugs. "You can wear the things you want, and you can give whatever doesn't fit to poor people. Surely there are still lots of people who can't go shopping freely?"

Me. I'm one of those people he's talking about. "I can't expect Kris to—"

"I'm about to be rich. I'll pay them back, and then you don't have to feel bad."

Ohmyword. "Grigoriy, look—"

He grabs my hand, not hard, not enough to dislodge it from its grip on my crutch handle, but firmly. "Say it again."

"Look?"

He shakes his head. "My name."

"Okay, this is weird," I say. "I don't know you."

"Your need woke me up," he says. "I'm absolutely positive."

"That makes no sense," I say. "I've been in trouble lots of times."

"But you haven't been about to die lots of times," he says. "I think that's what I felt. It was nothing but darkness and misery for me. Aleks says he doesn't recall much, but I remember pain. A lot of pain. Loneliness. Darkness. I've been miserable for a very long time, and then light exploded into my world. I was underground, which might have been a breeze for Aleks to deal with, but it was harrowing for me. I painstakingly dug my way out, one hoof scrape at a time, flailing, miserable, and then I felt something, pulling me toward you."

My heart's hammering again. Is any of this possible? Could he have felt me?

"I was finally free, and then I felt it—this incontrovertible pull. I ran toward it, and then I found you. Curled up, injured, and miserable."

I can't breathe.

He draws in a ragged breath. "You were brighter than the light in that dark place. You were what I'd been waiting on—an end to the pain. So I know you don't want my help, but just take it anyway. I owe you."

I let him lead me through the store after that, slinging mediums over his arm from every rack and stand. He chooses several purses, too. "It seems like you have lots of things to carry around these days. Phones, stuff for your lips and hair. I assume that, especially with the crutches, you need something to put them in."

He's pretty perceptive. "Yes, thanks."

"And it's better if they match what you're wearing, so maybe get a brown one and a black one for when you don't want to move stuff around, and then a few colors when you want to match."

I wonder how well I would adjust to a new time. Probably not nearly as well as he is. I'm sure having Aleks around helps, but he's clearly also very bright.

After we walk out, Kris and Grigoriy and Aleks offer to take me to any other store I want, but my leg's throbbing. I shrug. "We got a lot."

"Shoes, at least," Kris says. "You'll want some decent

shoes."

I begrudgingly nod. "But one pair is fine. You bought me way too much back there."

"I bought it," Grigoriy says.

Aleks laughs. "I think my credit card will beg to differ."

"I'll pay you back," he says. "I'm the one who insisted on buying all of that."

Aleks laughs. "It's fine. I told you."

Grigoriy shakes his head, apparently as stubborn as I am. "I'll reimburse you."

"Let's go to Rossita," Kris says. "Their window display had the most gorgeous boots."

"Or that A.S. 98 place was pretty nice," Aleks says.

Kris shrugs. "They're practically next door."

It's a car ride away, but when we get out, Aleks has parked right by an equine outfitter. I can't help the pang in my heart at seeing it. I'm surrounded by horse stuff day in and day out, but I never bother paying for expensive riding pants or boots. What's the point? I can't wear any of it for its intended purpose.

Something about seeing it all on display still pains me.

Even now, a decade later, I can smell the sharp new leather smell of the nicest boots. I can feel the tacky, grippy sensation of running my hands over the full seat pants. I can remember the way the best gloves grip your fingers, making them better able to hold the reins, even when they get sweaty inside.

I heave a small sigh.

"Let's step in here for a moment," Kris says.

I shake my head. "Can you go later?"

"I can," Kris says. "But you should come now."

"You know I can't," I say.

"But you can, now," she insists. "Weren't you on a horse this morning?"

I roll my eyes. "Only because I had no choice."

"You can't ride because a horse might spook or buck and you might fall, right?" Kris has a twinkle in her eyes.

"Right, and it's uncomfortable for me to even grip with my leg."

"But you're having a surgery soon, and on top of that, you have a horse that won't spook or buck, now. You have a horse you can trust to keep you safe."

What is she talking about?

"Me." Grigoriy smiles and starts toward the store.

"Wait." But I can't catch him. He's striding in way too fast, and he knows my size, and I wouldn't put it past him to just buy whatever he thinks looks nice, without even waiting for my permission.

I follow Kris inside, and the smell of boot leather and tack hits me like a fan to the face. I pause for a moment and breathe it in.

"—your most expensive pair of women's boots?" Grigoriy's asking the saleswoman. "And your nicest pants, jacket, whatever she will need. A few of each."

"Stop." It's embarrassing having him ask for me, like having my mom cut my sandwich.

"I would stop," he says, "if you would step in and order things for yourself, but the only way you'll get this is if I make you." He grins and switches to Latvian. "Have I told you how much I loved the feel of you *riding* me?" His grin is pure evil. "I'll buy whatever I need to feel that again."

"You knew that would sound dirty," I snap. "That's why you switched to Latvian."

Aleks looks supremely annoyed. "But I can still understand you." He shudders. "Knock it off, man. You sound. . .pervy."

He didn't sound pervy, not to me, but I'm not about to admit it. "Look—"

But the sales lady has returned, her arms laden with clothing stacked on two boot boxes.

"We'll take all of that, plus your nicest saddle," Grigoriy says.

"A Voltaire," Kris says. "Sized for a wide warmblood, with pro flaps."

"We'd need to see the horse," the woman says. "And our Voltaire rep won't be here for three more days, and even then it takes two months to—"

"You have some on consignment?" Kris asks.

The woman nods.

"Great. I'll pick one." She brushes past her toward the tack area, and none of them seem to be listening to me at all.

"But—"

"You went through something terrifying," Aleks says in a very low, very soft voice.

"I did," I say.

"We both feel awful, and we both feel a little at fault."

"It wasn't—"

Aleks waves. "The point is that, even if you hate this, it makes Kris feel a bit better. It's making Grigoriy feel better. Their trauma may not be as direct as yours was, but if it's not hurting you to watch them buy you things, let it go."

I stare at him.

"I have literal buckets of gems and precious stones. We have way, way more money than we will ever need. Don't stress about the cost. Whether Grigoriy repays me or not, it's irrelevant. It's making my betrothed happier, so I'd greatly prefer if you let us buy out all the boots in this store."

I close my open mouth with a click and stop arguing. It hadn't occurred to me that Kris and Grigoriy might feel unsafe or upset that I was attacked, or that I'm injured, and now that I see what's motivating them, and Aleks has assured me the money isn't an issue (which I struggle to even understand), I'm better able to let it go.

I cringe my way through another huge stack of clothing, which I'm worried won't fit in the back of the Range Rover, and then I grit my teeth and endure while we hobble into the store next door and buy a pair of sneakers, a few pairs of boots, and a few more things for Kris and Grigoriy, but then I'm done.

My good leg is trembling.

My bad leg is screaming.

I'll collapse if I can't sit down soon.

"I'd be happy to carry you," Grigoriy says. His arms are already heavy laden with bags.

"I'm fine," I say.

"Liar," Kris says.

"Here," Aleks says, moving toward me. "I can—"

But Grigoriy practically knocks him over, racing toward me.

I shove one hand against his chest—which is distract-ingly hard and well-muscled—and shake my head. "No. Respect my words and let me walk."

A muscle works in his jaw, but he listens, walking slowly at my side as we make our way to the Range Rover. Once we get the door open, Grigoriy insists on tossing my crutches in the back and helping me in again. Then he slides into the middle of the bench, right next to me, and buckles.

"What are you doing?" I ask, eyeing his proximity warily.

"There are three seats," he says.

"I know."

"I'd rather sit in the one that's closer to you." He shrugs. "Is that a problem?"

Kris is giggling in the front seat.

"I suppose not," I say.

And I hate that I mean it.

❧ 8 ❧

Home for me has always been where Kris is. I mean, it would have been nice if I grew up in the same place my entire life, like her. Or if I had lots of memories of the same house, like holidays in certain rooms with the same decorations.

But more than a location, home's a feeling.

It's being safe. It's being cared for. It's knowing no one wants to hurt you—anything bad that happens is inadvertent or fate.

The only person, since her mother died, who has loved me no matter what. . .is Kristiana. My sister always has her own fights to manage. My mom has always prioritized Mārtinš over everything else. No guy has ever cared much about me, except as something to control.

But Kris has always had my back, so with her, I'm home.

Which is why, when she grabs her purse and stands up, my anxiety rises. "I just put all my new clothes in that room." I swallow and force myself, painfully, to my feet.

"Oh, no, that's fine. Aleks and I will head back to his

place, which is only half an hour's drive, and we'll be back over tomorrow morning to take you to the doctor."

"Whoa," I say. "You're leaving without me?"

"My car's a two-seater," Aleks says.

"You could borrow the Range Rover for a day, right?" I hate how panicked I sound.

"Are you afraid of being alone with me?" Grigoriy stands. "Because you slept practically on top of me last night."

I swallow. "You were a horse."

"There are a dozen staff members here," Kris says. "Your stuff's here. We thought it would be easier if—"

"I'd rather go with you."

Kris frowns. "Aleks knows Grigoriy. They've been friends for years. I'm sure you'll be safe here."

I'm acting like a lunatic. My stuff's all in the drawers in an empty room. Kris and Aleks will be back in the morning. I know these things are true, but for some reason, I'm panicking anyway.

Grigoriy frowns. "You could change me back into a horse, if that will make you feel better."

"I'd prefer he's here as a man," Aleks says. "Remember what I told you?" He lifts his eyebrows meaningfully.

"What?" I glance between them. "What did you tell him?"

Kris sighs. "They have another friend who's still missing, and there are two more people like them who we think cursed them to begin with. They came after us once, right after the Grand National."

Came after them?

"I'm sure they'll be watching this place," Aleks says. "Just as they watch my place."

"How do you know?" Now I'm really nervous. What exactly is going on? Who are these people and why are they *watching* them?

"I've laid a few traps to see what might happen, and so far they haven't acted." Aleks sighs. "But when I was away from home, away from my wards, away from my support, that's when they moved in."

"But what does that have to do with me?" I ask. "Isn't that even more reason for me to come with you?"

"Aleks warded this place too," Kris says. "Before we ever stayed here. They won't be able to come inside."

All this magic stuff is bizarre, and I can't really trust it.

"Besides," Aleks says. "Grigoriy was always the scariest of all of us at combat. They won't come at him directly."

Grigoriy steps closer to me.

For some reason, it feels ominous. "What does that mean?"

"They're more likely to go after you," Kris says flatly.

"Why me?" I look around, searching all their faces for any answers. "I have nothing to do with him."

Aleks tilts his head. "You can shift him from man to horse."

"I mean, yes, I can. But who knows who else might be able to do it, too?"

"Only Kris could shift me," Aleks says.

"How many other people tried?" I ask.

Kris's shoulders droop. "None."

"So you don't know that she's the only one. Maybe lots of people could."

"I could only use my powers when I was touching her," Aleks says.

"Did you try with other people? Other women? Children? Anyone?"

Aleks clears his throat.

"Scientists you are not." I shake my head. "I don't want to stay here. I don't have anything to do with Grigoriy, and the last thing I need is a target on my back—"

Grigoriy touches my arm, and a sudden wind whips around the room. It lifts every single thing up off the ground. Picture frames. Chairs. Coffee table. Lamp. The curtains flap wildly. And then it all stops, and everything returns to its normal place, not a single thing a hair different than before. "I can keep you safe, but only if you're near me."

"Try it with her." I glare at Kris.

Aleks scowls.

Kris shifts awkwardly, but she nods.

Grigoriy crosses the room slowly, not looking too pleased, but he puts his hand on her forearm.

Aleks looks like he might hit him.

But nothing happens.

No one hits anyone. No wind whips around the room. Nothing.

"How do I know you're really trying?" I ask.

Grigoriy throws his hands in the air. "You're being impossible."

"Try with him." I toss my head at Aleks.

"Oh, please," Aleks says.

"Just do it."

Grigoriy stomps his way over to Aleks and yanks his arm toward him, holding both their arms up. "Satisfied?"

"Now try it." I practically bite out every word. "And I want to see you really focusing."

Both men sigh.

But nothing happens.

"Call one of the staff," I say.

"When are you going to be satisfied that we have some kind of connection?" Grigoriy releases Aleks and walks toward me. He's not stomping. He's not striding. He's not even stalking.

He's sauntering.

I hate how it makes my heart rate pick up. How it

makes my breath catch. And how I both want him to keep walking and want him to stop at the same time.

"Stop," I say, my cautious side winning.

"You stop." He does listen, but he's still staring right at me. The two feet between us doesn't feel like much of a buffer. "Until I can recover my powers, you're going to have to lend a hand for a bit." He smiles. "Consider it payment for the surgery and the clothes."

"See?" I fume. "I knew you'd bring that up again."

"Only because you're being so stubborn," he says. "You keep insisting there's nothing between us. You keep saying you want to go with her." He jabs his finger toward the door without even looking.

"You're a stranger to me," I say.

"And how will running away from me change that?" he asks.

"I'm so very, deeply sorry," I say.

"Huh?"

"Kris said that's what she said to get Aleks his powers back."

He shakes his head. "She said she *forgave* him and that's when they came back."

"How's this?" I sigh. "I forgive you, Grigoriy, for being pushy. I forgive you for not healing my leg. I forgive you for being overbearing. I forgive you for anything and every-thing for all time."

"For all time?" He's smiling and he takes a step closer. "I like that. Say it again."

"Try your powers." I fold my arms over my chest, leaning against the edge of the sofa for support. "See if they're back."

He frowns. "They aren't. Nothing changed."

"You did nothing that was really wrong. Of course nothing changed when I fake-forgave you."

"Say it like you mean it," he says.

"I don't mean it," I say. "You didn't *do* anything. Being overbearing isn't a sin that needs my forgiveness, but if it was, I can't pretend to give it."

He grits his teeth. "So you really *didn't* mean it."

I jab his chest with my finger. "Of course not. Stop bossing me around, stop grabbing my arm, and stop telling me what to do."

His hand closes around my wrist. "I'm trying to help you." He practically roars. "But you're impossible."

I shake my arm free. "That's because I don't want your help."

His voice drops until it's low, deep, and confident. "You didn't say that last night."

I can't help laughing. I mean, he's right. I was grateful for his help last night, but if anyone else heard, they would grossly misunderstand. I look behind us, because I just know Kris is laughing too.

But she's gone.

That jerk *abandoned me* while I was distracted. "They left?"

Grigoriy's smiling.

I slap his arm. Then I hit him again. And again, harder.

Now he's laughing. I'm abusing him, and he finds it humorous?

"Stop that," I say.

"You can hit me all day long," he says. "It's never going to hurt."

"Oh my gosh," I say. "What are you, ten years old?"

His face falls. "Oh, no." He sighs. "I think I'm more like a hundred and twenty-five. No, wait. I'm a hundred and thirty-two." He looks stricken.

I'm laughing again, and this time I can't stop.

"Why is that so funny?" He actually looks distraught. "You think being ancient's a joke?"

I shrug. "You look thirty, maybe."

"Well, I'm not. I was born in *eighteen ninety-one*." He groans. "This is horrible."

"It's not like the identification Aleks gets you will say that. And you were frozen or something." I poke the back of his hand where the skin looks perfectly smooth. Distractingly smooth. I shake my head. "You don't appear to have aged."

"Maybe all the years will show up at once." He blinks. "Between one day and the next, I'll age into a liver-spotted great grandfather."

I'm laughing again.

"You don't want to marry me because I'm ancient." He arches one eyebrow. "Admit it."

"I'm not marrying anyone," I say. "I already told you that."

"You sure did," he says.

"You don't listen very well."

He shrugs. "Neither do you."

Grigoriy has me there. "We should both get some sleep." I grab my crutches from where they're leaning against the sofa and head for the hall.

"Where do you want to sleep?"

I stop abruptly and pivot as quickly as I can on crutches. I shake my head slowly. "Why are you acting like where *I* sleep has anything to do with where *you* sleep?"

He frowns. "How can I keep you safe if you're sleeping somewhere else?"

"There are wards around the whole place," I say. "Kris said that."

"But what if someone inside the building tries to hurt you?" A muscle in his jaw works. "I don't know any of these people. I should at least be within earshot."

"You know where my room is," I say. "You can be anywhere but there." I start hobbling my way down the hall, but I turn to look over my shoulder. "I'll be locking my door."

His laughter follows me down the hall.

The next morning, when I finally emerge from my room, which thankfully has a connected bathroom, Grigoriy's eating breakfast in the dining room. "My mom always had breakfast in the sunroom." He points through the doorway at a tiny alcove with a much smaller table and a whole wall of windows. "But all of that furniture is long gone. The table Kris bought is quite small." He eyes my crutches. "I thought we might eat here instead."

He's learning. He didn't mention my leg or crutches or anything. He almost did, but I'll still give him credit. "Thanks." I lean the crutches against the table and hop as I pull out the chair and take a seat.

The muscles in Grigoriy's forearms are practically straining where he's gripping the table. I imagine it took all his restraint to keep from hopping up and circling the table to help me. But it shows that he can be taught.

"The woman who does the cooking said she wasn't sure what we liked, so she made a lot of things." He gestures. "There's buckwheat *kasha*, which might be good if you like gruel." He grimaces. "Pancakes with sour cream and raspberry syrup, which are pretty good. They're still a little crisp on the edges." He pushes his plate toward me, and I notice the remains of raspberry sauce. "*Syrniki*, which is even better."

I love the cheese pancakes, myself. My grandma used to make them. I grab a plate and reach across the table to snag a few of the *syrniki*.

"And she made *ponchiki*, but someone should have told her I don't like them cold."

"Oh, I do." I pile a few of the fried cheese donut holes on my plate. "They're my very favorite, hot or cold." I think it's the creamy cheese the Russians add that makes them taste a hundred times better than regular donut holes. I actually like them a bit better cold. They're stickier? Somehow it makes the sugar less overwhelming.

He smiles. "I was worried you'd want lentils."

I roll my eyes. "That's a misnomer. Latvians eat a lot of lentils, but it's not *all* we eat."

He stands and reaches all the way down to the end. With no warning, he tosses me a roll.

I catch the crusty, dark brown roll. "We also don't *have to have* rye at every meal."

"That's Russian black bread. It's far superior to your Latvian rye."

I doubt it, but I don't argue. "Oh." I notice a plate at the end. "Is that *zapekanka*?" My mouth starts to water.

"I think so," he says. "I hate raisins, though."

"You're wrong on almost everything," I say.

Before I can stand up and hunch over, he snags the plate and slides the others around to make room. I grab a slice, and it's even better than the *ponchiki*. "I should give my compliments to your cook." I sip on the tea—which is also quite good. Plenty of flavor, but not heavy, with a bit of sweetness that's clearly from a bit of added honey. "But if I stayed here very long, I'd become fat as a house."

He laughs. "I doubt that very much."

"I'm only thin because I've never had enough money to afford being able to gorge myself."

Grigoriy tilts his head, squints, and then shrugs. "I think you'll be very cute when you're chubby."

"Excuse me?" I slam my fork down on the table. "Just stop."

"Stop?" Grigoriy leans toward me, his eyes intent on mine. "Stop providing you breakfast? Stop telling you that you'll look good no matter how many stacks of *syrniki* you eat? Which part of that made you so angry? Or are you always this grumpy to people who save your life and have the audacity to try to flirt afterward?"

His words surprise me. He did save my life. And he's done nothing but try to help since, albeit in a bit of a high-handed way. He's right. I have been furious about it.

Why?

I hate circling back to the same thing over and over, but in this case. . . I swallow. "I think I might be nervous."

"Nervous?"

"My leg," I say. "It hasn't been strong and hale for more than a decade. It hurts all the time. I grew used to that. I couldn't ride—and for a while it felt like my life was over. It felt like I had no value and no future for a while, but I figured that out, too. I found a new future. I reconciled myself to never attaining any of my original goals. But then a freak accident wrecked even that." I sigh, poking at my *syrniki*.

"Those are *not* good cold." He pushes the raspberry syrup toward me.

"Thanks." I daub some on. "A surgeon in Latvia told me that the damage from that idiotic horse slamming me into a wall could be repaired. Probably." I drop my voice. "But he said there's a fifty-fifty chance it doesn't work, and if I fall on the wrong side of that. . .I'm crippled for good."

Grigoriy's eyes harden. "I hope Aleks found you a better surgeon."

"I'm nervous about what he'll say. I don't want to waste Kristiana's money, but if there's a chance I can fix my leg and get my life back, I selfishly want to take it."

"It's not a waste of her money, even if it doesn't work."

"It is, though," I say. "In a wheelchair, there's no way for me to earn the money back. I need to be able to teach horseback lessons, at least. That means that I need to be able to groom horses, lead them, lunge them. If I can't do even that." I throw my hands up in the air. "She says it's fine. She said she doesn't care, but. . ."

"Aleksandr knows that I'll pay him back once I have the money. I'm the one paying—so don't worry about paying it back. Without you, I won't even be able to earn the money. It's an even trade."

"Why are you being so nice?" I ask. "And why do you keep joking about marrying me? You can't really want to marry someone you just met. Is it because Aleks is getting married?"

"My parents died when I was sixteen," he says. "After that, I was raised by my aunt and uncle—my mom's brother and his wife. They were great to me. They were happy. They were kind. They worked hard. My uncle started pestering me when I was about twenty-five to get married." He shakes his head. "I had no idea how I was supposed to choose someone, so I asked him how he chose my aunt."

"And?"

"He said he met lots of women. Smart women. Funny women. Beautiful women."

"He liked them all?"

He shrugs. "He didn't say. But he told me that none of them were the right person. It wasn't until he met my aunt and his heart said, *'mine,'* that he knew. I've been looking and listening since then—with a hundred-year hiatus—and I've never met anyone that I cared about one way or another."

My pulse has picked up, and something he's saying is making me feel. . .tingly? Nervous? Excited? Terrified? All of those things. And others I can't describe.

I hate it.

And I love it.

"Okay."

"That night, when I saw you broken and bleeding, it was a dark night. I was a horse. I couldn't shift because my powers weren't working. I had no idea where I was or what was going on. I couldn't do a thing. So I crouched down by you and thought, at least I can warm her up. At least she won't be alone when she dies."

He looks like he might cry. Honestly. It's strange to see.

But then he inhales sharply. "But then, after I touched you, my powers worked, and I saved you." He shrugs. "I haven't wanted to share you since then. I figure that's my sign."

That simple. He saw me. He saved me. He wants me.

I'm not sure what I expected, but that's not it. "That's not a good reason to get married."

"What *is* a good reason to get married?" He looks serious.

"There isn't one." I cross my arms.

Kris pokes her head through the doorway. "You two look cozy."

"What time is my appointment?" I ask. "You didn't say before you left."

"It's in. . ." She glances at her watch. "Forty-one minutes."

I try to leap to my feet, forgetting in my adrenaline-laced panic that my leg is unsound, and I collapse on the floor. The pain's so bad, I don't even have space to be embarrassed.

"Mirdza." Kris crouches next to me, but a split second later, she's replaced.

Grigoriy's beside me, his face full of concern. His dark blue eyes are scanning me, and his hands brush against my forearms. "Do you want help getting up, space to breathe, or someone to curse at?"

It's a pretty comprehensive list, and making sense of it distracts me while the pain starts to ebb. "Someone to swear at."

He thumps his chest. "I'm ready."

But something about his concern-laden bravado makes me want to laugh instead. And it makes my heart flip over, too. "I'm sorry."

"For what?"

I can barely force the words out, and they aren't very loud. "For being so grouchy."

"If my body had betrayed me, I'd be crabby too." His fingers brush slowly down the side of my face.

Again, I both hate and love what I'm feeling right now. I'm not sure which one to embrace. "Alright. I'm ready for the help-getting-up offer."

He doesn't fuss or make a big deal out of it. He simply takes careful hold of my upper arms and lifts. Kris hands me my crutches, and I hobble my way down to my room to grab my purse and phone.

"I do have an ID for you," she says. "It's a copy they printed, with a signature from the Latvian embassy, but it's the best we could get for now. They're making you an expedited passport that should be ready in the next day or so." She offers me the temporary passport, and I take it gratefully and tuck it into my purse.

"We should have a new phone for you by tomorrow, but you may need to talk to them to confirm a few things. They were giving Aleks a hard time about having your plan transferred, since we're in Russia, I think. A non-EU country and an EU country. . .you know the drill."

Her fiancé's really connected. Or, as he already mentioned, he's quite rich and willing to spend that money. I suppose money's better than connections, anyway. I wouldn't know personally, of course, since I've never had either, but that seems reasonable based on what I've seen of the world.

"Hey, there." Grigoriy's leaning against my doorframe, and he's wearing new clothes I helped him pick yesterday. He was already quite striking, but now. . . His hair's pulled back with a rubber band, which I didn't think I'd like, but it works for him somehow, and in the dark jeans and black sweater that hugs his muscular shoulders and chest. . .he's dangerous. "Are you ready?"

I nod. "Yeah." And I realize that, for the first time since my accident, I actually am. It's time for me to be honest with Kris and with myself. "I need to tell you something."

"What?" he asks.

"Not you." I shift, and I meet Kristiana's eyes. "My surgeon back home told me that the surgery could possibly restore function to my leg, but because of how many pieces it was broken into before, and with the current damage to the bone shards because of all the pins and the screws. . ." I inhale and exhale slowly, "there's a fifty percent chance it fails entirely." I brace myself for her to be upset.

"Mirdza." Kris's entire face falls. "That's terrible. I'm so sorry. Hopefully this surgeon will have more confidence in himself and your odds."

"But if it does fail, and that seems likely." I look down at the beautiful new boots she bought me, the boots that help distract from the terrible twist of my thigh where the femur joins the hip. "I don't know how I'd ever pay you back. When I asked her for a loan, Brigita fired me. I have no job, and if I'm stuck in a wheelchair—" I choke up and look up at the ceiling to keep from crying.

"There's no way you can teach," Kris says. She's crying now, too. She finally gets it.

A terrible sound behind me has me turning around.

Grigoriy's hand somehow broke the wooden frame of the doorway, and it's come detached from the wall. "Your value isn't in being able to teach people to ride horses."

"Actually," I say, "it kind of is. Not everyone's a lost Russian prince whose best friend has bought his old family estate and has a plan to restore him to wealth." I shake my head. "My life, unlike yours, has never been magical, and

I've never been worth much." It hurts to say it aloud, but it doesn't change the truth.

"You do have a best friend." Kris is right beside me, now. She must have crossed the room while I was distracted by Grigoriy. "And I already told you that you don't need to pay me back. It's really not a big deal to us. Consider it the start of my apology for being so self-centered that I didn't even realize what you were going through."

"But—"

She drops her hand over mine. "No buts, Mirdza. You're my sister, and I'm paying for this surgery. And I'll be praying every single second that it goes well."

"We might be ahead of ourselves," Aleks says, leaning around Grigoriy. "We need someone to agree to do the procedure first. It was pretty hard for me to get us in to see this surgeon on such short notice. If we miss our appointment. . ."

"Let's go," Kris says. "And will you please tell Mirdza that you don't care about the cost?"

"If I tell her how much I had to bribe the front office to get the appointment, will that make her feel better or worse?"

"Way worse," Kris says. "Just tell her you don't care."

"I don't care," Aleksandr says. "And that's the truth. Kris's friend is mine too." He smiles warmly.

"Besides," Grigoriy says. "I already said that *I'm* paying, once I get my wind turbines running."

"The electrician called, actually," Aleks says. "Yours are operational. Now we just need to get that wind blowing."

When he beams, his already perfectly symmetrical face only becomes more breathtaking. "Excellent news." He turns back toward me. "If your appointment isn't too long, maybe you'll be up to going for a bit of a drive afterward and holding my hand for a little stroll?"

I roll my eyes. "I'm sure I can manage it."

"Great."

"You're sure you can make enough wind to power all those wind turbines?" Kris asks. "And won't that be tiring, always standing around making it blow?"

Aleks and Grigoriy share a glance. "It's fine," Grigoriy says. "Aleks explained what I need to do. Don't worry about it."

"Fine." Kris pushes past the boys and out into the hall.

The ride to the surgeon's office is a little tense. Partially because Aleks is going one point seven million miles per hour, but mostly because I can't seem to understand how they can all be insisting the money for the surgery doesn't matter.

Kris didn't even care that I might not be able to pay her back.

It can't be because she's rich now. I know plenty of rich people who won't share so much as a stick of gum with others. Finally, Kris turns around. "If I needed a surgery," she says. "And you had the money in savings—"

"I'd *loan* it to you," I say, "but I'd be nervous that you'd never be able to pay me back. That's how I expected you to feel."

Before she can reply, her phone starts to ring. Loudly. And it just keeps on ringing.

"Are you going to answer?" Kris asks.

I realize the ringing is coming from my new phone, not Kristiana's. "Only my mom and Adriana even have my number."

"Is it one of them?" Kris lifts her eyebrows.

I swipe to take the call. "Hello?"

"So is she loaning you the money? Because if so, I could really use my thousand euros back."

"Adriana, it's not a good time."

"For me, either," she says. "I really did want to help. I

mean, I still do, but if you can, like, wire me the money or something, that would be great. I have a race tomorrow, and I'm *sure* I'm going to win this time."

Adriana is always sure she's going to win. She does, occasionally, but she loses just as often. Only her optimism never changes. I sigh. "It wasn't a thousand, which you well know, and the thing is—"

"No, don't tell me the thing. I'll text you with the wire instructions." She hangs up.

And that's my sister. My real sister. Is it a shock that I feel guilty for taking advantage of Kris? This is what I'm used to. Although, I should be grateful. She *did* loan me five hundred euros when I had nothing.

"She needs money." Kris's voice—the woman who was just telling me that she won't let me repay her—is totally flat. She's not Adriana's biggest fan.

I don't really blame her.

"She'll be fine," I say.

"Forward the wire instructions to me," Kris says. "If she loaned you money, we'd better pay her back quickly."

Luckily, we reach the surgeon's office before I get anything from Adriana. Hopefully with all the distractions, she'll forget. Of course, it didn't occur to me that we'd sit and wait for over an hour.

Aleks finally gets fed up and marches to the front counter. I half expect us to get thrown out, but instead a lady in a bright green set of scrubs shows us back to a room. "The doctor wants all the tests done before he sees you."

I signed the release they sent yesterday. They should have them all from my doctor back home. "But my records—"

"Dr. Hubert only trusts tests he's had done himself."

I sigh.

"Hubert?" Kris asks.

"He's from the United States," the nurse says.

"What's he doing here?" Aleks looks suspicious.

"After his wife left him, he came on holiday," she says. "He never went back." She drops her voice. "Let's just say he appreciates Russian women and Russian vodka."

Grigoriy stands up. "We need to find a new surgeon."

"Only on the weekends, I assure you," the nurse says. "He's very professional. We're lucky to have him here."

His nostrils flare, but he sits down. "You want a surgeon who's from some tiny country that threw a tantrum when its mother imposed a few taxes?"

Kris snorts.

"We have a lot of things to talk about over the next few days about how the world has changed since 1917." Aleks pats Grigoriy's knee. "The United States isn't small anymore, for one."

Grigoriy shakes his head.

And while they bicker, I'm wheeled off to be poked, prodded, scanned, and x-rayed within an inch of my life. But eventually, we do work our way back to the exam room.

"—that ridiculous sport where men ran round in tiny shorts caught on? Everyone plays it?" Grigoriy rolls his eyes. "Impossible."

"It's the most popular sport in Russia," Aleks says. "I had trouble believing it, too."

"And the church is just okay with it?" Grigoriy looks incredulous.

"The church leadership was, apparently, eliminated when the communists took over." Aleks looks baffled as well.

"The doctor will be in shortly." The nurse wheels me into the room, pivots on her heel, and leaves.

"How much did you pay for this appointment?" Kris asks. "Because I'm beginning to think you were ripped off. We've been in this room for two hours."

Aleks whips out his phone, presumably to raise some Cain, when the door opens.

A short man with almost no hair on his head breezes through and grabs a stool. "I'm Dr. Hubert," he says in awkwardly accented Russian. "Sorry to make me wait." Clearly, although he's hopefully a competent doctor, he's yet to master the language here. And he has yet to look up from the tablet he's holding, either. He swipes, and swipes, and zooms in on something, squints, and swipes again.

Aleks clears his throat.

"How nice to meet you," Kris says.

If he heard either of them, he doesn't show any sign of it. He keeps on flipping through things, entirely intent upon his tablet. Finally, he looks up. "Alright. I review scans."

"We all speak English," Kris says in a clear, American accent. She sounds so much like her mom when she switches to English that it makes my heart twinge a bit.

"Oh, praise be." The doctor tosses the tablet down on the counter behind him. "You have no idea how nice it is when I find patients who do." He sighs. "I'm afraid the damage from whatever percussive impact you suffered is quite extensive. I didn't really need your office's work up, but I did want the old scans from before your accident." He wheels toward me quickly, and I shy back.

It's impossible to move away quickly in a wheelchair.

But suddenly there's a brick wall between us. A very Russian, very threatening brick wall. When Grigoriy reaches for my hand, I yank it away. "No flinging my surgeon around," I hiss in Russian. "He just startled me. Get out of his way."

Grigoriy scowls, but he moves.

The doctor cranes his neck to look up at him. "You're the husband, I assume. I understand being protective of your wife, but I assure you that I'm the best doctor for at least two thousand miles. Maybe more."

"He's not my husband," I say.

"She's mine," Grigoriy says, "and you'd better be telling the truth."

Dr. Hubert's tiny. He's lost most of his hair. And he's living in a country, the language of which he doesn't speak. But when he says the next words, he sounds utterly, entirely, massively confident. "Then you should be thanking me. Because there's not much good bone left, but I can put Humpty Dumpty back together again, and when I'm done, she'll be able to walk without those." He points at my horrible crutches and wheels backward. "Now, muscle man, are you ready to stand down? Or am I going to have to call security?"

❦ 9 ❦

When Kris hugged me, I felt painfully hopeful. I had someone on my side, someone willing to risk their money on me. When Aleks found a surgeon who would meet with me, I felt even more delighted. The idea of having the surgery here, where there are people who will care for me afterward. . .it's almost overwhelming.

But when the surgeon tells me I'll be able to walk again, I begin to shake all over.

With joy.

I hadn't admitted to myself how terrifying the prospect of being wheelchair-bound really was. I'm not someone who's brilliant. I'm not nearly as beautiful as Kris, at least, not in the striking, look-at-me way that she is. And I'm not exceptionally talented at, well, at anything.

Not anymore, anyway.

But I'm an active person who finds a lot of peace and comfort in movement. In being and doing and going. I may not be able to ride horses anymore, but I groom them. I lunge them. I lead them around. It's what keeps me sane. It's what makes it alright that I only teach and never ride.

Being around horses, leading them, petting them, and standing with them centers me.

I can't even fathom a life without my pushy, idiotic, hare-brained angels.

And this surgeon says he can give it back to me.

"How soon can we schedule the surgery?" Kris asks.

She and Aleks ask all the hard questions, pelting the doctor with pointed demands and pinning him down.

It's a Tuesday now.

He agrees to shift things around to do it on Friday.

In my wildest dreams, I never thought I might have the surgery in three days. "What's the recovery time?" I ask.

Aleks waves him off. "We can talk about that the day of the surgery. No worries about that."

"What about the second surgery?" I ask.

The surgeon smiles devilishly. "Those surgeons weren't as good as me." He wiggles his eyebrows. "I'll do it all in one. And since I'll use a graft, the recovery results will be better than what any of them predicted."

"That's amazing," Kris says.

"Now, let's talk about how many days you'll be here and your rehab schedule."

"We have another appointment," Aleks says. "We can finalize that information later."

Kris grabs the handles of my wheelchair, and Aleks grabs my crutches, and we shoot out the door.

"Wait," I say. "I didn't even have the chance to ask—"

But we're leaving the front office. . .and even Grigoriy isn't objecting.

"How am I supposed to know how soon I can get back to work?" I ask. "Brigita's holding onto my horses for now, but if I don't get back in time, the contract says—"

"You won't have any recovery time," Kris whispers.

"What?" I throw my hands down on the wheelchair

outer bar and stop myself forcibly. "Someone explain what you're talking about."

"Aleks's magic allows him to accelerate the healing of anything," Grigoriy says matter-of-factly, like I should just know this.

"I told you. Remember?" Kris asks.

I blink.

"The second you're discharged, he can heal you right up." Kris beams at me.

Is she serious?

"It's like how Grigoriy healed you, but a little different," Kris says. "Trust me. The recovery will be a snap as long as the procedure goes well."

Some woman rushes through the door, notices us, and slows down to a trot. "We need to finish the paperwork and take payment, if you're wanting to move ahead with Friday."

"Paperwork?" Aleks asks. "We're paying cash. Can't we just bring it—"

"The screws and plates are regulated," she says. "To place the order for them, we'll need a patient name."

It takes us almost forty-five minutes to fill out the paperwork, and by the time we're done, we're all starving.

Aleks looks practically insane when he catches Kris's eyes and lifts his eyebrows up and down. "Lamb *chebureki*?"

I can almost hear her eyeroll, it's so pronounced. "Fine. It's on the way anyway."

"On the way to what?"

Kris turns all the way around in her chair, gripping the side of the seat to hold herself steady. "Aleksandr said you were okay with going the long way home and stopping by the wind farm?"

Right. My leg's throbbing, and my head's starting to hurt, too. It could be hunger, or perhaps the fact that my worst fear's finally somewhat less likely.

Relief headaches.

They're a thing, right?

"Sure," I say. "It's fine."

"We can wait until tomorrow," Grigoriy says, "if you're too tired."

"It's fine," I say. "Really. All I have to do is be there, right?"

He nods. "Exactly."

I really hope, for his sake, that Aleks isn't overestimating what he can do. Once, for a party, my mom asked me to blow up a bag of balloons. The first one was super easy. The second was fine. But by the time I finished blowing up one hundred balloons, I was lightheaded, and my head was pounding.

I nearly passed out.

My mom freaked out, worried that the cheap balloons that were made in China might have poisoned me. In the end, it was just the sustained expulsion of air that left me drained. I think about the idea of someone creating enough wind to move the turbines on a huge windmill. . .and I worry.

Just a bit.

I mean, it's not like Grigoriy's my problem.

And even if he's broke, Kris isn't. I'll get my surgery either way. He seems so confident. I hate the idea of his confidence being misplaced, but I've met too many guys who could swagger, but couldn't back it up.

Aleks must have some faith, because he spent who knows how much on all those turbines. As we approach, I realize that I had *no idea* how much he'd spent.

I expected twenty or *maybe* thirty wind turbines.

There are at least two hundred of them.

"I thought they had to be spaced out," I say.

"Normally they do," Aleks says. "In fact, the install guys

were not happy with me. I'm not complying with most of their rules."

"Aren't these hugely expensive?" I can't stop gawking at the turbines. They're so much bigger than I realized. Massive, really. Hundreds of feet higher than anything else in the area.

"The Russian government made some promises to the United Nations and to Germany in their latest trade agreement, to move to using a certain percentage of renewable resources in the next five years." Aleks laughs. "They're way, *way* behind. Let's just say that these should be two or three million *each*, install not included, and I bought two hundred and eleven for two hundred *thousand* euros each."

"I'm not great at math," I say. "Because when I did that in my head. . .it seems like you spent forty million on them."

"Forty-two," Aleks says. "But don't worry."

If I had a paper bag, I'd be hyperventilating into it. How could he have spent that much on them and still have even a single ruble left to pay for my surgery? My mind is *reeling* right now.

"Not only that, but a few weeks later, a private party reached out. They had bought eighty-seven turbines and then been unable to find places to install them, so I bought those for only a hundred thousand each. They're being installed on my property right now."

"But you hadn't found Grigoriy yet," I say. "When you bought these, I mean."

Aleks smiles. "Some things you take on faith."

"Don't believe a word of that," Kris says. "He was *panicked* when months passed with no sign of Grigoriy. He had to sign a pledge to generate a certain amount of energy, and he's already four months behind." She sighs. "His penalty fees if he doesn't meet those quotas are. . .painful."

"But we will, now," he says. "No risk, no reward."

"You got lucky," Kris says. "You know how I feel about gambling."

"Says the woman who bet every euro she had on a losing horse."

I really, really like the two of them together, now that I know enough to understand what makes them work.

"Let's do it." Grigoriy reaches for my hand.

"Wait." I snatch it back. "That's it? We just do it? Just like that?"

His expression's bemused. "What did you expect? Should we have some performers come and celebrate this momentous event, first? Or perhaps we should open a bottle of champagne?"

"No, we do that afterward," Kris says.

"It just feels like a big deal. I read about wind turbines last night, and one of them can power fifteen hundred homes all year."

Aleksandr smiles. "These are a bit bigger, actually. Try two thousand homes at average capacity."

"Don't you need to, I don't know, prepare? Draw a warding circle in chalk, or something?"

"Where do you get these ideas?" Grigoriy laughs. "My magic, more than any of the others, is part of who I am."

"Let's not get carried away," Aleks says. "*More than any others?*" He rolls his eyes. "I think you meant to say that your magic, like mine, does exhaust you sometimes, but it's exhilarating too. And you know your limits well, because you trained to master it for a decade."

"More than a decade," Grigoriy says. "Now."

When he reaches for my hand this time, I let him take it. "Good luck."

"I won't need it," he says. "But thanks." He's not even looking at me when he reaches for my hand, but I can't seem to look away. His big, strong hand moves toward me smoothly, confidently, and slowly, his big fingers slip over mine. Even though his is covering the top of mine, his hand shifts a bit, and his fingers slide through the gaps between mine.

A shiver runs up my spine, and I suppress it, hoping he won't feel it.

He's far too focused on the vast army of wind turbines stretched out in front of us to even care what I'm doing, I'm sure. I crane my neck up, up, up, and then swivel back and forth a bit, trying to take in the hundreds of acres on which the wind turbines are placed.

"How big is this estate?" I ask.

"The turbines take up more than two hundred and fifty acres," Aleks says. "It was the closest I could get anyone to agree to install them." He sighs. "But Grigoriy has several thousand acres, so it's not a huge inconvenience."

"I can't believe we can see them all," Kris says.

"The human eye can see several miles before the curvature of the earth obscures their view," Aleks says.

"You can't trust everything you read online," Kris says.

"But." He shrugs. "Two hundred and fifty acres, evenly distributed, is just under three miles, and. . ." He points. You can barely make out the ones at the end.

"Now that we're here, looking at them, I'm a little nervous," Kristiana says. "That's going to take a *lot* of wind—"

She cuts off, because the sound around us is terrifying. It's like the screaming of a thousand sheep. Screeching saws from a hundred different blades. And then the closest wind turbine in front of us begins to turn, slowly at first, but then gaining momentum, and the others in the row soon pick up speed as well.

Aleks, Kris, and I all stand utterly still, watching gape-mouthed, as wind tears through the air above our heads. Trees creak and moan. Birds shriek and dive away. A chipmunk chirps and darts around us, racing away.

I wish I could run.

It's not like that's Grigoriy's fault, per se. I mean, he does need me here to do this horrifyingly scary thing, but even if he didn't, I can't run anywhere right now.

"Are we sure it's safe to be here?" I ask.

Aleks nods, his hair whipping around his head. "He has total control. It's just that, to power these, he has to lock in a very large, very concentrated amount of wind."

The hair tie flies off Grigoriy's knot, and his beautiful, dark brown hair looks just as tumultuous as his friend's. I wonder how desperately tangled my hair will be by the time we're done.

"Lock in?" I'm screaming now, just to be heard.

"We talked about it. We're going to do twenty-one hours on, three hours off, then twenty-two hours on, four hours off, then twenty hours on, one hour off, in rotating waves. That will look strange to the auditors, but at least it won't be as cut and dried as some kind of clockwork wind that never ceases."

"He can do that?"

"It's a combination of mathematical principles and the laws of physics," Aleks says. "And—"

"Boring," Kris says. "Stop."

Aleks laughs.

"Almost done." Grigoriy's still looking at the turbines, but now they're all turning, and the ones near us have picked up the pace. They don't quite look like a sideways ceiling fan, but they're closer than I'd have thought possible.

"This will keep going, even when you're not here?"

"It's about creating a sequence of tunnels in the air around us that will—"

"Ohmygosh," Kris says. "The answer is, yes. They'll keep going."

"Yes," Grigoriy says. "Sorry. That's the answer."

It takes him another ten minutes of total focus, but then he exhales and releases my hand.

I pretend it doesn't bum me out.

"Can you two get in the car?" He tosses his head. "I need to walk around a turbine or two and check some things. I don't want to send Mirdza back, in case I need her, but it's distracting with all the chatter."

Kristiana's eyes widen. "Fine." She and Aleks trot back, glancing over their shoulders most of the way.

"Should I come with you?" I ask.

He shakes his head. "I actually didn't need them to leave for anything related to that." He glances up at the closest turbine.

"What? Why, then?"

He smiles, but his words when he speaks are carefully enunciated to be audible over the strong winds. "We both got great news today, you about your surgery, and me with this." He waves his hand around. "Aleks had explained his plan, and I *thought* I could do it, but I wasn't entirely sure."

"So you are human after all," I say.

"I'm a stallion shifter, actually." His smile's back to being cocky. "And I did just power up two hundred and eleven turbines." He exhales. "By Aleks's estimations, they should run about three times the capacity of a normal turbine. That means they'll power six thousand homes worth of energy apiece. And we get paid about ten to twenty percent of that cost." He smiles. "It's going to be an absolute gold mine."

"I'm happy for you," I say.

"A gold mine in the sky." He shakes his head. "Trust Aleksandr to come up with a way for us to do that."

"Is he good at business?"

Grigoriy laughs. "He's lucky in that regard. He has an earth magic that allows him to find gold, oil, precious gems, you name it. He can even summon them to himself, which means he has limitless resources at his literal fingertips. Forget working in mines and taking risks and hoping and praying. He can just. . ." He waves his hand over the ground in front of us. "Print his own money."

No wonder he and Kris are rich.

"But my power's never been like that." He sighs. "It's always been the most useless."

"Useless?" I look up at the massive windmills churning. "It looks pretty useful to me."

"Now, but a hundred years ago, all I could do was make sure bad weather blew away and rain came toward my people." He shrugs. "Useless."

"Well, good thing you have Aleks, then."

"I still can't believe he set this all up before he even found me."

"He must have been pretty lonely," I say.

"Lonely isn't the right word," Grigoriy says. "He had Kristiana. He's happier than I've ever seen him. But Aleks has a very deep-seated sense of duty, and I think it pained him to think of us in that weird stasis, never living, but not quite dead. He wanted to save us in the way Kris saved him."

"But she told me he was a horse when she found him, and she had no idea for days that he could shift."

"True," Grigoriy says. "But she blew all the money she needed on him, which was out of character. He intentionally threw a race so she could win. They clearly both felt *something* from the start." He steps closer to me, his eyes on mine.

"I guess."

"Do you really feel nothing for me?" His eyes drop to my mouth.

My heart's a disloyal fiend. "Like what?" I try to lighten things by shrugging and pretending I don't understand him.

He lowers his head toward mine.

My heart gallops away with my brains.

"It's like that feeling just before a lightning strike. I think it's called *ozone*," he whispers, his lips now hovering over mine. "It's a feeling of expectation. Like whatever happens between us will be *incomparable*." The corner of his mouth curls up, and I look at it.

It's a mistake. His lips are so full. They're so confident. They're so *close*. I sigh involuntarily.

And he *knows*. Without another word, without a warning, without asking permission, he kisses me.

Kiss is the wrong word.

It just means pressing your lips to someone else's. It implies a kind of intimacy, a give and take.

But this isn't a kiss. It's a *claiming*. When Grigoriy said he looked at me and his heart said "mine," he meant it. His body angles over mine, his arms both bracing me and pulling me closer. His lips completely cover, and then coax, somehow in the same moment.

I'm such a liar.

I can't believe I looked at him with a straight face and pretended I felt *nothing*. My entire body sways toward him, like a tree craving the touch of the wind. My heart pounds, just for him. My soul longs for more.

And then, far too quickly, he releases me.

I drag in a breath that's so ragged, it should be thrown in the rubbish bin. "That." I swallow.

"Yes." His smile isn't halfway now. It's full-fledged, it's cocky, and it's very, very intense. "That."

Somehow, with that one word, I surrendered. There's no way he will believe me if I say I felt nothing. "Fine."

"You want me, too."

"I want you," I say. "But there are plenty of things I want that aren't good for me. I'll add you to the list."

He moves so fast, he should have a lightning power, sliding his arms under my knees and behind my back, and snagging my crutches as he does it. He carries me toward the car boldly, unashamed. "You're mine. You know it, even if you won't admit it yet. But that's okay. I'm patient. I'll wait."

Faced with a force of nature like Grigoriy, I don't even bother trying to argue. I just lean against his chest and close my eyes.

❧ 10 ❧

"I guess you got that turbine issue worked out," Kris says. She's trying not to smile, but she's terrible at it.

"We did," Grigoriy says, placing me gently in the seat. He tosses my crutches over the back. "Let's head back."

When he closes the door, I realize just how much background noise I'd become accustomed to out there. It's so quiet in here that there's absolutely nothing to distract from the heavy, almost oppressively awkward, silence.

"You know, I've been thinking." Kris pointedly turns around and faces forward. "With Aleks to help the process of mending your bones along, and Grigoriy who can repair any recent injuries. . ."

"What?"

"If this surgeon does what he says, maybe. . ."

"Maybe what?" If I'm a little snappish, well. Grigoriy apparently finds it funny.

"Maybe you could ride again."

I roll my eyes. "Let's not get carried away. No one's handing out invites to Hogwarts or magical wands."

"What's Hogwarts?" Aleksandr asks.

"He hasn't seen *Harry Potter* yet." I shake my head. "Tragic, and yet, I'm somehow also jealous."

"But, kind of they *are* handing out wands," Kris says, totally ignoring both me and her fiancé. "We have two mages. They can shift into horses, and that makes me even more positive. I saw you riding him yesterday. Remember?"

"I thought I was dead anyway," I say. "And I was in the middle of nowhere in a strange place, and a horse kept insisting that I ride him."

"What about now?" she asks. "You'd be able to ride a horse who won't spook, who knows you're injured, and who will be very careful with you. Right?"

"I could still slip," I say.

"And if you did, it would be a recent injury, and he could heal you. What else you got?"

I sigh. "Let's see how the surgery goes," I say. "Then we can talk."

"And we will talk," Kris says.

She's like a border collie stuck inside while a barn cat paces along the windowsill—she just can't let things go.

We don't have far to drive. We are, after all, already on Grigoriy's property, but we've gone less than a half mile when he reaches out and takes my hand, his fingers slowly sliding between mine.

I inhale, but I don't stop him.

Why don't I stop him?

I should.

He seems to want to own me, and that's never been a good thing in my life. People can't own people. Or, they can, but they *shouldn't*. At least the other guys I dated weren't blatant about wanting to possess me.

Maybe that's what feels different.

He's not just telling me what I want to hear—his

confession that he saw me and his heart said *mine* felt raw. Honest. Real. It almost feels like he's as lost as I am, just trying to navigate new waters, and for some reason, his words make me believe he wants something different than what I've had before.

I should be anxious about our kiss, about his fingers being tangled with mine, but for some reason, for the first time in my life, I'm *not*. Holding his hand feels right. It feels. . .safe.

When we finally reach his monstrous mansion and Aleks pulls into the garage, Kris and Aleks hop out and disappear faster than I even thought possible. I'm not even out of the car yet when she's waving her phone at me, and they're heading out the side door.

She pauses before leaving entirely. "I'm so very excited about your surgery." She smiles. "Text me that info for your sister, and I'll send her some money right away."

After Grigoriy's explanation about Aleksandr's powers, I decide to go ahead and do it. If he can literally pull gold out of the ground, maybe they're serious about it not being an imposition for them to help.

"I'm starving," Grigoriy says.

"We just had lamb *chebureki*," I say. "How could you possibly be hungry?"

"Did I mention that working magic leaves me ravenous?" His eyes drop to my mouth as the corner of his mouth turns up. "Though, now you mention it. I bet we have food inside."

My stomach's doing flips now, thanks to his smolder. "We could go out," I say, "but you don't have money."

"Aleks gave me money." He pulls a wallet out of his back pocket in a remarkably awkward way and flips it open, splaying a thick stack of bills. "And I have these little cards that everyone seems to take as well." He seems baffled about why credit cards are accepted.

"It's not that the card is money," I say. "It's that you pay with the card—that company pays for you—and then you pay all of the things they paid for back at the end of the month."

He frowns.

It is kind of strange, now that I think about it. I wonder who came up with that?

"What kind of food do you like?" he asks.

"I have a smart phone," I say. "I can see what places are close that have good reviews."

Grigoriy snags the keys off the hook by the back door into the house and trots toward the drivers' side.

"Whoa," I say. "Not so fast."

"Not so fast?" He turns. "Oh. Right."

I expect him to give me the keys, but instead he comes back to stand near me and does nothing else. "What are you doing?"

"Waiting for you to reach the car so I can take your crutches."

I whap him with a crutch. "I don't need that."

"Ow," he complains.

"Give me the keys."

He cradles them next to his chest. "Why?"

"Because you don't have a license, and even more importantly, you have no idea how to drive."

He frowns, and then he ignores me, heading back toward the driver's side. "First, you don't have a license either. Everything of yours was taken. Secondly, yours is from Latvia. I doubt it even works here. And finally, I do so know how to drive."

"Impossible," I say.

"They had cars before I was—er—frozen."

"Cars that went twenty miles an hour," I say.

"I'll have you know that I had a Stutz Bearcat—imported from America—that went sixty plus miles an hour." He straightens up. "I'll be an excellent driver. I assure you."

After a little more back and forth, I give up. He's unwilling to budge, and knowing he at least has sat behind the wheel of a car makes me slightly less terrified.

"I'll navigate," I say, "and you have to listen to me on things."

"Fine," he says. "Deal."

But from the second the engine purrs to life, he stops listening. "No, you need a blinker," I say.

"Why? People can see that I'm turning."

"But if you use your blinker *before* you turn, they'll figure it out faster."

We're nearly to the restaurant when I tell him to turn.

And he hits the gas instead of the brake.

I nearly faint.

But just in time, he switches, and we don't crash into the delivery van in front of us. "On the way home," I say, as we pull into the parking lot, *"I'm driving."*

He just smiles.

"Say yes," I say. "Or I'm not getting out of this car. You can eat alone."

He laughs.

"Grigoriy Khilkov, Prince of Dolgovo, stop laughing and agree with me. Actually, forget that. Hand me the keys." I extend my hand, palm up.

He sighs, and then he rolls his eyes, but finally he drops the keys into my hand.

"Really?"

"How will I get better if you never let me drive?" He leans closer, his eyes intent, but when he's only a few inches away, his gaze drops to my mouth.

I shoot out of the car so fast that I momentarily forget about my leg. I have to clutch at the doorframe to keep from falling. Grigoriy's there a second later, his arms wrapping around me from behind. "Be more careful."

"Why?" My voice is breathy. I hate it.

"Because it kills me to see you hurting more than you have to be."

Why is my stupid stomach flip-flopping? I must be hungrier than I thought. I slip the keys into my purse, and then I bend forward, moving away from his way-too-large, way-too-muscular body to grab my crutches. "Let's go," I say. "I'm starving."

He's grinning in a very proprietary way when we reach the front door. "You look great in those new boots, by the way," he says as he opens the front door and gestures for me to go in first.

The hostess looks at me, and then glances back at him, and immediately looks confused. I know just what she's thinking. *What's that crippled girl doing with that demigod?*

If I were her, I'd be wondering the same thing.

It's a fluke, really. He's just woken up from some kind of painful half-sleep, and I was the first person he saw. He wants to fix me, but when he can't, he'll get bored, and even if he can, I will no longer be interesting.

I'm not a complete idiot. I know these things.

And yet, having him completely ignore the lovely hostess and stare only at me is intoxicating.

"Table for two," he says. "Somewhere quiet, please." He still doesn't glance at her. He's staring at me boldly, and I should be embarrassed. Men stare like that at knockouts. At movie stars.

They don't stare at mousy little cripples at all, unless we get in the way. Which is fine. If any other man I've ever dated did that, it would make me ragingly uncomfortable.

But with Grigoriy, it's different somehow.

As she shows us to our table, I can see the hostess's attention shift. At first she was baffled. She thought she could get his attention and shift his focus. But he never wavers, and she begins to wonder. *Who is this woman? Why's he so intent on her?*

And just like that, I become someone important.

That's it, I realize. When I'm with Grigoriy, I feel important.

It's dangerous. If he changes his mind, which he surely will sooner or later, then I'll become nothing again. And it'll hurt way more because I'll remember what it felt like to be someone special.

That risk might make him the most dangerous person I've ever been out to dinner with.

When our waitress shows up, setting glasses of water in front of both of us, she makes the same immediate conclusions about Grigoriy and me, smiling at him brightly and ignoring me entirely. "Are you ready to order?"

But he turns her back toward me. "My fiancée always orders for me. I'll eat anything, you see, so I let her choose. I eat whatever she doesn't like."

That takes me off guard—and the waitress too, judging from the look on her face. "Okay."

I briefly consider correcting him. I'm definitely not his fiancée. But arguing with him about it might be worse than just ignoring him. "I'll have the *solyanka*." I love that soup, but the smell is strong. Onions, pickles, cabbage. It's so pungent that it'll surely keep him away. "And some *pelmeni*," I say. "They have the three-way filling, right?"

"Three-way?" Grigoriy asks.

"Beef, pork, and chicken?"

The waitress nods.

"And some beef stroganoff," I say. "It's just not the same in Latvia."

"You're Latvian?" The waitress curls her lip.

"And you're rude. Not wise for someone who works for tips." Grigoriy's finally looking at her, but only to glare.

She scampers off.

"That was right, wasn't it?" he asks. "Aleks explained the etiquette a bit, but I'm not totally sure I remember it all."

"She does work mostly for tips, but now I'm hoping she won't spit in our food. Maybe the stroganoff wasn't a great idea." I pick up my water and take a sip, just to have something to do.

"Are women often rude to you because you're prettier than them?"

I snort water through my nose.

My nose.

I feel like that's enough of an answer, but Grigoriy just shifts his chair and pats me on my back. "Are you alright?"

Once I stop coughing, I manage the word, "Never."

"You'll never be alright?"

He's so obtuse that it's actually funny. "Never in my life have women been mean to me because I'm more beautiful than they are."

His frown surprises me. "Then the world has changed a lot while I've been hibernating."

I think about that word—hibernating—and decide it fits. He may shift into a horse, but as a human, he reminds me more of a bear. "I doubt it's changed in that way, but very few people in the world have cause to be jealous of me."

"I doubt that," he says. "But even if it's true, I intend to change it."

Luckily, our food comes out quickly. I'm not sure how much of that kind of talk I can handle. It's a lot closer to the idiotic things Danils used to say, and it only makes me more wary of the man across from me. Luckily, if the waitress did anything to the food, I certainly can't tell. I'm not sure why we came out to eat when we have a woman whose entire job it is at home to cook for us, but maybe it's like the driving.

Poor, hibernating Grigoriy needs to get out and do things so he can acclimate to the new world order. He's definitely right at home ordering people around.

"What did you do before you went into hibernation?" I ask.

He blinks, and I realize he thought it was obvious. "I was a prince."

I mean, he said that, but I kind of thought it was a joke. "An actual prince?"

"The Czar rules in Russia, er, *ruled* in Russia." His brow furrows. "But princes were like. . .earls in other places in Europe. We were royalty, from whom others took orders, but I wasn't in line to rule and my family hadn't been for a long time." He shrugs. "My people loved to serve, because I took care of them. We never had droughts in Novgorod."

"You and Aleksandr both were princes? Near Novgorod?"

"Do you know who King Rurik is?" He looks curious, not irritated.

I shake my head.

"He was the king who united the Slavic people—the Vikings, really, called the *Rus*—who had moved into Russia. There are literally hundreds of families who called themselves princes, but only five original families could claim a true line of ancestry that ran back to King Rurik."

"Okay," I say. "I guess that's cool?"

He throws his head back and laughs. "You're very hard to impress. Back before my hibernation—" His eyes twinkle. "Lots of women found me attractive. It figures I'd fall for the one who can barely tolerate me."

"Oh, I find you attractive."

He straightens, the laughter evacuating his face. "You do." It's not a question, but it is. Almost.

"But about Novgorod?"

"That was the capital city for King Rurik," he says. "He

placed the capital here, near the Volkhov River, just below Lake Ilmen. Two of the sons stayed close, even when the capital moved to Kiev, and then Moscow." He shrugs. "The Volkhovs and the Khilkovs have always been close friends."

"Was it hard, having a rich friend?" I can't help thinking how, even though he was clearly never poor, my rich friend Kris is marrying his rich friend Aleks.

"It wasn't ever hard. Aleks never cared, and he'd always give me anything or everything. It wasn't ever something he even thought about." He sighs. "But I didn't have to think about it either. I can't dig gold or gems from the earth, but I've always been able to make sure our crops grew well, and when I was alive, that was the most critical thing—feeding your people. A drought year could bankrupt most anyone."

"But you could blow rain toward your people from anywhere." I saw that firsthand.

"Sometimes it meant traveling a very, very long way."

"So being able to transform into a horse was handy."

"Not as much in my lifetime—I'd always choose a car for long trips."

Our waitress brings the check, and he throws some bills down on the table. He's adjusted remarkably well for just waking up. He stands and offers me his arm.

I wave him off and force myself to my feet.

"Your roads are dramatically better," he says. "I'll give you that."

"Your roads?" The waitress is still hovering, apparently, and our conversation is not quite normal. "Whose roads?"

"He meant our roads in Latvia." I beam at her obliviously. "They're so much smoother than they are here. Probably because we have less snow and ice."

The look the waitress shoots me would wither most girls I know.

Good thing I'm tougher than most girls.

In the end, he's so insistent, I let him drive. . .again.

Thankfully, the ride home's much better, even though it's dark. "Maybe I'm less scared because I can't see everything you're doing wrong," I say.

"I'm not doing anything wrong," he says. "I'm an excellent driver." He stretches and drops one hand on top of mine.

"Nice try." I slip my hand free. "Grab that steering wheel, mister."

"That's 'Your Majesty' to you," he says.

"Yeah, I'm not saying that," I say. "Ever."

"We'll see." He's still smirking when we pull into the garage of his house. And that's when it hits me.

We're sleeping in the same house again. "Where did you sleep last night?"

His eyebrows rise. "Why are you asking?"

I roll my eyes. "I'm just curious." I frown. "Please tell me it wasn't on the floor outside my door."

"I'm not that masochistic. I slept in the room next to yours."

"Why?" I glare. "I told you I was locking the door."

He laughs. "If I wanted to get in, do you think that flimsy lock would stop me?"

I think about the way he ripped that doorframe off this morning, without the use of even a scrap of magic. "I guess not."

"The answer is that, wards or not, you can't even run. I'm sleeping close in case something happens. At least I'll hear you."

Like the rays of the sun melting the frost from the grass, my heart warms a bit. He may tease me, and he may be a conceited, overbearing prince, but deep down, I'm beginning to think Grigoriy might be a good guy.

So when I reach my room, instead of ducking through and slamming the door in his face, I release my crutches, lean them against the wall, and turn around, bracing my hands against the busted doorframe. "Thanks for dinner."

"You're welcome." His eyes are so very, very blue—a dark blue that would make the most brilliant sapphire weep with envy.

I bite my lip.

He smiles, and his head starts to lower.

"This doesn't mean anything," I say. "We aren't engaged."

"Mhmm." His head keeps lowering, his eyes moving from mine down to my mouth.

"You're not my fiancé, or even my boyfriend."

His voice is a deep, gentle murmur this time, that makes my stomach do a somersault. "Okay."

"You should stop telling people stuff like that."

"Uh-huh."

"And—"

But this time, before I can nervous-chatter anything else, his mouth covers mine, his hands pressing against the wall on either side of my head. He somehow manages to apply no pressure whatsoever to my fragile and precarious body, while also engaging the nerves in every single square inch of my skin.

I'm tingling.

I'm pulsing.

I'm alive in a way I never have been, not in thirty years of life.

His mouth on mine is *everything* I needed. I had no idea I could *yearn* for something even while experiencing it, but that's what's happening, because I know that any moment, it will end.

Unless. . .

I shake my head.

And he misinterprets that and stops.

I'm my own worst enemy.

He inhales slowly, his eyes lifting from my mouth to my eyes again. "Sleep well, Mirdza. I'll see you in the morning."

And then he's gone.

My heart and my head usually agree, but right now, my heart is ticked off. I wonder which one is right.

For several years after Mārtiņš shattered my leg, I dreamt every night that I was riding on Blanka—my heart horse. The grey mare who changed everything for me in the show jumping ring. It's no surprise that most of the time, we're at the Olympics in my dreams, representing Latvia and sometimes even winning a gold medal.

At first it hurt, dreaming of something I could never have. Eventually I came to look forward to my nightly rides. They were the only way I ever sat on a horse. But over time, that dream came to me less and less often. It's been weeks and weeks since I dreamed of being on horseback.

Until tonight.

Only, when I go to sleep after having dinner with Grigoriy, after being thoroughly kissed in my doorway, and while knowing he's sleeping next to me, I'm not riding Blanka, my Dutch warmblood.

I'm riding Charlemagne, the dark bay with that perfect blaze down his face, and the deep blue eyes that are so rarely seen on horses. He's smooth and fluid, but still a big mover. He's responsive in a way very few horses are, and he's almost unbelievably powerful.

When I rode him the other day, I was tentative, nervous even. I clung to him with my body as much as my legs, hunching forward to grasp chunks of his mane. I worried I'd upset him, or that he'd react badly to my cues based on past experiences, but he had been steady and true. We did nothing exciting. Barely any trotting, no cantering, and certainly no sharp turns or jumps—with the exception of his temper tantrum, where we hopped that downed fence and raced up to the main house.

But in my dream, my leg's hale. My limbs are powerful and strong. I cling to him like I used to, with my upper thighs, keeping my heels down and the weight in the balls of my feet light and even. My hips move with him perfectly, and when we clear a jump, it's nirvana.

I forgot the feeling.

The glorious, freeing rush.

He speeds just a hair as we approach, and I apply pressure. Not a half-halt—just a hair's bit of restraint. And then his head lifts as his haunches bunch, and we're in motion.

Watching a slow-motion jump as a bystander is an awe-inspiring thing. Horses literally launch twice, or very nearly. Their front end lifts away, like a coiled spring, leaping up and outward, but then their back end also compresses and practically explodes, especially on the talented jumpers, propelling them upward and forward in a way that's like poetry in motion.

But from their back, you're an active participant. Your most important job, other than lining them up, is not getting in the way while you sail over the obstacle. You don't want to pull on their mouth, but you can't chuck your hands forward either.

As with everything related to good horsemanship, balance is the key. Working as one with the animal. After years of riding Blanka, we moved very closely together. But sometimes I had to correct her, and sometimes I over-adjusted.

At times, we were at cross purposes.

But not with Charlemagne.

We sail over jump after jump, and then we pivot and come after the next. It feels like I'm riding a deer, to be honest. A powerful, majestic, responsive deer. Until a strange sound—a buzzing, ringing, jarring sound —wakes me.

I nearly bawl when I realize it was all just a dream.

Because now it's over.

The alarm on my new phone is the most grating sound ever. Now that I'm awake, my leg joins the chorus to scream good morning as well. I toss back a few NSAID fever reducers to bring the swelling down and force myself to leave the warmth of the fluffy, cloud-like bed.

As tempting as it is, I can't just lie around all day.

It hits me while I'm in the shower that this might be my last day alive. I mean, I'm not trying to be melodramatic, but the doctor read me an impressively long list of possible complications, and the most significant was that a relatively large number of people, compared to, say, your risk of dying in a plane crash, die from complications caused by the anesthesia.

I've never been someone who has good luck. It's not a stretch to think I might be one of the unlucky few. The thing I'll regret the most if I do die, if I'm lucid enough to regret anything at all, is not riding before my surgery.

I never rode because of the risks. But what if I die from surgery? Then how stupid was my ten-year sacrifice? I wasn't even *on* a horse when the worst happened and my leg was shattered again. Avoiding riding feels silly, now.

But what choice do I have?

I blow-dry my hair, swipe on a bit of makeup, and dress,

surprising myself by struggling into a pair of the new riding pants Kris chose. By the time I start to zip up my boots, the painkillers are finally starting to kick in, and my leg isn't even complaining as much as usual. The throbbing's almost bearable when I strap on my leg brace, grab my crutches, and venture out.

Like before, Grigoriy's waiting for me at the table. But this time, the table's holding only the things we ate yesterday. The things we didn't touch weren't made again, apparently.

"Dasha says that if there's something we just didn't have room to eat, but that we want in the future, to tell her and she'll be sure to make it from time to time."

He says that like I'm going to be a permanent resident. "We already can't eat all this food." I gesture. "It's already wasteful. The last thing we need is to add more."

He shrugs. "Then tell me what you want for tomorrow."

"I'll be fasting tomorrow," I say. "For my surgery." That's a sobering thought. "Actually, I'll need to be up quite early, if it's like the surgeries I've had in the past. Assuming it goes well, if you just sleep in, it might almost be over."

"As if I'd let you go without me." Grigoriy shudders. "It was rare for someone to be operated on a hundred years ago, because it was quite dangerous. I hope their success rates have improved as much as Aleksandr says."

"We've learned a lot about medicine and the human body since then," I say.

"If Alexei were here, none of this would even be necessary," he says.

"How so?" I hate that his words make me hopeful. But if I don't hope, doesn't that mean I've given up? Besides, I watched him power up a few hundred gargantuan windmills yesterday. I'd be pretty obtuse if it didn't occur to me to wish they could just heal my leg with magic.

"His power's water, and that alone can heal illness—

stopping typhus, for instance. If he hadn't been cursed and disappeared, those twenty thousand people wouldn't have died of typhus during the Russian Revolution."

He's an expert on the Russian Revolution, now? "What have you been doing while I was sleeping each night?" I grab one of the Russian cheese pancakes and coat the *syrniki* with raspberry jam and sour cream.

He shrugs. "I'm not sleepy. Maybe it's because I've slept for so long, but I haven't been able to sleep for more than about an hour. Aleks left me a computer and showed me the basics, so I've been studying up. It's like trying to drink from a lake, though. The more I learn, the more I have to look up."

I'm sure that's true. There are so many preconceived notions he has to divest himself of, and there's so much history to learn. I bet studying some of that feels more real to him than our modern-day problems, at least, the records dating back to the world wars and the Russian Revolution. I still struggle to wrap my head around the idea that he knew the Romanovs.

He may be a prince, but they were the Czars of Russia. A hundred years later, their story's still being told. . .and as we talk, I discover that apparently history got a lot of it wrong.

"The most irritating part to Alexei would definitely be all the images and records saying he was a small, weakly child." Grigoriy snorts.

"I take it he wasn't?"

"The worst part about history is that the ones who are around get to reframe it in any way they'd like."

"But those images," I say. "How could—"

He frowns. "You're really asking me? I've seen clips and videos of *dragons* and *unicorns*."

"You're implying that those aren't real, but you're a man who can control the wind, fly, and shift into a horse."

Grigoriy blinks. "I suppose that's true."

My phone chirps, and I realize I've lost track of time entirely. When we aren't arguing, he's not bad to talk to.

It's just Adriana, asking me whether I've got a surgery scheduled, but it reminds me I have no idea what time my pre-op appointment is today. "Do you know what time I need to be at the hospital?"

"Aleks sent me a message on the hand-held computer telling me they'd come to pick you up around two o'clock for the pre-operation testing."

"Phone," I say. "The hand-held computer's a phone." But as I say that, I realize that our phones today do so much more than just call people. They really are more of a hand-held computer than a device for calling others. I finish off my *syrniki* and grab a salami and cucumber sandwich. Grigoriy seems to love them, so there's only one left.

"What did you want to do until then?"

I glance at the window, noting the beautifully sunny weather. "Well."

He straightens up. "You have an idea."

"Actually, I've been wondering how the windmills are going. Are they all working?"

He whips out his phone and taps some things. An app pops up, and he swivels it around so I can see it. "You can tap on the different ID numbers and each one brings up a new wind turbine. This application will show me the various energy levels generated by each one."

"And?"

"Aleksandr didn't exactly set them up optimally, but it's fine. A few of them could operate more efficiently if we move them around, spacing them out a bit, but they're all working at more than double the typical levels." He nods. "Soon, I'll be a very rich man again. Not like Aleks, but comfortable in a way most people will never fathom."

"I'm glad," I say.

"But wait." He takes his phone back. "What did you want to do with your day? Shopping?"

I open my mouth, but he interrupts.

"Aleks said they got your official replacement passport and a phone that's linked to your old account. He's bringing it all at two."

"Oh, that's great."

"We could pick it up earlier, if you need something sooner."

"We don't need identification for my idea," I say. "And it's probably not a very good idea."

"Oh?"

"Actually." My cheeks heat up. "It's probably a terrible idea."

"I like the sound of that." Grigoriy leans back in his chair, just slightly, shifting his legs out and tilting his head. I've never met anyone with better bedroom eyes.

"Not like that." I would kick him, but it would hurt me way more than him. "I was wondering how hard it is for you to shift into a horse."

"Look, I know I tease you about being pushy, but I'm not actually a threat. You don't have to shift me into a horse, I promise."

"No, it's because I'd like to go for a ride," I say, my voice coming out much smaller than I intended.

He freezes. "Is that safe?"

"You tell me," I say.

"Why would you risk it the day before your surgery?" He closes his eyes. "Oh."

"Kris said that with you, it would be safe. You won't spook or buck, right?"

"No, but you can't grip with that leg at all, right?" He sighs. "I'm not sure it's safe, unless you agree to do nothing but walk."

"Let's say I fall," I say.

He's quick to argue. "Let's not say that."

"I'm not planning to," I say. "But even if I do, what more damage could it do? The worry before was that I'd dislodge a screw. Already done. Or maybe that I'd loosen a plate. Also, check."

"Huh. Well."

"Does that mean you'll do it?"

I expect him to argue more, but he doesn't. "It's your life," he finally says.

"So is that. . .a yes?"

He rolls his eyes. "I like to run as a horse. I definitely like to have you sitting on my back." His devilish smirk makes my knees a little weak.

"I doubt you have a saddle, seeing as there aren't any other horses on property that I've seen, and Kris took the one we bought back to her place."

"You don't need it. I won't let you fall," he says. "And you're right. I don't spook. Unlike most horses, I'm not prey."

He's definitely an apex predator.

"If we're doing it," I say, "we'd better get going, or we'll be late for my pick-up for the pre-op testing."

Grigoriy hops to his feet so quickly that it makes me a little jealous. I used to be able to do that. I'm sure he takes it for granted, but as I struggle to stand and grab my crutches so I can walk, I can't help comparing. It sucks being all broken.

By the time we get outside and circle around to the back where hopefully no one will accidentally see us, I'm starting to rethink the whole thing. It would be a terrible shame if I did significant damage somehow. What if the surgery becomes impossible because, after ten years of being smart, I do something stupid? I open my mouth to beg off, but as I lift my eyes, I notice something that squashes every single coherent thought in my head.

Grigoriy's stripping.

He peels his sweater off first. Then his shirt. I had, in only two days, somehow forgotten how glorious his body is. No one in Latvia really tries very hard. But with those muscular shoulders, massive chest, and clearly defined abdominals, it's clear that Grigoriy tries *very* hard.

My mouth goes dry.

When he reaches for the button on his pants, I almost choke. "What are you doing?"

"These clothes are new," he says. "I don't want to ruin them."

I cover my eyes with one hand, balancing on my crutches with pressure from my armpits. "Kris said Aleks lied to her—that you can shift with clothing on."

Grigoriy's laugh is low and deep, and it's slowly moving toward me. "It wasn't a lie when he said it. You can only shift with clothing intact once you've fully mastered your magic, and right now, I'm not the one shifting my form, remember?" He's right next to me now. I can practically feel the heat rolling off his naked body. "That's why our people grew accustomed to it—as we learned to master our powers, we couldn't shift with clothing. Once I regain my magic, I'll be able to do that, but unless you know how to change me without shredding my clothing, we're stuck doing it *this* way."

Both my hands are trembling now, the one wrapped around the handle of the crutch and the one covering my eyes. I hear the sound of his pants falling to the ground, and my heart hammers even harder inside my chest.

"Did you change your mind?" His voice is soft and close against my ear, and a thrill runs up my entire body, like a shiver and a sugar rush all hitting at once.

But even better.

Is this what desire feels like?

With Danils, my initial delight quickly gave way to pressure and fear. I usually felt trapped. With every other guy I've dated, I've felt chased, and cornered, and, frankly, unsafe. Why don't I feel that right now? My leg's not sound, and a magical naked man's standing at my side. I should be terrified.

Instead, my hand itches to drop so I can touch his bare chest.

And not only because I want to ride his secret horse.

That sounds. . .not right.

Because I want to ride him?

That might be worse.

"Okay, well." I lift just my bottom two fingers and peek out, being sure to keep my eyes aimed upward. "What exactly do I do now?"

"First, you have to touch me," he murmurs.

"Right." When I uncover my eyes entirely, I can't seem to help letting them roam over him one more time. He's magical. He's well-connected. He's about to be rich. And he's powerfully strong and perfectly built. It seems a little unfair, frankly.

Although, I suppose he did just spend a hundred years being tortured in some kind of bizarro time-out.

Maybe life is fair.

I slowly move my hand toward him, my fingers splayed, my breathing a little too short and shallow, and finally, I make contact. His chest is surprisingly warm, given the brisk weather and the length of time I made him wait.

His eyes are warm and calm as they hold my gaze.

Before I have a chance to flog my brain into coming up with words, he covers my hand with his. It takes me by surprise, for some reason. It's a gentle gesture, and he's not a gentle man. Maybe that's why—the incongruity between his behavior and attitude toward me and the way he behaves out in the world.

Finally, I mumble, "I want you to change into a horse."

I'm not actually super confident that it'll work. I figure I'll probably have to try a few times, or focus really hard, or learn how to do something special, but it *does* work, a little too quickly. I stumble backward and land hard on my butt, my crutches clattering on either side of me, right in front of the massive stallion, who's now standing on the hard-packed ground behind Grigoriy's mansion.

His head immediately drops to my face, his big, soft, baby fine fur-covered lips rubbing against my cheek, my chin, and then my shoulder.

"I'm okay," I say. "No undue pain in my leg." Just my butt. And my pride. It's more than used to being abused.

Charlemagne pushes my crutches closer with his nose as I struggle back up to my feet. "I don't need them," I remind him. "I'm about to climb onto you."

I'd have told you yesterday that horses couldn't flirt, but I learn today that it's not exactly true. He literally tosses his head and expels air from his horsey nose, and I know just what he's saying.

It makes me roll my eyes.

He's a powerful mage with the sense of humor of an eighteen-year-old boy.

Getting on proves easier than I expected, thanks to a well-placed boulder and a horse who *wants* me to climb on his back. He stands steady and still, even when I grab a fistful of his mane to compensate for not being able to really use my bad leg to vault onto his back.

Without a bridle or a saddle, this is still going to be a strange ride.

"Hey, before you were frozen, or whatever, did anyone ever ride you?"

His whole head curves around to look back at me, and he shakes his head back and forth slowly.

"So you wouldn't even know what I was trying to tell you if I had the bridle on?"

He snorts.

I suppose it's not hard for them to figure it out. They move away from pressure. But still, it's an interesting situation to have a horse who understands what I'm saying, but has never been trained to be ridden. I'm definitely more of a passenger than I've ever been in my life.

It occurs to me then that riding Grigoriy—Charlemagne? What do I call him? Does Kris say Obsidian Devil when he's in his horse form? Or Aleks? It's confusing. But riding him is an act of trust.

Other than Kris, I trust no one.

Certainly no men.

And yet, I've just climbed up on the back of a horseman, and I'm expecting him to take care of me. I don't really trust the man-form. Why should I trust the horse one?

Maybe it's because, as a horse, what he wants from me is so much more pure than what men usually want from women. He wants to give me a ride, and he's not trying to use me. I wish I could be sure that was true for the human Grigoriy.

"Okay, let's take this really slow," I say.

For some reason, in my head, I can't help seeing the human Grigoriy's face if I had said that to him earlier. I shake my head to clear it. I need to stop thinking about him and enjoy this while I can. He walks out smoothly, carefully threading his way around to the front of the massive house.

When we encounter the same man I saw on the first day, the butler startles. "Oh."

"I'm so sorry," I say. "I should have warned you that I wanted to come out for a ride."

"But." He frowns. "Where did that horse come from?" He arches one eyebrow. "Where has he been?"

"I think he's been wandering around the property eating," I say. "He's a little skittish of most people."

The man somehow manages to frown even more. "But why didn't Master Grigoriy inform me of the horse's presence? Master Aleks had the stables restored, and there's a groom and a trainer out there with no horses to tend to."

A groom? A stable? How vast is this property? I suppose Grigoriy did mention it was quite large. I can't even see the windmills from the main house, thanks to the rolling hills. "I'm sure he'll let you know soon."

"No one has even seen him," the man presses. "And there haven't been any reports of manure, either. I'm sure someone would have told me."

Oh, geez. "Uh, well, he is a dark horse." I grimace. "Maybe he kind of *blended in?*"

"Or perhaps he hopped that same fence and left the property for the past few days." He shakes his head. "You should be very careful. Master Grigoriy told the entire staff to give you anything you want at all times, which means that he values you. He'd be distraught if you were to hurt yourself because you were on such a terrible beast."

Charlemagne paws the ground.

I can't help laughing. The poor guy's trying so hard while simultaneously insulting his own boss. "I'll keep that in mind," I say. "And actually, a few days in a stall might be good for this guy." I pat his neck.

Charlemagne tosses his head and starts to move again, practically running the butler guy over.

"I should probably know your name, right?" I turn around, craning my neck to see his face.

"It's Sergey," he says.

Right. I did hear that the first day, I think. The butler's name means servant. It's still kind of funny, even now. I mean, it's a common Russian name, but still. It's pretty on-the-nose. "Thanks for your concern, Sergey. I'm actually really happy to know there's a barn and hopefully some tack I can use in the future."

Charlemagne takes off at a trot. I'm a little hard pressed to hold on at first, but then I acclimate, my hips moving naturally with his rhythm, which is quite comfortable for a trot. Once we reach the front gate, which is helpfully open, the ground flattens out, and he starts to canter.

It's not a race. It's not choppy or unsteady. It's smooth and even nicer than the trot. With the wind on my face blowing my hair behind me, I realize that I haven't been this happy in a very, very long time. I'm not sure how long we canter like that before he pulls up short. He glances up at the sun—starting to rise higher in the sky—and tosses his head.

He thinks we should head back.

I can't argue with him, so I nod and pat his neck. "Okay."

He turns around carefully and slowly moves back into a trot, glancing back to make sure I'm fine. I'm more than fine when he finally starts to canter again, and I try to savor every last moment. The muscles in my legs that are hardly ever used are complaining, of course, and even with a steady and smooth canter, each time we hit the ground, my injured leg jars and pain shoots upward, but it's worth it.

I'd nearly forgotten how much being astride fills me with utter delight. But too soon, we're back, dropping to a trot to enter at the gate and head up the drive.

I worry that we'll see Sergey again, or that a groom will show up and try to take him, but it doesn't happen. We circle around back and find his pile of discarded clothing behind the hedge where he tossed it.

"I suppose I should change you back," I say.

He whinnies.

"But this was exactly what I needed," I say.

He whuffles.

Once I'm back on my feet and I've secured my crutches under my now-sore legs, I hop-slide my way over to the hedge, and then I point. "You go here, and then I can shift you and—"

But he bumps me, and when I turn, his big horsey face is waiting to nuzzle my cheek with his face. Without thinking, I wrap my arms around his neck and hug him, pressing my face against his round-cheeked, stallion face. Unlike most horses, he doesn't seem to mind.

The only horse I own—of the six—who lets me hug her is my heart-horse, Blanka. She's so accustomed to me hugging her, loving on her, and generally needing to be *around* her that she will stand calmly and let me just *be*. That kind of connection is special. No matter how bad my day has been, a little time with her almost always resets it. Thanks to her, I can find my balance again.

I know that Charlemagne is really Grigoriy. I *know*, but even knowing that, it feels different when he's a big, powerful, shiny bay stallion. He's as calm as Blanka, and he seems to understand that I need to feel this connection with a horse. I need to feel the peace and comfort that they bring that can't really be explained.

Maybe because he *is* a horse sometimes, he gets it. I don't know.

But when I release him, I'm literally crying tears of joy. For the first time since that incident on the train—no, since the horse rammed me into that wall—or maybe before all that, maybe for the first time in years, I feel ready to move forward.

I have a surgery planned. I rode again, and not in a desperate attempt to stay alive. I rode for fun.

When I reach my hand out and splay it against Charlemagne's gorgeous, dappled back, I'm actually excited for what the future holds. It's bizarre. My life has taken a very strange turn, but I'm hopeful that good things are ahead.

Is that completely crazy of me?

I'm imagining a future with this crazy horse-mage-prince. It's nuts, but something about him, in spite of his power and domineering attitude, makes me feel. . .safe.

"I wish you would turn back into a man."

The change feels like it happens even faster this time. He shrinks down from a massive beast into a human man in the blink of an eye. He's still massive and muscled, but he's much closer to my size. He's staring at me in much the same way he did after that first transformation, his eyes boring into me without any sign of turning away.

His head drops near mine again, like he did when he was a horse, but instead of comfort, the proximity sends electric jolts through my body, radiating outward from my chest like pulses of light. His lips are full and perfectly curved, and I realize he's about to kiss me.

And the biggest shock of all is that. . .I want him to.

Until I remember that he's utterly and completely naked, and I shriek like a little girl seeing her first spider.

He claps one hand over my mouth. "Hush. Do you want people to—"

But it's too late.

Sergey, followed closely by what appears to be a gardener and maybe a guard or something, comes sprinting around from the front of the house and they pull up short, their mouths gaping, their eyes wide.

Luckily they're all men, but I still *feel* my blush start in my toes and flood my entire body. I'm sure I'm absolutely beet red.

"Master," Sergey says, finally realizing who the naked man is. "You're—" He swallows and stammers. "N-n-naked."

"I am." Grigoriy decides to lean into it, I guess, spreading his shoulders and setting his feet. Unfortunately the motion has me looking down, and I nearly jump out of my skin, trying to avert my eyes and shift away from him.

"Aren't you cold, sir?" Sergey appears to be regaining his composure.

The guard person shrugs out of his jacket and starts walking toward us.

"No, it's alright. I have clothing here." Grigoriy points to the hedge. "I was practicing the ancient Chinese art of Hengshu."

The three men all frown in a nearly identical way.

"It's almost too late in the season to do it," Grigoriy continues, "but I forgot my timer. And then I saw Miss Strelkova, whose horse had just galloped away. I thought she might help me by timing me. You have to spend at least ten minutes in the winter elements in order to steel your body against the changing whims of the earth that can't be controlled."

What in the galoshes is he saying?

"How much time do you have left?" Sergey asks.

"Six minutes to go," I say. "And now that you're here, you can take over."

I can't help a little laugh as I hobble away on my crutches, leaving Grigoriy to freeze to death, naked, in front of his new group of employees. I feel a tiny bit guilty? But he's the idiot who made up something as stupid as the ancient art of Hengshu.

By the time he comes back in, he looks pretty upset, so I duck into my room to hide.

"Hey." He bangs on the door.

"I'm just calling my mom and sister real quick."

He grumbles a bit, but that works. Which means I really ought to go ahead and call them. I dial my mom first, but she can't talk. Apparently she's busy baking rye bread—Mārtinš is very particular about it and won't eat store-bought. Jerk. "Well, it was good to hear your voice, Mom. Be safe while I'm in Russia."

"I don't like that you're getting that surgery there," she says.

For a split second, my heart swells. She's worried about me. "I'll be fine, Mom. I swear."

"I'll be praying for you," she says. "Like always."

My mom may not stand up for me, and she may not choose me over her husband, but at least she does love me. And prayers from your mother are better than nothing, which is exactly what some people have. "Thanks."

It looks like my call to Adriana's going to roll over to voicemail, but at the last second, she picks up. "Hello?"

"Hey, it's me. I just wanted to say that I'm going in for surgery in the morning. I have pre-ops in a bit."

"Oh." She's silent for a long moment. "Why aren't you doing it here?"

"Kris is here. She's my support system," I say.

"You have one here." She let me move in with her when Kris sold her barn, but I'm not sure I'd call couch-surfing at her place a 'support system.'

I don't bother arguing. "I saw a surgeon here, and he's an American one. I think he's pretty good. He says he thinks he can fix it. The guys in Latvia just told me they were hoping I might not need a wheelchair."

"Fix it?" Adriana asks. "What does that mean?"

"I'm not sure yet," I say. "It'll obviously still need screws and plates, but he thinks in time, I might be sound enough to really use my leg, without much pain." It would be a miracle if it was true.

"Could you ride again?"

It almost pains me to say the words. "That's the hope."

Adriana swears, and even though her dirty mouth gets us both in trouble a lot, it kind of warms my heart. She's more than someone who roots for me. She loves me with her whole little warrior's heart.

"Thanks."

"And hey, listen. I know you only owed me five hundred. I just wanted to say thanks."

"Huh?"

"It was so nice of you to have Kristiana send two thousand instead."

"To have. . ."

"I paid rent first, I swear I did, but I have a race tomorrow, and I can feel it. This is the one."

Oh, no. "Kris sent you two thousand euros?" I groan. "I didn't tell her to do that. Did you really think you should get four times what you loaned me?"

"When I win tomorrow, I'll pay her back and I'll give you the five hundred, okay?"

For the love. "Please be smart," I say. And then I hang up, because with Adriana, it's a waste of energy to argue. She always does what she wants, no matter what anyone else says.

The pre-op appointments are pretty boring, and they take forever. We pick up Italian food on the way home, and since I have to wake up at four-thirty the next morning to get ready and be at the hospital by five, I head for bed almost as soon as we get home.

Before I can duck into my room, Grigoriy catches my wrist. "I just wanted to say that it's going to be fine." His voice is low, his expression intent. "Don't get scared now that tomorrow's almost here."

"It's hard not to worry, but I appreciate your vote of confidence."

"Why do you think I'm insisting that I go?"

I shrug. "You're a good friend?"

He laughs, low and long. "Sure. A friend you walk around the grounds naked with."

Hey. "What did you tell those guys?" It did feel like he wasn't out there for quite six minutes.

He shrugs. "I might have told them Hengshu was made up, and that you got nervous when they all showed up."

I slap his shoulder.

Grigoriy just smiles. "I'm insisting on going tomorrow, and we're paying extra to be in the gallery. I told you already, but my healing power's able to repair anything that has just happened. So if he does something horrible or screws something up, I'll bust through the window if I need to, and once I'm touching you, I'll have access to my magic. I can heal you from any blunders he makes."

Is that really true? I must believe it, because when I go to sleep, I'm actually able to stay that way all night without tossing and turning for once.

❧ 12 ❧

A lot of the peace I found the day before is gone when I'm sitting in a hospital gown, about to be cut open. I mean, I know it's just my leg, but I kind of need it to work.

Also, I really don't want to die.

I don't spend a lot of time thinking about that, usually, but when you have to sign a release saying you know about 100 different complicating factors, all of which might kill you, it sort of starts to feel likely.

"It's going to be fine," Kris says.

"If Grigoriy tries to leap through the door and into the operating room," I say.

"Oh, don't worry, I won't let him interfere."

I shake my head. "Actually, I was going to say to help him."

Kris blinks. "What has been going on between you two?"

I shove her arm. "As if you didn't intentionally leave me there with the hope that we'd flirt."

"Flirt?" Kris sighs. "Aleks had a lot more faith in him than he should have, I guess."

"What?"

Kristiana shrugs. "He said that all the women were just obsessed with him, and that he was quite the ladies' man. Maybe it didn't really translate to this century."

A ladies' man, huh? "Did he have a lot of girlfriends?" For some reason, that really concerns me.

"Well, they didn't really do girlfriends back then. It was more like, women of the night or future wives."

"Women of the night? Really?" I roll my eyes, but I can't help asking, "Did he have either?"

"I'm not going to claim to be an expert, but Aleks said his buddy never had any interest in anyone."

That, at least, jives with what Grigoriy told me himself.

"It bodes well that you're asking, though." Kris is looking at me with a knowing glance that I don't want to deal with.

Luckily, the surgeon comes in and saves me. "It's a good morning to change someone's life," he says.

"Are there bad mornings to improve lives?" Kris arches one eyebrow.

"There are two men out there who both look really nervous," Dr. Hubert says. He looks just as bald, just as short, and just as unattractive as he did the last time I saw him, and I'm okay with that. I just want him to be a magician with bone repair. "They're insisting they be allowed to watch from the observation deck."

"It's fine," I say. "I know they're desperate for it."

"They need to know that they will absolutely not be allowed through the OR doors under any circumstance," Dr. Hubert says.

"They know," Kristiana says.

"Are you ready to begin?" Dr. Hubert looks suddenly serious.

I nod.

"Let's go." He introduces me to the anesthesiologist, and moments later, my world goes dark.

Of course, an instant after that, someone's snapping in front of my face. Recovery from surgery's pretty awful, every time. You're not in control of your body, you're disoriented, and for some reason, I'm always filled to the brim with panic and terror.

Probably because it's almost exactly how I felt on the day my leg was shattered originally. It's not a comfortable feeling. But eventually, I manage to make it through that horrible haze, and I start to surface from the fog and misery of post-surgical recovery.

"Hey there." Kristiana perches on the chair by my bed. "I'm so happy to see you looking so alert."

"Thanks." My voice is scratchy and sore. Anesthesia's a modern miracle, but even it has its costs. "I'm happy to be awake. Did he tell you how it went?" I struggle to sit up, hoping to see what my leg looks like.

Kris's smile doesn't really move. That makes me pretty nervous.

"Just tell me."

"There was more damage than he thought," she says. "You'll be fine to walk, and he doesn't think there will be any ongoing risk of infection, but. . ."

"But I won't be able to ride again?"

She swallows.

"Why not?"

"It's just not as stable as he'd hoped it would be," she says. "The configuration he wanted to use didn't work."

I should be fine.

This is what I was *hoping for* last week. But the opposite of hope isn't resignation.

It's despair.

I wish he hadn't even mentioned it was a possibility if he wasn't *sure*. "What's the good of all those tests if they can still be surprised when they go in to operate? You should get a partial refund."

Her smile's pained. "I'm sorry, M."

Me too. I'm sorry, too. But I refuse to dwell on it. My dearest friend in the world got me the surgery I need to keep living my life. To teach lessons. To care for my horses, even if I can't ride them. She gave me my life back, and I'm not going to repay her generosity by moping around and wallowing in ingratitude. "He thinks it'll recover well enough for me to walk, and that's all I had for the last decade. It's fine. It's better than fine. This is still good news."

"But—"

"Mirdza!" Aleks's voice booms, from the second he walks through the door to the recovery room, his friend on his heels. "So good to see you awake."

"They tried to tell us only one person was allowed in here at once," Grigoriy says. He shakes his head like he pities their stupidity.

"How did you get in?" I ask.

He leans down closer, having reached my bedside, and whispers, "I told them I'm your doctor back in Latvia, and that I need my assistant here too. They believed it, because I was allowed to stand behind the window and watch the whole repair."

That makes me chuckle, but that, in turn, hurts my throat and my leg.

"Let's do it," Grigoriy says. "Now."

"Right here?" Aleks glances around.

There's another woman, a much older lady, in the corner of the recovery room, with a younger man hunched in the chair next to her. Probably her son. Maybe even her grandson, judging by his age. And only one bed over from us, there's a man in his forties who looks asleep. A nurse comes by periodically and glances at his machine.

"No one will see anything," Kris says. "It just takes a moment."

The next thing I know, Aleksandr's reaching for my arm.

"Wait." Grigoriy grabs his forearm. "You're sure this won't hurt her in any way."

Aleks laughs. "I can't decide whether I like this new Grigoriy or whether I'm disgusted. Where's Ilmen's Gale? What happened to the Zephyr of Zhabitsy?"

Grigoriy glares.

"I've done this hundreds of times, and several this century, so calm down and let go of my hand."

He finally releases Aleks's hand and leans back, kicking up one heel to press it flat against the wall. He's trying to act tough, but he looks worried.

That makes me stupidly happy.

It's been a long time since anyone other than Kris, my mom, or Adriana cared what happened to me. I love them all, but I'm not even a top priority for any of them. It feels nice to have someone put me first.

Aleks lowers his hand slowly until he can wrap it around my forearm, and then he inhales and exhales slowly. "This is going to be fast, and it's going to be uncomfortable. I wish I could have done it while you were still unconscious, but they'd never have let me in."

Uncomfortable isn't promising.

"Kris, you make sure to distract anyone who comes this way, and Grigoriy, your job is to physically stop them if it comes to that."

Before I have a chance to object, Aleks tightens his hand, and it starts. A thousand little people with hammers are banging on the bones inside my leg. And one person with a nail gun is giving them some places to focus on. I open my mouth to cry out, but then I think of the sleeping man, the nurses coming and going, and the woman with her son a few beds down.

I bite down on my sob, and just a few moments later, the pain just. . .disappears.

Aleks looks like he might pass out at any moment. The blood has drained from his face. Even his lips look pale, and when he stands, he literally sways like a tree in a tempest. "Whoa, there," I say. "Maybe sit a little longer."

"I'm going to take him to the car," Kris says. "I have some juice and snacks out there, and no one has to watch him looking like this while he recovers."

"Recovers?" I struggle to a halfway seated position. "What's wrong?"

"It's taxing to use your powers in that way," Grigoriy says. "It depletes us."

"No one told me—"

Kris pats my hand. "It's fine. He wanted to help. And the good news is, the second they release you, you should be fine to walk and do whatever they said you'll be doing when the recovery is done. That's our real gift." This time, her smile's genuine. "Not the surgery, but the lack of a grueling and miserable healing and rehab period."

It's a pretty darn good gift. A moment later, they're gone and Grigoriy takes the chair next to me. His hand slides slowly over mine.

"I think my leg's about as good as it's going to get," I say. "I probably don't need comforting." But I don't pull my hand away. His huge fingers wrapped around mine feel too nice.

"You know, I came to watch because I couldn't bear the thought of something happening to you," he says. "I wasn't sure whether I would be able to save you—I've never had something like this happen, with a surgery and possible complications—but I hoped. But that doubt left me much more distressed than I expected." His nostrils flare.

"I'm fine," I say. "I think the surgery was a success. I mean, maybe it's not better than before, but at least my leg will be stable. And thanks to your friend Aleks, I won't even have to suffer through the weeks of healing and misery. I can start getting back into shape today."

"Maybe tomorrow," Grigoriy says. "Even accelerated, that kind of healing takes its toll. You and Aleksandr will both be very tired."

As if his words caused it, a wave of exhaustion rolls over me. I lean back against the pillows of the recovery room bed. "I do feel like I could take a nap." I realize that if I do, he'll be stuck here, and Aleksandr and Kristiana will, too. They all drove up here with me, and they've already been waiting for quite some time, I imagine. "Or I could get to the car now, if you help me, and then I can take a nap once I'm home."

"There's no rush. Rest here for a bit, and when you wake up, we'll get you home." His hand's still on mine, and something about his presence lets me rest better than I imagined.

I think about protesting—I'm sure they're all eager to leave—but I am so tired. The old woman's just getting to her feet, with the young man helping her gather up her things, when I drift off.

Angry voices and the tightening of Grigoriy's hand on mine wakes me. I'm bleary again, almost like I'm just waking up from the surgery. But I know where I am—still in the hospital recovery room—and I can feel and hear Grigoriy beside me.

"I already told you," he says. "I'm not leaving. Not without Mirdza."

I force myself to sit up. "What's going on?" I look around the room, noticing that the other patients have gone. The old woman left, as did the middle-aged man. No new surgeries ended either, apparently.

But then, who's Grigoriy talking to? I crane my neck to look around him. He's shifted forward so his body's mostly blocking me from whoever entered, but I can make out several men, and I can clearly see the one in the very front.

His beard is closely trimmed, with just a bit of grey. His eyes are flinty, and his hard gaze is focused on me. "I'm not going to ask again," Yevginiy says. "Leave this room, or you'll become collateral damage."

Grigoriy snorts.

"You may think you're an impressive fighter." Yevginiy smiles. "You may even be able to take me, though I doubt it. I didn't get here by losing to tough guys. But even if you could defeat me, did you forget that I came with friends?" He tosses his head and his men step closer.

There are seven of them.

All of them wearing black.

They all look just as scary as they did on the train. Except for one of them, who has his arm in a sling. It must be Durak, whose clavicle I snapped.

My heart hammers in my chest, but I feel strangely calm. "Just go," I whisper. "This isn't your fight."

Grigoriy laughs then. "Actually, this is exactly my fight. It's a fight I thought I'd have to work much harder to find." He stands up, his hand still in mine. "And I should thank you, Yevginiy, did you say your name is?" He tilts his head. "You saved me the trouble of finding you. They really do deliver everything in this day and age."

"Deliver?" Yevginiy laughs. "You were coming to look for me? Why?"

"I detest the smell of rotting garbage," Grigoriy says. "Actually, I hate everything about refuse. I always make sure to burn my trash, so it can't cause problems for the people I care about."

Yevginiy's lip curls. "Garbage? Are you saying—"

"Are you really confused?" Grigoriy asks. "You abuse

women, and when my woman stands up for the poor lady you've claimed, you try to kill her."

Yevginiy shakes his head. "Stands up for?" He sneers. "She broke Durak's clavicle, and we did kill her. I have no idea how she survived that fall from the train after being stabbed twice, let alone in the middle of nowhere. At night. In the cold."

"Yes," Grigoriy says. "Keep telling me the details of exactly what you did. That helps me feel better and better about my plan for today." He looks behind him. "And how many of these men were with you that day?"

"What?" Yevginiy frowns.

"How many of your seven friends were on that train?"

"All of them," he says.

"Excellent," Grigoriy says. "And my last question is, how did you come to be here, in the hospital? There are security guards outside that should have at least tried to stop you."

Yevginiy laughs. "You don't even know who I am? I own Saint Petersburg. When my men went back to collect that filthy cripple's body, it wasn't there. That's when we started to look for her—we had her bags, you know, with her identification in them. That doc put in a request for medical hardware, and her name popped up." He smiles.

"But how did you get here?" Grigoriy asks again, doggedly.

"That was the easiest part. Your doctor's greedy. A little bit of money and he brought us here himself."

"Thanks," Grigoriy says.

"For what?" Yevginiy starts toward us, pulling a knife from somewhere. "Do you make it a habit of killing people who are about to kill you?"

Grigoriy frowns. "That would be a difficult habit, unless I was a vampire or zombie. Otherwise, how could it happen more than once?"

I can't help snorting. Yevginiy is a real idiot.

Grigoriy pulls a knife from a sheath on his hip I hadn't even noticed. I can't help staring at the symbol on the hilt. Crossed axes.

"Wait, that's—"

"This is the knife that was inside my woman when I found her," he says. "Normally, I'd take my time carving all of you up." Grigoriy shakes his head. "But she's with me, and I don't want to scare her too badly."

Grigoriy throws his hand to the side, and the doors leaving the recovery room slam closed.

"What's happening?" Durak asks.

The other men murmur, glancing back at the doorway.

A howling sound fills the room, and I realize why Grigoriy hasn't left my side. He needs to use his powers, and he needs to be touching me to do it. The man who powered up two hundred industrial windmills could easily crush all these men.

But I don't want him to kill them. That's as bad as what they want to do to me.

"Just get us out of here," I say. "Can you do that?"

The look he turns on me is full of regret. "They're terrible people," he says. "Any man who will kill an innocent woman or who stands by while someone else does deserves to die."

I try to yank my hand away, but he tightens his grip.

"Please don't," I beg, my heart racing, my pulse pounding so loudly in my ears that I can't hear. The adrenaline, the panic, the misery—it's just like the day Mārtiņš was so angry. The day my life changed forever.

"I don't care about carnival tricks," Yevginiy says, gaining confidence now that I've distracted Grigoriy. "But they won't be enough."

"How about this one?" Grigoriy asks. "If you'll agree to fight me yourself, after I kill you, they can all walk out of here."

To fight him, Grigoriy would have to release me. He'd be without any magic at all. Then he'd be the one at risk. "No," I say in Latvian. "Just make them leave. Blow them out the door or something."

"What nonsense is she saying?" Yevginiy asks.

"I won't offer again," Grigoriy says. "Fight me, and your men will live. I'll lay all the blame on you."

"I'm not so stupid as to give up my advantage," Yevginiy says. "You may be able to defeat me, but you can't kill all of us."

"Fine," Grigoriy says. He shifts so that I can see his face. "I tried." His free hand twists again, and the dagger with the crossed axes flies through the air.

Time slows down.

The men are confused when the dagger cuts a path through them. Blood blooms along the arc, springing up on a shoulder, a thigh, a cheek, and a hamstring. The men shout and swear and clench fists and collapse on the ground.

There's blood spray on the wall. On the ceiling. On the other men.

"What are you doing?" Yevginiy asks. "How did you do that?"

But Grigoriy doesn't stop.

The dagger keeps flying back and forth. Durak, the idiot with the arm in a sling, jumps in front of it, and it buries itself in his chest up to the hilt.

"Ah, see?" Grigoriy says. "It's gone home. How nice." Then he whips his hand backward and it flings back out, only to arc around again, painting more of the wall and floor bright red.

The men are panicking now, with several of them collapsed on the floor, unmoving, and one breaks for the back door.

"It won't open," Grigoriy says. "I warned all of you." But

the dagger is now focused on the one who ran away. "How does it feel to be a horrible person and *also* a coward?"

The dagger slices the backs of his legs, and he falls to his knees.

Grigoriy twists his wrist with two fingers and it slices his throat. He topples forward, a pool of red widening around him.

"You're controlling it," Yevginiy says. But then his eyes widen. "Why can't I move?"

"A horrible person and also quite slow," Grigoriy says. "It's not quite the ending that you all deserve, but I'm having to work within my limitations, you see." He squeezes my hand as if he's making a hilarious joke.

I'm shaking, now.

As if he's just noticing that, too distracted by massacring so many men as slowly as possible, Grigoriy glances at me. Then he turns and says, "Time to wrap this up." The dagger slices through the last two men's throats, blood spewing out all over the front of their bodies, and they collapse forward at almost the same time.

Barn cats can be quite feral. They play with the mice and rats they find, often ripping their extremities off one by one. Only once the poor things can no longer move do they wander off, happy to let them bleed out in any way they see fit.

Grigoriy looks just like that.

As if the murder of seven people while their boss watches is all in a good day's fun.

"You're disgusting," I say. "A sociopath."

This time, he doesn't turn toward me. I only know he heard it because I see him flinch.

I can't even handle looking at the recovery room floor. What began as a shiny, pristine surface is now splattered and coated with intermittent pools of spreading blood.

Until now, I never realized that blood from different

people would be different colors. I hate that I know that now.

"I think the last question I have is whether you want to fight me, man to man." Grigoriy's smile's predatory. "Or whether I should carve you up like your friends." The dagger's dripping red drops onto the floor in front of Yevginiy, where it's hanging in the air.

I pull as hard as I can to free my hand.

Grigoriy lifts his free hand and the dagger flies back to it. And then he releases me.

Yevginiy stares blankly at his men, unblinking, as if he's in shock.

"Filth," Grigoriy shouts. "Will you fight me? Or will you die like a cow on a block?"

I scramble backward in the bed until I'm crouched against the wall.

"Fine. I'll just execute you." Grigoriy walks toward him slowly, as if the fact that he no longer has his powers doesn't matter.

"Wait." Yevginiy turns slowly. "Who are you?"

"Your judge," Grigoriy says, "your jury, and your executioner." He smiles again, and there's no doubt on his face. Not a hint of fear. Just rage. Consuming, all-encompassing rage.

A dark chill races up my spine.

Yevginiy's scary, but at least he's human—containable. I realize in this moment how horrifying Grigoriy the mage truly is. What was I thinking, feeling safe at his side?

The one truth with powerful men is that danger always surrounds them. He could have simply protected me. Scared them away, called the police, or warned them off. He could even have simply left me. I would have been alright with that. At least nothing would have blown back on Aleks, Adriana, or Kris.

But he couldn't help himself.

He had to kill them all, and now he's playing with this last one, and dressing it all up as though he's got a right to do it because of what they did to me.

The reality is that he's not a judge. He's definitely not a jury. But he's about to execute him anyway.

"Please don't," I beg.

I can't help thinking of how the poor woman on the train begged Yevginiy. Unintentionally, I now sound just like her.

"Can't you let him go?" I ask.

"Listen to your woman," Yevginiy says. "You don't want to kill me. I have more men back home. Lots more. They'll come after you if you kill me, but if you don't, I'll hire you instead. You can have untold riches if you come work for me—no." He throws his hands up, palms out. "Work *with* me. We can be partners. You can share everything I have."

"You think I want anything that's related to you?" Grigoriy laughs. "You're dying today. You can decide whether you die trying to survive, chanting a rosary, or staring at me like a coward."

Yevginiy hurls a small dagger at Grigoriy then, so fast I nearly miss it, and I remember that Grigoriy now has no magic. Luckily, he moves fast all on his own. He shifts and the knife flies past him, sinking into the wall a few feet away from me. He lunges for Yevginiy next, and they're brawling on the floor, punching, shoving, kneeing, groaning, rolling, and smashing.

It seems like the one being broken each time is Yevginiy. Or at least, he's the only one shouting.

I close my eyes then, but I can't block out the sounds.

Bones breaking.

More cries.

Soft swearing by Grigoriy.

And then a soft sound of triumph. When I open my eyes, Grigoriy's holding Yevginiy in a headlock. "They teach you these moves as self defense," he says calmly. "But Mirdza is distressed, and I'm bored. So." With a quick movement of his hands, he snaps Yevginiy's neck.

Right in front of me.

The man who terrorized that poor woman and her child and ordered others to kill me and then tracked me here and came again slumps to the ground, his eyes glazed, his head at an unnatural angle.

"You'll never have nightmares of him hurting you again," Grigoriy says. "You saw for yourself that he's dead."

My hands are shaking.

My stomach's churning.

My head's pounding.

But I force myself to my feet and start for the door.

"Wait," Grigoriy says. "We can't leave yet."

"I'm going," I say.

"But that doctor welcomed them in," he says. "He can't be allowed to—"

I stop, fighting briefly against my entire body, which is screaming for me to run. "If you harm the doctor, I'll never see or talk to you ever again."

Grigoriy sets his jaw. His brow furrows. "He knew they would kill you," he says. "He allowed those men into the hospital, and he's a physician. I saw the paperwork on his wall—he took an oath to do no harm."

"More violence won't fix anything," I say. "All it does it hurt people."

Grigoriy jerks his thumb at the dead bodies in congealing pools of blood. "Violence stopped them. They won't throw any more women out of trains."

"But who will take their place?" I ask. "Someone else will simply step into the power vacuum that killing Yevginiy made," I say. "You fixed nothing. You just made room for a new leader to terrorize the women in Saint Petersburg."

Grigoriy shakes his head. "That's not true. These men

can't hurt people anymore. Eliminating them was the right thing to do."

"What's going on?" Dr. Hubert jogs through the operating room door and pulls up short, his eyes widening in horror. "What happened here?"

"You caused this," Grigoriy says. "You accepted payment from the mafia to come after the woman you had just taken payment to repair."

"Don't," I beg. Again. "Please, don't."

"I had no choice," Dr. Hubert says. "They said if I didn't help them, they'd kill me."

"You always have a choice." Grigoriy smiles.

"So do you," I say. "Let him go."

As if I'm watching a movie in which I have no role, they act like they can't hear me.

"They told me she had run away from home," Dr. Hubert says. "They said they were just looking for her."

"You didn't believe that," Grigoriy says. "You knew they wanted to hurt her, and you took their money anyway."

Dr. Hubert doesn't argue. He gulps.

Grigoriy walks toward him, leaning over in a fluid movement to yank the knife Yevginiy threw at him out of the drywall.

Dr. Hubert backs up quickly, scrabbling backward as fast as he can without taking his eyes off of Grigoriy.

But it's futile. Grigoriy speeds up to a jog, and I watch in horror as he slits Dr. Hubert's throat with his own hands. I can't decide what's worse to watch. A phantom dagger, massacring seven men slowly, or a man, a man I cared for, using his own hands to slit one person's throat.

"You were running from something when you came here," Grigoriy says, "but when bad people leave, they don't change. You made poor decisions here, too, and now they've caught up to you."

There's no way Dr. Hubert can understand a word of what Grigoriy's saying.

But I can.

I bolt through the front door as quickly as I can move on my recently healed leg. It's not strong. I'm not agile or balanced, but I make it to the car, where Aleks and Kris are waiting, chatting happily in the front seat of the Range Rover.

Kris reacts immediately to the panic on my face. "What's wrong? Where's Grigoriy?"

I leap into the car. "Drive!" I shout. "Go, now."

Bless him, but Aleks doesn't insist I answer any questions. He just leaves.

Ten years ago

Mom's wearing a turtleneck again. I promised to leave her alone. I told her I'd stop arguing about him, but I can't help it. I can't just bite my tongue anymore.

"I talked to Kris," I say.

"That's good, since you're living at her place."

"I'm not in her house," I say. "I'm in one of the two-bedroom apartments. It has a really cute little kitchen they just remodeled. It's on the back side of the barn. The one with its own parking spots."

"I don't like you living in the main barn. I'm sure lots of the grooms are thinking inappropriate thoughts about you," Mom says.

It's like he's talking to me through her, like Mom's become his puppet. "I'm sure that none of them are, but who cares if they are? They're polite, and I have privacy, and I love it there. They can think whatever they want, as long as they don't act on it. And since I'm starting a lesson program at her barn, my rent is *zero*."

"I'm happy for you." But her tone doesn't match her words. She doesn't sound happy at all.

"Did you hear the part where there are *two* bedrooms?" I ask. "Because there are. You can have one."

"Have one what?" Mārtiņš stomps through the doorway from the bedroom, and I startle.

"Oh." I swallow. "I thought you were at work."

"I'm sick," he says. "I stayed home."

I grab my purse, my hand trembling. "I hope my voice didn't wake you. Sorry if I was too loud." I absolutely loathe how I turn into a slinking dog around him, but I can't seem to do anything about it. Even my voice shakes when he's near.

Mom's not much better, but now I understand why she wouldn't even entertain the idea of moving in with me. Her lousy husband was in the next room. Why didn't she send me some kind of message? Or warn me when I first came through the door by mentioning that he's here?

Mārtiņš looks casual as he walks toward me, but nothing is ever casual with him. Or even if it is, you can't enjoy it, because you're always waiting for the moment it all changes. "You have a two-bedroom place, huh?"

I nod tightly.

"Why?"

I shrug.

"I asked why." His voice is deceptively calm, but I can tell from his narrowed eyes and his clenched hands that he's angry. He heard more than he's admitting to hearing.

"It's the apartment Kristiana had available," I say.

"I said not to say her name in this house," he says.

It's not a house. Mom and Mārtiņš live in a lousy little apartment, but I don't point that out. I may have been unprepared to deal with him—I dropped by specifically because I thought he'd be gone—but I'm not stupid enough to intentionally provoke him. "Sorry."

"You should move back here," he says. "You don't even have to run a lesson program here, and you won't have to pay rent." He eyes me from my head to my toes, and even though he's never done anything sexual, it still feels appraising in a way that doesn't sit well with me.

"I'll think about it," I lie.

"Come back tomorrow," he says. "My friend was asking about you."

"Your friend?" I ask.

"Danils," he says. "You never should have left him."

I'm surprised he's putting it that way. The public story is that Danils dumped me, but I didn't mind. I was relieved, to be honest. After I found out he was cheating, I disconnected, and after that happened, I realized what a mess our 'relationship' was anyway.

Not that his infidelity was an excuse in Mārtinš's book. No woman should ever leave a powerful man, not for any reason, not even if he dumps her. Even if he cheats. No matter what, she should slink around forever, licking his boots and hoping he'll take her back. "It's too bad I had such poor judgment," I say, hoping he can't sense my sarcasm.

"It is," he says. "But I think he might take you back yet." He nods. "That was not quite what he said, but almost."

Not for anything in this world would I go back to Danils, but I don't say that, either. "I'll let you know," I say. "But I'd better get back. I have my first lesson in an hour."

He scowls, but he doesn't make a move to stop me.

The moment I'm out the front door, every muscle in my body turns soft. I very nearly collapse against the front door, drawing in ragged breaths, waiting for my heart to stop pounding in my ears and my legs to stop shaking.

"Why didn't you stop her?" It's faint, but I can still hear

Mārtinš through the solid wooden door. He must be really angry.

My mom says something, but I can't make out the words.

"I didn't hear you ask her to move back. I told you Danils said if she goes back to him, he'll hire me."

Mom tries again, but it doesn't seem to help.

Because the next sound I hear is a crash.

It's not like Mārtinš has even been an amazing bread-winner, but with the sheer volume of belongings that he breaks, it's a wonder they have any furniture at all. At least when he's breaking things, he's not hurting Mom.

In the end, though, there's not much I can do. I keep asking her to leave him, but until she's ready to do it, nothing will change. The only thing that happens when I visit is I wind up in the crosshairs. I call the police on my way back to Liepašeta. Hopefully, if he does start breaking more than lamps, the surprise arrival of the police for a sound disturbance will cool him down instead of riling him up.

Usually when I was around, a visit from the police would buy me a few days of polite behavior.

Sometimes it went the other way.

When Mom calls me the next morning, she sounds utterly drained. That's not a good sign. "Can you pick up some food for me?"

That's not either. Because when she's black and blue, she can't go out, but Mārtinš still expects her to make his dinner. "Mom."

"Please?" He definitely beat her. Badly.

During my two-hour break, I drive out and pick up rye bread, lentils, smoked mackerel, sour cream, eggs, and a few fresh greens. It's not a lot, but I don't have much money to spare. There's no way she'll be able to pay me for any of it. He's always expected her to perform miracles like she's Jesus, blessing the loaves and the fishes.

I almost leave the bags on her front porch, but I think about the sour cream and the eggs and change my mind. I hate seeing her all bruised, but I'd hate if all the food I could barely afford went to waste.

I knock, and then I wait.

Horrifyingly, it's not Mom who opens the door.

Mārtiņš is spoiling for a fight from the second I see him. His knuckles are bruised and one of them's bleeding. His eyes are bloodshot—which means he's been drinking—and he has a little bit of spittle on his chin. He's clearly been ranting, too.

"Here." I hold out the bag. "My mom couldn't go shopping, since you beat her black and blue." When I'm not in the house, and my car is mere steps away, sometimes I have the confidence to get a little mouthy.

Which is really stupid. His face contorts.

Screw the sour cream. I should've dumped it and run.

When Mom stands up behind him, her face is more purple than flesh colored. "Mirdza, thank you."

Fury and rage bubble up inside of me. "You're a sick human being," I say. "You should be in jail." My hands shake. My blood boils. For one split second, I wonder what would happen if I hit him, for a change. Could he take a hit, or can he just inflict pain?

"Get out of here," he says. "I'll tell Danils what a pile of filth you are. Forget about that second chance with him." He shakes his head and curses me under his breath.

I'm stupidly desperate to do something.

With every single fiber of my being, I want to hurt this man who has done nothing but damage my poor, widowed mother, but right alongside my rage is a very real, very old fear.

But something new occurs to me.

I have no idea what would happen if I struck him in the face, but even if I can't beat him, even if he handles pain just fine, maybe seeing him hit me would galvanize my mother. She might leave him, finally.

But it's a lot of maybes.

And I already know what happens if I drive away. I'll be safe. It's also what my mother would want. So even though it pains me, I step back and pull my keys out of my pocket. I'm less than one step away from my car when I hear it.

My mom's whimper.

He didn't close the door all the way, so this time, I can hear everything. His cursing. His demeaning verbal attacks. His accusations that she wanted me to come over here and intervene for her. "You called the cops," he says.

"You can check my phone," she says. "I didn't."

"Then you sent your daughter a message somehow," he says. "You made her call them."

I'm a little embarrassed that we never thought of that. We should have had some kind of message, something we could say in front of him that meant something else.

But the sound of his fist against something soft, the splatter-thunk sound of my already purple and horribly damaged mother being beaten again by her husband, it takes the almost equally balanced rage and terror inside me and it tips the scales *just enough*.

Before I have time to even think about what I'm doing, I push through the almost-closed front door, and I grab the busted lamp off the ground. I don't stop moving. While Mārtinš is staring at me slack-jawed, while my mother watches in abject horror, I stride toward him, lift my arm, and slam it downward, aiming for his ugly face.

But I don't succeed.

The lamp's a wooden block with a shattered glass bulb on top, and it would really hurt if it smashed into his jaw.

His hand, however, seems to have almost no trouble stopping me.

And then he laughs.

I'll never forget that sound.

Laughter should be bright, and happy, and infectious.

This was infectious alright, but in the same way that tuberculosis or the bubonic plague are. It's certain death to all joy. He drops my mom's hair, which he had been holding her up by, and stands. "Look at this. Your little girl finally came to play." Faster than I thought possible, he yanks the lamp from my hand and slaps it against his free hand. "And you even brought me a toy."

I think if I hadn't grabbed the lamp, things might have ended differently. I might not have been beaten as badly. Or maybe it wouldn't have mattered.

As much rage as I held inside, as much pent-up fury and repressed hatred as I had, Mārtiņš apparently had even more, and he'd had years and years of practice converting that rage into meaningful action.

It's the lamp, in the end, that he uses to shatter my femur. By then, that horrible pain's just more noise. I don't know who calls one-one-nine to report the emergency. I don't know what the paramedics who come to get me look like. I do hear my mother telling them that I got in a fight with *her* after she broke my lamp.

It's so ludicrous that I start to laugh, but even that slight effort on my part causes my split lip to bleed profusely, flooding my mouth with an iron taste and choking me. I spit it on the disgusting rug I'm lying on, and I stare right at Mārtiņš. "He hit me," I manage to say. "With that lamp. My mom did nothing."

After that, I pass out.

When I wake up, I'm in a hospital bed, all alone. I call out, but no one comes. It's just me and a beeping machine. I don't even realize that my leg doesn't work. I just look around, call out another time or two and go back to sleep.

Almost ten days later, when I'm finally discharged, my leg in a cast after a sequence of three surgeries, my sister Adriana's the one picking me up. "The police still haven't come by," I say.

"And they won't," she says. "Mom has given several statements that you two had a fight and that she hurt you. Mārtiņš gave one that backs up her story. Your only option will be to press charges against her, but she says you started it. Since you're the aggressor, they're not inclined to do much to her."

I can't speak at first, as her words sink in.

Deep down, I always thought that if it came down to it, my mom would pick me. That helped me survive years of watching Mārtiņš beat on her. If she had to, she'd protect me. If he ever threatened us, she'd leave him, because in the hierarchy of her love, Adriana and I came first. I believed that.

But now my leg's shattered. My face is swollen like a balloon, and she hasn't so much as come by my room or brought me flowers.

And she lied to cover for him, the man who did this to me.

"We need a code," I say. It's the only thing I can think to do.

"A code?" Adriana snorts.

"If I ever call and ask you to get me Polish sausages, I need help. I need you to call the police. I'm in trouble. Someone bad, probably Mārtiņš, is going to hurt me."

"You hate Polish sausages," Adriana says.

"Exactly," I say. "That's why it works. It's not something I'd ever ask you to do, but no one else will know that."

Adriana smiles. "I like it."

She helps me struggle into the passenger seat of her car.

"As soon as I can walk again," I say, "maybe we should take a self-defense class."

My sister shakes her head. "Screw self-defense. I'm taking Krav Maga. I'm not going to protect myself. I'm going to beat any man who attacks me into a Polish sausage."

I never do take those classes, but Adriana does.

❧ 14 ❧

It takes *days* for us to deal with the fallout from the way Grigoriy handled Yevginiy's appearance. I'm forced to lie to the local police and say that after I left, Grigoriy went back inside to look for some things I thought I left behind. Luckily, the mafia had already taken care of any video camera feeds, presumably through the good doctor as well. They probably did it so that no one would have evidence of them murdering me.

Ironically, the idiot doc's actions prevented his own murderer from being caught.

Grigoriy had the presence of mind to dump the dagger he used into a vat of some kind of cleaner and then knock it over sideways, leaving no trace of his fingerprints on the murder weapon, which was marked with the sigil of Yevginiy's men anyway.

The local newspaper finally reports the deaths of the eight mafia members and the American surgeon this morning.

ST PETERSBURG MAFIA KINGPIN MURDERED BY AMERICAN

On Friday of last week, in a shocking turn of events, the

man rumored to be leading the mafia in Saint Petersburg, one Yevginiy Stepanchikov, attacked a local hospital. An American physician who had been taking bribes from Mr. Stepanchikov fought with him, presumably regarding a payment dispute. Both are now deceased, but prior to his passing, the physician killed seven of Stepanchikov's associates. Nothing has yet been discovered about the nature of their relationship or the method by which the physician was able to accomplish such a feat. Authorities suspect he employed the use of some kind of paralytic to carry it out.

The police officially cleared Grigoriy yesterday, and he's no longer being supervised or considered as a suspect. I wouldn't have minded him being behind bars for longer, but Kris and Aleks were quite distressed, and that made me sad. They've done so much for me—I can't really blame them for being worried about another friend.

In my heart, I know that Grigoriy thought he was doing the right thing. He thought he was protecting me. I'm not even angry with him, not really.

I'm just terrified *of* him.

"But how can you just leave?" Kris asks.

"I appreciate everything you've done for me," I say. "I really and truly do, but I need to get back home quickly. I don't have a lot of time before Brigita starts selling my horses."

"I'll call John and have him go get them," Kris says.

"That would be great," I say. "I would love to know they're back at your barn, but I still need to get home. I have a life there. I'm so happy that you found Aleks, but I can't just relocate to Russia."

"I understand," Kris says. "I was planning to head back soon, anyway."

"That's a relief."

"The thing is." Kris drops into a chair in the corner of

my room. "The guys don't want you to leave. . .unless they come along."

Not this again. "We've been through this. I know Grigoriy can't use his powers without my help, but—"

"It's not even about that," Kris says. "You aren't safe."

"I'm never safe," I say. "I'll take my chances."

"The mafia bosses always report to someone else," Kris says. "That means Yevginiy had a boss, and he didn't bring all his people. You even said there were more people on the train that day. One of them could come after you, or tell his boss who to come after."

"So could your magical men—the ice and fire people."

"It's electricity and fire," Kris says, as if that sounds less insane.

"I can't spend the rest of my life looking over my shoulder," I say. "I live a small life, and I'm ready to go back to it. Surely the mafia people would know that if I was going to talk, I would have. And the magical people will come after Grigoriy, so him coming along actually makes me *less* safe, not more."

"But he can't defend you unless he's with you."

"It's a real conundrum," I say. "I get it. Without me, he has no magic. But with me, he draws the bad guys to me." I shrug. "I suggest he stays close to Aleks and hopes his buddy can keep him safe."

"If we all stay close, then I can help Aleks when they come." Grigoriy steps through my destroyed doorway, pushing the door open as he does. "I think we should all go back to Latvia."

"You've never even been there," Aleks says. "So you can hardly say you're going back."

My palms start to sweat, my heart rate spikes, and my hands start to shake the second they step into my room. "I believe I've been quite clear."

"I have an idea," Grigoriy says.

"Actually, it was my idea," Kris says.

I feel a little betrayed. If it were anyone else, I'd just get a train ticket and leave on my own. But it's Kristiana, my best friend, and she's having ideas about how to convince me to let them tag along. "What?" If I sound a little terse, I think I'm justified.

"You aren't scared of him as a horse." Kris shrugs. "Shift him and let him stick around in horse form."

"In horse form?" I ask.

"Shift him now," Aleks says. "We'll drive back to Latvia with him in a trailer."

"I'm sure he'd love—"

"It's fine," Grigoriy says. "I'll do it."

"You'll spend however long I say as a horse, because you scare me as a man?"

He nods.

"Is this some kind of joke?"

"Some of our happiest moments at the beginning were when Aleks was a horse," Kris says.

"I'm not going to wind up engaged to Grigoriy," I nearly shout. "I wish you'd stop comparing us." I can't bring myself to look at him. I know he'll be hurt, but I just can't. Every time I see his face, I see him dragging that knife across the doctor's throat. I can't help my shudder.

"Change me now," Grigoriy says. "See if you feel better." His eyes, when I glance that way, look tortured.

"Fine." I point. "Go out back. I'll be there in a few."

He and Aleks both disappear, leaving Kris to smooth things over, I assume.

"You could have warned me." I sound a little petulant, but Kris understands. She saw me at the hospital after Mārtiņš beat me. She gave me a place to live, and she knows I didn't leave her compound for months after I was released from the hospital.

"You have to make your own decisions," she says. "I didn't want to manipulate you into it."

Kris always reminds me that I'm strong, even though she knows as well as I do that it's not true. "When I still want to claw my way up the wall to get away from him, even when he's a horse, will you let it go then?"

My best friend stares at me for a moment, and then she nods tightly.

"Great, then let's go." I realize as we're walking outside—my leg is sore, but doing much better—that I'll have to touch him to shift his shape. I practically recoil in horror, and I'm not anywhere near him yet. "I don't think I can." I stop walking.

"He'll shift immediately, and then if you're still upset, you just have to change him back and Aleks and I will take you home."

"With or without Grigoriy?"

"He'll have to come with us—he's a sitting duck out here alone. But we'd have rules. Once we're there, he won't be allowed on your side of the property."

Great. We'd be like a divorced couple, but at Kris's place. Maybe over time, he won't fill me with as much terror and dread. Maybe. It's hard, marching behind Kris into the clearing out back. Aleks is standing in front of Grigoriy, who has already stripped down.

"Hey," Aleks says. "You turn around."

Kris is laughing when she does an about face. "As if I didn't see him already that first day."

"No reason you need to be blinded again."

No one's worried about *me* being blinded, obviously. But Aleks does block most everything from my view as I approach, and he stays in place, even when I'm only about two feet away.

"I'll stay here," Aleks says. "You can reach around me."

Kris must have explained what I've been through. I kind of hate that he knows, but at least he's not abandoning me.

"I won't hurt you," Grigoriy says. "I never would."

He doesn't get it. He'll probably never get it. He already has hurt me—by hurting other people.

I don't bother trying to explain. I just reach around Aleks's solid frame and extend one single finger until it's touching some kind of skin. "I wish you were a horse."

There's a tiny whoosh of air, and suddenly, it's the horse, Charlemagne, standing behind Aleks. It helps to think of it by a different name.

I remember different things with him than I do with Grigoriy. The wind in my hair. A gentle nudge of his nose. His movement beneath me, carrying me, saving me that first day. Warming me the night before. Healing me when I was almost dead.

I have no bad memories with Charlemagne.

"I need you both to call him Charlemagne," I say.

"Charlemagne," Aleks mouths. He frowns.

"It's what I named him that first night, before I knew."

"We can do that." Kris walks closer. "You don't mind, do you boy? It's a good name." She reaches out a hand and rubs his nose, just like she would with any horse. Her hand slides up, then, rubbing along the flat front of his face and ruffling his forelock.

He whuffles.

Even Aleks, who usually doesn't like having Kris anywhere near Grigoriy, doesn't seem to mind.

Because it's not the same. My heart decelerates more every moment.

He's a stallion now, not a man.

He can't talk.

He can't drag daggers across people's necks.

He can't even argue with me.

"Okay," I say quietly. "We can take him with us."

It takes us a day to get things gathered and ready to leave, and even once we're ready to go, the drive is long. I sleep through part of it, but I take my fair turn behind the wheel. We're only a few hours from Daugavpils when Kristiana's phone rings.

"Hello?"

"I have bad news." I can barely hear the voice on the other end of her phone over the hum of the truck engine, even though her speaker's clearly set to max. It's John, her trainer. Bad news about horses is always really bad. If it wasn't, he wouldn't be calling.

"Did someone colic? Was it Five? Or did Dad gamble again?" Kris doesn't sound nearly as nervous as she would have before, and I can't tell whether it's because she owns the land and the barn now, or whether it's because Aleks is rich, or perhaps if she's just started to care less about the father who's always caused her so much grief.

Are we ever really able to care less about the ones we love so much that they can hurt us? Probably some people can. I'm not sure Kris is one of them.

I know I'm not.

"Nothing like that," John says. "In fact, it's not really your bad news at all."

My heart sinks. If it's not hers. . .

"What's wrong?" Kris asks.

"I went by to get Mirdza's horses, but Brigita insists they're all hers now. She waved a contract in my face and told me off." He sighs. "She wouldn't let me take any of them, not even Blanka."

❦ 15 ❦

The last time I walked into this barn, I was using crutches and a leg brace, and still, I could barely move. I begged for a loan and was fired instead. Brigita, for whom I had worked for months, and whom I had known for more than a decade and a half, told me I had a month to find a new place for my horses. It's been less than two weeks, and she wouldn't surrender my horses when John went to collect them.

"Are you sure you don't want me to come in with you?" There are wrinkles at the corners of Kris's eyes, and her brow's locked into a furrowed position.

"I need to face her alone," I say.

"But she won't be alone," Aleks says.

The window on the back of the truck is open, and I can see Charlemagne, hanging his head out. He tosses it. Clearly he thinks I should take the backup they're offering.

"I want to give her a chance to do the right thing," I say. "Taking you in with me will only put her back up."

Kris compresses her lips, but she doesn't argue. "Go, then."

"If you're not out in five minutes," Aleks says, "we're coming in after you."

He's been watching too many American films in an effort to catch up with modern culture. It's making half of what he says unbearably cliché. Not that Kris seems to have noticed.

Love really does make you blind.

"I'll know in less than five minutes, I imagine," I say.

"I'm ready to barge in and yell," Kris says. "More than ready."

I appreciate her support so much that it hurts. It was her idea to stop here on the way home. "We have the trailer hooked up already, and I know you're worried. Let's get those babies and bring them home."

The word *home* makes my heart expand.

It hasn't felt like I had one since Kris had to sell Liepašeta.

But now I do again. I think about her face as I march inside. It's a miracle that I'm able to walk in, frankly. I should be more grateful. Isn't it funny how quickly miracles stop mattering once the limitation they repaired is a thing of the past? Humans don't retain our gratitude for very long.

We're all quite greedy.

"Where's Brigita?" I ask one of the grooms.

He points at the main arena.

I figured that's where I'd find her, but I must've been harboring hope that we could have this face-off without an audience. No luck. I square my shoulders and push past the wheelbarrow and toward the arena.

Brigita's facility is set up with two outlying barns that feed into the main barn. The main barn, in which I'm now standing, is shaped like a large letter T. It has stalls all down the main row, with a wide alleyway, and a huge covered arena that abuts the line of stalls, but branches off away from them at a ninety-degree angle, forming the bottom of the letter.

She's riding Blanka when I arrive.

My horse. My beautiful, grey mare sails over a four-foot jump right in front of me.

All my practiced calm evaporates.

"Get off my horse, you thief," I shout.

A dozen heads turn toward me. Six equine, six human.

It looks like she's showing off on Blanka to the class she's teaching. Three of those riders were my students. I hate that she's using my horse to impress my own students, but even more, I hate that they're all here to watch this.

Brigita hauls on the reins, pulling Blanka up short and making my blood boil. I wonder how she'd feel if I stuck a steel bar in her mouth and ripped it into her face like that. The thought of doing it makes me smile.

"What's so funny?" She moves toward me on Blanka at a very brisk trot, hauling on her again just in time to keep from crashing into the side wall of the arena. Blanka's a very literal horse, and she'll do anything you ask, even if it's smashing into a wall. A competent rider would already have figured that out and wouldn't be punishing her horse for her own failings. "Is calling me a thief some kind of joke I don't get?"

"That's my horse," I say. "Get off her immediately." I open the gate and walk through.

"No, this is *my* horse," Brigita says. "If you'd read your contract, you'd already know that. She was abandoned at my facility after you were terminated for cause. It's all laid out in article six."

"I wasn't terminated for cause," I say. "I was injured here, at your facility, by a horse you manage. Poorly manage. I forgot that part."

She shrugs. "Have your lawyer contact mine. Until then, I'll keep riding *my* horse." She yanks hard on the right side, forcing Blanka to pivot and head back toward the group gathered in the center of the ring.

"Oh, you'll be hearing from my—"

One of the loudest whinnies I've ever heard sounds from the alleyway at the far end of the barn, near the entrance.

Brigita freezes except for her head, which whips around to see what made the noise.

It's Charlemagne. Of course it is. Even from here, he looks breathtaking, his sides heaving, his nostrils flaring as he paws the concrete floor.

Brigita forces Blanka to trot back toward me. "What in the world—"

"You will give my friend her horses back." Kris's hands are on her hips, and she looks as angry as Charlemagne, who is currently wearing a halter that looks more like a face decoration than a method of control. "Or I'll see to it that your entire lesson program moves to my barn. I'll be offering *free* lessons for three full months, *and free board*, to anyone who moves to my much nicer facility, just to ensure that happens."

Brigita's eyes widen. "You wouldn't dare."

"Oh, I think I would."

"It doesn't matter," Brigita says. "Even if you offer free board, my clients have signed agreements with me, just like your friend. They aren't at liberty to just leave."

"How do you think it will sound to the horse community that you stole her horses?" Aleks asks.

Brigita slides off Blanka's back and hands the reins to her assistant, Alvīna, who has also dismounted. "Hold her." She strides toward us then, her eyes flashing. "If you think you can browbeat or threaten me into giving you those horses back, think again. You already know that Danils and the mayor—"

"What do you want?" I ask. "You only do stuff like this when you're upset about something."

"I don't want anything," she says. But she glances back over her shoulder, and I think about what she was doing. That may be the most telling thing of all.

For the last decade, Brigita has competed when I could not. She has ridden in every competition she could sign up for, but she's always been *just* below where she needs to be to win enough Longines points to qualify for the Olympics.

And at the last Olympics, for the first time ever, Latvia actually had a qualifier. Brigita wanted it to be her.

I know, because that was my dream too, long ago.

Blanka was the horse I thought could get me there. She sails over four-foot jumps like they're nothing. She clears five-foot jumps competently, even in sequence. And her horizontal clearance is unparalleled.

She wants my horse.

The World Cup show jumping competition in Riga is barely more than two months away. She's hoping to gain enough points there to qualify, and she needs Blanka to do it.

So pushing her other buttons, or threatening, or yelling and blustering—none of them will change her mind. She's already got her hands around her end game, and she's not going to let go unless something even better is within reach.

"How dare you bring a horse onto my property without my permission. Whose horse is that?"

"I want my horses back," I say, ignoring her. "But you have law enforcement in your pocket, thanks to your boyfriend." I cross my arms.

Kris and Aleks are walking closer. I hear them behind me, or rather, I hear Charlemagne's huge hoof falls.

She shrugs. "You could buy the others back, but I'm afraid Blanka's not for sale."

I want to call her a string of names. I want to slap her across her greedy face. But none of those will solve my problem.

At least, not until something occurs to me.

"What if we had a little competition of our own?" I glance behind her to check, and sure enough, every single person in that lesson is listening, including her gossipy assistant. Even two grooms have stopped working and are leaning against the walls.

Perfect.

"What kind of competition could we possibly have?" She scoffs. "You can't even ride. I've already beaten you in every possible way."

"I had a surgery," I say.

"Mirdza," Kris says. "Why don't you come with me to the trailer, and—"

"See? Even your friend thinks this is a bad idea," Brigita says. "Maybe you should stop before you embarrass yourself more."

"I'll show you right now what I have in mind. I just need to borrow an oversize bridle."

"Excuse me?" Brigita arches one eyebrow.

I look back at Charlemagne, desperately hoping that he's got my back, even if Kris doesn't. The doctor said I couldn't ride, yes, but it was for the same reasons as before. Any quick, sharp spills could cause terrible damage. If I'm okay with the risk—and for Blanka, I am—then I can ride.

Right?

"I have a saddle and bridle in the trailer," Kris says.

Tears spring into my eyes and I brush them away. "If you really think you're such an amazing rider and I'm a joke, then you should be able to outjump me right now, on my horse." I toss my head. "I'll ride that one, who's never been in a single show in his entire life."

"You must be kidding," Brigita says.

"I'm not." I stare at her.

"I own her," she says. "I'm not going to risk her like an idiot."

"So you think she can outjump you?" Kris asks. "You think it's a risk?"

"I have nothing to gain," Brigita says.

"But surely there's no way you could lose, either, right?" Kris's expression is pure mocking, and I want to hug her.

"Who is that horse?" Alvīna asks. "Where did you get him?"

"I found him in Russia," I say. "Right before I had my surgery."

"Can you even ride?" Alvīna asks. "You just had surgery."

"I'm not supposed to," I say. "And you all know I haven't ridden in ten years. Don't you think, if I can beat Brigita, who's riding my horse, she should give her back?"

There's a lot of murmuring.

"A few jumps mean nothing," Brigita says. "Besides. You aren't supposed to be riding at all."

"How about a sanctioned event?" Alvīna asks. "The Riga World Cup. If you both compete and she beats you there. . ."

"She can't even get in," Brigita says. "She hasn't ridden in more than ten years! You said it yourself."

"Surely you could get her in," Alīna says. "It would make the whole thing much more interesting for the rest of us to watch. And we'd be certain that staying at your barn is the right move." She tilts her head, and I have never liked her more.

"You did say you're a way better teacher," little Ludmila says.

I want to kiss her face.

"There's still nothing in it for me," Brigita says. "Only a fool gambles something valuable for nothing."

Kris looks furious. "I'll be happy to—"

Brigita shakes her head. "I don't want one of your charity horses."

"What do you want?" I ask.

"You'll be riding that horse?" Brigita eyes Charlemagne carefully. "Right?"

I grit my teeth.

"It's only fair if we both offer our horses," Brigita says.

"But yours is Mirdza's horse." Kris looks ready to punch her.

"Not anymore," Brigita says. "Like it or not, Blanka's mine. So if you want a chance at winning her back, I'll give it to you. I can get you into the competition, but you have to put that big guy at risk to do it."

I glance back at Charlemagne, who probably has no idea what we're even talking about. He tosses his head, his eye perfectly steady on mine.

"I'll be generous," Brigita says. "I'll give you an out. If you can't find a doctor to clear you to ride, I'll let you out of our deal." She glances around the room. "See how kind I am?"

"We'll come up with another way to get Blanka back," Kris says.

But I know that there isn't another way. For her, maybe, but my life doesn't work like that. If I walk away, I'm saying goodbye to Blanka forever, and worse, I'll be leaving her to the most awful person in Daugavpils.

Charlemagne takes another step and presses his face against my arm. He exhales slowly. When I look down at him, he nods again.

If I wasn't quite sure he was in, now I am.

"Deal," I say.

It's not until I walk back out to the truck, my recently repaired leg trembling from overuse, that I completely lose it. Not only do I have to interact with Charlemagne every single day if I want to have any hope of beating Brigita, but I've put his life at risk. A human.

Over losing a horse.

I'm as selfish as Adriana. Maybe worse.

❧ 16 ❧

I have exactly one way to get out of this, which is why I'm sitting in this miserable place.

Doctor's offices have never been good for me. Actually, hospitals haven't been that great, either. I know they're supposed to heal us, and I know that without medicine, the world would be even nastier, more brutish, and shorter than it already is.

But it is definitely not my happy place.

"This is taking forever," I say. "We should just go." I can call Brigita and tell her I couldn't get cleared. I can beg off. The thought of losing Blanka makes me panic, but it's the smart thing to do. People don't risk their entire lives over horses. They just don't.

Kris scowls.

"It was a stupid bargain to strike," I say. "I should use this to back out."

"None of those students will ever leave her barn if you do," Kris says. "Everyone will have heard about it by now. You'll have to figure out a new career."

Aleks laughs. "Besides. Grigoriy will destroy her."

It's good that he has faith in his friend, but I'm not entirely sure it's not misplaced.

Kris was even more adamant than Brigita that I get cleared to ride before I climb on Charlemagne. Brigita wanted to save face, or possibly she didn't want it to come back on her if I wasn't really safe to ride, but Kris is genuinely worried.

The problem is, I'm pretty sure I already know what the docs are going to say. No one wants to take the risk that if my leg isn't ready, they said I'd be fine.

"Doctors are going to want to protect themselves," I say. "It's their job. It's not as bad here as it is in the United States, but what does it benefit them to clear me?"

"Maybe with Aleksandr's help, your leg healed better than we thought it could," Kristiana says. "Maybe there won't be any risks, and then we can all sleep well at night while you practice."

"You can already sleep well." I look pointedly at Aleks. "You have a big, hot—"

She slaps me right as a nurse finally shows up. "We're ready to take you back for your scans."

I wasn't nervous in Russia, where apparently the mafia was already actively looking for me, but for some reason, I'm terrified right now. As I'm sitting utterly still, I realize the reason.

I'm hopeful.

I hate admitting it, even to myself, but like Kris, I'm desperately hoping that the surgery went better than stupid Dr. Hubert thought. He was the best of the best at orthopedic surgery, even if he was a gross human being. What if *he* thought it wasn't good enough, what if *he* thought it was a failure, but what if really, it's mostly fine?

Besides, with magical assistance in my recovery, could the bones have fused better than they would have, healing the slow and miserable way? The doctor said something about bone edema and infection risk and space around the screws and blah blah blah. Without any of that, maybe my leg's more stable than they thought it could be.

I'm trying to rein myself in, but it's not working very well. I'm not admitting it to Kris, but part of me is happy to be here: desperately hoping yet again for a miracle.

Because I'm greedy.

I don't just want to win Blanka back.

Watching her sailing over those jumps with Brigita on her back, my old dream to ride in the Olympics flared up again. My jealousy that Brigita can do with my angel horse what I never can was practically a tangible thing.

Because if I can't ride her, am I even justified in taking her back from Brigita? As much as any I've ever seen, my horse *loves* to jump. She's always been so talented, it's almost cruel for me to keep her from achieving whatever she can, from living her best life.

I'm tired of being in the way of everyone else because of my limitations. So when the doctor finally shows up in the room where we're waiting, I'm equal parts hope and desperation.

I hate every second of this agony.

Unlike Dr. Hubert, this guy sits down, sighs slowly, wheels a little closer to me on his tiny stool, adjusts his glasses, and then clears his throat.

"What's the news?" Kris asks. "How did it heal up? Can she ride horses again?"

He flips his chart open and starts to look at something intently.

"Doctor," Aleks says.

His head whips up. "You say your surgeon did this how long ago?"

I swallow. "Three months." That's how long he said my recovery should take, and with Aleks healing me, it seemed best to go with that.

"The thing that's strange is that I'd expect to see more muscle mass than I do, if it was that long ago. It's like the bone has healed, but the muscle has atrophied."

"But the bone looks good?" I ask. "Could I ride a horse on it? Maybe that will help strengthen the muscle."

He frowns. "I'm surprised your surgeon didn't tell you this himself." He turns his clipboard around and points with a pen toward a paper printout. Latvia is many things, but high tech is not one of them. No iPads here. We use photocopies of the actual scan. "See this?"

I lean forward, my heart in my throat. Be good. Be something good. Please. Something good that Dr. Hubert didn't share.

"It looks like he intended to use a bone graft on this area," he says. "Based on the scans in our system from the last time you were seen, it's what I'd have recommended as well." He frowns. "But the last scans we had were from a few weeks ago, so I don't see how—"

"The critical point," Kris asks, "is whether she can ride? Or is it too dangerous?"

"He didn't do the graft," the surgeon says. "He could barely rejoin the bone fragments, and it looks like he found evidence of a bone infection, based on the amount of bone he shaved before reattaching the new plate. I'm assuming that's why he backed out on the graft and didn't add as much hardware as he told you he would." He drops the clipboard holding the scans on the counter.

"So, she can't?" Aleks asks.

"She can do whatever she wants to do," he says. "I've heard of people riding horses without having legs. You could probably make her a brace that would even allow it to be more comfortable, but it would be very stupid for her to do that when she can actually walk on her own right now. If she fell, or if she even pushed too hard, the results could be catastrophic."

It's what I expected him to say. I'm not even surprised. But I am disappointed.

We're not even to the car when Kris says, "The only way I'll support you in this is if you ride with a brace like the one he mentioned, and that you ride Grigoriy and no one else."

"So we have him make the brace—"

She shakes her head. "We had to get out of there, because he had noticed too many things. There's no way for us to explain what Aleksandr did to you after that procedure. We will commission a top-of-the-line brace from that company he mentioned. But it's not because he'll be safer that I want you riding Grigoriy."

"You mean Charlemagne."

Kris stares me dead in the eyes. "You *do* know that Grigoriy and Charlemagne are the same, right? It's not like he's actually a horse."

I drop my eyes. "Of course."

"Okay, as long as we know we're being silly." She shakes her head. "It's fine—I even get your need to pretend he's something else. But in this instance, it's *because* of who he is that it's fine for you to ride him."

"His powers," Aleksandr says, "include healing injuries that have just been suffered."

Which means, if I fall off, he could fix it. Probably. Assuming it works to heal damage from past issues, which it might not. Even so, I can't argue that it's not my best shot.

"Plus, I'm sure he's a heck of a jumper," Kris says.

"Why do you two think—"

Kris shrugs. "They aren't real horses, and Aleks is the best jumper I've seen."

Her future husband looks really, stupidly hot most of the time. But when he's preening because his fiancée complimented him for jumping really well as a horse?

He looks decidedly dopey.

My lip curls. "But if I agree to ride him?"

Kris smiles. "Then I'll do everything in my power to get you ready for that World Cup competition."

"I really want to win Blanka back."

"I like Blanka," Kris says. "But what *I* really want is to watch Brigita get destroyed. It's really important to me that happens, and that as many people as possible see it happen."

Aleksandr laughs. "My tiny little fiancée is such a delicate flower."

Kris stomps. "Just because I'm small doesn't mean I'm delicate."

"Don't I know it." He steps toward her possessively, and I'm worried he's going to pounce on her in the parking lot.

"Can you two at least take me home before you start acting so disgusting again?"

"We should." Aleks still isn't looking at me. He's fixated on Kris, like she's the only thing that matters. "I'm sure *Charlemagne* is freaking out right now." He laughs again. He seems to think it's hilarious that I keep calling his friend a made-up name.

"Should I start referring to you as Obsidian Devil?" I ask. "Will that help you focus?"

"I think you should." Kris isn't looking at me either. She's directing a disgustingly come-hither look at Aleks.

"Okay, that's enough. I have some hard-core rehab to do, and I don't have very long to do it."

That seems to snap them out of it. Kris starts for the car. "You do need to get on that saddle every single day, for as long as you can manage."

"Speaking of getting on every day," I say. "I was hoping you might be willing to train me."

Kris freezes, her hand on the handle of the car door. "Train you in *show jumping*?"

"I know you've never done that, *per se*," I say, "but—"

She turns, one hand flying to her hip. "Not per se," she says. "I haven't done it *ever*. I only know racing."

"I can't afford anyone else," I say. "And even if I could—"

"No one else will understand the Grigoriy thing," Kris finishes. She sighs. "I've got to be the least qualified, least competent person for the task."

"But I know all the rules," I say. "I've won several of the World Cup qualifiers, and one of the Nation's Cup competitions, all on Blanka, before my accident."

"No, I know you have." Kris shakes her head. "But you have to listen to a trainer. That's the point. And if you know more than I do, I'm not sure how I can possibly be of much use."

"You can see what I can't about what I'm doing wrong. You're smart. You're talented at both riding and equine care. I can't think of anyone better."

"And your fiancé can magically remove her soreness each day," Aleks says. "A buildup of lactic acid is the cause, and it's something your body will heal on its own, so." He wiggles his fingers.

He's an expert on lactic acid now? "How much time does he spend researching things online?"

"Way, way too much." Kris finally gets in the car. "I may need to install some parental limits on you, mister."

They banter back and forth the whole way home, and I appreciate it. It gives me a little bit of time to think about how I'm going to face Grigoriy now that I've offered him up as the collateral on my bet. I have an out right now, if we claim I can't get medical clearance. If we proceed, if we share the letter from the doctor saying I can ride, then I need him to be on board.

Kris hasn't once mentioned the risk of losing Charlemagne if she beats me.

It can't hurt that he's so massive, so talented, and so smart, but why aren't they worried about it?

"Are you concerned about me losing?" I ask.

"You won't lose," Aleks says. "Not on Grigoriy."

"But if we do, Brigita gets Charlemagne," I say.

Aleksandr laughs.

"Why is that funny?" I ask.

"I mean, presumably you could change him into a human a day or two after she takes him," Kris says. "And then her horse is just. . .gone."

"But if he's ever a horse at our place," I say.

"Then we'll say it's not the same one," Kris says. "It's not like he plans to live here as a horse. It's fine."

"And he's not going to lose," Aleks says. "Trust me."

He did just win the Grand National with Kristiana, in spite of people tampering with their tack.

"Hey," I say. "What ever happened with the investigation into whoever cut your strap?"

Kris sighs. "It's pretty disappointing, really. They found quite a bit of evidence that it was Rex McComb, *and* he rammed into me during the regirth, right before the race began. But it was deemed inconclusive, and I think they're going to let it go."

"That last letter intimated that it didn't matter anyway, since you'd won," Aleks says.

"It's an email," Kris says. "It came electronically, remember? And the reason they're letting it go is that they found hair from Earl Grey on the girth—and Jackson Buley's a real piece of work, too. Since they couldn't determine, decisively, which of the two might have done it, it wasn't right to come down on either of them."

"I still think it might be that Finn guy." Aleks frowns.

"Finn McGee?" I ask. "Isn't he your best guy friend of, like, more than ten years?"

"Thirteen," Kris says. "Aleks has this unreasonable dislike of him."

"First of all, he's a terrible rider, always yanking on my face," Aleks says. "And besides that, he called Kris up when he found out she'd already left and *told her he loved her.*" He scoffs, paying far too little attention to the road, if anyone asks me. Which they never do. "Tell me that's not disturbing."

"Isn't the friends-to-lovers story like the oldest one ever told?" I shrug. "I always thought he had a crush on you, and as far as he knew, Obsidian Devil wasn't an impediment to telling you how he felt." I can't help smirking. Stirring Aleks up is too fun.

"See?" Kris shrugs. "I said that, too. I mean, I told him I'm with Aleks, and he was disappointed, but he let it go. There's no way he would have cut my girth. He'd have cut his own first."

"There's something off about him," Aleks says.

"You're just jealous," I say. "Which is cute, but misdirected. Kris would never date a guy who was the same size she is. She likes her men big, rich, and bossy, apparently."

Kris snorts.

"I'm not bossy," Aleks says. "I do as I'm told."

"Agree to disagree," Kris says.

And then we're turning down the drive of Kristiana's family farm. Liepašeta is the closest thing to home I've ever had, and I can't help it that my heart swells when we turn down the driveway. I have no right to feel this way, but I'm proud every time I see it.

But it also means I'm about to have to confront Grigoriy and ask him if he'll help me beat Brigita. I'll need to ride him every single day, sometimes for a really long time, and put a pounding on his joints going over hugely high jumps.

And that's not even the hard part.

He's going to be at risk. No matter what Aleks says, Brigita will not be keen to let me anywhere near her new horse, and she will throw an all-out fit if he disappears. I'll be her number one target. This could go very, very badly all around if we don't win. It feels like Grigoriy will be risking more than anyone else.

Plus, I imagine Grigoriy will be worried about my leg, just like Kris. I wouldn't be surprised if his biggest hang-up, instead of being the risk to himself, is the possible damage to my leg. Why didn't that stupid dead doctor do the bone graft? Why couldn't he have done what he said he'd do—and then it hits me.

"Do you think that maybe Dr. Hubert did a lousy job on the surgery. . .because he knew those people were just going to come and kill me anyway?"

Aleks slams the car into park.

Kris spins around in the seat and stares at me, her mouth dropping open. "No. He wouldn't, right?"

"Would you spend a lot of time fixing up and remodeling furniture you knew was going to be destroyed?"

Kris's shoulders slump. "Do you really think he knew they were going to kill you?"

"I have no idea," I say. "But it seems strange, doesn't it? He didn't do the surgery he said he'd do, the surgery he prepped to do, and then it turns out he was being paid by the people who came to kill me?" If that one interaction on the train caused all these problems for me. . .

I like to think that I'd have done the same thing anyway.

My leg may not work right, and it may still make my life harder, but I'm proud of who I am, and I can look myself in the mirror without guilt. Even if standing up for that poor woman was futile in the end, I'm still glad I did it.

I let Mārtiņš turn me into a coward for far too long.

It's time for Mirdza Strelkova to be brave again. I

unbuckle my seatbelt, and march—as smoothly as I possibly can—toward the old barn where Charlemagne's staying. I stumble once, okay, maybe twice, but I keep going. And finally, I reach the front.

But there's no horse inside.

Where in the world is he?

A lot of my pep and resolve has fizzled by the time I find him, grazing on the lush green section of grass that no horses have access to in front of the back pasture. I can't help rolling my eyes.

"Really?"

His head whips around.

"I let you out in the morning *and* all night. You have to escape from your stall in the afternoon, too?"

His ears swivel around, and I realize he's hoping someone else is around to defend him.

"It's just me, your Royal Prince. There's no one else around to save you." I put one hand on my hip. "The good news is, no one else caught you. How am I supposed to explain that you, of all the horses on the property, don't need to be kept inside a fence?"

He snorts, and I know what he's thinking. Obsidian isn't ever tied or restrained.

"But Aleks can change himself into a man when he needs to," I say. "So it's not the same."

He walks toward the barn, head down, almost chagrined-looking, for a horse.

"Wait." I clear my throat. At least there are bushes here he can stand behind. Maybe I should just ask him out here. "I need to talk to you for a minute."

He freezes, his entire body utterly still.

"Just for a minute."

The thought of being face-to-face with Grigoriy, not Charlemagne, brings back all the memories. He's slicing throats. He's fighting with Yevginiy.

He's ignoring me completely to destroy.

A shudder runs through my entire body, but I will it to stop. I won't think about that, not right now. What I have to focus on is asking him to do me this favor. Asking for his help, in a form where I can be totally sure of his answer.

"I'm only changing you so I can talk to you—so I can make sure you're willing to do this. Then I need to change you right back. Okay?"

He stares at me for a moment, and then he nods.

I point to a big bush that's finally filling back out, thanks to the spring rains. "Go stand there. That should be enough to keep things mostly decent."

He circles around and then arcs his head toward me, ears up.

I place one hand on his neck, trying not to think about what he's about to be—a huge naked man with the power to knock over every tree and building in the area. A man who can and has murdered lots of people.

Another shudder.

I must focus. I have to do this. I'm the one asking a favor. I close my eyes and say, "I wish you were a man."

And then he is.

I didn't see it happen, because I'm looking away from him, but my hand's suddenly against a very warm, very smooth neck.

I yank it back.

"I have a favor to ask," I say, keeping my eyes averted.

"Okay." His voice is deeper than I recall it being.

My hands are shaking, so I press them against my breeches and push until they stop. "I need to beat Brigita at the showjumping World Cup in Riga in seven weeks." I swallow. "You heard what she wants at the barn." I exhale forcefully. "And you know what that means, I think?"

I wait, but he doesn't say anything.

"If we lose, she wins *you.*"

"Okay."

"Will you do it?" I turn toward him slowly.

"Do you think I can?"

"Aleks does," I say. "And more importantly, Kris does."

"Okay."

"And you're already in decent shape." I can't help a downward glance at his chest and shoulders, confirming that statement. I feel the heat rising in my cheeks.

"Okay."

"But you're the one who's really risking everything. I mean, if we lose, it would be awkward at the least. Dangerous at the most." I inhale sharply, now concerned that he's going to say no. He should say no. "Besides. I'm in terrible shape, and I haven't done this in a long time. Even if you're perfect, we could still lose."

"I'll do it," he says, "but I have a condition."

"A condition?" I turn to face him.

His eyes are wide and sincere. "I can't live the rest of my life as a horse. And you can't bear to be around me as a man, but you're the only one who can change me."

I notice he doesn't mention that he misses me. He doesn't say that he wants to be near me. I'm just his key to freedom. Is that what it was all along? Was the rest all some kind of act?

It doesn't matter.

"What do you want?"

"I'll do anything you need, but I get two hours a day as a human."

"And you stay entirely away from me?"

"No dice," he says. "I have to be close to you, or I can't keep you safe."

Keep me safe? "I'm not in danger here. Aleks is here." I turn away from him again. Looking at him is hard, but I can't tell whether it's because I sort of miss the Grigoriy I knew before, or whether it's my fear from the Grigoriy he really was underneath that veneer he used around me.

"For now. But he can't stay here forever. I need to regain my powers and be able to protect you myself."

Protect me? This is all really confusing. I keep staring at the ground as if it may hold the answer.

My boots are shiny and new, but they don't help at all. I have to discover my path myself. "I'll do half an hour."

He grunts, and I realize he's going to argue.

"It's what I can manage," I say.

"Fine."

I snap my eyes back toward him, and he's smiling. "I'd have taken ten minutes."

"Ten minutes, then."

He shakes his head. "No way. You agreed to half an hour."

Backpedaling now would be even harder, so I just reach out for him again. I expect to feel his shoulder, his bicep, or maybe his perfectly sculpted chest.

He takes my hand in his.

It reminds me of that time in the car, and my heart pulses in my chest. *No.* I can't do this. "I wish you were a horse."

And then he is, a gorgeous, breathtaking horse who's willing to risk his own freedom for me.

But a tiny part of me wishes he was still a man.

17

I've wasted an entire week, because neither Charlemagne nor Kristiana will let me ride until I've gotten my leg brace. So here I am, sitting in a doctor's office yet again. There isn't much to do in doctor's offices, but they usually have some interesting reading. Some people like to read celebrity magazines.

That's not my thing.

With Kris and Aleks meeting with some important officials, they forgot about my appointment. That means I actually snuck away by myself today. Kris will likely be upset when she finds out—I feel like I'm in witness protection right now—but it's nice to be free, even if it's only for a bus ride and an hour long wait in a doctor's office.

Usually I manage to find a medical magazine to read. Sure, they can be a little confusing sometimes, but I've also learned a lot. When you have a major injury, the more you know about how science and medicine work, the better you can advocate for yourself. In a country with mostly socialized medicine, that matters more than you'd think.

Today, when I pick up the newest publication of *Internal*

Medicine Europe, one article jumps out at me. "Pain: Is it Real?"

Of course it's real.

Right?

It has to be.

I've dealt with pain intimately for years, so I know just how real it is. So many human decisions are made because of pain, either as a direct response to it, or out of the fear of causing more. Inexplicably, people see capitulating to it as a sign of weakness—a flaw. But it's also the primary motivating force for most humans.

This article asks some interesting questions, and answers them with even more shocking examples. It shares quite a few case studies, but two really stand out. They both involve construction workers who were making use of nail guns. It's a tool that dramatically reduces the amount of work and time required for building a new structure, but they're apparently pretty common causes of injury worldwide.

The first person was using a nail gun to put boards down on a floor or something. Sweaty palms plus a nail gun were a bad combo, and a nail shot right though his boot. Of course, with a lot of workers on the site, plenty of people came over to freak out with him. According to the case notes, half a dozen people accompanied him to the emergency room where he was cared for, and everyone was suitably distressed about his significant injury. Upon examination, the injured man rated his pain as a ten out of ten. I doubt many people would be inclined to disagree. After all, a nail through the foot may not be something we've personally experienced, but it sounds pretty painful.

The second case was a worker who was nailing drywall into wall studs. In this case, something caused the gun to slip and pivot so that it was facing toward him. I'm sure that was plenty frightening, but when the gun fired, the worker saw the nail shoot past his face. His injuries were sustained from the weight and force of the gun slamming against his jaw. It busted his lip, and he had blood in his mouth, but it wasn't major. He took himself to the emergency room, declined any X-rays, and left the ER with an ice pack. He rated his pain as a two out of ten, most of it from a headache the blow caused, and agreed to take over-the-counter pain medication as needed.

The article then circles back to the guy who had the nail in his foot. It alternates between the two cases, because they both involve nail guns. Apparently all the screaming caused things to take a bit longer, but eventually they had to cut the boot off of his foot. The fascinating part is that, once they removed it, they discovered that the nail actually went through the space between two of his toes. He had a tiny scratch on the side of his big toe that barely even bled enough to turn part of his sock red.

That's it.

That was the extent of his injury. A minuscule scratch a small child could easily handle without tears.

But here's the important point.

His ten out of ten rating for the pain was, as far as anyone can tell, quite real. But that pain was caused not by the injury itself, but by his belief that there was a significant injury. Once he realized he was fine, the only pain he had was from his wounded pride. I'm sure the other guys who went in with him were not very kind, but the article believes that the pain he felt was real. Being a tough guy, he would not have wanted to blow that injury out of proportion, even when he knew it was a nail to the foot.

And now we're back to the follow-up care for the guy who saw the nail fly past his face. He went almost a week before finally checking in with his dentist for chronic, low-level tooth pain. He was convinced that the impact from the nail gun caused some kind of trauma to the root of one of his teeth and after nearly a week of persistent irritation, his wife made him get it looked at.

Only, when the dentist took a look, he discovered that a two-and-a-half-inch nail had gone through his mouth, into his jaw, and had been lodged there for a week already. The minor pain the man had been enduring, and treating with over-the-counter pain meds, that he was still rating as a chronic one to two, was in fact caused by a nail lodged in his head.

Holy cow, right?

The guy who had nothing wrong was in terrible pain. The man who had a legitimately horrifying injury was dealing with nothing more than mild pain.

If pain is the body's signal to the person that something is wrong, that there's a problem, then what does this tell us?

The guy with the nail in his foot knew that if there was a nail lodged in his foot, his whole life might change. He could be crippled for life, possibly, depending on the prognosis and the damage from the nail.

The second guy didn't think anything about his life was going to change. He anticipated a very short-term impact and didn't see any trajectory shift.

As I sit in that office, waiting for my brace fitting, I wonder about my own pain. Has it also been tied to my vision of the future and my ability to reach my dreams? Maybe that's why my leg has hurt so badly all this time, and why it has barely bothered me since my surgery.

If any part of that is true, I vow not to let it stop me anymore.

I've given up enough of my life. I spent the past ten years living without taking any extra risks. I've been afraid of Mārtiņš, afraid of pursuing my dreams, because the last time I took a risk, it led to a lot of pain and misery. How much of my pain has been of my own making? I'm not sure. But I'm not going to do that anymore.

"Mirdza Strelkova," a woman in pink scrubs calls.

I stand as smoothly as I have in years and force a smile. "That's me."

She leads me to a small room and points at a stool instead of the squishy bed I'm usually told to sit on. "The doctor will be in momentarily to check the fit of the brace."

It's a bit more than momentarily, but he does come inside, carrying a rather unwieldy black brace that's as long as my arm.

"Does it have to be that large?" I ask.

He rolls his eyes. "In order to stabilize something, you need a brace that runs from one solid thing to the other. For you, that's below your knee to your hip."

It's not lovely to fasten in place, with more straps and buckles than punk rockers wear at a concert. But once it's in place, appallingly ugly over my brand new jeans, the difference is amazing.

"Will this keep me from developing muscle?" I ask.

His eyebrows shoot up. "After a week of riding, you tell me."

Seven days later, I have no thoughts of calling the doctor to do anything but say thank you. But my thighs are *screaming* their disapproval.

"Why'd you drop down?" Kris asks. "You're supposed to hold two point for ten laps."

"I can't hold it that long," I say. "I was pinching with my knees, and my leg was falling behind."

"I know," Kris says. "It's pushing to exhaustion that's going to improve your muscle tone the fastest."

She's trying to help, but it bloody well hurts. I slide forward, back into two point, but my horse stops.

"Charlemagne," Kris says. "You can't do that."

He snorts.

This may be the first time in history that a trainer

addresses a horse as often as the rider. "When I bought Obsidian Devil, he had been stuck as a horse for months. He knew how to be ridden. He understood the cues. He'd been broken, at least enough to ride in chases. But you don't know any of that. While I appreciate you wanting to help, you need to let me tell Mirdza what to do, and then you need to learn to listen to her. Stop making up your own mind. It's not your job."

He stopped because I'm tired. It's kind of sweet, but also, my issues are my issues, not his. I pat his neck. "It's fine, boy. I can do it."

He turns his head and eyes me as if he's deciding for himself whether Kris is being smart or cruel. Something he sees must satisfy him, because he turns back toward the arena and starts to trot again.

He has a beautiful trot, but he's such a big mover that it's horrible to sit. It actually feels a bit like I'm riding Tigger, the bouncy tiger from my favorite children's cartoon. In that regard, two point is at least easier on my backside.

It's just my thighs, calves, and my lung capacity that are unhappy.

That, and my leg, which even with the brace aches so constantly that I've almost learned to ignore it.

Almost, but not quite.

It's like someone's stabbing me in the eye over and over without stopping. Except instead of my eye, it's my leg. But according to Aleks, I'm not doing any real damage.

"Nerves are regrowing," he explained last night, as if he was a doctor himself now. "It's natural that as they do, they'll fire a bit more than normal, especially since you're putting them to work."

Even with the attendant pain and sore muscles, being on horseback in an arena again is glorious.

If my students could see me right now, they'd probably

laugh. It's been six days already, and Kris still won't let me go over anything larger than basic cross rails. And even then, she's only setting them up now, at the very end of nearly an hour of flat riding.

"I could go over these in my sleep," I complain.

"Yes, you could," Kris says. "And each week, we'll add a few inches."

"We have to be able to clear combinations and jumps up to six feet in less than six weeks," I say.

"We'll get there," Kris says. "I'm not worried about the height." She scowls.

"What are you worried about?" Even asking that question makes me nervous. Because if Kris is worried about it, I probably should be too.

"You two don't look connected," she says. "More than anything else, a horse and rider combo has to have a connection." She sighs. "It's why Obsidian and I lost the King George."

"We'll figure that part out," I say. "It's just that Charlemagne's new and I'm just getting back into it."

"Maybe," Kris says. "But for now, do the flowers, the blue stripe line, and then circle back around and come over the raw wood jump."

"Fine." I doubt that doing little four-jump combinations is really going to prepare us, but if I'm fighting with my trainer in the first week, I really am doomed. I ask Charlemagne for a canter with a squeeze on the outside, but he ignores me. I press again, and he looks back at me.

"I'm asking you to canter," I say. "Remember? The squeeze on the outside means you should lead with your right shoulder."

He snorts.

I have to circle, which makes Kris scowl, but after another bump, he picks it up. Annoyingly, the second he picks it up, Kris shouts.

"Stop."

"What now?"

"I want you to trot into the first jump," she says.

"You only do that to keep the horse calm," I say. "It's not like he's going to race away with me."

"It's not the only reason," she says. "Just do it."

Which is why I'm trotting up to a tiny x like a total novice at her first lesson when Brigita approaches, leading my oldest lesson horse, Buckwheat, with a smug smile on her face. She's wearing one of her stupid little baby-doll dresses. She's always thought that dressing up like a teenager makes her look younger. It's especially idiotic, given that she's leading a twelve hundred pound horse. "Looks like I'm about to own this horse, too."

Charlemagne pulls up short, pivots, and snaps at her, almost catching her shoulder.

She jumps, her eyes wide.

It's satisfying, but I can't have him doing that. Not really. She might change her mind, and then I won't even have a shot at winning Blanka back.

Even now, he's glaring at her.

I kick his side, hard. Stallions should not be glaring at people. It was one of the strangest things that horse on *Tangled* did. That, and have eyes on the front of his head, like a dog.

"We'll be ready," I say. "It's just that Charlemagne's green broke, so we're taking it slow."

"You want to run a green horse in the World Cup?" Brigita's smirk irritates me. "Hoping to break your other leg, too?" She eyes my brace intently. Too intently. I don't like her paying attention to anything to do with me this closely. "I just came by to bring you a token of my genuine concern." She holds out Buckwheat's lead rope and drops it.

Kris jogs out of the arena and takes it—luckily he

ground-ties quite well. "You brought back her twenty-four-year-old lesson horse? Why? Is he lame?"

Brigita rolls her eyes. "All her horses are lame, just like her."

"Oh, great, then we'll just pick them all up, including Blanka, and this dumb contest can just go away."

"Nice try," Brigita says. "If you don't want him, I can just take him back."

"No," I say. "I want him. And any others you want to bring so that you have an excuse to spy on my progress. Feel free to do that any time."

Before she can react to me calling her out on her supposed generosity, a huge gust of wind rips past her, blowing her skirt almost up over her shoulders. Brigita frantically presses it down, but no matter which side she pulls, the other side goes flying up, almost as if. . .

"Grigoriy," I hiss. "Knock it off." Since I'm touching him, he has access to his powers, and I'm quite positive he's messing with her.

The wind immediately dies, so I was right.

Horses can't laugh, but I could swear his sides are shaking as if he's huff-laughing at her frustration.

"I certainly didn't come to check on your progress." She rolls her eyes. "As if I even care."

More wind gusts blow her back toward her truck and trailer, and she trots along, trying to keep her balance while somehow staying decent.

"This weather is the strangest thing," Brigita shouts. "I hope your horse doesn't spook and kill you. That would be a real tragedy."

I don't try to stop him from ushering her along. She's far enough away this time that I can just laugh.

"That was childish." Luckily, Buckwheat is as calm as can be, so Kris isn't in danger. I notice that the corner of her mouth is twitching. "And pretty freaking hilarious."

If Charlemagne sails over the tiny cross rails that afternoon with a lot more clearance than he did yesterday, well, I don't blame him. Brigita may have come to spy, but all she did was strengthen our resolve. Maybe Kris will notice and give us larger jumps tomorrow.

As if she knows what I'm thinking, she adds an extra workout later in the same day, and we aren't allowed to jump after it *at all*. When Aleksandr comes by to heal me up from my sore and aching muscles, Charlemagne follows him inside my apartment, tracking mud and debris right into my family room with his huge hooves.

"What are you doing?" I ask. "Why's there a *stallion* making a mess in my house?"

Aleks shrugs. "He was grazing outside your window and followed me. I figured you knew."

I glare, as if that will have any effect at all. "I told you to stay in the barn, or people will notice that you're not quite normal."

"Frankly, I think the grooms already know," Aleksandr says. "They've been making a lot of jokes that he's just like Obsidian and that Russian horses are crazy." He shrugs. "It's hard to disguise a Horse Lord as a regular horse to anyone who spends much time around them."

My exasperation bubbles out. "He *is* a regular horse."

"Speaking of." Aleksandr pulls a thick white envelope out of his back pocket. "This came in today. My guy gets better and better with this stuff."

"What's that?" I ask.

"Charlemagne's papers," Aleks says. "Won't you need them to register him for the World Cup?"

Duh. "Thanks."

"I wonder whether he followed me inside because he's sore, too," Aleks says. "I kind of thought he might be, but it's hard to ask."

Charlemagne bumps Aleks's shoulder.

I groan. "Fine. He can have his half hour right now."

"You're going to change him here, are you?" Aleks asks.

I nod.

"It's just that, I think one of the grooms might have seen him walk in with me." Aleks frowns.

Which is how it turns into a forty-minute ordeal. I have to walk him back to the barn, shift him, wait for him to change, and then walk him back to my apartment. But at least when other people are around for the thirty minutes Grigoriy spends as a human each day, I don't feel nearly as nervous or uncomfortable as I would if we were alone. And, if I'd just changed him in my apartment, he wouldn't have had any clothing that fit.

Once we're back, Aleks works his magic, which really is astonishing, and then stands to leave. "It would be easier if you'd just move into that apartment above the old barn," Aleks says. "Then you'd always be near him, in case either of you had a problem, and you wouldn't need to go back and forth."

"I keep telling her that," Grigoriy says.

"But this apartment's nicer," I say. "Much nicer."

"I'll happily pay to have that one fixed up," Aleks says. "But that takes time and a lot of people will have to come and go."

"I'll think about it," I say.

"I'd be more than happy to move all your things over there," Grigoriy says. "You wouldn't have to do all the work yourself."

I can see it now. Giant heaving wind gusts, transporting all my boxes and bags across the courtyard like we're on some kind of Disney cartoon. No one would notice *that*, I'm sure. "It's fine," I say. "If I go, I can do what I've always done and handle it myself."

"Kris says she wants to start tomorrow at seven, sharp. She has some vet visits she needs to make before lunch."

"It's a wonder she has any clients left, with how often she's been gone for races and your extended trip to Russia," I say, sort of hoping to keep him here, chatting, for another few minutes.

"She'll sell her practice soon, actually," Aleks says. "She said once we figure out where we'll be, she can restart it, but she thinks the inconsistency isn't fair to her patients."

Kris loves taking care of horses, but she'll always put their safety first, so I'm not surprised. Hopefully she can work out where they'll live soon, and hopefully it'll be here, not an entire day's drive away in Novgorod.

Once Aleks is gone, Grigoriy sits down on my sofa and looks around. He's altogether too comfortable in my apartment, and it makes me uneasy.

"If you don't want to move to the old barn, I could come here. I like your apartment, and I could easily move my clothing here. You have stalls just outside your door over there. You just moved that horse Brigita brought to one of them. You could relocate me there too, and I could always hear if something bad happened."

Oh, goodie. I could have *more* Charlemagne in my life. Just what I want. "But looking out my window at Buckwheat makes me happy," I say. "He's close enough for me to see the one horse that's mine whenever I want."

"Maybe that moron will bring more over so she can spy again." He shakes his head. "I still think you should just go take them, no matter what her piece of paper says."

Which, frankly, makes me nervous about his willingness to go through with the bet. "In the modern-day world, if the paper says she owns you, she does." I can't help frowning. "If we lose this bet, she'll own you. And we can't just say no and walk away."

"I've talked to Aleks. If I behave poorly enough, she'll sell me for sure."

I shake my head. "She could put you down," I say.

"People do that to horses. She could do it, and no one would stop her. You couldn't even stop her, not without your powers." I'm starting to feel extremely uneasy about the whole thing, now that it's getting closer.

He stands and crosses the room, extending one finger toward me.

My entire body tenses, and I'm flooded with adrenaline. It's not as bad as it was, but being near him still panics me.

His index finger presses against the spot where the skin is furrowed between my eyebrows. "Stop worrying." He smiles. "We're going to be fine. I know it."

I back up, still scowling. "You don't understand how the world works now," I say. "And I still don't get why you need to spend your thirty minutes as a human with me. I'd give you more time, like the two hours you asked for, if you'd just stay away. I'll promise to stay on the property, even."

"No." The corner of his mouth turns upward into a half-smile.

"Wouldn't you rather, I don't know, catch up with your friend instead? Or search the internet like Aleks is always doing to learn new things?"

"No, I wouldn't." He steps toward me.

I stumble backward, bumping into the wall next to the front door. I'm so very grateful for this apartment, but it's not very large, and Grigoriy *is*. "Stop," I say.

He does, but he narrows his eyes. "Why?"

"I feel weird when you're too close."

His mouth curls all the way up into a smile.

"Not good-weird," I clarify. "I feel like I might puke."

The smile disappears. "I know you're upset about what I did in the hospital, but it was to protect you."

"Said every single villain ever."

His hand clenches at his side. "I'm not a villain for killing the men who tried to kill you. I think most any man you've ever met would agree with me."

"But I don't."

"It wasn't even the first time they tried." Now he's standing right in front of me, a muscle in his jaw pulsing. "You would have died if I hadn't found you that night before you bled out."

He's right about that, but he's missing the point. "Protecting someone's not a free pass. If you really want to take care of me, you have to do what *I* want. Not what *you* want."

"What would you have had me do?" A lot of the tension has gone out of his body, and he's looking at me with curiosity. Wonder, almost.

"I don't know," I confess. "But I would not have had you play with them until they died." I still see that in my dreams. When I close my eyes. All the time. "It haunts me."

"I'm sorry. You should know that I wasn't playing. I was punishing, and they deserved that and much, much more." His hand floats upward, like he wants to stroke my hair.

Which is disturbing, since he was just talking about punishing people by slicing them up.

I flinch.

And he drops his hand. "I don't know what to do to show you that I'm sorry."

"Nothing," I say. "Do *nothing* to me, *nothing* for me, and *nothing* with me. That's what I want."

"Is it really?" That muscle's working again, and it just accentuates his powerfully square jaw.

"Yes."

"Fine. I'll be here, by your side, but if you don't tell me to do something, I won't do it."

I wish I could believe him. Knowing that he would listen to me, no matter what, would do a lot to ease my anxiety about the future. Proximity to violent men always leads to more danger, and men like him are never able to keep their promises.

Never.

Just like the nail guns that make houses go up so much faster, there's a danger in being near him that no one, not even the man himself, can quite control.

One stray nail is all it takes to cause a lifetime of pain.

18

Finally—*finally*—a solid month and some change into our training, we're jumping oxers and doing a few small combinations. We're only jumping two and a half feet, but it's progress.

I understand Kristiana's main motivation: to keep me safe. But with Charlemagne's skill level, we can clearly move up faster. I need to be practicing patterns, not incrementally doing small runs like the ones I teach my kids.

"See?" I ask. "We can go higher. Let's just do three feet."

Kris looks like she might throw something at me. I'm lucky she's only holding a coffee. There's no way she'll part with that until the last drop is drained. "Just do as I tell you and stop complaining."

So we do.

I've noticed that Charlemagne's paying attention whenever she gives instructions, and it's a very strange experience, having a horse who knows where to go as well as I do. The only time it causes problems is when he decides to get somewhere a little faster. He hasn't done many courses, so he doesn't always understand why we need to take the longer way round.

"Blue to red, then the purple line," Kris says. "After that, I want you to make a hairpin turn and hit the flowers."

A triple with two box oxers. Even if it's only two and a half feet for each, I'm excited.

"Once you come off those, I want you to circle and do the purple line one more time," Kris says. "That'll be a nine-jump run, and next week, we'll start working twelve-jump runs, set up more like the ones they may have in Riga."

A little thrill runs through me.

Sure, coming up with things to keep me busy and occupied so I can essentially ignore him entirely while also spending my half an hour a day with Grigoriy has been tiring. Sure, my body's completely exhausted every single day. Kris keeps working us both harder and harder. And some days, when we work on flat work only, it's also really boring.

I swear I'm doing two-point in my sleep.

But my leg's getting stronger every day. My fear that something will go wrong and I'll fall or snap the confetti bone shards into more ruins fades a little more with each passing day. Charlemagne's learning his pacing, and I'm almost able to guide his strides and keep his speed consistent. With Kris's help, we're figuring it out.

It almost feels like I'm floating as we take off, circling around to approach the first blue vertical.

Blanka's a wonderful horse, but even she can't compare to the feeling I have when I'm on Charlemagne's back. For the first time, I admit to myself that I'll be disappointed when he finally gives up and leaves. Could that be the reason I haven't tried very hard to break the curse and let him regain his powers?

If so, it's a terribly selfish reason. I should try harder to release him.

And I will.

As soon as I've defeated Brigita and won Blanka back, I'll focus on nothing else.

We sail over the blue jump, though Charlemagne picks up the wrong lead on the other side. He changes when I ask, though, and we approach the red one perfectly. . .and then we sail right over it. One short moment later, we're coming up on the purple line, and even though he knows to moderate his speed, Charlemagne's moving pretty fast.

Like me, he likes the jumps.

Sweat glistens on his neck.

As we sail over the first and then the second jumps in the line, my spirits soar. This is why I love it. I'd almost forgotten, after so many years on the ground.

My pulse beats in my ears as we spin around and head for the combination—a single, and then two oxers, only two strides between each one. He's going too fast, and I balance up on my toes in a passive two-point and lean back a bit, pulling slightly with my reins too, for a half-halt.

He ignores me, of course, and plows right into the first jump. He's going so fast that we barely fit one solid stride before the first oxer, clipping it on our way over. Luckily he slows a bit and we manage two, much more even, strides before the final oxer. When I turn back, I notice we dropped a pole in that middle jump. If we were at the Riga show, we'd have four faults right now.

On a two-and-a-half-foot jump.

"Alright." Kris crosses her arms. "What did you do wrong?"

"Chose a steeplechase jockey for your trainer?" The loud and clear voice comes from the other side of the arena. Charlemagne spins around so quickly that I fall forward over his mane.

I certainly don't look graceful when I glare at my sister, Adriana.

"And who should I be asking?" I arch one eyebrow. "My sister, who can't jump worth a bean?"

"Oh, I can jump a bean," she says. "I just don't like anything that slows me down."

She has always had a need for speed. More than anyone else I know, Adriana hates stopping, and she doesn't even like to slow. "What are you doing here?" I ask. "Other than hassling me."

"Didn't John have a wife for a while who was a show jumper?"

Kris shudders. "Don't mention Amēlija. She might come back and haunt us."

"Wait," Adriana says. "Is she dead?"

"I wish," Kris says.

"Okay, that's. . .disturbing." Adriana's annoyed with Kris at the best of times, but right now, she looks downright frayed. "Can we talk?"

"You can go," Kristiana says. "I'll cool Charlemagne down."

"Oh, good. The queen says it's fine." Adriana's lips compress.

She's lucky *the queen* hasn't slapped her yet for being a brat. When I start to sling my leg over Charlemagne to dismount, the jerk dances to the side. "What the heck?"

Kris starts walking toward me.

And my idiot horse takes off for the gate.

Which is closed.

Apparently he hasn't gotten Kristiana's memo that we can only jump small jumps, because when we get close, he sails over the fence surrounding the arena, which is much closer to four feet than two. He finally stops, his sides heaving, right next to my sister.

"What the heck kind of horse are you riding?" Adriana glares at Kristiana. "Did you forget about my sister's leg? You can't let her borrow a horse that's less insane?"

"Excuse me," Kris says, opening the gate slowly. "That's *her* insane horse. You can take up the decision to ride him with her."

Adriana's eyes widen. "You're broke. How did you afford a horse like that?" She narrows her eyes. "Crazy or not, he's clearly worth a lot of money."

I don't like her appraising look.

He probably is worth quite a lot, but I can't sell him so it hardly matters. Kris is pinning his bizarre behavior on me, but I don't even really own him. I suppose I don't blame her—it's not like she should have to make up lies to tell my pain-in-the-rear sister.

"Look," I say. "I'll explain everything in a minute. Let me get him cooled down and put away, and I'll meet you in the old barn."

"Can you handle that alone?" Adriana's looking at Charlemagne sideways, and I know that look. It's the one that says she thinks a horse needs a good lunging and a lot of tough-love training. "He doesn't look very broke to me."

"Nothing you ride is broke," I say.

She shrugs. "That's part of the job. You don't want racers to be too broke, but you do want the show jumpers to listen to you. Right?" She looks at me with her face kind of squinched up.

"Just leave it be. I'll see you at the apartment in five minutes."

"If you say so," she says. "But this can't wait, so hurry."

My pulse picks up. "Can't wait?"

"It's Mom," she says. "We need to get her out of there. Today."

I'm a little preoccupied as I walk Charlemagne around and around, and then ask him to turn into the old barn. I can't help wondering what's wrong with Mom. There's no way it isn't Mārtiņš's fault. It has to be.

I really ought to hose Grigoriy off, but maybe if I

change him, he can just shower himself. I yank the saddle off and put it away quickly, and then I point at the stall he goes into before I change him. The latch doesn't work right and he can open it, so he never argues about going in there.

Once I've shifted him, I waste no time telling him what I need. "I'll give you extra time today," I say.

The pants that hang over the side of the stall disappear, so at least I know he'll be decent when he emerges.

"Can you shower while I'm gone? I'm not sure what's wrong with my mom, but I can't—"

"I'm coming." His gaze is intent as he walks out of the stall.

"No way," I say. "This is a weird family thing and—"

"Your stepdad beat you." His words are curt, the vowels clipped, the tone abrupt. "I overheard Kris telling Aleks. There's no way you're dealing with him alone."

I grit my teeth. "I won't be alone. Adriana will be with me, and—"

"No." He stares me down.

"You're the last person I would take with me." I cross my arms. "You know why."

"Because if someone tries to hurt you, I'll kill them."

A chill runs down my spine. Because for most people, that would be a figure of speech.

For Grigoriy, it's not.

"This is why I can't be around you," I say. "You don't respect my boundaries or my rules."

"Not when you're in danger, no. I don't." He steps closer.

His pecs are glistening, and the muscles in his shoulders and arms bulge heavily. He may have pants on, but it's not nearly enough.

I look at the ground. "You should get the rest of your clothes on."

He grunts. "I need to shower first." He steps closer still,

his half-naked body so close that I can smell him. Sweat. Pine shavings. *Man.*

I can't think when he's this close, but this time, it's different. It's more like it was before. I no longer feel like I need to vomit. Now I feel. . .jittery and unsteady and *hungry.*

I hate it.

"What's gotten into you?" I point with one hand. "Go shower, and we can talk when you're done."

He laughs. "How stupid do you think I am?" His hand wraps around my wrist and gently drags me closer. "You come with me into the room, and I'll put on some clothes. How's that for a compromise?"

"But you stink," I lie. I mean, he smells sweaty and a bit like a horse, but then, so do I.

He snorts. "If I go shower, you'll disappear, and I'll be left wandering around like an idiot while you're in danger."

"Just let go." I hate the note of pleading in my tone.

He drags me even closer, until the side of my body is touching his. As ripped as he was before, the month of non-stop training has only made the lines on his body even tighter, leaner, and *larger.*

"Whoa," Adriana says from the entrance to the barn. "What happened that stallio—uh." Her nervous giggle is new. "Who on earth is this?"

I drop my hand and stare at her in horror.

Grigoriy straightens. Honest-to-goodness, we're caught standing in a barn, all sweaty, with his hand around my wrist, and he *straightens* and *smiles.* "Grigoriy Khilkov, Prince of Dolgovo."

"I should have known," Adriana says. "He's gorgeous, he's naked, and he's *insane.*"

"Actually, only two of those three," I say. "He really is a freaking prince. You should see his house. It's actually a palace."

Adriana blinks.

"So you think I'm gorgeous?" He's no longer looking at my sister. He's smiling down at me.

I spring away from him as if he might burn me.

But now my sister's view of him is entirely unobscured.

"Why's he wearing nothing but jeans?" she asks. "Not that I'm complaining." Her appraising once-over is the dirtiest thing I've ever seen her do.

I ignore her, focusing on the idiotic prince in front of me. One thing at a time, after all. "Go change. Now."

"I'm going with you," he says.

"No," I say. "You're not going anywhere."

"Why's a Russian Prince living in Kris's barn?" Adriana asks.

As if he's counting on her to keep me here, Grigoriy glares pointedly at Adriana, and then pivots and heads upstairs.

"It's a long story," I say. "But it turns out, her super hot fiancé Aleksandr is also a prince, and he has a few high maintenance friends."

"Wow, well, you know that I never date, but if I was ever going to break my rule." She whistles.

"Stop," I say, terribly worried that he might be able to hear.

"I'm actually really proud of you." She winks. "I thought you'd never date again. I mean, two or three dates a time or two in the ten years since Danils." She grimaces. "And if you ever did find someone, I assumed he'd be weak. You know, someone you could boss around." She chuckles. "Boy was I wrong."

I march toward her, ready to strangle her if she doesn't shut up. "Stop. We aren't dating."

She waves me off. "Fine. Fine. Look, I wasn't kidding. I came after you here because we don't have long." She looks around a little distractedly. "But where did that big horse go?"

"I put him out in the pasture. Why don't we have much time?"

"That was a short cool down." She shrugs. "But listen, I have a big favor to ask."

"I'm still broke," I say. "And you can't keep all that money Kristiana sent. You have to pay her back."

Adriana cringes a bit. "Yeah, I mean, I definitely will. I can't right now, precisely, but soon."

"What happened to it?"

"That bast—"

"Never mind. I don't actually want to know. Look, what's up with Mom?"

"He made a mistake." She smiles. A genuine smile. "And she wants to leave."

I look her over, head-to-toe, searching for more information. He's done nothing but make mistakes as far as I know, and she's never left.

The shower kicks on, distracting me a bit. He must have the door open, or I wouldn't be able to hear it.

"We should go," I say. "You can explain the details on the way." I grab her arm and head for the exit.

"No way." Pulling on her is like pulling on a brick wall. Which is nuts, because she's not very big. She can really set her feet, apparently.

"What?"

"I want that big, scary guy to come with us."

"Why?" I shake my head. "That's a mistake, believe me. He's worse than Mā—" I can't quite bring myself to say that. "But he's worse than Danils. Trust me on this. We are *not* dating, and you do *not* want him to tag along."

"But I do." Adriana's voice is small. "No one is worse than our stepdad, and I think your prince might intimidate him."

"Why does Mom want to leave now?" I almost don't want to know. When he beat me into jelly with the very lamp I tried to use to attack him, she defended him. She chose him over me. What on earth would make her leave him now? Out of the blue?

"He cheated on her," Adriana says.

I didn't think I could despise my mother more than I do. I mean, I also love her. She gave birth to me. She cared for me. She cleaned homes for me. She fed me and rocked me to sleep and sang to me. But she also picked the worst possible man to remarry, and then she chose him over her girls repeatedly. Even when he attacked us.

What kind of person does that?

But, then what? She'll leave him because he *cheated on her*? Isn't beating her so much worse than that?

I do not get it.

"I'm ready." Grigoriy jogs down the stairs, until he hits the landing in the middle. Then he vaults the rail and drops the last three feet to the floor.

"Oh yes, he's coming with us." Adriana's actually smiling at him. . .in a very flirty way.

That makes me want to puke again.

"No." I glare at him. "We already talked about this. You will stay here."

Adriana grabs his wrist just like he took mine. "He's coming with me, then. You can stay here if you feel so strongly about it."

Before I can even argue, she's marching out the door, dragging Grigoriy with her. He could easily stop her, but he doesn't. And when I catch his eye, he's *laughing*.

Fine. You win this round, you jerk, but you will pay for it later.

"You need my truck?" Kris is dangling keys from one finger when I reach the front driveway of Liepašeta. "It might make things easier."

"Wait, what things?" I ask.

"Your mom's moving out of her place, right?" She looks practically giddy, which is probably how I'd feel if I weren't too nervous to really hope for it.

Mom's never even agreed to leave before, so it's hard to imagine she'll really go through with it. It's likely to be a threat to bring the world's nastiest guy running back to her.

I struggle to understand my mom. She's like someone who wants a hairless cat as a pet. I don't even begin to get it, but those people exist.

I take the keys, though. "Thanks."

I climb into the driver's seat of Kristiana's truck, and there's a bit of an awkward moment when both Grigoriy and Adriana head for the passenger side, but to my shock and horror, Adriana gives way with a smirk.

"No," I say. "You can sit up front."

"It's fine," Adriana says, climbing into the back seat and moving Kristiana's piles of vet supplies and paperwork over to clear a spot to sit. "I was just surprised for a moment, that's all."

"I'd be happy to drive," Grigoriy says, "but I don't know where we're going."

"You're along strictly for moral support," I say. "You don't need to drive, talk, or even come inside."

Adriana laughs.

I glare at her before backing out and turning down the driveway. As we approach Mom and Mārtiņš's place, my hands grip the steering wheel tighter and tighter, and I realize that it's not Grigoriy who's making me uncomfortable. Somehow, after my experience with that horrible Russian mafia guy, I'm even more nervous about being anywhere Mārtiņš might be.

"Don't worry," Grigoriy says. "No one can hurt you when I'm here."

I ought to punch him. I definitely don't want him along,

and I don't need his help. But at least he's making me angry instead of sick to my stomach.

Is that progress?

Probably not the point right now.

When we arrive, I park, but even after Adriana hops out, I'm still gripping the steering wheel. "You can stay here," Grigoriy says. "I can go inside and help move anything your mother wants."

"She won't want to take much," I say. "But I doubt she'll even come. I bet *he* shows up and begs her to forgive him. Then she'll make a big production out of it, and he'll ratchet it up a notch or two, and then she'll decide to stay."

"You said he's horrible," Grigoriy says. "Why would she stay?"

I turn on him. "What reason has she ever had to stay before? Did you think before you came into my life, it never occurred to me to tell her to leave him? This isn't our first time trying to get her away."

"But it's her first time wanting to leave," he says quietly. "I heard that much."

"*Because she thinks he's cheating on her.*" And suddenly I'm sobbing, my forehead leaning against the steering wheel, and big, ugly tears rolling down my face.

"She should have left him for you." Grigoriy strokes the back of my head. "She's a terrible mother, but she's still your mother."

"Hey." I lift my head. "She's not a terrible mother."

He keeps stroking my head. "She's not a terrible mother."

"Actually, she is." I sigh and drop my head back onto the steering wheel.

He keeps stroking my hair like nothing crazy is happening at all. "She's a terrible mother."

I laugh then, but it doesn't sound happy at all. "I'm a crazy person."

"You're not crazy. You're complex, and that's one of the things I like the most about you." He's quiet for a moment, and then he continues. "My life hasn't been simple, either. My parents died in front of me when I was sixteen, and I couldn't save them. I had to learn how to master my magic and step into my role of ruling our people from my uncle, who wasn't magical. Shortly after I felt like I had a handle on things, I was cursed and stuck in an uneasy sleep-that-wasn't-sleep for more than a hundred years."

"That's nothing like my life."

"But you understand that things can be very black and white."

"Everyone understands that," I say.

"At the same time."

"That's just grey."

"Not quite, no. Your mom's terrible, and she isn't terrible. The world is good, and it isn't good. The light is bright, and it also creates shadows. Dark only exists because light also does. You probably appreciate your leg more because it doesn't work quite right. You understand the complexities and confusions of the world that most girls never will."

Before I can reply, there's a loud crash from somewhere inside the apartment. I don't even think. My hand just yanks the handle open, and I'm rushing inside, my heart galloping at a dead sprint as my legs desperately try to catch up. Grigoriy reaches the door before me, and as I push it open, he takes my hand.

I know why, and I should pull away.

But I don't.

"What was that?" I ask.

"Why is *she* here?" Mārtinš asks.

"My mother's moving in with me," I say. "Didn't you hear?"

He frowns. "That was a misunderstanding. She's decided to stay."

My heart sinks even though I knew this would happen.

Only, behind him, Adriana's still gathering up Mom's things as if she doesn't know it's not happening. And then Mom's head pops out from behind the back door. She looks. . .resolved.

"Where are you going?" Mārtinš asks. "I told you. I already went to the store."

"I'm moving in with Mirdza," she says, her chin lifted. "She needs help, since she just had surgery."

"She ran in here without crutches or a brace," Mārtinš says. "She's clearly fine."

"You're supposed to pretend to believe them," Grigoriy says. "It's the only way for you to keep a scrap of pride." He's staring at Mārtinš like he's a particularly vile bug.

"Who are you?" Mārtinš spits on the floor. The floor that, if my mom doesn't come with us, she'll have to mop up later.

"Does it matter?" Grigoriy asks. "I doubt we'll have much to do with one another after today."

Mārtinš straightens up, his brows drawing together. "You're standing in the doorway of *my* place. Tell me your name."

"I'm your step-daughter's fiancé, if you must know. I'm Grigoriy Khilkov, Prince of Dolgovo."

Mom gasps.

"That sounds just as cool the second time," Adriana says. "Especially since now I know it's actually true."

"A filthy Russian," Mārtinš says.

"Wait, he's a prince?" Mom asks.

"I was more surprised by the fiancé part, honestly," Adriana says. "My own sister didn't even tell me."

I don't know how to respond to his ridiculous claim. He hasn't said anything that stupid since the day after we first met. Although, he has spent most of his time since then with four hooves and no powers of speech.

"Mom, are you coming?" I ask, ignoring all of them. "I brought Kristiana's truck."

"No," Mārtinš says. "She's staying."

Grigoriy steps closer, still clasping my hand in his. "You will sit down." A blast of air punctuates his command, and my step-dad flies backward into his weathered armchair with a whump.

"What was that?" Mārtinš leaps to his feet. "What did you do?"

"He's standing right by me," I say. "What could he possibly have done?" I squeeze Grigoriy's hand and shake my head slightly, in case he wasn't sure what to do.

"I'm just here to make sure you stay polite and calm while we remove your wife from this miserable little apartment." Grigoriy smiles. "Though, I must admit." He drops his voice and shifts a little closer. "I'm secretly hoping that you do something very, very stupid. Ever since I found out how you damaged my Mirdza, I've been fantasizing most every night about beating you to death." His smile's terrifying.

My stomach turns, and I try to pull my hand away. This is exactly the Grigoriy who makes my blood run cold. It's the reason I've kept him around only as a horse.

But my uncle's sputtering is a reaction I've never seen before, and it distracts me. "You've been. . .what?" He fumbles and nearly drops his phone, he's so desperate to extricate it from his pocket. Then he frantically dials numbers on it.

If it were anyone other than my stepdad, I'd think he was calling the authorities, but he would never.

No, he's calling someone else.

"Danils," he hisses. "Yes, it's me. Mirdza's here with *her fiancé*, and he's threatening to beat me to death." He pauses. "Yes. Of course." He hangs up and puffs out his chest. "He'll be right over."

"Oh, good." Grigoriy's smile never wavers. "Her ex-boyfriend is the other person I've been wanting to meet."

Mārtinš clearly does *not* understand. "You *want* him to come? What did Mirdza tell you?"

Grigoriy shrugs. "Nothing, but her friend Kristiana told me enough."

"Did she say that he treated Mirdza badly? Because he didn't. Danils dumped her for being boring. Mirdza's been too pathetic to date anyone else since then."

"It's been a very, very long time," I say. "And I didn't refrain from dating because I was upset. I was just so disappointed with men in this area that I gave up."

"What Danils hasn't told her yet is that he still wants her," Mārtinš says.

"That's definitely not true," I say. "Have you been drinking?"

"But it is." Mārtinš has pretty much always been drinking. He keeps vodka on his nightstand. Today, though, it seems that's not his primary problem. "Danils has been waiting for her to grow up a bit and become more interesting, but if you think he's going to let you show up and marry her?" He snorts. "He was furious when he heard about you."

"He's delusional," I say.

"You'll see," Mārtinš says. "He's been checking up on her for years, biding his time."

This is all ridiculous, but at least Grigoriy doesn't seem to care much. He releases my hand and drags me under his arm. He leans his cheek against the top of my head. "It's not even my birthday, and yet, things just keep getting more and more fun."

"This isn't fun." I shake him off. "Mom, let's grab your things and go. We can come back for the rest later."

"I'll buy you anything you want," Grigoriy says. "You don't really need to bring anything with you." He glances around the apartment. "It doesn't look like there's much worth taking anyway."

Mom's finally letting us load her backpack and two duffel bags into the back of the truck when a large Mercedes Benz GLE rolls up. It feels like a movie, because everything feels like it's dropped into slow motion when Danils opens the door and climbs out.

I'm not one of those girls who's surrounded by drama. I'm a cripple who can barely keep a job. I live in an apartment provided by the charity of my friend. I've pretty much only dated one person in the last twelve years, and he's practically ignored me ever since we broke up.

This cannot be happening to me.

"Are you alright?" Grigoriy reaches over to take my hand again. He's either undeterred by my persistent brush-offs, or he's preparing to blow the house down.

Both possibilities annoy me. "I want to leave," I say. "Right now."

"What's this madness I hear?" Danils is staring right at me, wearing his usual—a perfectly tailored suit. His pristinely beautiful face and shining blond hair look exactly as they always do, but they're contorted into some kind of fury, the likes of which I haven't previously seen. "You're not engaged. Right?"

I should tell him that Grigoriy was kidding. The last thing I need is for that delusional Russian prince to start harboring hope that we're together. But the only thing worse than pretending to be engaged to him is giving Danils any reason at all to hope that we might date again. I'm sure that Mārtinš is just being insane, or that he misunderstood an offhand comment Danils made, but just in case. . .

I lie. "I know it's a surprise, but it happened fast." I lean against Grigoriy with a girly sigh, batting my eyes for good measure. Then I whisper, "Let's get out of here before I ruin this farce by kicking you."

Grigoriy laughs as if I've just said something hilarious, and slides his arm around me, dropping his face right next to mine. "Sadly, we have no plans to invite either of you to the wedding."

He presses a kiss against my cheek, and I do my level best not to shudder.

But Danils? That idiot looks like he's about to explode.

＊ 19 ＊

Once, one of Mom's clients gave her an entire box of bananas. And not a tiny box. It was a *huge* box, the size of a muck tub. At first, we were giddy. Apparently, they had somehow procured way too many, and they were giving them to everyone. We felt so lucky to be included.

I hadn't had many bananas. Fresh fruit was too expensive and we didn't often even see it, much less have any. I still remember eating that very first one—firm, but sweet. So stinking sweet. It felt like nirvana, or as close to it as I would ever come.

But then Mom didn't want us to waste any.

So we ate more bananas and more. More and more and more. And my stomach, unaccustomed to any bananas, much less dozens of them, was very unhappy. It protested. A lot. Frequently.

Now even the thought of bananas makes me want to hurl.

That's how Danils is, too.

When he first showed interest in me, both Adriana and I were shocked. After all, she's the prettier sister. I was always very thin, with a lot of hair, and very large brown eyes, and not much else. No other boy had even bothered to taunt me.

I found out later that Danils had laid claim on me at least a year before he even approached me. He was that kind of person.

But the day he smiled right at me? The day we first spoke?

It felt like I was eating that very first banana.

As time passed, my entire life felt like a bite of that first banana.

Until it didn't.

What was great at first was ultimately very bad for my body, my heart, and my soul. In the end, when he dumped me, I felt nothing but relief.

The notion that he might still have harbored some feelings for me is ludicrous. He and his girlfriend worked together to inflict misery on me, and now she's stolen my favorite horse.

"You can't marry him," Danils says.

A genius, he never has been. I shake Grigoriy off and take one step closer, holding up one finger to wag it at him. "Whether I do has nothing to do with you," I say. "Go home so I can finally free my mother." I glance back at where Mārtiņš is hiding behind the front door, only his head visible.

"Bring your mom to my house," Danils says, as if that's not the dumbest thing I've ever heard. "I'll keep Mārtiņš away from her, if that's what you want."

Mārtiņš's mouth dangles open.

"Thanks for the offer," I say, "but I'll pass."

"Not a Russian," Danils says. "Even if you're still upset with me, you can't date a *Russian*."

"What's wrong with Russians?" Grigoriy asks.

"We don't have enough time to even get into that," Adriana says.

That makes Danils beam. "Exactly. See?"

"I'm not lumping him into your idiotic generalization," Adriana says. "So stop gloating and get out of here."

"I've been meaning to find the time to come over and chat," Danils says. "But you haven't been responding to my messages or calls."

"He calls you?" Grigoriy takes my hand again, like he might lose me if he's not touching me.

"Get in the car, Mom," I say. "Ignore the men."

As if on cue, three more men climb out of Danils's car.

"Oh, for the love." I point. "They have nothing to do with us."

Mom glances back at Mārtinš as if he's the safest place around here.

"Tell your men to get back in their car," Grigoriy says. "They're making Mirdza's mother nervous."

"You don't give orders," Danils says.

"But Mirdza does," Grigoriy surprises me by saying. "And she just told her mother not to worry about something that's obviously worrying her."

"So you just do as you're told?" Danils smiles.

Grigoriy frowns.

"Looks like I've hit a sore spot." Danils steps closer. "You're some big man in Russia, but you're in Latvia now. You're surrounded by other big men, and you, apparently, take orders from your woman." He arches one eyebrow in disdain.

"Your men don't scare me, and you certainly don't either." Grigoriy shifts until I'm standing behind him. "But violence upsets Mirdza."

"Oh." Danils laughs. He uses a high voice to mock. "It upsets my girlfriend."

"Not girlfriend," Grigoriy says quietly. "My *fiancée.*"

Danils scowls. "She is not going to marry some pathetic, leashed man. Trust me. She'll call it off."

"You think she wants someone like you instead?" Grigoriy asks. "Her stepfather seems to think you still like her."

"I do." Danils puffs up his chest and looks right at me, where I'm peeking around Grigoriy's arm. "I never stopped. But she needed to learn how to behave."

"Doesn't look like she did," Grigoriy says with a smile. "I think your plan failed. If anything, she's become less likely to let you order her around."

"You have a girlfriend," I point out. "You have no business even being here, so go home."

"Brigita?" Danils laughs. "I dumped her after she fired you."

Is that true? Did he, really?

"Come back to me, and I'll make her give your horse back. I hear you can ride again."

"Not really," Grigoriy says. "She's only been cleared to ride *my* horse. No others."

"That's ridiculous," Danils says.

He's right, obviously, but I can't exactly explain.

"Your error all along was that you put strings on everything," Grigoriy says. "If this, then this. If you don't, then you won't." He snorts. "That's not how love works."

"You'll let her lead you around on a leash, then?" Danils scoffs. "Like you're her little dog?"

I wait for Grigoriy to slam him back against his car with a puff of wind. Or lunge at him and crush his throat.

He shrugs. "If that's what she wants." He smirks, just a bit. "I'm open to nearly anything she wants, including leashes. And a lot more."

"Ew," Adriana says.

"No woman wants a man she can order around," Danils says.

"It's true that no woman wants a dog," Grigoriy says.

"But if he's powerful, but he's also a gentleman who respects her right to make the important decisions for them as a couple, then yes. Women do want that. Or at least, I think that's what Mirdza wants. It's taken me some time to figure it out."

Is that really what he's doing? What he's offering?

"Think about it." Danils stares at me intently. "Do you really want to waste time with this filthy *Krievu* when you could be with me again?"

I can't help it.

I laugh.

Danils's nostrils flare and his hands clench. He steps toward me aggressively.

Any questions I had about what kind of man he's become evaporate. If that's how he reacts to me laughing at him, then I already know. I shouldn't be surprised, since he seems to get along with Mārtiņš.

Before I can say a word, Grigoriy releases me and grabs Danils around his throat, lifting him a good foot off the ground, the muscles and veins in his forearm straining. "You will never touch her again. You won't approach her or talk to her or ask her any questions, not unless she talks to you first. And no more calling or texting. Am I clear?"

The three men advance, two of them pulling weapons.

Grigoriy brushes his free hand against my arm, and the men go flying. The knife and the gun two of them had clatter against the rocky ground, several feet away from the men.

"What just happened?" Mārtiņš shouts from the doorway. "Something strange is going on."

Another burst of wind, and the front door slams, leaving my stepdad inside.

Meanwhile, Danils's entire face is purple and he's flailing around like a fish on a hook.

"I'll put you down once I'm sure you understand me. I

know your brain is quite small, so I want you to try and focus." Grigoriy lowers him a little, but his feet are still kicking against nothing. "When I release you, I'm going to ask you a question. The correct answer is *never.* Okay?"

Grigoriy drops him.

Danils collapses to the ground, dirt and debris soiling his formerly pristine suit. He's gasping, his hands both around his neck.

"Will you call or message my fiancée, Mirdza, ever again?"

Danils doesn't even look up.

Grigoriy kicks him.

"Never," he wheezes.

"Do you regret treating her so badly when you were dating?"

Danils looks up, his eyes wide, clearly nervous. Grigoriy didn't give him a script for this part.

"You do regret it," I say. "That's why you came here to beg me to take you back."

Danils's lips compress into a white line.

"You don't have to say it," I say. "I don't expect obedience from dogs. Only from boyfriends." I can't help smiling.

Grigoriy, though, he's beaming. "You may think it's an insult to say she's leashed me." He shakes his head. "It's not. I'd rather be leashed by her every day of the week than left. Like you." He holds out his hand.

I start to place mine on it.

He shakes his head with a smile still broad across his face. "The keys, sweetheart."

Something about the way he says 'sweetheart' makes my knees weak. I toss him the keys.

And finally, Adriana and my mother climb into Kris's truck. Grigoriy climbs into the driver's side, and I take the passenger seat. And then we leave this horrible place, while

Mārtinš hides inside and four men crawl toward their car, slowly.

Without asking any other questions or even saying another word, Grigoriy drives Mom and Adriana back to Liepašeta. He helps Mom carry her things into my house. "What about you?" he asks Adriana.

"I'll collect my stuff later. It's at another friend's house."

"Grigoriy and I need to talk," I say. "Get settled, and I'll be back in a moment."

I march to the old barn without stopping to see whether he followed me. I can hear his footsteps behind me, after all. But once we reach the old barn, I spin on my heel and face him. "Engaged?" I roll my eyes. "That was pretty high—"

He steps closer then, right into my personal space. "You didn't say we weren't." His eyes are on mine, intense and focused. And then they drop to my mouth.

My heart hammers inside my chest, and my breathing becomes shallow. "There were too many people and too many things going on."

"No one else is here now." He's definitely thinking about kissing me. He's even leaning closer and closer and. . .

I shake my head and take a step back. "Which is why we can talk, finally. We're clearly *not* engaged. You're not even spending any time as a human man. Remember?"

"But your mother and your sister—"

"I'll tell them we broke up," I say. "It's fine. They won't even be surprised."

"They'll be disappointed," he says. And then his voice drops lower, and it's husky and rough. "Are you sure they're the only ones who'll be sorry to hear it?"

My mouth is dry. My knees are weak. "I. . . Yes. They are."

"Really?" His eyes drop to my mouth *again*, as if I'm some incredibly distracting supermodel or something.

"Look," I say. "You and I both know that everything you said back there was a lie."

"What part?" He straightens, his eyes shooting back up to mine. "I didn't say a single untrue thing."

I inhale sharply. "That I leashed you?" I snort. "Please."

"That's true," he says. "I realized that's what you want—no, it's what you need. After the miserable men you've been around your whole life, *you don't feel safe* unless you're the one calling the shots. So that's what we'll do."

"You're saying that from now on, you won't do anything violent or bad unless I *tell you* to do it?"

He nods slowly.

"That's nuts," I say.

"It's my offer." He steps a tiny bit closer, and it reminds me of this kid's game we used to play. Mother May I. It's like he's trying to follow all the rules, but reach the front of the line so he can collect his prize. "I want you to feel safe around me, safer than you've ever felt. And if the only way to do that is to let you decide how I act, then we'll do that. Consider me your pet, if you'd like."

"You are my horse." My hands long to touch his cheek. But that's insane. He still makes me nervous. Too nervous.

"I want to be your *everything*," he says. "Your ride. Your protector. Your man."

What can I say to that? "You can't really stand aside and do nothing if I ask you to, though. Obviously, you'd stop listening to me and do whatever you want. Like going with me to my mom's today." Ha. Now I've got him.

"I didn't say I'd become a doormat." He shakes his head. "Nothing matters more to me than your life. That's why I killed those men. It's why I want to kill your lousy stepdad. I wanted to kill your idiotic ex, too. But I didn't do either of those things." He lifts one finger and touches the side of my eye. "I didn't even beat him until he was bruised and broken. Because you didn't want me to do it." He runs his finger downward, trailing it along the side of my face to my neck.

And then he stops.

So does my heart.

Waiting.

To see what he'll do next.

"You're the boss, now," he says. "Because I discovered that more than keeping you *alive*, it's my job to keep you *happy*. I think that's what real love is. When nothing matters more to you than the other person's happiness, you're in love. So now, if you're alive but not happy, that means that I've failed."

"That's ridiculous."

He lifts his hand and cups my jaw. "Mirdza, I don't intend to fail ever again."

20

or the next two weeks, I make up reasons not to turn Charlemagne into a human. Or to keep him in the barn during his thirty-minute stint, while I'm pulled away to deal with other things. It's fairly easy, between my mom and Adriana being *everywhere,* and Kristiana increasing the length of our workouts. Plus, with one lesson horse back, I start teaching a few of my students who are already sick of dealing with Brigita. It feels nice to be back to normal, at least a little bit.

By the time we finish our flat work, we're usually both exhausted.

And when we circle back in the afternoon to work on jumps, after a little TLC from Aleks, Kris pushes even harder.

"It's pretty neat that we can work this long, really," Kris says. "If you tried to do this with a real horse, there's no way he could hold up."

Charlemagne's ears both swivel forward and there's a little more spring in his step.

"Then again, real horses *listen to their rider* better." Kris scowls at him, but then turns the same look on me. "And other riders *make the horse* listen when he ignores them by using their spurs or a crop."

That's been our biggest issue, really.

It's a little like having two drivers trying to control the same car.

"You need to do your job." Kris glares. "And you." She chucks a pebble at Charlemagne's butt. "You need to remember you're not the boss. She's driving."

He snorts.

"This is a team sport, but only one person can be making the decisions about where you go, how fast you get there, and when you turn. The other teammate is supposed to be listening." Kris has taken to pacing back and forth along the side of the arena and barking commands like she's the second rider. My poor friend, who's supposed to be selling her practice and planning a wedding, looks stressed to the max.

I wish there was someone else who could coach us, but no one else really understands the fairly important dynamics of why our partnership exists.

Kristiana whips her head around and pins me with a stare. "Can you treat him like a real horse?"

I nod.

"And can you actually listen to her?" She drops her gaze to Charlemagne's beautiful head.

He tosses his head and paws the ground.

"Is that a yes?"

I shrug. "Maybe."

"Alright, let's try this again, but at speed this time." She tosses her head toward the starting jump.

Before I can even ask for anything, Charlemagne's cantering toward it, and I'm left scrambling to stay in my seat. We clear the first vertical, but I nearly topple over his ears when he pitches forward too much, and I'm not ready.

By the time we hit the combination, a single into a

square oxer with two strides between, we're going way too fast, and I fall forward, my hands scrabbling at Charlemagne's mane.

"You two are *ridiculous,*" Kris says.

"It's his fault," I practically spit. "He just took off."

"And did you stop him?" Kris asks. "Did you even try a half-halt?"

"I mean, I can't go hauling on his reins. It's not really a horse. He's a person."

Kris throws the crop she's been slapping against her thigh onto the ground. "I quit."

"What?"

Charlemagne whinnies loudly.

"Neither of you listen, so there's no point in me wasting my time out here."

I've realized lately that it's not just Blanka I want to win back. It's my *life*. More than a decade ago, I lost everything that mattered to me. I couldn't ride. My dreams of the future were gone. Everything went down the drain.

For the first time since that horrible day, it has felt like I'm really living. I might ride into the ring and complete a circuit in a Grand Prix... I might win my horse back, my heart-horse, and I might qualify for the Olympics. While I was training years ago, anything seemed possible.

It's felt like I'm getting my life back, only now, Kristiana's giving up on me. I slide off Charlemagne's back and try to run after her.

But my leg isn't having it.

After riding all day, I don't have the strength to race after her. My leg gives out, and I drop to the ground and start to bawl. Charlemagne bumps me with his nose repeatedly. I shove him away. "Just stop."

He bumps me again.

This time, I shove my hand on his face and say, "I wish

you were a man." Because then he'll be naked, and he'll have to go away and leave me alone.

It works.

A split second later, a very naked Grigoriy's standing in the middle of the arena, naked as a jaybird, except for a saddle pad he's holding around his mid-section.

"Have you lost your mind?" He glances around. "Anyone could have seen that. Grooms. That trainer John."

"No one's here," I say. "It's blisteringly hot, and we're the only idiots stupid enough to be out here. Now go away."

To my shock, he listens, stomping off toward the old barn.

Only my saddle and bridle remain, lying in the dirt forlornly. That leaves me to haul them to the tack room myself. English saddles aren't too heavy, but with my over-worked and complaining leg and the sun beating down overhead, I'm sweating and swearing up a storm by the time I finally reach the tack room.

The grooms are looking at me like I'm nuts, but I don't even care. I drop off my tack, wipe it down, and start stomping toward the corner of the barn where my apart-ment's located. I'm almost there when I hear him.

"Mirdza." He doesn't sound angry, which surprises me.

"I don't have the energy right now." My leg's throbbing, and I'm sweaty, and I stink, and I lean against the door-frame of my place and close my eyes, trying my hardest not to cry.

He's closer than I thought he could be when he whis-pers, "Mirdza, look at me."

I don't want to look at him. That's always when I get confused.

"It's my fault," he says. "I can feel that you're scared. I can feel your hesitancy, and I want to show you that it's going to be fine. That's why I rush toward the jumps."

"But it's not safe when you do that," I say. "You're the *horse*, not the rider."

"I know."

"And it shows that you don't really listen to me." *You big liar.*

"I know."

"If you know everything," I say, turning to glare, "then why can't you just—"

He takes my hand. "Because being around you, touching you, it makes me lose my mind just a little bit." He sighs. "Or maybe a lot."

I don't even know what to say to that.

"I'll figure it out," he says. "I'll get it under control, and I'll stop trying to take care of you. I'm working on it, okay?"

In that moment, I realize that when he's a horse, I absolutely *have* to think about him as a horse. I can't even consider him as anything else. I need to use my heels and the reins and *make* him turn when *I* want him to turn. Not a second sooner. I have to ride him like I used to ride, without worrying about my leg or his feelings or anything else.

That's the only way we can win.

For the first time, instead of just feeling guilty at the prospect of losing him to Brigita since he's not a real horse, I feel *sick* at the idea of her touching him. Of her riding him. Of her having anything to do with him.

Because he's mine.

"It's my issue," I say. "I'll fix it tomorrow, I promise."

He takes my hand again. "Can we just—"

I yank my arm free. He may be mine, but I'm not about to admit that to him. "No, we can't *just* anything. You're helping me so that you can get your powers back, and once I've won, I'm sure I'll be able to say it. I'll be able to convincingly forgive you for all that mess you created. Once

I can do that, you can get your powers back and leave, okay?"

"I don't want to leave," he says. "I meant it when—"

"No more of that," I say. "None. If you keep talking, I'll change you into a horse again right here."

"But—"

"No buts. You get to go do whatever you want with your free time, but I have to walk to the corner where the bus comes, wait for half an hour, get on the bus, and head for the grocery store. Then I have to shop for me and my sister and my mom and come back and make food for them. My mom's barely holding onto her resolve, and I'm exhausted and broke, and I don't have the energy to deal with this right now. Got it?"

Grigoriy frowns, but he doesn't argue any more. I decide it's too hard to switch him back to a horse right now, so I just walk inside and slam the door instead.

"Are you alright?" Mom's head pokes around the corner of the door to the second bedroom. Adriana and I are sharing, since that seemed more polite than asking my sister to share with my mother. It might have been a mistake. She mostly hides in her room all day, and neither of us have an excuse to go inside.

"I'm fine," I say.

"Was that your fiancé?" Mom perks up. "I haven't seen him at all since. . ." She swallows. "You should invite him inside."

My voice is flat when I say, "We broke up." She may as well get used to the idea now. How horrible would I be if I encouraged her enough that she started, like, shopping online for wedding dresses or something?

Not that any of us could even afford one.

"Why would you do that?" Her entire face falls.

"Mom." I straighten and cross the room. "It's for the best. He's not the right kind of guy for me."

"What does that mean?" She frowns. "He's rich."

"Oh my word, Mom. Is that really your number one criterion?" Is that why she married Mārtinš? Because if so, he's been a huge disappointment.

"Not only that," she says. "He's handsome. He's powerful."

"Mom, he makes decisions for me, and even though he knows I hate it, he can't seem to help doing it. He's pushy and domineering, and we argue all the time."

"I never argue with Mārtinš," she says softly.

That takes the oomph out of my ranting. I collapse into the chair in the corner of the small kitchen. "We aren't a good fit, okay? Just give it up."

"If he's not going to be around," she says, "maybe I should go."

"What?" I stand up. "Why?"

"I felt safer, knowing he was here. He scared your stepfather."

He scares everyone. That's part of the problem. "Mom, scary guys are *bad*. We're better off without them."

"But he was the good kind of scary. The kind that listens to you and also keeps you safe."

As if my mother would know a good guy if he slapped her across the face. "I'll keep myself safe."

"You're stronger than I ever thought you might be." She sits at the chair next to me and drags it closer to the table. "I bet you're wondering why I never left Mārtinš before."

If a cloud opened up and a rainbow Pegasus floated down out of it and pooped cotton candy on my head, I couldn't be more shocked than I am right now. My mother's asking me if I know why she never left my abusive sack-of-trash stepdad?

She never talks about hard things. She always just hides.

"I didn't think you and your sister could ever forgive me for what I'd done." She starts crying then, but it's like she hasn't even realized it. Big tears are rolling down her face, and she's still talking. "That day he beat you—" She draws in a ragged breath and carries on. "I wanted to stab him with a butcher knife. I wanted to chop him into pieces. But I knew that I was as bad as he was, for letting that happen to my little girl. I deserved to keep being beaten by him forever." I can barely hear the last sentence she says. "Until he killed me."

"Mom."

She shakes her head. "I stayed with him, and I didn't send him to jail, because that was what I deserved. To be punished forever for bringing him into your lives."

She can't really think that, right?

"But if I knew that I had also ruined your future with my terrible choice. . ." She wipes at her tears. "Your man is a good one," she says. "He loves you and he fights for you and he listens to you."

She doesn't know anything about Grigoriy or what kind of man he is. But I can't just let this go, this stuff about how she feels about herself. "Mom," I say. "You have to divorce him."

"I can't," she says.

"You have to do it," I say. "Swear to me that if I hire someone, or if I get online and find the forms, you'll do it."

"It's been so nice, hiding here with you," Mom says. "But I can't stay here forever. Eventually he'll get tired of torturing that new woman, and he'll come looking for me, and without your fiancé around, he might even hurt you again."

"Mom," I say.

She shakes her head. "I should probably go back tomorrow, but I want you to remember this. You deserve better than me."

"Mom, you're wrong," I say. "About a lot of things, but

mostly about this." I take her hand. "I still love you. I always will. You're my mom."

Her quiet tears take over then, wracking her entire body.

I stand up and drag her against me, cradling her against my chest. "You have to leave him, Mom, and whether Grigoriy's around or not, trust *me* to keep myself safe. It's time for you to worry about keeping *you* safe. You don't deserve to be treated badly. None of us do."

She stays there like that, hugging me, and I repeat the same thing over and over. Finally, I hope a tiny part of her starts to believe me, because she pulls back and says, "If that's what you want, I'll file for divorce. If you're sure it's what you want."

"It is," I say. "It is what I want."

Before she can change her mind, I search online and download the forms. Three hours later, I've had it notarized, and hired a courier, and I'm handing the forms off as Kristiana comes out of the big house.

"I'm sorry," she says. "I overreacted."

"It worked," I say. "I think both of us needed that kick in the pants."

"Are you sure?"

I nod.

"Because Aleks just took Grigoriy out drinking, and I wasn't sure why. Isn't he only allowed half an hour a day as a human?"

I laugh.

"No?"

"I mean." I sigh. "I'm an idiot." Apparently I come by it honestly, because my mom's a moron, too. But if she can learn and grow, maybe there's hope for me yet.

"So you still want me to train you?"

"Do you hate it?" I ask. "I know you're already struggling to find time for your practice, and with the wedding—"

Kris hugs me then, cutting me off entirely.

"Oh."

"I love you, Mirdza."

I choke up a little bit, then. Even after hugging my mom and telling her she's not trash for a long time today, I didn't realize how much I needed to hear the same thing.

She finally releases me. "I love helping you. I love *you*. You're kind and hard-working, and you care for your family and friends, even if there are precious few of us in the world who have been kind to you. I don't know many people that would still be a light in the world after all the darkness they've encountered, but you're one of them."

"Thank you." I drag in breath.

"Now tomorrow, you get in there and you kick that man if he's being an idiot."

"Do you mean Grigoriy? Or Charlemagne?"

Kris laughs. "You know, I did it too, using different names for Aleks when he was a horse or a man, but it's kind of crazy."

"What?"

"He's the same both ways," Kris says. "He's not ever really a beast. He's always a man."

"Some men are beasts," I say.

"But not this one." Kris's voice is small, but her eyes are intense. "He loves you, I think."

"He said that."

"Kick him in the arena, but be kind when you leave it, if you can possibly manage it."

With that, she heads back toward the house. And I'm left with nothing but a pile of thoughts I don't know how to sift through.

21

The next day's training goes *much* better. I treat Charlemagne like a horse, and he acts like one. But in spite of our seeming breakthrough, Kris works us harder than ever before. To make matters worse, Aleksandr has something going on—he's still hunting for any documentation or family records or something that will explain why Boris Yurovsky and Mikhail Kurakin's powers did nothing to Kristiana—so we don't even have anyone to take our soreness away.

And since I bailed on the grocery store yesterday, for a noble cause, but still. . .I'm stuck going today. Now that I'm buying groceries for three of us, I have to bring home a lot more than I used to. It's hard, with my leg, but I don't want Mom to leave, and Adriana's gone a lot.

The bus, as usual, is running late.

Which wouldn't be *so* bad, but I bought sour cream. It's been sitting a while already, so long that it's not even sweating. It's just dropped to the ambient temperature, which is pretty hot since we're outdoors.

I finally decide to walk to the other line, in case this

one has a bus that's out of commission or something. It's not as convenient, and the walk from the bus stop to Liepašeta is an extra mile, which is going to *kill* my bad leg, but at least I have some hope I'll actually get home. I sling my purse crossways across my body, gather up my bags—four in each hand—and start to cross the road.

That's when not one, but *two* of my bags decide to break at the same time. A jar of pickles shatters as it hits the road, creating a dark puddle that spreads all over the asphalt. A bag of lentils busts and scatters, some of them sticking in clumps in the pickle juice puddles.

Cars start honking.

I want to sit down and cry.

Before I can, a large black sedan pulls up close and turns sideways at the last moment, blocking everyone else who was honking. Then the driver's side door opens.

"Mirdza?" Danils is wearing his suit, a pair of designer sunglasses, and a half-smile. "Need a ride?"

I might have taken a ride from the devil himself—no. Even in that moment, I'd spit on Mārtiņš before I'd have gotten in his car. But most anyone else? Yep.

The bizarre thing is that there's no way all the people in the road know who he is, but not a single one of them honks now that he's gotten out to help me. It takes him thirty seconds to grab all the things that are salvageable from my bags and load them into the back seat of his plush car.

"You have two cars?" I can't help asking.

"Excuse me?" He opens the passenger door for me.

"I asked whether you have two cars," I say. "Though it's a silly question, I guess. Clearly you do."

"I have four cars," he says. "It's a stupid waste, right?"

Not many people in Latvia have cars, and most of the ones that do have old ones. We have the lowest number of cars per thousand people in all of Europe, and the oldest fleet of vehicles, too.

Stupid Danils has four new ones.

Of course he does.

He doesn't say much on the way to Kristiana's farm, thankfully. I'm a little surprised he knows the way without my help. "Thanks," I say when he stops. "I really appreciate it."

As if he didn't even hear me, he says, "Your stepdad's going to make things hard on your mom."

"What?" My hand was gathering up my bags of groceries, but I freeze.

"He called to tell me that she filed for divorce—your doing, I suppose—and he's livid."

That's no shock. "I don't care how much he—"

"I can convince him to let her go," Danils says.

Hope springs up inside of me. I hate how much I want that for my mother. Even so, I can't quite bring myself to beg for his help.

"I have a confession," he says. "I was actually driving over here to find you, which is why I knew where you were living. I looked it up."

"You. . .why?"

"Your stepdad called me about the divorce, but he happened to mention that you broke up with your fiancé." He meets my eyes, and his are hopeful. "That guy." His hands tighten on the steering wheel and his gaze shifts toward it. "I hated him, but he was right about one thing." He still isn't meeting my eyes. "I don't think I regret anything in my life as much as losing you."

"Danils, that was a million years ago," I say. "We were kids."

"I've regretted it all the same," he says. "And after that loser hurt you, I brought him into my organization so I could make sure he never did anything but fail."

What? He did. . . "Mārtinš works for you because you wanted to punish him?"

"I didn't realize until recently that hurting him might also be hurting you. . .because of your mom."

I have no idea what to say to that.

"Will you give me another chance?" he asks. "Now that you're not dating that other guy." His hands tighten again and he grits his teeth.

"Danils, I—"

"Can you just think about it?" He finally turns to look at me again. "Just one date?" He sighs. "I wanted to say that you *had* to let me take you out if you wanted my help, but that feels like the wrong move. I'll just say this. I've left you a gift at your barn. I tried to get Blanka back for you, but Brigita likes her more than I knew. Or she's angrier with me. Either way, she wouldn't budge."

What's he talking about?

"And I'll deal with Mārtinš. He'll let your mother go quickly. I promise." He sighs. "But will you just consider that sometimes people are wrong, but they can change? Will you just *think* about letting me take you out again?"

"I mean, I can't really—"

A terrible screaming whinny comes from across the yard, and I realize that Charlemagne's racing toward us, his tail shooting up and outward, his mane flowing out behind him, his nostrils flaring. He dead sprints until right before he reaches the car and barely manages to stop before plowing into us.

Danils throws the car into reverse and starts to back up.

"Wait," I say. "It's fine. That's my horse."

"That's. . . What?!"

"He gets worried whenever I leave," I say. "But honestly, it's fine. He must have realized I was back."

It takes a little more finagling, but finally Danils lets me go, pulling down the drive slowly with a lot of backward glances. The second I'm out of the car, Charlemagne latches onto my sleeve with his teeth and won't release me.

"Just let me put these away, and then I'll follow you to the barn to talk."

He stamps his foot.

"No, I won't go hide in my apartment. I'm just going to put these away, and I'll join you, okay?"

He fumes, but he releases me.

My leg had a bit of a rest in the car, but not enough. It's cramping when I finally get the groceries put away, and I hobble into my room for a moment to sit down. When I pull the blinds up, there's a horse head pressed up against the glass.

I nearly fall over on my butt. "Charlemagne!" I slam my hand against the glass and he backs up. One inch.

"Oh, for the love. I'm coming, alright?"

Two minutes later, I hobble my way outside.

"My leg hurts, you jerk." I slap his powerful chest.

He drops down to that weird horse-kneeling pose that he did on the very first morning in Russia, tossing his head.

I reluctantly climb onto his back because he's agitated enough already. Since he's the one insisting I do this debriefing, he may as well make it easier on me by giving me a ride.

But by the time we reach the barn, he doesn't look any less upset. I slide off his back, but he's still tossing his head, neighing, and nostril-flaring—generally being a big, fat baby.

"If you don't cool off, I'm going to leave you a horse and just walk back to my apartment." I put my hands on my hips.

It takes a moment, but he finally calms. He even sniffs pointedly once, which I take as a sign that he'll be polite. I point at the stall where he hides when I shift him, for decency's sake. Horses can apparently roll their eyes, which almost makes me laugh.

The very second he's human, he yanks the pants hanging over the stall on and comes shooting around the corner. It's hard for me to focus on what he's saying when I'm staring at beautifully full and rounded pectoral muscles, which are currently bouncing as he trots toward me, and gleaming abdominal muscles, all shifting in perfectly sculpted lines.

"Mirdza!"

"What?" I force my eyes to his face.

"Are you even listening?

"Huh?"

"I humiliated that man, and then you just get in a car with him?"

"He heard we broke up," I say. "He was just being friendly and offering me a ride when my arms were full of groceries. Actually, if you must know, he saved me."

While Grigoriy splutters, I go back to ogling his shiny, beautiful muscles.

"When did we break up?"

"Huh?" That's what he's worried about? "I told you I was going to tell my mom that."

"We didn't break up," he says. "We're doing better than ever."

"Since we were never dating, 'breaking up' is the best term for what we did." I cross my arms.

"Mirdza Strelkova, I'm starting to get really upset."

I can't help laughing. "You're not upset enough already? Please." I take a step closer and jab the center of his chest with one finger. If it lingers a bit, oh well. "If you can make up stupid lies, so can I. I couldn't let my mother plan a wedding that was never going to happen. I improvised, alright?"

"Next time you *improvise*," he says, "let me in on the play. I could have ruined things by not knowing."

"Stop being ridiculous," I say. "I made up that story to explain to my mom why she never saw you. Now, if we're done. . ."

His hand flattens against the wall behind my head, trapping me in place. "We aren't done."

I swallow, his proximity changing my flirty, admiring feelings to low-key panic. "Grigoriy."

His voice is a purr. "Mirdza."

I exhale gustily. "I'm not just saying your name. That was my way of asking you to move so that I can leave."

"I wasn't just saying your name either," he says. "It was my way of saying, no, I don't want you to leave." His head drops until it's level with mine. "Mirdza."

"What?"

His voice is a low, raspy whisper. "That time, when I said your name, I was saying that I wanted to kiss you." His breath is warm on my face.

I can't help thinking of the last time our lips touched. My heart accelerates, and a zing races up my spine.

He lowers his head half an inch. Then a bit more. . .and then his lips nearly reach mine. "Is that a yes?"

"No." My voice is stupidly breathy, but I can't seem to make it behave.

"Is it a firm no?" he asks. "Or is it negotiable?"

"What does that mean?" Nothing in the world makes sense right now. I want him to kiss me. . .badly. But I can't say that. I'd sound like a lunatic.

"I'm either going to kiss you right this moment, or you're going to tell everyone we're *not* broken up."

"Isn't that backward?" I ask. "If we're not broken up, isn't that when we'd be kissing?"

His devilish eyes sparkle. "Good point." His mouth

closes over mine, angling and possessing, and shifting me until his hands are resting against my body on either side, and I wonder whether a person can actually melt into a wall.

It's either that, or I'm going to become a puddle.

Nothing inside of me is doing what it's supposed to. Every single part of my body feels too hot, and too gooey, and just too much. I should shove him away.

I told him I don't want this.

So of course, my hands cup his face and drag him closer, my right hand traveling up even farther and twisting into his hair. I open my mouth to moan, and I almost say, *"Mine."*

What's wrong with me?

I want to crawl inside him and start putting up flags, marking him as taken for everyone to see. Which is absolutely *insane*.

"Wow, this barn must be hotter than it looks from the outside," Kris says. "I could swear that Aleks pressed me against that very wall."

More effective than a bucket of ice water.

No, two buckets.

"Oh." I slap Grigoriy. "Why did you do that?" I straighten up and throw my hair behind my shoulders. "He just doesn't listen." I feel the heat rising in my cheeks.

"Nice try," Kris says, "but I noticed your hand grabbing him by his hair. Nice move, by the way." She coughs. "Either way, sorry to interrupt, but we got your confirmation. You're in." She waves a paper at me and beams. "You're officially racing in the Grand Prix in just over a week."

I can barely contain my squeal.

"And that's not all," she says.

"Not all?" I don't understand.

"I thought you'd be happy to know that your other four

horses, the ones Brigita *didn't* return so that she could spy on you more?"

"Yeah?"

"Apparently Danils bought them for you and had them delivered. They're all back, in the stalls across from your apartment. You can run your whole program properly again, if you still want to."

❦ 2 2 ❦

The next morning, my mom's squawks wake me up.

"What's wrong?" I rub my eyes as I drag myself out of bed. Adriana's already gone. She's always been an absurdly early riser.

"He signed." My mother's hand is shaking. "I just got a notification from the court that the petition for divorce, which was only just served a few days ago, has already been signed." She blinks. "Once the requisite thirty days have passed. . .it'll be official."

He did it.

Danils brought all my horses back, well, except for Blanka. And he got Mārtiņš to sign—exactly what he said he'd do. I'm not sure how I feel about it, except that I'm utterly grateful. It's been a very long time since anyone other than Kristiana has done something so kind for me.

When I leave my apartment, helmet in hand, I'm already running late. I'm never late, so in spite of all the good news, I'm a little flustered. But when I start across the courtyard for the old barn, I pull up short.

There's a beautiful, shiny, powder blue Ford Bronco in

the parking space right outside my apartment with a big red bow on the hood. My name's scrawled across the front windshield.

I can barely force myself to take the steps required to reach the driver's door, and when I open it, there's a card on the seat.

Mirdza.

My name is the only thing on the windshield, and it's the only thing on the front of the card, too. It's written in a slashy, masculine hand. My fingers shake as they open it.

Mirdza,

Since we 'haven't broken up,' I decided I should take better care of you. It's not safe to take rides from strangers.

Don't take the bus anymore, either.

-G

PS- I figured you needed a car with space for lots of tack and a horse on its butt.

I circle the vehicle slowly to see what he means, and sure enough, there's a bucking horse emblem on the back bumper, right next to the spare tire. It's cute, really. And it's an American import. I never in a million years dreamed of owning a car, much less a car like this.

But the papers in the glove compartment have my name on them.

Mirdza Strelkova.

Is all of this because he doesn't want me taking rides from Danils? It feels like it. And for some reason, that pisses me off. It makes me mad enough that I pick up my phone and dial.

"Mirdza?" Danils's voice is so hopeful that I almost hang up.

But then I think about my mother's face. "It's me," I say.

"You heard he signed?"

"I did."

"I had to promote him to get him to do it, but don't worry. Once it's final, I'll be sure to fire him."

"Don't do that," I say. "Keep on paying him. My mom should get a cut of whatever he makes for the next two years, according to the paperwork."

"You're tougher than I realized," Danils says. "I like that."

"I'll do it," I say. "One date."

His exhalation into the phone makes me wonder what he's doing. Dancing? Pumping his fist in the air? Laughing?

"Just one time, though, and it doesn't mean anything."

"Sure," he says. "Just one date."

"I'll text you details." I hang up.

When I reach the arena, Charlemagne's already waiting. I can tell he's hoping for some kind of reaction, and that makes me want to deny him, for some reason, but I can't help it.

I'm mad at him for trying to manipulate me, but I'm too excited about the car to be truly angry. "It's beautiful." I rub his face, and he leans into my hand.

"He wanted to get you a red one," Kristiana says. "But I told him blue was more your speed."

"Wait," I say. "You talked to him about it? How long ago did he order it?" I figured it was bought yesterday, on a whim, after he saw me in Danils's car.

"American imports take forever, even when you're willing to pay a hefty premium. He ordered it, what? A month ago?" She looks at him for confirmation.

Regret steals its way through me. I reacted badly, thinking this was some kind of petty power play. But it wasn't. He wasn't reacting to Danils. He was just being thoughtful. And now I feel like the lousy one, for calling Danils and agreeing to go on a date. It's not like I owe Grigoriy anything, but it'll upset him.

Actually, that's reason enough for me to go.

I'm not my mother. I won't tiptoe around a guy, worried something I do will hurt his feelings. His feelings are his to manage, not mine. We aren't dating, we aren't engaged, and we definitely aren't married. If I want to go on a date with an ex to thank him for his help with a terrible situation, I'm more than entitled to do it.

Even so, I don't mention it during our workout for the day, not during the flat, and not during the jump courses, which we've thankfully improved at, quite a lot.

"You only knocked two poles the entire workout," Kris says. "Nice work."

I peel off my riding gloves and tuck them in my pocket, then I reach down and pat Grigoriy's sweaty neck.

A sudden gust of wind flies by and places the pole we knocked down on our last run back in the cups.

"Whoa," Kristiana says. "I just thought of something."

"What?"

"You guys could totally cheat," she says.

"What?"

"If you could figure out some way of touching him, he could make sure no poles fall. . . at all. Isn't that kind of his thing?"

Charlemagne tosses his head and neighs, clearly on board.

"But we'd be cheating." I shake my head. "That's not what I wanted. I want to win because I'm an excellent rider on an amazing horse."

"Okay, but come on," Kristiana says. "You're already *kind of* cheating. Your horse is not a normal horse."

I rub his neck. "He looks and feels perfectly normal. Obsidian Devil passed all the drug and chemical tests they do."

Kris rolls her eyes. "Sure, he did. But a magical horse isn't really a regular horse."

"Do you think I shouldn't compete at all, then?" I ask.

"I think." Kris folds her arms. "When I needed the money, I guess I thought it was totally fine." She laughs. "I don't know what I think. I was just arguing for Grigoriy winning by using magic, so I could be the wrong person to ask."

"It's fine," I say. "I'll just hop in my new car and head for the library to research the ethics of magic horses in the real world."

"Wait, I know you're kidding about the library, but are you really going for a drive?" Kris asks. "Because I want to go with you if you are."

"When did they even get it?" I ask.

"Remember when I said they were going out drinking?" Kris shrugs. "That was a lie. They went to get your car."

"That's a pretty good surprise."

"Speaking of magic," Kristiana says, "Aleks brought something up last night."

"Okay." I slide off Charlemagne's back and exit the arena. "What?"

Kris starts walking too, so I assume she's alright with following me to the old barn. "He said that when you first tried 'forgiving' Grigoriy, there was nothing for you to forgive. Maybe that's why it didn't work."

I think about what she's saying. "You're telling me that maybe I should try again? That maybe I could restore his powers and break the curse now." I don't tell her that I'd already thought of that, but that I wasn't really feeling ready to try. It makes me sound like kind of a brat.

She shrugs. "What could it hurt?"

"What do I have to forgive him for?"

Kris arches one eyebrow.

So she knows, too. It's the murdering and general violence, and that's going to be hard, if I have to be honest.

"He did it to save your life and to keep those men from coming back again."

"That's what he says."

"It's what we all think," Kristiana says quietly. "If you knew everything, you might think better of him, too."

"What do you mean, 'if I knew everything?'" I don't like the sound of that.

"Nothing," Kris says.

"Tell me." I tilt my head.

She sighs. "He had Aleksandr help him track down that woman and her child," she says. "He had money from the first payment he received on that wind energy sent to her, and he put out word that the same man who slaughtered all those men will eliminate anyone who touches her, without warning, if she's not allowed to leave peacefully."

"A violent man made more violent threats?" I'm not surprised he threatened to kill more people. But I am surprised, and impressed, that he remembered what I said about Yevginiy's wife and her daughter and took steps to keep her safe. But admitting that I'm happy with that feels. . .I can't do it.

"I know your history isn't mine," Kris says, "and I know it's very real. I still think that, as you get some distance, you might understand that he was trying to help you the best way he knew how."

"He killed the doctor," I say. "And that guy had only helped me."

"I mean, not really," Kris says. "He accepted a bribe so some people could come kill his patient, and that may not be all of it, right?"

I frown.

"You said yourself that he promised you the world before that surgery, and he didn't deliver. Is it a stretch to imagine that he didn't bother working so hard, knowing you were going to die?"

"Regardless, he didn't pose an ongoing threat."

Charlemagne bumps my arm and whuffles slowly. If a

horse could apologize, I imagine that's about how it would sound.

"The thing is. . ." I don't freeze up around him anymore. I don't have nightmares. Yes, it was harrowing. Yes, he made it worse. But he also saved my life, and I haven't thanked him.

Not once.

"I am grateful that he was there and that I'm still alive."

"Hey," Kris says. "That's progress."

"It may be all I can handle right now," I say. "But I'll think about the apology thing."

"That's more than I expected, to be honest," Kris says. "I think Aleks will be pleased."

Charlemagne drops his sweaty, huge head on my shoulder and lips at my face with his fuzzy, foamy mouth.

"Eww, really?" I shove him away.

"You're going to shower anyway," Kris says.

"Yes," I say. "I am. I have a date later."

Charlemagne freezes.

At least I can't be accused of lying to him or hiding things.

"Mārtiņš, as usual, was making our life a misery. I finally convinced Mom to divorce him, but he was planning to drag his feet and make her as miserable as possible." I drop my voice. "I was worried that if it took too long, she might change her mind. He's really done a number on her. She believes she's the trash he treats her like."

"Okay. How's that connected to a date?"

"Danils gave me a ride home the other day, and he offered to help." I shrug.

"Wait." Kristiana's lip curls. "You traded your mom getting a divorce for. . ." Her jaw drops. "And the horses?"

Charlemagne's pawing at the ground, his nostrils flaring.

I shove her and walk away from both of them. "Please. Stop it, both of you. He did *both of* those things as gestures.

He didn't have stipulations or requirements. He simply said he did what he should have done all along, and that he would love a date if I ever changed my mind."

"Whoa." Kris's shoulders slump. "Did you change your mind? Because—"

I hold my hands up, palms out. "Stop. Geez. Have a little faith in me. I didn't change my mind, but I've known him for almost my entire life, and he just did me two huge favors. The least I can do is let him buy me dinner and thank him for his help. It's the courteous thing."

"Let him buy you dinner?" My best friend is beaming. "I like this new Mirdza. You're repaying him by allowing him to be in your presence." She mock bows. "I'm impressed, Your Majesty."

I roll my eyes.

She bites her lip and then smiles even wider. "I mean it. You're finally starting to see what everyone else already sees. You're amazing, and he's lucky to be around you. Good job."

When she puts it that way, I feel a little bad.

"Just be careful," she says. "The ringleader sometimes sets the tone for his minions, and Danils's minions all over town aren't wonderful."

She's not wrong. I know he's a powerful man, and in Daugavpils, or really anywhere in Latvia, powerful often means dangerous. I think about that a little more, and it leads me inevitably to think about Grigoriy.

Only, instead of thinking about how I need to be wary around him, I'm thinking about how I may have misjudged him. I don't like it, but Kris might be right.

I might have overreacted that day because of my past.

Because of Mārtinš.

I hate the thought of that man causing my life to take shape a certain way. The thought of him damaging my future or my relationships disgusts me. But if it weren't for him, I'd probably have forgiven Grigoriy long ago for being high-handed in the way he saved my life from the villains who came to murder me.

"Wait," I say. "I'm about to change him." I clear my throat. "And I guess I should probably try apologizing or whatever."

"Do you mean you should try forgiving him?" Kristiana asks, her eyes wide. "You said you'd think about it, but I didn't think you meant you'd decide that fast."

"Sure," I say. "Forgiving him, too."

Charlemagne tilts his big, beautiful, round-cheeked head and my heart stutters just a bit. If someone told me a year ago that I'd meet a man who was strong, brave, powerful, and kind, I would have laughed in their face. If they told me he'd propose, I'd probably laugh until I wet myself. But if they told me he'd also be able to shift into the most beautiful horse I'd ever seen? I'd have called them certifiable.

But here we are. He's standing right in front of me. I've let my past get in between us for too long.

I point at the stall, a pair of jeans draped over the edge.

He circles around and stands still, just his head hanging over the edge of the stall wall. I place my hand on his neck and shift him.

"You can go shower first if you want," I say, nervous now that he's right here in front of me. Epiphanies are great, but when life gets real, it's hard to follow through. This is the scene in all the rom-coms when the heroine chickens out.

Only, I've been a professional chicken for a long time. I try to steel my nerve. The second he's clean, I'm going to—

"I have time." Grigoriy shrugs. "Say what you're going to say."

"Okay, then, I guess we'll do this now." I sigh. "I. . .my

uncle—who is also my stepdad." None of this is coming out right.

"Mārtinš is a festering boil of a person," Kristiana says. "He beat her mother for years, and then a decade ago, when Mirdza tried to intervene, he beat her half to death, shattering her leg. You already know how that's ruined her life ever since."

I blink.

"I heard most of that from Aleks." Grigoriy circles around, walking barefoot out of the stall to stand right in front of me. "I'm sorry that I reminded you of him." His lip curls even saying that, but I can tell he means it.

"It's just that violence," I say, "all violence, really." I sigh. "It's hard for me. I hate it all equally."

"I'm sure being stabbed and tossed off a train wasn't great either," Grigoriy says. "I know that thinking about those men who did that to you was hard for me, and I didn't even live it."

I realize what he's saying. I went through so much, all in quick succession. . .and he understands that it might have all been conflated. No wonder he's been patient.

He's a genius.

"I should explain something I never really elaborated on." He tilts his head, and it looks much more natural coming from a human than from a horse. "In 1905, when I was sixteen, the Imperial forces in St. Petersburg were being swarmed by protestors. Their commander that day was young and scared. He had his guards open fire, killing a terrible number of unarmed protestors."

Kristiana glances at me, her eyes wide. I can tell she's wondering whether she should leave. It does feel like a pretty personal story, even though, so far, he's telling it like he'd read a newspaper article.

"There was a large outcry, unsurprisingly, and another sequence of rebellions rapidly followed. The Czar reached out to my parents and asked them to talk to some of the insurgents. My father was quite a talented speaker, you see, and he handled a lot of negotiations for Nicholas as well."

"I take it that plan went badly?"

"My parents were attacked, shoved into an enclosed building, and while they were still inside, Yakov Kurakin torched the place. I screamed and cried and begged and pleaded, but he couldn't hear me. I had to watch as they burned alive."

Oh my word.

"When you say you abhor violence, I hear what you're saying. In my life, the only way to end the horror, the only way to protect myself and the people I care about, has been to become stronger than the people who want to inflict harm. If I'd been powerful enough that day, I could have blown the building down. I could have knocked Kurakin over. Or blown out the fire. But I knew nothing. I'd spent my time playing around instead of becoming strong." His lip curls in disgust. "I started practicing that night, and I never stopped."

Except now, he has no powers at all, not without touching me. Yet, he hangs back from me right now, standing several paces away, giving me my space. In the weeks since he woke from his strange sleep, he hasn't once pressured me or badgered me to forgive him. He hasn't even complained about being stuck as a horse almost every single day, all day.

"I'm sorry I've held you accountable all this time," I say, "for a situation you didn't create. I'm sorry that I've blamed you for the horror that came from it, even though it wasn't you who made the world such an ugly place."

"It's alright," he says. "You don't owe me an apology for being hurt."

"I do though, for blaming you."

"I'm sorry that I caused you all that trauma," he says.

"I'm sorry that I didn't listen when you told me to stop. I'm sorry that I don't trust the government to take care of the villains of the world, and I'm sorry that I wasn't always around to keep you safe." He steps toward me then, his eyes intent on mine.

"I forgive you," I say simply. "For murdering those men to save me. Even for killing the doctor. You did what you thought you had to do, and you aren't someone who can stand by and watch while terrible people keep on doing terrible things. That's better than the alternative."

"Do you mean that?" Grigoriy steps closer still, his bare chest gleaming with sweat from our ride. "You're not upset anymore?"

I shrug. "I may always be upset about it, but it's not fair for me to blame you. The world's a dark place, but that's not your fault. You're dealing with it as well as you can. So." I reach across the foot or so that separates us and take his hand. "I forgive you, Grigoriy Khilkov. For everything."

Kristiana starts clapping, and I startle, dropping his hand and scrambling backward.

I'd forgotten she was there.

"Okay, that was really good, but I think the reason it didn't work is that it was really specific. So maybe try it like this." She walks toward Grigoriy. "I forgive you, Grigoriy Khilkov, for anything you've done, and for anything you will do. I forgive you for hurting me, for failing me, and for being a scary man, and I also forgive you for what you've done in the past."

Kristiana freezes then, and then she kind of bows back- ward and then collapses forward, shuddering and shivering like she's caught some kind of horrible illness. Then I feel a strange sort of. . .pulse or something, and Grigoriy cries out.

Not in pain, I don't think? Maybe he's in shock?

"What's going on?"

"I don't think it was her," Grigoriy says slowly, his gaze intent on Kristiana. "I think *you* just restored my magic." He blinks, extending his hands slowly, staring intently at his fingers.

And then a light breeze ruffles my hair, sends shavings flying in swirls and streaks, and whistles through the top of the barn and outward.

"Whoa," I say. "Do you have your powers back?"

"Yes." Grigoriy beams. "I think I do." He throws his hands outward and flies up into the air, hovering a few feet off the ground. His hair whips around his head, but nothing else in the barn shifts at all.

And then he whoops, loudly.

"How did *I* do it?" Kristiana looks dazed, like she's utterly perplexed.

"You're the one who helped Aleks too, right?" I ask.

"But you were the one who could shift him." She shakes her head. "It makes no sense."

"Wait. You said the powers from the bad guys didn't work on you," I say. "But what about Grigoriy?"

Kris blinks. "He's never tried to hurt me."

"But what if he *did try* to do something?"

"Aleks has healed me," Kris says. "So it's not like I'm some kind of null who no one can touch."

"But I wonder." I wave at Grigoriy, who's now zooming upward and diving down toward the ground, tilting every which way like a superhero from a comic book. "Hey, come down here, Bumblebee Man."

Grigoriy looks annoyed when he lands. "What did you call me?"

"Nevermind that," I say. "I need a favor."

"What?"

"Now that you have your powers back. . ."

His chest puffs up. He's clearly very pleased.

"Can you lift me in the air?"

The smile steals across his face. "Of course."

I try my best not to panic when gentle pressure from all sides wraps around me and I float up into the air more than a foot. "That's plenty. Please put me down."

He does, but he looks disappointed about it.

"Now. Do the same thing to her." I point at Kris.

Her eyes widen. "But why?"

"Just do it?"

Grigoriy shrugs. And then he scowls. And then he leans forward a bit, his brow furrowing even deeper, his body angling more, like a runner about to take off. "What's going on?"

"It didn't work, right?" I ask.

Kristiana blinks.

"See?" I shake my head. "It's more than just the villains. None of their powers work on you. . .except for Aleksandr's."

❄ 23 ❄

"I have to go tell Aleksandr you have your powers back," Kris says. "And I need to tell him about what we just tried, too. But you." She beams at Grigoriy. "I'm so happy for you. And also, no floating or flying or zooming where anyone else can see you. Stay inside the barn if you're floating, am I clear?"

She's downright frightening when she's giving orders.

Grigoriy salutes her. "Aye."

She rolls her eyes before trotting out the door.

And the second she's gone, the huge, half-naked mage lands right behind me.

"I'm happy for you," I say, but my tone is flat. I'm clearly not happy.

But why not?

"What's wrong?" he asks, his voice low.

"Nothing." I poke his shoulder. "You need to go shower."

"If I do, you'll leave."

I shrug. "I have a date to get ready for."

He grits his teeth. "I forgot about that."

"What do you care?" I ask. "You're leaving soon anyway."

"Leaving?" He frowns. "Why?"

"You can change back and forth any time you want, and now you can use your wind power whenever."

"That's true." His brow furrows. "But why do you sound all grumpy about that?"

He won't need to hold my hand anymore, and he won't need to follow me around. Or stay where I am. Am I actually upset because I don't want him to leave? That's stupid. I want my life back. Now that my leg works, I want. . .

What do I want?

"I'm going to shower. We can talk about it more later."

I expect him to stop me, to complain that I'm going, or to insist that I stay and talk it out. But he doesn't. He lets me go. And even after I'm ready for my date with my makeup done and my hair styled, I don't see him.

Which means I was right.

He was the monumental nuisance that he has been because he needed me that whole time. Now that he's been restored, I'm free to do as I'd like. Just like every other man I've met, he wanted something from me, and once he got it, bam.

Done.

I drag a few breaths in and out, until I'm sure I won't start crying, and then I slide into some cute flats for my date. Maybe one day I'll risk heels again, but with my leg, probably not. The fashion's really not worth that kind of pain.

I'm on my way out—it'll be my first time driving my new car—when Adriana reaches the apartment. "Wow. You look pretty fancy to be teaching lessons."

"I don't have any set up for today," I say. "So far, I only have them on Tuesdays and Thursdays."

"Enjoy that while it lasts," Adriana says. "I'm sure Kristiana will be working you to the bone again soon enough."

"She never—"

Adriana waves her hand through the air. "I know, I know. She walks on water. She sweats sunshine. Whatever. The point is, you look really nice. Are you going somewhere?"

"Actually."

Adriana grabs my wrists and squeezes, her eyes lighting up. "Please tell me we're going out. You're ready to get over that hunky, too-good-too-be-true prince guy, and we're going drinking?"

My sister rarely drinks, but when she does. . . The mornings after I drink with her have been the worst hangovers of my life. I shake my head. "Sorry. I've got a date."

"A date?" Her face falls, she drops my hands, and her shoulders slump. "Well, that's depressing."

Only my sister would think a date was depressing. "You're supposed to say, 'good for you, getting out there again.'"

"Dating's stupid." My gorgeous, smart, petite, blond-bombshell sister drops onto the end of the sofa. "Boys are stupider, and any girls who date them are the stupidest."

"Wow, that's a lot of stupid for one sentence."

She sighs dramatically.

"At some point, you might actually meet someone who could change your mind."

She holds up a finger. "Dad died."

"Okay, but—"

She waves a second finger. "Danils screwed you."

"Well, the—"

She melodramatically holds up a third. "Mārtinš. . .I think the name is enough." She shudders.

Maybe she's right.

"And now, even the fairy tale prince—gorgeous, rich,

and chivalrous—has let you down." She waves her hands in the air. "Just get out of here, you never-ending font of ridiculous hope."

I grab my purse and head for the door, a smile playing at the corners of my mouth.

"Wait."

I turn around slowly. She's flipped around on the sofa and she's hugging the back, her eyes intense. She spears me with a very pointed look. "Who's the date with?"

Aww, crap. I almost made it out without having to tell her. "Just someone I know from school."

She frowns. "You're not exactly Einstein. I know everyone you knew from school, so that fact that you're being vague means. . ." Her jaw drops. "It's not Henri, right?" She pulls a face. "Because his breath."

"Judging people for how they looked or sounded in grade school seems pretty unfair," I say.

"Not looked," she says. "Not sounded, either." She stands up and stomps around the couch. "Is it Henri? Because I swear—"

"It's Danils, okay?"

She throws her hands up in the air. "No." She shakes her head. "I forbid it. Do you hear me?"

I roll my eyes. "You're worse than Kris. Look, it's not serious. He returned my horses, probably at a significant cost, and he pushed he-who-shall-not-be-named into signing the divorce papers. He at least deserves a dinner."

"Thank you," Adriana says.

"Huh?"

"Oh," she says. "I'm sorry. I thought maybe you forgot how to say it. That's what he deserves. Those two words and nothing more. He certainly has not earned a date with you. Because that's going back to the bad place, and we don't go there."

She's still ranting when I walk out the door, slamming it in her face. I really don't think she gets to stay with me for free, sponging off me, or at the very least sponging off Kristiana—a friend she's always abusing—while simultaneously ripping me a new one about my personal choices. I didn't ask her why she's flat broke, again. I didn't press her about how she lost her job. She can leave me alone about where I go for dinner.

But of course, slamming the door doesn't work. She just opens it and shoves right through, doggedly following me out to the parking area.

"—until you understand that it's the same as with Mom. He's the kind of guy who—"

I press a button and the car lights up and beeps at the same time. I can't help a giddy smile. I open the driver's side and slide into the seat, my bum smoothly shifting into a comfortable spot.

And the smell.

The new-car smell is heavenly. I've never really experienced it, only heard about it.

"What on earth are you doing?" Adriana gapes, as if she just noticed I'm sitting in a brand new car. "Did you steal this?"

I laugh. It just bubbles right out of me.

"Wait. Did Danils *buy you this*?" she asks. "That filthy, disgusting pig. I'm going to castrate him, I swear. Where does he get off, thinking he can *buy* you—"

"Adriana!"

She finally shuts up.

"This is a gift from Grigoriy, and I'll explain it all later, okay?" With that, I close the door and put the car in reverse. Watching her expression as I drive away is now the highlight of my day.

My life's confusing, but at least I'm not the only one left reeling.

By the time I reach Skovorodka, one of my favorite

places, it's totally slammed. I should have known—it's a Friday night, after all. Of course, Danils is waiting for me, and when he sees me climbing out of my new Bronco, he waves and heads over to meet me.

"This is a nice car," he says. "Where'd you get it?"

"I thought it was a gift from you," I say.

He blinks.

I head for the door, towing him behind me like a kitten following its barn-cat mother. "I'm kidding. Grigoriy gave it to me."

Now he's frowning. "I thought you broke up."

"We did," I say. "But I guess he hasn't given up yet."

His frown deepens. "That's concerning. There's something off about that guy. I swear, no matter how many times I go over it, it's like he had some kind of pressurized air or something. Like a leaf blower in his pocket, or..." He shakes his head. "I hated him."

"He didn't like you much, either," I say.

"Let's not talk about him anymore."

"Done."

The maître d' seats us right away, as I'd expect with Danils, no matter how busy it is. There are a few perks to going out with someone who has connections in the modern world.

"I assume you still like *šašlik*," Danils says. "But if that's wrong, I can also personally recommend their burgers and their spiced chicken with *adžika*."

"Sounds like you know the menu better than I do," the waitress says with a smile.

I hate being out with someone with whom everyone flirts. It always happened with Danils, and recently, the same thing happened with Grigoriy. I mean, it's probably all powerful men, but why can't women just do their jobs? Why do they always have to be flirty with men when they're out with other women? I don't even *like* Danils and it still annoys me.

The waitress hands Danils his menu first and then drops mine on the table.

I pick it up. "I still like *šašlik*, but I'll take a look and let you know what sounds best."

"Sounds like you two are getting to know each other again?" The waitress asks.

"I'm hoping to win her back." Danils half-smiles at her. "What do you think my odds are?"

The waitress looks between us, her eyes dropping to my leg. That means she noticed my limp on the way in. I can tell she's evaluating my face—not bad—and my figure—slim, but not very curvy. "I'd say you look like you'd have your pick of any woman in the room, Mr. Andris." She smiles. "Including your current date."

"Waitress," a man with a deep voice says. "Excuse me." He points at a table. "The host said I could sit here?"

He's so loud that I can't help turning to look as well. And that's when it hits me—I turned because I recognized the voice, too.

Grigoriy Khilkov, dressed in an impeccable suit I'm quite sure I never saw him purchase, is sitting down at a table not three feet away from us. I have to do a double take, because he's gotten a haircut. What used to be a shaggy mess is now the latest style. Longish on top, swept sideways, and close cut on the sides.

The waitress rushes over to hand him a menu. "Certainly, sir."

I look away immediately, but it's too late.

He saw me looking. And his knowing smile tells me he's pleased.

Somehow, miraculously, Danils didn't notice. For the first time since meeting him, I wish Grigoriy had a phone of his own. He'd be getting a blistering text.

I have to settle for messaging Kris instead.

"Is something wrong?" Danils asks.

I slide my phone back into my purse. "No, I'm fine. I think the chicken *šašlik* will be perfect. With the fries and soup."

"I'll get a burger and you can try it."

He's showing off, and it's kind of cute. I knew the teenage boy who had his parents' money but not much confidence, and now I can watch the man he's turned into. I almost wish poor Henri could be here, too. We should set up some kind of reunion for all our high school friends. I barely see any of them around, which is silly. I'm sure they all live relatively close.

The waitress shows up a moment later to take our order. "Unfortunately, we don't have any burgers." She sighs.

"What?" Danils asks. "How can you not have burgers?"

"It was a really bizarre thing, actually," she says. "It just happened in the last few minutes. The grill fire just blazed up, and every burger our chef put on burned up over and over. It was like there was someone blowing on the fire to make it too hot every single time."

Blowing on the fire? I glance sideways.

Grigoriy's smiling.

I don't like it.

"The spiced chicken with *adžika*, then," Danils says.

Not two minutes after she leaves, she returns, a smudge of something across her forehead. "I'm so sorry." She shakes her head. "This is so strange, but a wind gust blew a bunch of leaves and trash through a window and it landed right in the pepper sauce," she says.

"You're kidding," Danils says. "How could that happen?"

She shrugs. "I'm so sorry. Can we try just one more time?"

"You like borscht," I say. "Right?"

I know Grigoriy likes it, so he's unlikely to ruin something he'll want to eat himself.

"Why don't you order that, and the *šašlik*, like me," I say. I glare over Danils's shoulder at Grigoriy.

"Sure, sure," he says. As the waitress is walking away, he says, "After this, we can head over to Cafe Imbir. I know you love their cake."

"Do they still have that orange cake? The one with the mousse topping?"

"Just last week, I saw it through the glass."

"I've been craving that, actually," I say. "I can't believe you checked on it."

"Every time I see it, it reminds me—" His glass, for no apparent reason, topples over, spilling water all over him. Danils leaps to his feet, and I realize it all landed on his crotch.

I can't help it. I laugh. But I clap my hand over my mouth the very second I do, so hopefully he doesn't realize I'm laughing.

"I'm so sorry," I say. "I wonder if this table's uneven."

"Maybe I should head to the bathroom," he says, "and see if I can clean this up."

"Good luck," Grigoriy snickers. "Once he comes out of there, everyone will assume he wet himself."

The second Danils is gone, I round on Grigoriy, gripping the back of my chair. "What are you doing here?"

He shrugs. "I was hungry."

I roll my eyes so hard, I worry they'll pop out and fall to the floor. "You followed me here."

"So what if I did? Isn't Latvia a free country?"

"I'm here on a date," I hiss. "And I can hardly pay attention—"

"Don't look now," Grigoriy says. "I think your pee-pants prince is on his way back."

I spin around so fast it wrenches my neck.

And there's no one there.

I'm going to kill him. I turn back again. "Do not call him pee pants, and do not do anything else, or I swear, I will—"

"What?" He leans closer. "What will you do?" He lifts both eyebrows, his eyes dancing.

"Just, don't do anything else, okay?"

"But it's so hard," he says. "He's trying his very best to impress you, and he's just so. . .what's the word?"

This time, it *is* Danils coming back. I see him out of the corner of my eye.

"Oh. Right. I remember now," Grigoriy says. He hisses the last word, right as Danils comes close enough to hear. "Boring."

"Boring?" Danils glances his way, and his eyes almost bug out. "What's he doing here?"

"Just pretend he's not here," I say. "That's what I'm doing."

"I can't do that," Danils says. "He needs to leave."

"I'm having dinner, just like you." Grigoriy lifts his water and smiles.

Luckily, our food arrives before Danils's head can actually explode. Every time Danils turns around, Grigoriy's humming to himself, talking to his food, or pretending that he's batting at invisible things around his head.

It's irritating.

It's distracting.

And it's pretty freaking funny.

I'm not sure when my irritation changes entirely into entertainment, but sometime before Danils asks for the check.

"Oh, I'm sorry," the waitress says. "The gentleman there already paid." She points behind Danils, as I somehow knew she would. Then she smiles at Grigoriy. And *blushes*.

"He *what*?" Danils's face turns bright red. "You can't just let people pay for other people." He crumples his linen napkin in his fist. "How could you—" He throws the napkin down and stands up. "I want to pay for his meal, then."

"He's already paid," she says. "I'm sorry."

Danils turns around to glare, but I touch his arm. "Can you just let it go?"

He yanks his arm away. "Fine. Let's get some—"

"Waitress," Grigoriy says. "Where did you say that amazing cake was?" He stands up. "I especially love *orange* cake, if you know of any place that sells that."

"Why yes, Cafe Imbir's famous for its cakes and pancakes," she says. "And I think these two were just talking about the orange cake earlier."

Danils swallows, his Adam's apple bobbing, and then he lets out a string of expletives unlike any I've ever heard.

"Sir." The waitress looks around, her eyes wide, her pupils dilated. "I'm going to have to ask you to leave. You're distressing the other guests."

Danils snatches his jacket, which he'd laid across the back of a chair, and marches out the door. I start to follow him, Grigoriy falling into step beside me.

"That man looks a little unhinged," he whispers. "I think you'd be safer going home with me."

I can't help looking at his face, which is a mistake. I've spent so much time looking at his horse form, or at his head right after a shift, with his hair askew and tousled, that I'm almost unprepared to see his human face straight on, with his perfect brows slanted over his spectacular eyes. His high cheekbones. His flawless skin, and his square jaw.

Just a little dark stubble finishes it off, and with his hair like this. . . Exceptional beauty tempered by almost overpowering masculinity. It leaves me a little breathless.

"I drove myself," I say.

"Perfect," he says. "I had a friend drop me off." His eyes

sparkle. His head cocks to the side. "And I've been *dying* to drive the new Bronco. I hear it handles great."

I laugh then, out loud, like a complete flirt. "It does, yeah."

"You like it, then?"

I dig the keys out of my purse and toss them to him.

"Please tell me this means you're letting me drive, and not that you're about to head out with that moron for cake."

"Hey, I like cake. It's not stupid to have a sweet tooth."

"Nothing you do is stupid," he says. "But I'll buy out the store as long as he's not with us."

I arch one eyebrow. "Be honest. If he came, you'd still buy out the store just to bug him."

"I would, yeah." His smile is almost too much. He looks like the guy who played Superman in the last movie. With the dimples and the blue eyes. "It's nice, this renewable energy thing. I've become a very rich man."

My heart is racing, and I need it to stop. *Get ahold of yourself, Mirdza.* I swallow. "I didn't really thank Danils very well for the help he provided with my mom's divorce," I say.

"That's why I paid for his dinner," Grigoriy says. "*And* I'm happy to thank him for you, right now." He turns us toward Danils's fancy German sedan.

I grab his elbow, and he freezes. When he turns back around, his eyes aren't dancing, and they aren't sparkling either.

They're smoldering.

Danger, Mirdza. So much freaking danger. My mouth goes dry. My eyelids flutter stupidly. And suddenly, I can't remember my own name. It starts with an M, I think. Or maybe an S.

"What?" He stalks closer, and I scrabble backward.

There must be somewhere safe. Somewhere I was

headed before. My body finally backs up against something cool and smooth. When I turn just enough to see that it's blue, I realize that it's my new Ford Bronco. My beautiful new car.

The one this man bought for me.

"Mirdza." His voice does something to me, something bad, something good, something I don't understand. I'm hot. I'm cold. I'm scared. I'm giddy. I'm up and down and all around.

A feeling of complete loss of control wars with total joy.

I lick my lips.

That's a mistake. His eyes dart downward and lock on, like a heat-seeking missile. "You pulled me back. You're staring at me. You laughed all night long." He lifts one hand and reaches out to touch my face, but his hand stops an inch before it reaches my skin.

Why did he stop? I need him to stroke me, to press his big, strong, powerful hand against my body. Now that he no longer needs to touch me. . .does he not want to anymore?

I inhale sharply, and the corner of his mouth turns upward. His head tilts. His teeth bite down onto his lower lip, and I'm transfixed. Like a deer staring unblinking into the headlights of the car that's about to mow it down, I can't look away.

"Mirdza." His voice, low and possessive, is like the caress he's withholding. "Tell me to go away. Tell me to leave you alone."

I exhale involuntarily. "No."

His hands slam down against the car's frame on either side of my face, bracketing me against the new car he gave me. "Tell me to go right now, or you won't be able to drag me away."

This time, my voice is breathy, but I shape the words. "I don't want you to go."

His smile's predatory, like a tiger who has trapped a gazelle. Like a falcon closing in on a cowering mouse.

But only if the mouse welcomed the dive.

I reach up then, before he can react, and pull his head down toward mine. When our lips touch, it's sunshine in the middle of a thunderstorm. It's a warm breeze on a wintry day. It's a healing touch when I'm trying to embrace death. It's black and white together. It's up and down at once.

That's what Grigoriy has always been to me.

Something that shouldn't exist. Something that changes my miserable existence into something safe and warm and whole. The tiger who loves the wounded gazelle. The falcon who picks up the mouse and flies her into the sky. I don't understand the why, but I know that something about him has transformed me fundamentally since the very beginning into more than I'm capable of being. He has healed me in a way I couldn't be healed.

On top of all of that, my body is *yearning* in a way it never has. I want to wrap my legs around him and hop up on the hood of this new car, heedless of who might be watching. I want to drag my nails across his broad, muscled back. And I want to press my body against his, curling into him, claiming him, disappearing in him from his head down to his enormous, clomping, boot-clad feet.

I think I might *love* Grigoriy Khilkov.

"So I guess this means you're back together?" Danils swears again from somewhere behind me.

By the time his words register and I pull away from Grigoriy, he's already turned around, headed for his car again.

The old Mirdza might have been embarrassed. She might have been mortified. She might have been angry with Grigoriy, or even nervous about his reaction. But in this moment, all I can feel is bubbly happiness, so I laugh.

"I guess it does mean we're together," I say. "Although, the 'back' is misplaced."

Grigoriy presses a kiss to my forehead. "Together?" He sighs, the breath from his mouth warming my entire face. "Are we, really?"

"Aren't we?" I ask. "Or do you only want things you can't have?"

"I want you," he says simply. "You're the only person I've ever wanted."

"I think you may be the only person I've ever wanted," I say.

"You think?" He raises his eyebrows.

"You are," I say. "But I'm new at this. Cut me a little slack."

He lifts me up and sets me on the hood of my new car. "Oh, I'll do anything to you that you want. And then some." And when he kisses me this time, it's even better than I imagined it would be.

$\maltese$ 24 $\maltese$

Eleven years ago, Blanka and I were waiting at the edge of the show ring, waiting for them to post the order. I was at my first World Cup qualifier, and I was shaking like a leaf in a stiff wind. The second they posted the route and the maximum time for the course, I started to review the best path in my head.

I remember chanting it like a rosary.

Round to the right. Cut through the green stripes. Circle the rainbow flowers and hit the blue vertical to start. Then out and around the black and white checkered jump to the black tuxedo jump, and then just six strides to the first combination.

Blanka stood utterly still, completely calm, trusting me entirely to tell her where to go and how fast to take it.

After the incident ten years, six months, and eleven days ago, I thought I'd never ride again. I thought my legs would never slide into tall, shiny black boots. I feared that my hands would never slide into tight, fitted gloves. I worried that my head would never be cradled by a sleek, shiny black helmet, and that my arms would never slide into the fitted show jacket that always makes me feel like a champion.

Because my leg would never be able to survive something as risky as jumping at speed.

But here I am, wearing the gear, standing with my hands clutched around the reins of an English bridle, and the horse standing beside me isn't Blanka, but he is utterly calm, just like she was.

Only, while I wait for them to post the route, I see someone I wish I didn't have to see.

Danils is sitting in the stands, which I should have expected. He's back with Brigita, according to my mother, and of course he has to come and cheer for his girlfriend. I turn away quickly, but not before I notice something strange.

He salutes me.

Why would he do that?

What could it mean?

I refuse to let him get in my head and make me nervous. I shake it off, and turn back to wait for the order to be posted. When the official in the white polo shirt and dark trousers marches my way, my heart picks up speed. I want to stay calm, but I can't expect the impossible.

It's a little like taking a position in front of a starting line, when they tell you what route you have to take. But as he approaches, I notice that the official doesn't have a paper in his hand.

I frown.

"Where's the route?" I ask softly, even though I know Charlemagne can't reply.

"Mirdza Strelkova," he says.

"That's me." Now my pulse is pounding like the galloping of hooves on cement. Loud and rhythmic.

"There's been a report." He arches one eyebrow and tilts his head.

To look at my bad leg.

"What kind of report?" I ask.

"That you're wearing a brace underneath your pants."

The outline of my stupid brace is clear. There's no way I could deny it.

"Yes," I say. "I am."

He shakes his head. "It's against regulations. You're not allowed to—"

"It's required by her physician," Kristiana says. "It's not to enhance her performance. It's to stabilize her leg."

"And if you were participating in the Special Olympics, that would be fine," he says. "But this is not that." His lips compress.

"What are you saying?" Kris asks, frowning.

"She takes that off, or she forfeits."

When I glance up at Danils, he's smiling.

I should have known they'd report me.

"It's fine," I say. "I can change. I'll ride without it."

The official marches off.

"No way." Kris is shaking her head. "We'll fight it. Once they understand—"

"There's not enough time," I say. "And I'm Latvian, and this is Riga, or did you forget? We're already the crappiest World Cup qualifier in Europe. They won't risk anyone saying that one of their riders had an unfair advantage."

Kris's entire face contorts. "No."

But Charlemagne stares at me steadily. And then he bobs his head up and down.

I toss his reins to Kris. "Grigoriy says it's fine. It's two to one." It takes me so long to change that I'm panicking. I know they'll post the route and rider order while I'm gone, and that'll leave me scrambling to memorize it in my head.

What if I'm first? How will I know the route well enough?

My leg actually feels better when I return, but I know

that's deceptive. It's easier to move, but there's no protection from the tremendous force of every single landing. No way to keep my leg from twisting if we land wrong at all.

It's stupid, riding without the brace.

And I plan to do it anyway.

The paper's fluttering a bit in the light wind. Charlemagne whinnies when he sees me. I lift my hand and move as quickly as I reasonably can to reach them. Before Kris has time to start yelling at me, I snap a photo of the route and order and turn away.

I worry that Kris is going to waste all my preparation time to argue with me, but she doesn't. She gives me some quick instruction and suggestions, and then she closes her mouth. Bless her, I'm lucky to have a friend like Kris.

I'm reviewing the pattern and looking at the ring and then checking the pattern again, trying to make my plan, when Charlemagne freezes, and then snorts. Loudly.

When I ignore him, he paws the ground and tosses his head.

Oh, for the love. "What?"

He tosses his head again, this time more pointedly. I follow his head toss until I notice two people sitting in the audience, both wearing unrelieved black.

"Okay. There are two men there. Should I be worried any time I see two men, sitting near one another?" I arch one eyebrow. "Do they *look* like your old friends?"

He whinnies so loudly that his nostrils expand and billow.

"Fine," I say. "I'll call Aleksandr—" I snap my mouth shut when an official glares. It's not super abnormal for someone to be talking to her horse at one of these things, but it is a little strange to do it so loudly and for so long. Certainly implying that your horse wants you to call someone. . .it's borderline.

Of course, people would be more likely to believe I'm

smuggling drugs in my saddle than the insane idea that my horse is actually a human male. I laugh it off and then surreptitiously pull out my phone and hit talk.

"Another sighting?" Aleksandr laughs.

"About two o'clock on the north side," I say. "Two men in black."

"I've been watching everyone who comes in," Aleksandr says. "Does he mean the blond and the brunette?"

I glance back again, trying my best not to look like an infatuated teen. "Uh. Yeah. Brunette has long hair."

"Nope. Not them for sure. One of them is *Polish*," he says, as if that tells me something meaningful.

"Okay, well, thanks."

"Can you tell him to relax? You're going to be fine, and we're expecting them this time, so if they show up, we're ready for it."

I'm not telling him that again. It's getting a little embarrassing. I end the call and shake my head slowly. "I'm not calling him again."

Charlemagne whuffles, blowing against my hand and bumping my shoulder with his big, furry face.

"No, sir." I rub his nose. "That worked last time, but it's not going to work again. You have got to stop freaking out about every single person in this show hall. I have a little story to tell you, actually. It's about a little shepherd boy who kept insisting that there was a wolf when there wasn't."

Charlemagne takes the bit and pulls me along, tossing his head for good measure.

"Ah, so you've heard the story," I say. "Because later, when there was a wolf, he'd claimed there was one when there wasn't so many times that no one believed him."

He looks away from me.

"Come on," I say. "I'm trying to help you. I'm a bundle of nerves. The last thing we need is for both of us to—"

"Mirdza." I hate that voice. It makes nails screeching their way down a chalkboard sound like a lullaby.

I grit my teeth and turn around, plastering a smile that probably looks more like a grimace on my face. "Brigita," I say. "Such a pleasure to see. . .Blanka here." My heart lurches a bit at the sight of my gorgeous mare, wearing a bright red bonnet that matches her saddle pad... standing next to the devil's concubine. "Too bad you're the one riding her."

"I hope you haven't gotten your hopes up too high," she says. "Because I hear this course was designed by Olaf Peterson, Jr. It's not like the ones your little friend set up for you at home."

"By 'my little friend,' do you mean Kristiana Liepa, the winner of the Grand National?"

"I hear the cups on that twelfth jump are shallow," Brigita says. "Good luck having a clean run on that nag."

Charlemagne shifts and steps on Brigita in the process.

I yank him back, but Brigita's mouth flies open and she collapses inward. I think it really hurt.

I feel a little bit bad, but mostly I focus on suppressing my laugh. "I may need to get my stallion here a red ribbon," I say. "He has a terrible habit of stomping on prissy little whiners."

"I was trying to help you," she says.

"Oh?" I can't help laughing. "You were trying to help me? Was that before or after you stole my horse while I was busy getting a surgery from an incident that happened at your stable?"

"Your leg wasn't my fault," she says.

"Pardon me if I don't heed your warnings," I say. "But if the cups are shallow on the twelfth, everyone will have the same difficulty in clearing them. Worry about yourself."

It's more likely that horses will struggle with that vertical because it follows a water jump, and a lot of the posh show jumpers aren't adequately prepared for those. Luckily, my horse knows that a little water never hurt anyone.

But of course, if he touches it, it's just like knocking a pole. Four penalties. We need a clear round to make it to the jump-off, and that means no time penalties, either. When I finally take a look at the order, I'm a little disappointed. I like to go first, before the jitters have set in, and before I have time to psych myself out.

So of course I'm dead last.

Twenty-one jumpers, and I'm the twenty-first. What horrible luck.

At least I can study what patterns work and which ones crash and burn. "Alright, let's not get too distracted," I say to Charlemagne absently. "I want to see whether people are able to cut that corner after the triple combination, or whether it sets them up to hit that vertical at an angle and they drop a pole while trying to cut time."

But when Charlemagne remains completely silent, I realize he's not even listening. Which means. . . I follow his line of sight and realize he's staring at two more men. "One of them's sporting a creeper-stache and wearing a fedora, for heaven's sake," I say. "And the other one's holding a paper dish with nachos in it. Do your fiendish enemies eat a lot of processed cheese?"

In the process of mocking his obsession, I notice something that *is* a bit strange. Next to the two men who are definitely *not* magical criminal masterminds is someone I know.

Or at least, someone I've spoken to before.

An old woman who smells like pumpkins. The memory washes over me like a wave trying to drown a small child—fresh, dangerous, and vaguely threatening.

It wasn't the old woman who wouldn't stop prattling about her cat that was terrifying that night, but it's a memory that's tied to the misery in my head. I wish I hadn't noticed she was here. She never mentioned horses, and so it feels strange to see her.

And now she's looking right at me.

I blink and look away.

Charlemagne bumps me with his wet nose.

"Hey," I say. "Don't get stains on the jacket."

He snorts.

"What now?"

He tosses his head, and I realize the woman has been climbing down ever since we made eye contact, and she's only a few rows away and headed right for me.

"You were in Russia," she says.

My stomach flips. It's all I can do to nod mutely.

"But now you're here, in Riga, of all places. What brings you out here?"

Is she insane? I'm holding a horse and wearing show clothing, complete with a number on my back. "I'm about to ride in the Grand Prix," I say slowly. "What brings *you* here?"

She cackles, and that sound definitely reminds me of that horrible night. "I'm here for the same thing."

"You're riding?" I ask, stupidly.

This time, her cackle's even louder. "You're a funny girl. It must be one of the things he loves about you. He's humorous, too."

"He?" I ask.

She looks pointedly at Charlemagne. "You know who I mean."

My heart stops dead in my chest and then rushes back to life in a staccato burst. "You mean. . .have you met my boyfriend?"

She cackles again. "Nice try, girl. I mean him." She points at Charlemagne and moves closer. "I warned you that night, remember?"

That night.

My pulse beats loudly in my ears, and Charlemagne pushes me to the side, angling himself in front of me, his nostrils flaring, his head up and tossing aggressively.

The woman doesn't look the least bit afraid. "He's a fine one." She sighs. "Not many made like him." She tilts her head and smiles. "Yes, I can see why you were won over."

"What are you talking about?" I ask, half afraid and half hopeful.

"Your soul bond," she says. "If I hadn't left you on that train, you'd never have been in trouble, and he'd never have saved you, and neither of you would ever have changed so gloriously." She doesn't cackle this time. She just smiles, revealing very shiny dentures that look too big for her thin-lipped mouth. "But I did leave you, and you were almost killed, and he did rescue you. It wasn't pleasant, but real change, soul-deep change, it never is comfortable. It can't be." She reaches for his nose with one wrinkled hand, and he actually lets her touch him. "I wonder." She snatches her hand back and turns to face me again. "If I gave you the choice, would you do it all again, just the same?"

I open my mouth, but they call the first jumper.

"Never mind, then, girl. It's time for you to go. You'll have to discover those answers for yourself. And maybe you can help the other. She's going to need it. Her road will be even bumpier than yours." And then she's cackling again. A sound that now sends chills up my spine.

"But wait," I say. "I have questions."

"Isn't it hilarious how young people always think that just because they have questions, they're entitled to the answers?" She smirks. "You have to earn the answers, girl. If you don't, they're meaningless anyway."

"Mirdza," Kristiana calls.

"I have to—actually, you should meet my friend." I turn

to wave Kristiana over, but when I turn back around, the old woman is *gone*. "Whoa," I say. "Where did she go?"

The strangest thing is that I'm not even surprised. It feels right, somehow, that she'd just disappear into thin air. An ominous feeling steals over me. I hope her departure this time isn't as unlucky as it was the last.

I watch as the first rider knocks two poles, essentially eliminating them from the finals. The second rider knocks three, but it's really her own fault. When her horse picked up too much speed, instead of slowing him down with her seat, she yanked on him. That only made him go faster, and then he overcorrected, plummeting after each jump.

It was painful to watch.

But the next two run clear, and I start to worry.

How many of us are going to make it to the jump off?

Brigita goes next, and she and Blanka are the third team to have a clean round. And they were fast, finishing with a second and a half to spare.

I plan out the route in my head again, modifying for the successes and failures I've seen. We can cut tighter corners than that second pair, and we always hit the base of the jump before we launch, now. Finally, it's almost our turn. Five pairs have run clean, so far. Brigita was right, though. The twelfth jump has been the most knocked of all. It's the highest on the course, at 1.6 meters, and although it's a vertical, it follows quickly behind a difficult triple combination. I think a lot of the horses underestimate the height because of the angle of the turn right before it.

I run Charlemagne through a few arcs and turns in the warm-up ring, and then Kris is calling us over. "You're on in two runs," she says. "Do you feel ready?"

I glance over at the crowd. Adriana's looking my way and she waves, but the seat next to her is empty. "Where's my mom?"

Kris swallows. "She, uh, she had something come up."

A ball forms in the pit of my stomach. "Not Mārtinš, right?"

My best friend drops a hand on my arm. "Nothing like that, no. It's just that she's scared. She wanted to come, but in the end, she was too afraid."

Nervous that I would fail and it would hurt her? Nervous that I'd be sad and she'd say the wrong thing? Worried she'd be embarrassed if I did poorly? Either way, it's yet another disappointment.

It's probably my fault for continuing to hope.

"You're brave, Mirdza," Kristiana says. "You have a leg that's not quite right and pains you all the time. Your mother hasn't always been there, cheering you on, and your sister is. . .erratic. And still, in spite of your miserable lack of support, you're here, doing amazing things. Even if you knock down every single pole, I'll still be ridiculously proud."

"Wait, do you really think I might knock down every pole?"

"No." She sighs in exasperation. "Mirdza, focus. You're amazing. That's the point."

"But do you think—"

"Oh, stop." She swats Charlemagne on the butt. "Get her out there, and don't give her time to overthink this. She only has forty-five seconds from the buzzer to that first jump."

And I only have seventy-three seconds to complete the entire course.

Brigita already jumped clear on *my* horse, but I still have the edge tonight. Charlemagne's been groomed within an inch of his life. His hooves have been polished. His mane's plaited in careful braids. His coat shines like a diamond. And when I ask for him to move, he practically floats. He moves off my slightest ask, curling around the opening at the one-third break and cantering easily toward the first vertical.

"Here we go," I whisper. "Stay with me, now. Don't take off."

And he does. We sail over the first jump, and in my head, the little timer that always starts rolling on the television begins to count upward. I ask for a bit more speed as we circle to our second vertical, the one with the crazy Egyptian dog heads on the standards.

Even the bright purple stripes on the poles don't phase Charlemagne, because he's not an idiotic horse, whose instincts are telling him that everything wants to kill him.

No, my horse is only scared of pairs of men wearing all black.

That thought makes me chuckle as we approach the first combination, an ascending oxer followed by a triple square with a two-meter spread and a height of one sixty. I shift forward and hold my breath as Charlemagne clears it with room to spare.

Thank goodness for magical ponies.

I ask him for a bit more speed, getting a bit cocky as we circle around the Egyptian dog heads to approach the vertical with the most poles—four—all lined up underneath. It's not that high, but it's a strange angle, right after we circle the last combo.

We sail over it, and my nerves float downward. For the next few obstacles, I'm not even anxious. I'm having *fun*. It feels *good*.

And then we're sailing up to the tenth vertical, which is a solo jump with flowers *and* a faux brick fence, but it's an easy approach and we clear it without a problem. Next we head for stupid number eleven, which is followed by number twelve, the jump with the most dropped poles in the entire arena. For a split second, I wish that I'd told Grigoriy to use his powers.

If we hit a pole, keep it in place. Don't let it fall. It would have been so easy to tell him that.

But I didn't.

My stupid pride.

The eleventh pole has a wide blue rectangle underneath it, full of brightly colored blue water. Time seems to slow as we approach, our cadence perfect, our timing spot on. Charlemagne's front hooves launch first, up, up, up and then over, his powerful back legs leaving a hair after, propelling us upward and out, like a rocket, really.

It feels like we're flying, and I revel in it, my heart racing, my stomach flipping, and my body floating.

Only, there's a huge crash in the audience just then, and I can't help turning to see what it is. Someone has lit something on fire, it looks like trash, and people are fleeing away, dropping bags of food as they flee.

Charlemagne turns to look as well, and the ground's racing up at us now, too quickly. He slams into the ground way too hard, which wrenches my leg, but I level out and grit my teeth against the pain.

That twelfth jump would have been hard even without a horrible approach, but as it is, I'm acutely worried.

In the audience up ahead, I see her.

The old woman.

Smiling.

Instead of freaking me out, it settles me.

I was alone that night, when I stood up for that little girl. She was like me, all alone, without a protector. But I'm not like that anymore. I'm strong. I'm healthy. And I have people at my side, ready to keep me safe.

Ready to lift me up and help me succeed.

So now, when I'm rattled and afraid, battered and nervous, I slide my hands forward and trust Grigoriy to make the jump on his own. He can do it even when I can't.

And he does.

We sail over that horrible jump, and he hits the ground hard, and then we keep moving. I sail through the next few jumps on autopilot, thinking about the crash and the fire and the old woman. They were things that could have ruined anyone's ride, but not me. Not anymore.

For years and years, I've lamented what I lost. For the past ten years, I've regretted that I would never again be able to ride like I did. I still can't ride like I did over a decade ago.

Because I'm stronger now than I was.

When we finish and turn to look at the scoreboard, I see that we had the fastest time on the course. Tears well up in my eyes. For a moment, I thought we were doomed, but I had faith in Grigoriy, and I let him ride when I couldn't, and it worked.

When the scoreboard leader list updates, we're at the very top. Kristiana flies toward me, arms outstretched. "Look at you, speed demon!"

I shake my head. "I thought we were doomed."

"That was your wonderful ex." She chuckles. "He's a real loser. Glad that date crashed and burned."

"Huh?"

"He was escorted out of here a few moments ago. If we wanted to really trash Brigita, we could tell them it's her boyfriend and get her tossed out, too."

But unlike her, I don't want to disqualify anyone.

I want to outride them.

When I look around, I don't see the old woman anywhere. It's too bad. I have so many questions I want to ask, and I'm willing to earn the answers. But I wind up settling for just sliding off Charlemagne's back. Instead of hugging or high-fiving Kris, I slide my arms around my big stallion's neck, and I squeeze.

"We did it," I say. "You did it. Thank you."

"Just one more race to win," Kris says. "You feel up to it?"

My leg is throbbing thanks to that horrible landing without my brace. My heart's racing, thanks to that stupid stunt Danils pulled. I just saw a creepy old woman who said odd things about me and Grigoriy and disappeared into thin air. And my mother didn't come to watch me compete.

"Sure," I say. "Never been better."

Because for me, this is about as good as it gets.

25

Sometimes the jump-off happens at the end of a long day, after riders have completed the event in batches, but not at a World Cup qualifier. It happens as soon as the course directors can modify the course, removing a handful of jumps to streamline it and make sure it's a little different, and then give us the green light.

I think it's normal to deal with some nerves during the waiting period, but as they announce our order, there's a bit of a distraction. When they post the list, Kristiana looks poleaxed.

She walks toward me slowly, her feet dragging. "First."

Most people are bummed about being first. I prefer to go first on the initial run, so my nerves don't get away from me, but on the jump off, the benefit of knowing how hard to press corners to make up time outweighs even the detriment to my nerves. So when I wanted to go first, I went last. And now that I'd like to go last, I'm stuck going first.

"It's fine," I say. "I really just have to beat Brigita, right?" I can't help laughing. Our fear, of course, is that although Grigoriy can jump like a deer, we haven't been as focused on speed. Tight turns and maneuvering are great, but it's hard to know how much he can shave on time, and for the jump-off, that's much more important.

Kris reviews the paper that tells her exactly what we're watching them do right now. "They're pulling the third vertical out of that triple combination," she says. "And they're changing the second oxer to a vertical."

She frowns. "And they're pulling out one other vertical." She flips through the papers again. "Is that really it? Nothing else?"

Which is why the time isn't coming down by too much. I lean closer and pat Grigoriy's neck. "It's fine. We'll keep those turns as tight as we can, and when we hit the big path before the rainbow jump and the stars, we'll carry as big a stride as you can manage."

He bobs his head.

"And then you just jump your heart out, and if you have to keep a pole from falling, well." I shrug.

For all my insistence that he not use his powers before, now that we're here and both his ownership and Blanka's are on the line, maybe my ethics aren't as rock-solid as I thought.

Charlemagne makes a snorty-whuffle-whinny sound that is quite strange, but I think it's his way of laughing at me.

"Go ahead," I say. "Just remember that I'm a woman, and we reserve the right to change our minds."

After a few more nerve-jangling moments, they signal us that they're ready. It's only a two-star qualifier, here in Riga, but it's still well attended. As we circle around to the lead-in for the course, I can't help looking at the audience. There aren't the sixty thousand spectators that Bordeaux France boasts, and it's certainly no Barcelona. But I'm proud of Latvia and the several thousand people who have gathered to cheer us on.

We may be small, but we are mighty.

And I'm a proud Latvian equestrian. Before I start, I take the reins in one hand and fist pump with the other.

"Tēvzemei un Brīvībai!"

It's unconventional at a dignified gathering like this, but other than Brigita, I'm surrounded by riders of other nationalities. We two are representing our entire country, and we both made it into the jump-off. Win or lose today, I'm still proud of myself and our country.

Apparently the crowd is too, because they go wild.

That gives me the energy and confidence I need to really squeeze Charlemagne's sides as we approach the first vertical. My hands are shaking, and my stomach's unsteady, but it's my dream—one I'd given up on.

And I'm here, doing it.

I tighten my reins just a hair and lean forward, ready to begin. Before I'm truly ready, it happens. Charlemagne launches and we're flying through the air. We're clear of the first jump, and into the seven-stride run to the next.

Only, my beast of a horse does it in six, and he clears the obstacle beautifully.

Now the biggest combination on the course is coming up fast, ready to throttle us. It's an ascending oxer, followed by a two-meter spread square, and my heart's in my throat, because Charlemagne has pulled out all the stops and he's practically sprinting toward it. I signal a half-halt, which he ignores, and I brace myself.

There's no way we clear this without a knockdown.

Except, somehow, we do.

His ears forward, his powerful muscles pumping, he takes two strides and sails over the massive two-meter spread of the triple oxer and doesn't even sink into a nose dive on the back end.

Instead, he pivots like a kangaroo or something, and I hear the dirt spraying behind us as he gallops toward the next vertical, clearing it so fast that I have to remind myself to breathe. Unfortunately, I'm not quite ready when we land, and I tip forward, my foot twisting in the stirrups. When he lands on the ground for his next stride, it wrenches, and the sound it makes is bad.

Like that noise when you pop the top on a jar of pickles.

And the pain, oh, the pain. I try to tell myself that the nail didn't go into my jaw. I grit my teeth and pretend that it went between my toes. But my leg's not getting the message. Something's wrong. Very, very wrong. I can't even pull my foot back out of the stirrups to reposition my weight.

I can't seem to move my leg *at all*.

But there's no time for pansies, not when that clock is rolling.

Charlemagne, clearly without any idea that my leg is jacked, rounds the bend, prepared to cut a stride yet again. We're barreling toward the next combination, and I'm genuinely worried we're going to crash into it, but when I ease back right before, he listens and we hit the base perfectly, springing over the first vertical, hitting two clean strides, and clearing the wide oxer.

But now it's time for another tight turn, and my leg's livid. It's messed up, and I'm worried that impact might have dislodged something important, like a screw. It feels like a hot poker's digging into my thigh, and someone whacked it with a hammer, all at once.

I can't grip Charlemagne on that side properly, so I try to compensate, but it leaves me canted in the saddle.

My horse has finally noticed. He glances back quickly, looking for reassurance I can't give him.

We're approaching the water jump, and I need to get

my head back in the game. *It's probably only fifteen more seconds. I can do anything for fifteen seconds.* I force my leg to squeeze, even though it feels like I'm pressing it against a cheese grater and holding it there.

If my life has prepared me for anything, it's the ability to endure pain. So when we reach the jump, I grit my teeth and slide into jump position, my hands trembling as they hold steady over Charlemagne's plaited mane.

The force of the landing resembles being smashed by a wooden mallet, a feeling I can sadly relate to quite well. And then we're headed for our very last jump.

Just don't fall off or screw this up. Don't screw this up, Mirdza. You may never ride again, and you want this last one to be worth it.

If I did wreck a screw. . . If that doctor's right, there's not enough bone left to reattach anything. But that's a struggle for another day. For now, it's just this one last obstacle, and I can stop squeezing. Stop breathing through the wall of pain rising around me.

My entire life narrows to this single point in time.

And I pitch forward, grabbing Charlemagne's braid nubs inelegantly, and holding on for dear life as he vaults over the last vertical. I don't mean to, but I wind up leaning heavily on my left side on the landing, trying to keep the weight off my bad leg.

I slide sideways as we race to the end and nearly topple off.

The crowd notices, and so does Charlemagne, but it doesn't matter. We're done, clear, and our time is fixed. I look up at the clock with trepidation. . .but it's a full three and a half seconds below what I hoped to get.

"Yeah," Kris shouts. "Just try and touch that, you prissy little snobs!" She's a little more suited to the mood of a race track than a show jumping ring, but the crowd mirrors her enthusiasm, at least.

I wheel us around to the edge of the ring, prepared to try and watch the others in the jump-off, but Charlemagne isn't having it. He keeps turning around to look at me, eyeing my leg, and whuffling.

I pat his neck. "It's fine, boy. Everything's fine."

But he can sense the lie. Probably because my leg's still essentially a lump of dead weight.

He whuffles again, and then he paws at the ground.

"You can't change right here," I whisper. "So you'll have to wait to take a look."

He whinnies softly, and the officials glare at me. If I'm not careful, they won't let us watch, and I need to see who wins. If it's not me. . .as long as it's not Brigita.

But when Charlemagne dances sideways again, I have to balance with my bad leg and tears spring into my eyes. I look up and inhale so I can keep them at bay.

Suddenly, a warm feeling spreads through my entire body, but starting with my thigh.

Grigoriy can heal damage that's recent! How did I forget that?

My head snaps down toward his, and he snorts. Then he shakes his head slowly, side-to-side.

The misery in my leg magically. . .disappears.

Can that *be*? I slide out of the saddle and swing off, landing hard on my legs, and the pain is the same as I've grown accustomed to enduring, no more. Now I really am crying, and Kris has noticed.

"Hey, are you alright? Your run was *amazing*. Did I not mention that? It was. Epic, really. If any first round run is going to win, it's that one."

"It's fine," I say. But in that moment, I wish desperately that Charlemagne could be human. I want to hug Grigoriy. I want his arms around me, not the warm, solid body of this massive stallion. But I can't have my cake and eat it too, so here we are.

And so I watch, one by one, as the other jumpers enter the ring, fly around the course as quickly as they can. . .and knock poles. The first to follow me knocks one down on the ascending oxer. The next bumps the second vertical. The fourth rider runs clean, but four and a half seconds behind us.

It's looking like we might actually. . .win.

But now it's Brigita's turn, and Blanka looks ready. Focused.

Part of me is a little bummed that she's jumping just fine for my arch-nemesis, but horses don't understand the concerns of humans. The best ones just like to *move*, to leap and bound and pivot and race. And Blanka's one of those. I can't really fault her for being amazing at what she was made to do.

After they clear the first two verticals and the oxer combination, flying around the difficult turns, my heart gets heavier and heavier. Because I can control how well I do, and I can push through the pain, but there's an element of chance with a jumping round that you just can't manage, and that's how well other riders manage it. Whether that horse is having an epic day. Whether the riders are in sync.

I'm watching their time, but I can't really tell exactly where they should be to beat us. It's a long course. When they hang a tight corner and duck around the water jump to reach the last—a pretty risky move—I hold my breath.

Because Brigita's taking Blanka at an angle into that jump, and it's 1.6 meters high, and that's not great. Even Blanka can't make it work. She shouldn't have tried to cut the corner.

I cringe when Blanka drops a pole.

Even though it means that I've beaten them.

To my surprise, when they finish, even with cutting corners and strides, they're almost two seconds slower than we were, too. As soon as they walk off the course, Brigita throws Blanka's reins at me. "Take her. She's defective anyway, just like you."

I'm so stunned that I nearly drop Charlemagne's reins.

Luckily, Kris takes them.

A few moments later, when the final contestant, a French pair, loses to us by more than two full seconds, I stand numbly as they announce Charlemagne and me as the Grand Champion of the two-star World Cup qualifier in Riga.

A lot of people appear, some holding cameras and microphones, and some just officials and trainers and breeders.

"How does it feel to be the first female from Latvia to win the World Cup qualifier in your host country?"

"Where did you locate this brilliant horse?"

"Were you nervous to ride a stallion in such a large event? Especially one who was untried?"

"What inspired you to make this comeback after more than ten years?"

Everything starts to blur together, but I answer the barrage of questions as well as I possibly can, dodging questions about why I'm now holding Brigita's horse. It would have been nice if she'd been less melodramatic, but the reporters seem to be assuming that we're close friends and she was just too upset to stick around.

Eventually, Kristiana starts answering for me, which is a real blessing. We're both holding horses, though, and we're both tired. So before too long, Kris cuts it short. "We'll make her available for interviews tomorrow," she says. "We really need to get these horses cooled off, tacked down, and in their stalls."

A moment later, Adriana reaches us, and I hand her the reins to Blanka. She's beaming as we exit the arena and head for the stables.

"You destroyed her."

I smile.

"It looked like your leg was hurting, though, at the end?" She peers down at my bad thigh. "Are you alright?"

She's too smart and she pays too close of attention sometimes. "It's fine," I say. "I tweaked it a little, but the pain's fading."

Charlemagne tosses his head and looks back at me.

"Do you want to take him?" Kristiana asks.

Adriana's brow furrows. "I still can't believe you were competing so soon after that surgery. But if you're walking on it, it can't be that bad, right?" She points at a chair at the front of the stables. "You should wait here. Kris and I can cool these two down, and you can take a little break. Join us when the twinge is gone."

"But I—"

She jabs her finger at the chair. "Sit."

It's easier to sit than to argue with her, and I am a little exhausted. I'm sure Charlemagne is, too. There are horses and riders walking back and forth in front of us, and it's not smart for Kris and Adriana to loiter around. Plus, the horses do need a cool down, water, and some rest.

"I'll be back in ten minutes," I say. "Thanks."

Of course, about four minutes later, two men with name tags and notepads realize who I am. "Mirdza Strelkova?" The taller one looks delighted. "You're sitting here. . .alone?" His Latvian is good—no accent at all. Grigoriy will be pleased that I'm paying attention—he does not sound Russian.

I laugh. "Just taking a quick break. I'll be headed back to check on my horses in a moment."

"Is it true you and Brigita are close friends?" The shorter one's not quite as tall as his companion, but they're both quite tall. Taller than Grigoriy, even. And they're both in the nerdiest looking tweed suits I've ever seen. They definitely wouldn't make Grigoriy nervous. No black at all.

"We've known one another for a long time," I say. It's what Kristiana said earlier, and it seems like the smartest thing to disclose.

A few other reporters around the corner notice we're talking and start walking this way. In a few short moments it'll be another feeding frenzy.

"Do you have time for a brief interview?" the tall one asks. He's quite handsome, even for a reporter in nerdy clothing. His jaw is square, his eyes are sky blue, and his hair's a striking golden-blond, military cut. "We could sneak back there."

I wave them off. "I really should be getting back."

"We're with *Horse and Hound*, and our editor wants to use you as our spotlight this month. Unfortunately, we have to leave on a flight in about three hours." The tall blond glances at the shorter one, who has russet hair.

Good heavens, he's stunning looking, too. Is everyone who works for *Horse and Hound* as fabulously shiny and handsome as their publication? It's probably the most famous of the magazines that covers show jumping. The thought of being on the front. . . "Why would you want to feature me?"

"Far more women than men ride at the lower levels, but the higher echelons of the sport have always been dominated by men," the russet-haired man says. His Latvian's also quite good. Maybe that's why they were sent to cover this. "Our editor's a woman, and she's keen on highlighting how that's changing. What better story to feature than one about a country that recently had its first Olympic contender, and the woman who just brought home the win at their local World Cup qualifier?"

My national pride swells up a bit, thinking about being the representative for Latvia. We've always been the stepchild of the European jumping circuit. We're not as wealthy, and we're farther away than most other counties from the majority of the shows.

"Aren't you also best friends with Kristiana Liepa?" the blond asks. "We've been trying to reach her for a feature for weeks and weeks now. The second woman to ever win the Grand National, and the first person from Latvia to ever take it. It seems like Latvia may be a sleeping power-house for equine sports." He beams.

"Fine," I say. "But only ten minutes. If I'm gone any longer, my best friend will worry. And if we hurry, she might be willing to give you a bit of time, too." I stand up and start following them out the back way, where hopefully there won't be quite as many other reporters heading for us like heat-seeking missiles.

"Is it true she's engaged?" the blond asks. "To some kind of magnate from Russia?"

I bob my head. "I mean, he's not a magnate, but he's pretty wealthy."

"So it is true," the russet-haired man says. His bright green eyes are sparkling. "Will they move to Russia? Or will he come to Latvia?"

"I think she'd be the better person to ask those ques-tions." My feeling are a little hurt that they seem more excited about her than me, but I suppose that's to be expected. Wining the Grand National landed her a million pounds, whereas my win made me thirty thousand euro. And this is only a regional qualifier—a two-star, at that. But still. I *just* won it. "Are you guys using me to get to her?"

"Of course not," the blond says.

But the russet-haired man looks a little uncomfortable.

Which should have been my red flag, if I were more careful. Because sometimes the boy who cries wolf. . .is right. Sometimes there are wolves lurking around the corner.

Of course, I don't realize it until the tall one grabs me and the russet-haired one holds a white cloth over my face.

By then, my limbs are slack and the world's already going black.

❧ 26 ❧

Waking up feels like swimming. . .through tar.

My eyes are burning.

The inside of my mouth and throat are as dry as cotton.

Every part of my body aches, but especially my leg.

The world around me is still utterly dark, but I realize that's because my eyes are covered with. . .something.

Unfortunately, I break into a coughing fit, alerting the people around me that I'm finally awake. You always think you'll be tough, when you see people in movies doing stupid things. Maybe I would have been tough, mentally, but my body's always been weak.

This stupid, delicate meat sack.

"Ah, welcome back." Someone yanks the blindfold away, and the blond one's in front of me, his head only half a meter from mine. He's speaking in English, and he doesn't even have a British accent. Why didn't I switch to English to confirm he was at least British? Ugh.

His outfit's entirely different now. No more stuffy tweed suit.

It makes my heart sink when I notice. . .they're in all black.

"Who are you?"

He looked good before, in the ridiculous costume he was wearing, but now? The blond one's clearly broad shouldered, in great shape, and the beauty of his face cuts like a knife. Impossibly high cheekbones. Startlingly ice-blue eyes. Full lips. Golden skin. An arrogance that reminds me of Grigoriy.

Without the kindness.

He gestures around the room. "It's been a while, and no one has noticed you're gone. . .or if they have, they don't know where to find you."

I remember my stupid boast that if I was gone more than ten minutes, someone would be worried.

"He'll find you," I say. "And he has his powers back. You'll wish you'd never been born."

The tall blond stands. "Grigoriy, you mean? Hardly."

The russet-haired one looks less. . .sadistic. He's behind the blond, leaning against the wall of the small, dark room where I'm stuck on the floor. "Just hand her the phone."

"The phone?" My hands are tied behind my back, which is probably why my right shoulder feels like it's been ground against the floor for an hour. My feet are also bound, but my bad leg has, blessedly, gone numb. I struggle until I'm at least sitting up, bracing myself on my good side. "Who do you want me to call?"

"We had to dispose of your phone, just in case your friends are tech-savvy." The blond one frowns. "Which is a real hassle. I hope you know Kristiana's number."

"Wait, Kris?" I blink, trying to make sense of what's happening. "Why Kristiana? You aren't really reporters, clearly."

The russet-haired one makes a sound that I think might be a laugh. "No, we aren't." He switches to Russian. "I'm

Mikhail Kurakin, and my stupidly pretty blond friend there is Boris Yuravsky." He drops into a crouch, his green eyes hovering in front of mine. "We're friends of your new boyfriend. He didn't say?" His hair's tufty now, no longer combed into neat lines. It falls all around his face like reddish straw, nearly obscuring his eyes.

How dare he claim to be friends with Grigoriy? I spit on him.

Which earns me a raised fist. To my shock, he pulls back. He grits his teeth, inhales slowly, stands up, and starts pacing.

He did say they were friends of Grigoriy's—could he be serious?

"You attacked Aleksandr after the Grand National," I say. "What kind of friends do that?"

"We didn't hurt him," Mikhail says. "We wanted to see what he could do and how much of his power had returned."

"But you've been hiding all this time," I say. "And you kidnapped me. What kind of friends do that?"

"Estranged ones," Mikhail says.

Boris has been quiet ever since Mikhail took over. Mikhail. . .Kurakin. The name's familiar. I know they're the other magical horse lords, but I can't quite recall who is who. . .until I remember. Grigoriy said that the Kurakins killed his parents.

Burned them alive.

I imagine he wasn't very close to the redhead after that. "You cursed them," I say. "They've been asleep for a hundred years because of you, and they still haven't found Alexei."

Their eyes widen, both of them.

And now I'm giving them information they didn't have. What's wrong with me? Apparently my body's not the only weak thing. I clamp down on my tongue, determined not to say another word.

"Is that what Grigoriy says?" Mikhail rubs his hand along his jaw, the pressure of his fingers making the tiniest scritching sound against the reddish stubble. "He thinks we cursed them?"

"Didn't you?" I ask. Maybe I can get them to share something, too. "For refusing to help your people grow crops in that famine, you found a witch and you made them pay."

'They did refuse us," Boris says. "That's true enough."

"But we didn't have the power to curse them, and no witch we could have found had more power than any of us." Mikhail's laugh is bitter.

"You clearly haven't aged," I say. "And you weren't sleeping."

"That's true," Mikhail says. "But it wasn't a witch who cursed them. It was—"

Boris shakes his head.

That's it. A tiny gesture.

"It was who?" I ask.

"Nice try," Mikhail says. "We need to see Kristiana."

"Why her?" I ask. "None of this makes sense."

"Just call her." Mikhail crouches down again, and this time, he dangles a phone from two fingers. "Tell us the number, and we'll dial."

"What am I supposed to say?"

"Tell her to come to an address we'll give you," Boris says. "Simple. Easy. Not scary at all. And the second she shows up, without your boyfriends of course, you're free to go."

I press my lips together and shake my head. "No way."

"It's a simple trade. Your life for hers."

My head snaps up. "You're going to kill her?"

Boris rolls his eyes. "You've been watching too many shows. We need to talk to her."

"Talk to her? Do I look stupid?"

"Have we hurt you?" Mikhail's eyes narrow. "No. We have some questions too, and we need answers. That's all. We aren't super villains, no more than your boyfriend is."

"Do you hold a grudge against them for not helping you in the famine?"

Boris and Mikhail lock eyes.

"Do you?"

"A grudge?" Boris shrugs.

"Yes," Mikhail says. "Not only that. We've known each other for a long time, and our last hundred years haven't been a walk in the park, either."

"But who—"

The phone rings. Before he snatches it away, I see the name of the person calling.

Rukovoditel.

He who controls.

"Yes." Mikhail's entire body stiffens, his eyes flinty. He stands up and begins to pace again. "No."

I strain to hear, but the volume must be set low.

"But she—" He grunts.

Boris is staring at him intently.

"Fine." Mikhail frowns. "I said I don't want—" His free hand tightens into a fist at his side. "Yeah." He hands the phone to Boris.

Boris glares at him for a second before taking the phone. When he does, his expression is just as grim.

They don't like this person, whoever it is that's controlling them.

"No." Boris pauses. "I agree."

What's going on?

"Fine." He hangs up, and he tosses the phone to

Mikhail. Then he picks up a chair, and he flips it upside down.

I expect to see something magical, but I'm disappointed.

He smashes the chair against the door frame, and it shatters more easily than I would have expected. It looked like a pretty sturdy chair. When he turns back toward me, I realize that I'm shaking. My entire body's trembling like a leaf in a gale-force wind.

Because he's holding the turned leg of the chair like a tiny club, and he's advancing on me like a man with no options.

"Call your friend," Boris says.

"Tell me you mean her no harm," I say.

He stops, his lips compressed into a white line.

"You will kill her," I say.

"You can't save everyone, you know. Sometimes you have to worry about yourself first." He reaches down faster than I can process and holds his free hand over my ankles.

There's a quick zap, and I yelp, and then the ropes fall loose around my feet.

He's freeing me?

"I could explain that I don't want to do this, and that I don't have a choice," Boris says. "But we all have choices, and we're about to give you one." He flips me sideways, exposing my old injury, lifts the chunk of chair leg, and before I can even scream, slams it against my thigh, shattering the papier-mâché bone.

The pain's like a lightning strike, which I suppose is fitting.

"In a moment that pain will recede," he says. "Or at least, it'll go down a little bit. I imagine that like us, pain is an old friend to you."

He extends his hand.

Mikhail places the phone in it.

He crouches down this time, his ice-blue eyes impassive, unconcerned. "Your boyfriend has the ability to heal anything that *just* happened. That means you have thirty minutes to get your friend here, or you're going to be in a wheelchair for life."

His finger hovers over the call keys.

"Tell me her number, and Grigoriy can fix your leg. The pain will go away."

But they're right.

I'm no stranger to pain.

In fact, more than anyone else, I'm uniquely suited to ignore it. Pain has been my most constant companion for more than a decade. If they think I'm going to trade my pain for my friend's, they don't know me at all.

My body's a weak meat-sack, but my will is strong.

"Go to hell. I'm sure they have a room reserved for you."

"If she's not motivated enough yet," Mikhail says, "we can motivate her more."

Motivate.

So they plan to torture me?

I'm not afraid. Eventually, after enough 'motivation' hasn't worked, they'll kill me. It'll all be over, but my friends will have no idea what's going on. They need to be warned, and Grigoriy deserves to know what happened to me.

"I'll call her," I say.

Only, the numbers I rattle off aren't Kristiana's.

Boris's index finger hovers over the talk button. "Nothing funny, hear me? You tell her that we have you. You tell her where to come, and you tell her she has to come alone."

I nod.

"Do you think she'll do it?"

I breathe through a wave of nausea. The worst injuries

always cause your entire body to turn on you. "She's my oldest friend," I say. "I'd come for her."

Boris laughs. "And yet you're calling her right now."

"I didn't say I'd tell her to come. You just told me to call her."

He rolls his eyes and hits talk.

"Hello?"

"Kristiana," I say as clearly as I can. "It's me, Mirdza." I hold my breath, desperately hoping that she doesn't say anything stupid.

"Thank goodness you're calling," my sister says.

"The men you were worried about have taken me after all, just like Aleksandr thought they might," I say. "But you're the one they want, Kris. Not me." I wait for her to process that, and silently pray that she gets why I'm calling her.

"Okay."

"They want you to come to the following address in the next half hour." I rattle off the numbers and street name they're holding in front of me. "But you know me. I hate the idea of someone trading themselves to save me as much as I hate Polish sausages. I've never wanted any, and I don't want you to show up in the next thirty minutes, either."

"If you don't come alone, we'll kill her," Mikhail says. "And if you're late, we'll kill her."

Before I can say anything else, Boris ends the call. "You're dumber than I thought. Why call her at all if you're going to tell her not to come?"

"Because she wants to be noble," Mikhail says, "but she's also hoping for a way out." He chuckles drily. "It's a real conundrum, deep-seated human loyalty combined with the very human desire to survive."

"Don't act like you understand me," I say.

I'm praying that Adriana remembers our code. She's never been a huge fan of Kristiana, so I'm sure she'd rather

Kris get caught than me, but she's the only one who knew the code. If I mention Polish sausages, it means to send for help.

But instead, I said that I hate them.

I don't want help.

I just want her to tell Kristiana that I called, once it's too late, so she knows what happened and something about where I was. But while I wait, the men both pacing, I can't help my mind from revving at a million miles an hour.

Why do they want Kris?

She's the one who restored Grigoriy's power. Their powers do nothing when directed at her. The wind dies away. The earth can't smother her. It can be wrapped around her, but not pressed against her.

What's special about Kris? How is she connected to all this? Apparently we're not the only ones who want answers. And I can't quite help myself. I keep badgering them for more, even knowing I'll never be able to share what I learn.

"What's the connection?" I ask. "How is Kristiana tied up in all this?"

Mikhail frowns. "That's what we want to know."

"You really have no idea?" Boris scowls. "You've been with her this whole time."

They know as little as I do.

I wonder what Rukovoditel knows. Who is he? Why would these two be scared of him? Could he be the one who cursed them originally? Mikhail said their past hundred years haven't been comfortable either.

It feels like every question I ask just births two more baby questions.

And my leg's throbbing, throbbing, throbbing.

I wonder how long it's been.

Surely once the time has passed, they'll kill me. Grigoriy and Kristiana will both be devastated. Aleks will be bummed too, I imagine. He's a decent guy. My mom will probably go back to drinking. And maybe to Mārtinš. Hopefully Adriana can keep her away from both.

And, oh, my sister's the one I worry about the most.

She's already so angry all the time. What will something like this—my death, and her being the only one who knew about it—do?

As the minutes tick by, I start to feel a little light-headed. Is my injury causing internal bleeding? Will I pass out before they kill me? That would be nice. I'd prefer not to be awake for the stab wound or the misery of being thrown from the window of a moving train.

On that dark night, I wished I could have ridden one more time.

At least I don't have to regret that. Not only did I ride, I triumphed.

And those guys weren't really going to feature me on *Horse and Rider* or *Fox and Hound* or anything else, but other reporters did want to share my story.

"It's time," Mikhail says. "It's been half an hour." He stands up.

And the phone rings.

Boris leaps to his feet and answers it, and then he nods. "Okay."

After he hangs up, I close my eyes. I didn't lose consciousness, but surely it won't be horrible, like stabbing or something. They're tough, but the two men don't seem ghastly like those Russian mafia guys.

They never bothered binding my legs again—after they shattered one, what's the point? But when I hear bootsteps approaching, I simply clamp my eyes closed tighter.

The little zap by my wrists surprises me. "You're free to go," Boris says.

"What?" I look up at him, confused.

"Your friend came." He looks a little disappointed. "I

guess you get to live another day. She must really like you. She came alone."

My heart breaks. "No." I try to stand and end up in fetal position, whimpering. "Why? Why didn't Aleks stop her?"

"She must not have told him," Boris says. "But he's going to hate you. It might even split him and Grigoriy up."

"That would be interesting," Mikhail says.

My entire body's shaking, and I'm worried that I'm going into shock.

Mikhail drops something next to me. "Here. Use it quick, before you pass out."

I hear them leave as tears run down my face. Only once the door closes behind me, do I turn to see what they gave me.

It's a phone. Not the one they used earlier. A different one.

I hate myself for doing it, but Mikhail was right. I do want to live. I dial Kristiana this time, hoping that she'll answer. Hoping that there was a misunderstanding.

But I know—

"Hello?"

It's her voice. Kristiana's voice.

"Hello?" I ask. "Are you there?"

"*Mirdza!*"

"It's me," I say. "Mikhail and Boris took me." I start to sob. *Why did they leave? Why did they give me a phone? How am I still alive? What's going on?*

Of course, the extra surge of adrenaline pushes my poor body over the edge, and I finally pass out.

When I wake up, I'm cradled in Grigoriy's arms.

My leg still feels like it's made of confetti. It's throbbing and I want to throw up.

"It was too late," he says. "I'm going to kill those—"

"Stop," Kristiana says. "You're not going to do anything. She needs you here right now."

In trying to orient on her face by following the sound of her voice, I realize where we are.

In a hospital.

"The best orthopedic surgeon in Riga's going to operate right now," Aleksandr says, standing behind Kristiana.

Grigoriy stands and places me on a hospital bed, his hand still in mine. "You're going to be fine. I promise, we will figure this out."

And then we're wheeling down a hallway, and he's pressing a kiss to my forehead, and a man in blue scrubs is telling me that he's going to count down from ten.

Again, in the same stupid day, I'm unconscious.

When I wake up this time, my head isn't pounding. My mouth is dry, and my eyes feel exhausted by the light, but the first person I see is Grigoriy, and he's smiling.

"Is it fine?" I ask.

"He said it was a success. He thinks you'll walk again."

"Walk?" My voice sounds like the croak of a frog.

"Isn't that great?" Kristiana asks.

"I guess?" I try to sit up.

Aleksandr presses me back down. "This is going to hurt a bit," he says.

And then I'm nearly drowning in an ocean of pain. My leg feels like hot pokers are being driven into it from all angles. My chest feels as if a thousand-pound plate is pressing against it. My entire body bows outward, like it's being pulled by a million iron cords.

But then it finally stops, and I collapse in the middle of the hospital bed. "Next time," I croak. "I want to wait a few days."

"It's not as effective if you wait." Grigoriy's huge hand strokes my hair.

A few months ago, my mom was with my stepdad. My friend had lost her farm and was AWOL. I was doomed to a wheelchair, and I hadn't ridden in over a decade.

Now I've won a World Cup qualifier. I've got a boyfriend, and I have a best friend at my side.

"I'm so relieved you're okay," I say.

"Me?" Grigoriy asks.

"No," I say. "Kristiana. If you're here, fine, how did you get them to release me?"

Grigoriy lifts one eyebrow as he meets Aleksandr's eyes.

Kristiana tilts her head. "What are you talking about?"

Oh, no.

This time, I do struggle until I sit up. "Where's Adriana?"

Kristiana blinks. "I don't know. Where should she be?"

"I called her," I say. "I called her and told her where they wanted you to go. I told them I was calling you. I wanted her to warn you. Kris, they were obsessed with you."

Kris frowns.

Grigoriy freezes.

"They have my sister," I say. "She must have pretended to be you."

"The question is, why did they want her, and have they figured out it's not her yet?"

"But it wasn't the guys who had her," I say. "Not Mikhail and Boris."

"What?" Aleksandr frowns. "Slow down. You're not making sense."

"They were taking orders from someone else." I collapse back against the bed. "Someone they had saved in their phone as Rukovoditel."

"The one who controls?" Grigoriy asks.

I nod.

"That's not good," Aleksandr says. "Not good at all."

Unlike the last time, when I leave the hospital this time, no one has died. No one shot at me, threatened me with a knife, or slit anyone's throat. All in all, it's a much bigger success.

And if my new-ish boyfriend insists on carrying me, well. I'm not going to complain about that.

The day I left the hospital last time, I was fleeing Grigoriy. He was protecting me, but I was too upset to see that. All I could see was how grotesque his form of protection was. I blamed the tiger for *being* a tiger, even if his reasons for mauling were solid.

Today, though, I need the tiger and his claws.

"I still don't understand how this could have happened." Kristiana's understandably frazzled. She's not someone who likes to impose on anyone, but hearing that my sister's been taken by a horrible person who's apparently controlling two shape-shifting mages has not been easy for her to process. "Why didn't you just call me?"

"I knew you'd come," I say.

"Isn't that the point?" Kris leaps in front of Grigoriy and throws her hands up. "Listen."

"I was listening." I pat Grigoriy's arm so he'll release me.

He shakes his head.

"Put me down already. I'm not a baby."

"You just had surgery on your leg," he says. "You're not going to start walking anywhere until we're sure it won't damage anything."

I feel so stinking stupid, being held like I'm three years old. "Kris, I called Adriana because I didn't *want* you to come save me."

Kris blinks.

Aleksandr's eyes widen.

And Grigoriy's arms tighten around me.

We're standing in a parking lot, staring at each other. This is stupid. "We need to go," I say. "We should be looking into whether Adriana's disappeared."

"Maybe they let her go," Aleksandr says. "They could have."

Grigoriy starts walking again, moving faster than before.

But Kris is like a dog with her eye on a milk bone. "You didn't want me to come? Why not? Because you thought I'd bring the guys and get us all killed?"

I shake my head.

"Because you. . . You'd rather die than risk me?" She scowls. "Is that it?"

"It's a simple math problem," I say. "I'm all broken and damaged and always have been. I'm poor and not well educated, and my family's a mess. You just won the Grand National. You're in love, and you're beautiful, and you're well educated and talented, and it did *not* make sense to call you. I knew what you'd do. It's why I love you so much. But I couldn't call myself a friend if I let you do something like that."

"But you called your own sister," she says.

"I knew that if I just died, you wouldn't really know what had happened. I thought this way, she could tell you what I'd said. You'd know what had happened. You'd be able to look into things with one more piece of information. She and I had a code—I used it." I swallow. "Only, she didn't listen."

"You expected your own sister to simply let you die?" Aleksandr asks.

"You don't know my sister," I say. "Not like Kristiana does. In her entire life, Adriana has always protected exactly one person above all others."

"Herself," Kris says. "That's true. You can rely on that. When you're born without a mother who will look out for you, you learn to fend for yourself better than most." She tilts her head and sighs. "She's not a bad sister, she's just not a very good one."

I feel pretty disloyal for confessing why it never occurred to me that Adriana might try to save me herself. She didn't understand how high the stakes really were—although the guys did say they'd kill me, repeatedly—she might have thought it was a joke or that they were exaggerating.

"She must have pretended to be me," Kristiana says. "She knows me well enough, and people have always thought we looked a lot alike."

"They'll figure it out quick," I say, "when she has no idea they're magical or that Aleksandr can shift into a horse."

"It's not going to go well," Aleksandr says. "Anyone who those two listen to. . . We need to hurry. Let's get Mirdza home, and then we can—"

"But I want to help," I say. "It's my sister."

"She's in danger because of me." Kristiana opens the car door and waits for Grigoriy to set me inside. "Aleks and I have a lot of resources. We plan to use them all."

"You need to rest and recover right now," Grigoriy says.

"And I can either help them, or I can stay by you if I have to, to make sure you do it."

That shuts me up. The entire way home, I can't help but run through ideas, possibilities, and possible situations she may be stuck in.

"Do we have any ideas of who this boss might be?" I ask. "Was there someone they listened to before? Someone they were accountable to?"

"The Romanov family ruled all of Russia," Aleksandr says, "though the Kurakins and the Yuravskis never really liked it."

"Was there another person who challenged them?" I ask.

Aleks shakes his head. He's driving a little too fast, and I worry that he may not be paying much attention to the road at all. "Not that I recall. Grigoriy?"

He's thinking, at first, but after a moment, he shakes his head, too. "I wish we had our old family records. Did you find anything back at your place?"

"They burned most everything during the Soviet regime," Aleksandr says. "They weren't much for freedom of expression."

We know that first hand. Latvia was dragged down by them as well.

By the time we reach Liepašeta, we still have no real leads or even good ideas. "Get her inside," Aleks says, "and meet us in the barn office." Aleks has taken over the main barn office and apartment for himself, since Kris's father vehemently objected to him staying in the house, and the old barn was taken by Grigoriy.

I want to argue, but I'm also exhausted. And I trust that Grigoriy and Aleksandr and Kristiana will be able to do more than I could, even on my best day. It's nice to have people you trust in your corner, especially when they're wealthy, powerful people.

"I could call Danils," I say. "He's pretty connected around here."

Grigoriy stops so fast that I nearly topple out of his arms and onto the ground.

"I really think I can walk," I say. "And if you're going to overreact to every little thing, I might be better off on my own feet."

"The docs said it will take a lot of rehab to—"

"But my muscle hasn't atrophied thanks to months of lying around," I say. "I'll be fine."

He ignores me, of course, plowing ahead.

"Hey," I object. "Why aren't we headed for the apartment?"

"You and I will both be staying in the big house," Grigoriy says. "We decided during your operation. Even if her dad objects with every cell of his body, Aleks is going to start sleeping inside as well. It's time to close ranks."

"They waited until we were in Riga," I say, "and until you weren't anywhere near. They didn't want to make a scene. They're hardly going to steal onto the property and sneak into my apartment. What am I supposed to tell my mother if I move?"

It hits me then.

"What if Adriana's in our apartment? I know she didn't answer her phone, but maybe she's home and we just don't know it."

Grigoriy reroutes then, heading for my place. He doesn't look too optimistic, but crazier things have happened. Clearly his two 'friends' don't want news of their existence out there, or they wouldn't have been so careful. Which means if they discovered they'd been tricked, they might not have wanted a murder on their hands, no matter how tough they seemed.

Hope surges inside of me.

But when we reach the apartment, only my mother's

there. She shoots to her feet. "I didn't expect you until tomorrow." She beams. "Congratulations, sweetheart."

"Have you seen Adriana?"

She glances at Grigoriy, trying to figure out what's going on.

"She owes me money," I say. "I'm worried she's going to hide at a friend's place because she's too embarrassed."

"I haven't seen her," Mom says. "I can try calling her."

I shake my head. "No, it's fine. But if you *do* see her, can you call me right away?"

Mom nods slowly.

Grigoriy turns on his heel and heads out the door.

"Wait," Mom says. "Where are you going, and why's that man carrying you?"

That man? "Mom, you've met him. He has a name."

"Are you dating him again?" Her stage whisper is ridiculous. Obviously he can hear everything.

"I am," I say. "It was all a misunderstanding before, but we have to go right now. There are a lot of things for us to handle, mostly related to other things that happened at the show. I'll be back as soon as I can."

Mom looks skeptical, but she doesn't argue. That's one thing about having a total wuss for a mom. She never makes things harder than they need to be, even when she disagrees with you.

"I really am so proud," she says. "I'm sorry I didn't go. I thought it might be hard for you to see me if it didn't go well." As if the thought's just occurred to her, she inhales sharply. "Did you hurt your leg at the show?"

I decide that at least one thing I say can be true. "I did," I say. "But I've already been to see the doctors and they said I can still walk. I'm just giving it a bit of a break for now."

"Smart," she says. "You're lucky to have found a man strong enough and patient enough to put up with all that."

"Actually," Grigoriy says, "I'm the lucky one. It's my pleasure to be around your daughter and to be able to serve her in any way I can."

Mom's staring, her mouth dangling open, when we head back out.

The cost of hope is often despair, and it hits me as we leave.

Adriana wasn't there.

She's really missing.

And it's my fault.

I underestimated her filial love, her devotion, and her bravery, and now I've put her in danger. She might even be dead. I'm crying again by the time we reach the house, and I've curled my head up against the side of Grigoriy's strong shoulder.

He jogs up the stairs as if I weigh nothing, and then he heads to the right, counting rooms until he reaches the fourth. The guest room. I'm fancy, now. I remember helping my mother clean this room as a kid. Or at least, I remember sitting in the corner quietly while she cleaned. I doubt I was really very helpful, in retrospect.

The room's bright, the bed in the center not quite as massive as I remember it being. But the bedspread is just as white and frilly as it is in my memory. And it still smells of jasmine—Kristiana's mother's favorite scent. No matter how long I live, I'll always associate that smell with her. It used to make me really sad to smell it. Now I can't help smiling just a little.

At first the pain of loss is almost unbearable. But at some point in our lives, the sentiment switches from the pain of losing someone, to the joy in the memories of them we yet retain. I suppose that's one of the most beautiful gifts of healing.

Joy is always better than pain.

And it outlasts it, in the end.

Grigoriy sets me on the edge of the bed carefully. "What can I get for you?"

"Nothing," I say. "If you guys won't take my help, at least you should go and see what you can do."

I don't tell him that there's no way I'll be able to sleep or rest, not while Adriana's gone. It sounds overwrought, and also, with as tired as I am, it might be a complete lie. But I don't want to divert resources, either. Grigoriy's smart, capable, and a little terrifying. If there's something he can do to help her, I want him doing it, not talking to me about what snacks I might want.

"What code did you give her on the phone?" he asks.

I explain the Polish sausages thing.

But recounting that gives me an idea. "Her phone records," I say. "They may be our only real lead. I called her from a phone they had, and I don't think it was a burner."

"Why not?"

"Because it had his number, whoever he is, saved in it. That sounds more permanent, doesn't it?"

He thinks about it.

"Aleksandr may have a contact that would be faster, but if he doesn't, I can call her phone service and ask them to email me some records."

"Good idea." He rummages around in a bag and fishes out a phone.

"What's this?" I ask.

The jerks either stole my phone or left it in a bucket of ice water somewhere. But as far as I know, Grigoriy never got one of his own.

"Aleksandr told me I have to have one, so this is mine. You can use it, until we get you a new one."

"Thanks."

I check to make sure it doesn't need a code, and of course it doesn't. And... his banking app is right there, on the second screen. "Grigoriy, when we find my sister, we need to talk about technology and how to safeguard your identity."

He arches one eyebrow. "You sound like Aleksandr."

"In this case, I'll take that as a compliment."

I expect him to leave, but he doesn't. Instead, he circles the bed and sits down. Then he drags me over next to him and wraps his arm around my shoulders.

"You could have died."

I can't argue with him. I definitely could have.

"You were badly injured."

Can't argue with that either.

"You should have called me."

"They wanted me to call Kris."

His arm tightens on my shoulders. "You thought I was crazy, eyeing everyone like they could be a threat, but I knew. I knew you were exposed, and I knew I could only keep you safe if I could keep you in my sight."

I thought he was being paranoid, but in the end, he was right. I've become so accustomed to thinking he's a lunatic, ignorant about the modern era, that I may not have given him enough credit for his knowledge of the people we're dealing with or the magic they possess.

"I'm sorry."

"Don't ever do it again," he says.

"What?" I ask. "Follow two extremely handsome reporters for an exclusive interview?"

"Handsome?" His hand drags my chin around until I'm looking up into his face. "You thought they were—" He sputters.

I can't help my smile. "In a pretty-boy, lightweight kind of way."

Now he looks like he might choke.

"But compared to you? They looked. . .insubstantial." I smile. "And I like my men to be substantial."

He frowns. "That sounds vaguely like an insult."

"You're the best-looking man I've ever met," I say. "I realized earlier that you're a tiger, and I never should have been insisting that I should be able to leash a tiger. Now that my sister's in danger, I want you to attack."

His gaze becomes almost predatory. "A tiger?" He chuckles. "I prefer to be called a big bad wolf."

"What?" I ask. "Why?"

"Have you ever heard the story of the three little pigs?" He lifts one hand and papers from the top of the armoire blow around the room. "Do you recall what the big bad wolf threatened to do?"

"Huff, and puff, and *blow the house down.*" I can't help laughing. "You're saying that's you?"

"Our family crest is a wolf," he says. "It seems ridiculous, because we're horse lords, but in reality—"

"It totally fits you," I say. "You could blow any house down, and on top of that, you're not a tiger." I lift just one finger and run it over the line of his upper lip. "You're a wolf." I drop my voice to a whisper. "My wolf."

He actually growls.

I laugh. "I'm glad you're my wolf."

"Now that you've admitted it, you have to promise me something." He looks so intense, so sincere, that I know he means it. It's not just a joke.

"I will," I say. "Anything."

"From now on, you will value your life more than you did when you called your sister. And you'll have more faith in me, too, to keep you safe."

"But—"

He presses his finger to my mouth. "No. No buts. You will have faith in me and my ability to protect you, and you'll value yourself enough that you'll never again think of making such a stupidly noble sacrifice."

"Any way you look at it," I say, "Kristiana—"

He kisses me then. Not a gentle, take-care-of-this-girl

kiss. No, it's the predatory kiss of a wolf, claiming me as his. I forget where I am, what I'm doing, and why I'm doing it. There's only his massive strength and my limitless yearning.

Until he pulls away.

I can't help my whimper.

"Tell me." His voice is low and urgent. "Tell me you will never again undervalue yourself."

"Grigoriy," I say. "You're—"

"That's not the answer I need." And he kisses me again. Short, urgent, demanding.

My hands grab his collar, dragging him closer.

And he finally releases me. His eyes are intent on mine. "You're beautiful. The most beautiful woman I've ever met. You're smart, and doggedly determined, and loyal, and you're kind. And you love unconditionally, including caring for people who have let you down repeatedly. The world doesn't deserve to have a Mirdza Strelkova. I don't deserve her, but I've convinced her that she's mine, so I need her to say it." He looks at me expectantly, his beautiful eyes unwavering.

"I'm valuable?"

"Is that a question?" He quirks one eyebrow. "Because—"

I shake my head. "No. It's not. Don't kiss me again, as much as I like it, because you have to go help them find my sister."

He smiles, and it's not a friendly, boy-next-door smile. It's a wolfish, gloating, predatory, possessive smile. "You're worth more than one thousand Brigitas. And as much as I admire Kristiana, you're worth a dozen of her."

I can't help rolling my eyes.

"She had everything handed to her, but you've had to work for every single scrap."

"But—"

"No buts, I said. Don't make me kiss you again."

If this were any circumstance other than the current one. . .but Adriana's missing, and I can't keep him here. "I love you," I say. "And I may not think I deserve you right now, and I may sometimes have trouble accepting you just as you are because of my past. But I know that if I weren't valuable, you'd never love me back. So how about this? Now that I know you're waiting for me to come back home, I won't devalue myself anymore, because I trust your judgment."

"It's not enough," he says. "But it's a start." He gathers me in close to his chest. "And I plan to spend the rest of my life writing the happily ever after."

"Together," I say.

"From now on, never apart." He kisses me again, but this one is a definite goodbye.

At least for now.

❦ 28 ❦

ADRIANA

My entire life, I've been surrounded by women who don't really think they deserve what they have. My mother was always thanking people for everything, profusely, ridiculously. She cleaned for people as her job, but did that mean she had to be their *servant?*

It always annoyed me.

Mirdza grew up just like her, a doormat who was always worried about the feelings of everyone else.

I went another direction.

My very first promise to myself was to never, ever let anyone take advantage of me. If all the world's either victims or Vikings, then by golly, hand me a sword. In every instance in my life when I made a choice, I always chose myself.

The worst one of all was the day I walked home and rounded the corner and heard a lot of yelling coming from the apartment. *His voice,* like always, was so very loud. It was loud, and terrible, and it featured in every single one of my nightmares.

"Look at this," I heard him say. "Your little girl finally came to play."

I knew, in that moment, that Mirdza had finally snapped. She stood up and fought back against him for our mother's sake. I was proud of her decision, and I knew that I should join her. We were twins, but I was the strong one. I was the one who always went in swinging.

But then I heard Mārtiņš say, "And you even brought me a toy."

It was an ugly thing to hear, coming from him. Nothing he thought of as a toy could be something good. And the thwack I heard, and the slither of someone falling on the ground afterward. The moans, and the horrible, terrible, gosh-awful meaty sounds of someone being beaten. . .I'd heard them all before.

I should have intervened. If our roles had been reversed, mousy little Mirdza would have come running to step in front of me.

But I ran away.

That night, on the night of the one beating that changed my twin sister's life forever, I was there.

And I *ran away*.

Sometimes it feels like I've been running away from that night ever since. When she tries to help me, I can't accept it. Not when I could have saved her and didn't. When a man would try to date me, sometimes even a guy I sort of liked, I would always think, *Adriana, do you deserve a great boyfriend?* The answer was no, of course. To the world, I was a scrappy fighter, both confident and talented. Beautiful, even.

But deep down inside, I knew: I was a terrible coward when it really mattered. I failed the one person in my life who always did anything and everything she could do for me in every way.

So when she calls me and pretends I'm Kristiana, the

friend who has really and truly saved her whenever she needed it, the friend who has always been there for her, the one person she could always trust to not ever let her down, when she calls me knowing she'll die, because she wants to spare her friend's life, I can't do it.

I can't stand by that cracked door and listen and do nothing again.

I may be a selfish, useless piece of trash. But I did learn that night that the only thing worse than taking a brutal beating is standing by and watching while someone else, someone you love, takes one. So instead of waiting half an hour, instead of *not* going for help, like she begged me to do, I paid every last dime I had to the first cab I could hail. Then I sprinted to the place that horrible man said I had to go.

And when the man in the ebony suit approached, all smooth movements and complete confidence, I didn't struggle at all.

"What's your name?" he asked, his Russian accent pronounced.

"I'm Kristiana Liepa," I lie.

It's the easiest lie I've ever told.

I've wanted to be Kristiana all my life. Not because she's rich, or because her dad loves her, or because her mother did, too. Not even because she owns a million beautiful horses, is living my dream, or has a billionaire fiancé. She's also won the biggest horse race in Europe, but that's not it either.

No, I spend my life wishing I could be her, because she's had the luxury of caring for my twin sister in a way I never did.

When important, powerful people care for you, you can spend your time protecting others. When no one cares whether you live or die, it turns you into a selfish beast.

Pretending to be Kristiana Liepa is the easy part.

Convincing them not to kill me like they're planning? That's the hard part. But other than coveting my neighbor's life, that's probably the one thing in the world that I'm the best at—surviving, at any cost.

"Come with me," the man says.

I don't argue, but I'm already making a plan.

** **I** HOPE YOU ENJOYED MY DARK HORSE PRINCE!

Are you ready for Adriana's story? I'm including the (very rough!) first chapter of the next book, My High Horse Czar if you keep scrolling.

You can preorder it right now. Here's the blurb:

Adriana's stuck between a rock and a very hard, very dangerous place. It's not the first time she's ever been in trouble, but it is the worst.

When her twin sister calls and tells her she's going to be killed unless Adriana surrenders herself in half an hour, she figures she doesn't have much to lose.

But Adriana has no idea how much excitement her future holds, or whose protection she's about to awaken.

The scrappy fighter who has vowed never to date or marry is about to meet her match in the highest horse-shifter in existence—the displaced Czar of Russia himself, Alexei Romanov.

My
High Horse
Czar
THE RUSSIAN WITCH'S CURSE BOOK THREE
BRIDGET E. BAKER

❧ 29 ❧

ight or flight.

They say humans experience one or the other under stressful circumstances. As a female who weighs less than 6 stone, I should really have learned to run. It's not like I'm equipped to take out mean men who are twice my size.

But my twin sister got all the flight response.

Mom always says I'm fifty pounds of dynamite in a five pound bag. And I don't have a very long fuse, either. I just wish I was more like a thousand pounds of dynamite in a hundred pound bag. Then maybe I'd have seen another way out.

My step father really caused everything. If he hadn't been so unbearably gross, I never would have felt compelled to move out of my mom's apartment. That meant I needed to find another place to live, and being on your own is expensive. It's worse when you have no education or skill set, other than riding. It didn't leave me a lot of options.

My sister's best friend gave me two horses who weren't good at jumping, and I used them to run races, earning money more often than not. At first it was enough, but as bills began to pile up, I needed a bigger win.

To really make enough, I needed more money than I had, so I borrowed it. But then. . .I didn't win. I lost. And then I was really in a bind. I kept paying things forward, staying a half-step ahead of where I needed to be all the time.

Until I wasn't.

The first time I met Nojus, I thought he was cute. He had a little-boy air about him. I must have been delusional, because the second time we met, when I had to tell him I didn't have his money, he was busy gutting someone when I walked through the door. I nearly lost my breakfast, and I couldn't bring myself to tell him the truth. I lied and said it had been stolen. I think he knew, but he gave me an extension with outrageous interest, which would double the amount due. It felt better than being gutted, anyway.

Only, now, almost a year later, after throwing a race to cover some of the compounding interest, he basically owns me.

All he has to do if I stop listening to him, aside from killing me, is hand in his evidence of my criminal activity to the policija. Which is how he's been able to use me to run his errands, threaten people in higher positions where the more obvious goons could never sneak through, and dig up information from people who would see his jackets a mile away.

Even so, I'm past the grace period.

"Adriana." Nojus's hand strokes the top of my head and my heart races.

I can't help looking around desperately for anything I could use to defend myself.

"You still haven't repaid me."

"I've done you a lot of services."

"None of that discharged your debt." His hand slides

down my jaw slowly and hooks beneath my chin. "I've told you what you can do." He lifts my face toward his. "I can't figure out why you keep refusing. It's making me self-conscious, to be honest. Do you not find me attractive?"

He makes my skin crawl. He makes me want to claw my own nails down my face until I'm so hideous no one would look at me. He reminds me so much of Mārtiņš, my step-father, that the thought of him touching me makes me want to throw-up.

"It's nothing personal," I say. "I vowed years ago never to date, never to fall in love, and never to marry. You've met my step father. You know why."

"What I know," Nojus says, "is that I'm *right here*, telling you that you can pay me back, or you can die."

My hand itches to slap him, but I doubt I could defeat him, even with my jujitsu classes. And seeing as he's got at least six men in the next room, I know that even if I could, I'd still lose. "My sister has a new boyfriend," I finally say, my voice trembling. "She just won a huge jumping contest. It's why I was already here in Riga when you called."

"And?" His hand slides over my shoulder.

I think about something else. Anything else. If I can't distract myself, I'll punch him. Or I'll puke. Either one will likely get me killed.

"If you let me go see her, I'll come back with your money."

"You think your crippled sister's boyfriend is just going to give you half a million euros?" His laughter grates on my ears. "What an optimistic slut you are." Without warning, he slaps me across my face, sending me sprawling across the floor. My hair falls loose, the rubber band holding it back snapping.

But I welcome the violence. It's so much easier to handle than the misery-inducing caresses he usually employs.

"You have one hour. If you're not back here in one hour, I'll send my men to either collect you or kill you, Adriana. You will be given the choice. If they collect you." His hand drops to his crotch and he rubs.

I drop my eyes so he can't see how disgusting I find him. Few people are worse than Mārtiņš, but Nojus, the Lithuanian arms dealer who supplies the criminals on the eastern side of Latvia might be one of them.

"One hour."

"Don't forget to keep this with you." He sets one of his burner phones in front of me. "I'd hate to have to add the cost of locating you to your already increasing debt. You might never repay it."

I've barely reached the street outside an unknown number calls. I'm pretty sure I know who it is. It has to be either Mirdza or Kristiana, calling from the arena. After all, when Nojus called me, I almost threw Blanka's reins at Kris and ran away.

Mirdza's probably pissed.

She just made a huge comeback, the likes of which I never imagined, and not only did her boyfriend not go to see it, our mother skipped, too. And then her sister ran away and left her instead of celebrating. I'd be super duper pissed.

Maybe she'll forgive me. My twin sister's nothing like me.

She's the one everyone loves. The one people want to be like. The one people want to help. She's also the reason Kristiana ever gave me anything at all, and without those two horses, I'd never even have been able to race. I should be grateful to have a sister like her. I know I should. I'm the worthless sack of crap, and I'm the one always taking, taking, taking, but for some reason that knowledge just makes me angrier.

Every time I think about Mirdza, I'm overcome with

the same guilt. The guilt I've always carried around. She's crippled because of me. Because when I should have stepped in to help her—I'm the fighter—or help my mother, or call the authorities, or. . .well, anything. I should have done *something*, but instead I ran.

Her life was forever wrecked because of me.

Until Mr. Handsome Prince showed up, I guess. He seems willing to cut the world in pieces and run it through a blender for her if she just mentions she'd like an earth smoothie. When she moves around a room, his eyes track her every movement, like he's a magnet, but instead of tracking north, he tracks Mirdza.

I know Aleksandr is rich. I hear Grigoriy is, too. He's a prince, for heaven's sake, or he says he is. He must have money. Is there any chance she might be able to get. . .but *half a million euros?* How could I even ask her for that?

Just before the call's about to go to voicemail, I swipe to answer. "Hello?"

"Kristiana," she says. "It's me, Mirdza." It's definitely her, but why's she calling me Kristiana? She didn't stutter or stammer or correct herself. And she doesn't sound mad that I left, either. What's going on?

"Thank goodness you're calling." I open my mouth to force the words out—to ask her for money. Maybe I can drill down to the final amount later. After she's agreed to talk to Grigoriy. I'm going to have to tell her the reason, and that makes me want to scream.

"The men you were worried about have taken me after all, just like Aleksandr thought they might," she says.

What? What men? Before I can ask, she dives back in.

"But you're the one they want, Kris. Not me."

Whoa, she knows I'm not Kris. She wants me to get a message to Kris, clearly. But why didn't she just call Kris? Or why not just tell me that? "Okay." My mind finally wraps itself around what she said. Those men Aleksandr was worried about. . .took her?"

My brain rebels against the thought. I deserve to be taken, beaten, whatever. But not Mirdza. She's never done anything bad *ever.* How dare Aleksandr and Kristiana endanger her life.

"They want you to come to the following address in the next half hour." She pauses, thankfully, and I flip the phone to speaker so I can enter the address she reads into a note. My heart was beating fast before, but now I'm probably close to the heart attack range.

I need to get there in a half hour. . .or what?

"But you know me," Mirdza continues. "I hate the idea of someone trading themselves to save me as much as I hate Polish sausages. I've never wanted any, and I don't want you to show up in the next thirty minutes, either."

Polish what?

I remember it, then. Our stupid code she made up after Mārtiņš nearly killed her. Something about Polish sausages means I'm supposed to call the police.

But she said she hates them, and that she doesn't want any. Then she told me NOT to come. Does she mean to tell the cops, but not to go?

It hits me then, why she's calling me and not Kristiana. I really am a moron. I should have known from the start. If she called her best friend, she'd rush to her side. Then the men might kill them both. Or even if they released Mirdza, they'd kill Kris.

My sister would *never* trade herself for someone else, and I'm probably the only person she could trust to pick myself over her. She's sending them a message. . .through me. She won't want me to share it until the time has past.

"If you don't come alone," a man's voice says, "we'll kill her."

A chill races up my spine. This man sounds worse than Nojus.

"And if you're late, we'll kill her." The man hangs up.

With shaking hands, I look up the distance to the address and find out that, shockingly, it's a five minute walk. That gives me a little time. I stop at the local post office, scrawl out a hasty note, and mail my own phone to our apartment at Liepašeta.

I was never going to get the money.

Part of me knew that already. There's also no way I was going to repay Nojus in the way he wanted. If I'm doomed to die today, I may as well do it for a good cause.

I'm terrified as I march into the park where the men told me to go. My heart's racing. My palms and pits are sweaty. My head throbs from dehydration, too much panic, and the incessant darting of my eyes, looking for the horrible mastermind who's planned all this.

What do they want with Kristiana?

I expect a dozen men in all black. I expect knives and guns and flinty eyes. I don't know what kind of people Kristiana pissed off—or maybe it was her husband. They're probably Russians, right? The Russian mafia? Maybe he borrowed money, too. That's rich, if I'm killed for the same thing I did, only by someone else's villain. Won't Nojus be shocked when he can't rape me? I hope he finds out that I'm dead—I want him to be deprived of the satisfaction of harming me himself.

Or maybe he'll spend years and thousands of dollars searching for me. That would be even better.

As I glance at my watch, I realize that if I can just delay whoever it is that comes for Kris for twenty minutes or so, Nojus's lackeys should show up to collect me. That might be interesting.

And of course, as always, the second I see a glimmer of hope. . .

I start to make a plan.

The people who wanted me here will be strong. Powerful. Probably scary looking. And I have no idea why they want me. Mirdza knew something, which means Kristiana would have an inkling of who they are. Other than her dad's gambling, her life was pretty blasé before she got engaged.

Plus, Mirdza said, 'like Aleksandr thought they might.' It has to be related to him. He's Russian. The guy will likely be Russian. It's probably about money.

I start watching people intently in the park.

No one's wearing black. No one's carrying any weapons I could make out. No one even looks ominous.

Actually, there aren't really any men.

There's a woman her two young children. A lady carrying a bag of groceries walking past. There's a teenage kid with a dog. And there's one man, talking on a cell phone. He's wearing a bright blue scarf, he has hair so dark that it's almost black, and when he looks up at me, his eyes exactly match his scarf.

He's drop-dead gorgeous. Like a print ad model for Calvin Klein. He smiles, and even though I never date and have no intention to, my heart still swoons.

I can't help smiling back.

A moment later, he hangs up his call and stands. Then he starts to stroll toward me. I mean, this happens sometimes. I'll meet some stranger's eye and he'll approach me. Ask for my number. I may be a mess, but like Mirdza's bestie, I'm blonde, thin, and pretty.

It's just a really bad time to deal with this.

I'd hate for the beautiful stranger to get caught in the crosshairs of this mess. I glance at my watch and realize it's now only five minutes until Nojus's deadline, and the stranger is a few paces away and closing.

"I'm dating someone," I say. "Sorry."

"I know," he says. "I wish I could give Aleksandr my regards. Maybe someday soon."

The bottom falls out.

How could this man be the one threatening my sister? He looks like he could be mugged by a Backstreet Boy with a pair of safety scissors. I'm suddenly much more worried about the men Nojus is sending, and annoyed by the fact that I *mailed* my cell phone to myself with a dramatic note.

"Is this some kind of prank?" I ask. "Because Mirdza—"

"I just told my men to release her." He tilts his head sideways, examining me. "You're taller than I thought from the photos after winning the Grand National. And have you gained a bit of weight?"

This guy is *rude*, too. "Now, listen here."

"Oh, I am delighted to listen to anything you care to say," he says. "You're really a marvel to me, you know. When the men told me their powers just dissolved when they touched you, I thought they were lying. They're creative in excusing their failures, you know, always have been. That's the problem with people who were raised wealthy. They're always full of excuses."

Raised rich? Kristiana was raised rich, too, but not like, Aleksandr levels of rich, I guess.

"What did you want to tell me?"

I decide I should tread lightly. Maybe he has men stationed where I can't see them, in the buildings all around the park or something. He looks like a trust baby people might report to.

"Why did you want me when your problem's with Aleksandr?" There. That's a good question. Maybe he'll tell me something I can use.

"My problem isn't with Aleksandr, actually. It's with someone named Baba Yaga, if it's with anyone, but even she did us all a huge favor." He gestures at the bench.

I think he might be insane.

If the men following him are also crazy, that would explain their threats. No one was really in trouble, but when someone threatens you, it's hard to realize that. Especially Mirdza. She's been afraid of everything and everyone since the Mārtinš incident. Once you start running, it's hard to stop.

"Baba Yaga? Are you kidding?"

When he smiles, he looks even prettier than I realized he could. "You don't believe me?" He sighs. "It's a shame that the revolution I started created so many complete zealots, but when you light a match, it's hard to control the flames entirely. They burned so many things that we really should have kept."

Revolution? Fire? What's he saying?

"Here's the thing, Kristiana. I'm genuinely worried you're a threat to me. So while you arouse my curiosity, I think I'm probably safer just killing you."

The idea that this fop might kill me is laughable.

Then again, he thinks I'm Kristiana. She hasn't trained in martial arts. She hasn't thrown a high-stakes horse race, or cut off someone's finger when they were groping her. Luckily, that made Nojus laugh—he was actually angrier at his man for doing it than he was at me for defending myself. He kept thinking I would someday come around to wanting him.

As if my thoughts summon them, his men show up right then. I'm actually impressed to see that he sent a dozen men. I've met all but three of them, and the ones I've met are all decently strong and reasonably competent. The others look like kids who probably tagged along to learn something.

"Who are they?" the print model asks. "I thought Aleks might be somewhere near—hoped he would, if I'm being honest—but it didn't occur to me he'd hire goons to come after me." He laughs and it's surprisingly melodic. "What's the point?"

"Who are you?" I ask. "Aleksandr doesn't know."

"I'm Leonid Ivanovich, the true heir to the Russian throne. My great, great, great, great grandfather was locked up by the Romanovs when they stole the throne. Your darling boyfriend Aleksandr was Alexei's best friend, and Grigoriy was always following them around, too. If they'd just sworn to me a hundred years ago, things wouldn't have gotten nearly as nasty."

Oh, no. He's a raving lunatic.

He may be gorgeous, but I've learned that sometimes lunatics are the scariest people of all.

"We have a chance here to set things aright, five hundred years late, but better than never."

"A chance?"

He stands. "It's either that, or we'll have another bloody battle to fight. I don't actually care which. I think they both sound fun, and the end result won't change."

"She's coming with us," Nojus's second in command says. He's tall, he's stupid, and his Latvian is terrible. He usually keeps things pretty short, which is his best quality.

"She's definitely not." Leonid glances back at me. "They're with you? Really?"

I shake my head. "I don't like them. They're here to kill me too, though, so maybe you have more in common than you think."

"You want to kill her?" Leonid's eyebrows rise. "Really?"

The men glare. About half of them don't speak Latvian. Lithuanian is similar, but I can only catch snatches of it here and there. I'm guessing it's the same for them.

"They don't understand you," I say.

"You're positive they want you dead?" Leonid asks.

I nod.

He sighs. "This is tedious, and I hate doing things out

in the open like this." He glances around slowly, and I notice that everywhere he looks, there are electric sparks.

He glares to the east, and there's a popping sound and sparks fall from a camera mounted on the side of the brick building. Then he looks to the east, and the same things happens to a traffic camera on a light post. Again, and again, ten little pops and sparks.

"What are you doing?" I ask.

"Do you really not know?" Leonid looks even more annoyed now.

"She comes with us," Nojus's cousin says. He's smaller, but he is covered in tattoos. I've always thought he was one of the scarier lackeys. He's also really handy with a switchblade.

"Yes, you've said," Leonid says. "And now that I've made sure—" He cuts off with a grimace and there's a spark and a shout from a man standing on the closest corner. "Move along, loser!" Leonid waves, and the man actually scampers away.

"Okay, *now* that we're finally not being filmed, I can eliminate one more nuisance." He lifts his hands, and all twelve men are suddenly engulfed in flames.

I can barely believe what I'm seeing.

They're screaming and stumbling and the *smell*. I do retch, right over the side of the bench.

"I know. Burning people alive is so messy and disgusting, but honestly, I did not expect this of Aleksandr." He sighs. "So what's his plan, then? He just sent you here like a sacrificial lamb?"

"No," I say. "I'm not a lamb."

"Oh no?" Leonid smiles.

There are a dozen men who are literally burning into piles of ash behind him, and he looks like he's forgotten all about it.

"Tell me, then. Why was he okay with sending you here

alone like this? With just a few helpless, walking firewood sticks as company?"

"Those men weren't sent by Aleks," I say. "They were coming to kill me because I owe a very bad man a lot of money."

"Wait." Leonid looks truly baffled. "If you owe someone money, why hasn't Aleks taken care of it."

"For someone who seems to think he knows everything," I say, "you're not very smart."

When his eyes flash, I realize I should not be baiting him. What is wrong with me? Why do I always take swings at lions?

"I'm not even Kristiana, you idiot." Hopefully it has been long enough that Mirdza's safe. "I'm Mirdza's criminally worthless twin sister, Adriana."

Convinced yet? Preorder My High Horse Czar now.

ACKNOWLEDGMENTS

My husband is a rock star without a guitar (or any hair... or a drug addiction.) Actually, he's not much like a rock star. But he is amazing. Without him, my male leads would be boring, and my days would have far less laughter. Also, I'd be poor. Thanks for keeping me around.

My kids act like they're my little broke friends who think I'm rich, but I love them to pieces anyway. And they're usually the first ones lined up to read and gush about my books. THANK YOU for being patient with me when I'm writing, for bringing me food (mostly Tessa and Dora!) and for being excited for my stories.

My mom is my second biggest fan, right after Whit. It's an honor to have had such a supportive mother my ENTIRE life. I hope she sticks around for at least another year or two... All joking aside, how about another DECADE or three?

My PA Sharon helps me pretend to be a business professional. My cover artist Lara is patient and hilarious. (And talented!) My editor Carrie is so supportive and helpful.

My best writing friend, Elana, keeps me from going nuts and always encourages me to do better.

Last, but not least, to my ARC team and my readers. Te amo. Je t'aime. Jag älskar dig. Я тебя люблю. Es mīlu Tevi. I love you. I just do. More than words can say. More than I can express, I LOVE YOU GUYS!! You help me to achieve all my dreams by supporting my stories and caring about my characters. I still wake up every day, amazed that I earn my living by making up fake people and writing about their lives. AMAZING! THANK YOU THANK YOU THANK YOU!

PS- To Leo (my horse), Chewy (my puppy), Wicket (my dog), Lucky (my other dog), my two annoying cats, and all my chickens, YOU SUCK! I love you beyond belief, but you did your very best to make sure this book was never finished. SHAME SHAME on all of you, especially Leo for the shenanigans with the blanket. For the love. But really, I still love you. Thank you for making me much happier almost every day.

ABOUT THE AUTHOR

Bridget's a lawyer, but does as little legal work as possible. She has five kids and soooo many animals that she loses count. There are for sure looots of horses, dogs, cats, rabbits, and way too many chickens. Animals are her great love, after the hubby, the kids, and the books.

She makes cookies waaaaay too often and believes they should be their own food group. In an attempt at balancing the scales, she kick boxes (almost) daily. So if you don't like her books, maybe don't tell her in person.

Bridget's active on social media, and has a Facebook group she comments in often. (Her husband even gets on there sometimes.) Please feel free to join her there: https://www.facebook.com/groups/750807222376182

She also gives a free book to everyone who joins her newsletter at www.BridgetEBakerWrites.com

Renounced (4)

Reclaimed (5) a novella!

A stand alone YA romantic suspense:

Already Gone

I also write contemporary romance and women's fiction under B. E. Baker.

The Finding Home Series:

Finding Grace (0) Prequel!

Finding Faith (1)

Finding Cupid (2)

Finding Spring (3)

Finding Liberty (4)

Finding Holly (5)

Finding Home (6)

Finding Balance (7)

Finding Peace (8)

The Finding Home Series Boxset Books 1-3

The Finding Home Series Boxset Books 4-6

The Birch Creek Ranch Series:

The Bequest

The Vow

The Ranch

The Retreat

The Reboot

The Setback

The Scarsdale Fosters Series:

Seed Money

Nouveau Riche

Loaded